"You have plenty of reason to be worried," Sean reminded Emily.

"Don't make this into a worst-case scenario." Emily continued to hold his hand, and he felt the tension in her grip.

"Seriously, Emily, you *do* need a bodyguard."

"I agree, and the job is yours."

He'd expected an argument but was glad that she'd decided to be rational. He glanced toward the dining room. The snowstorm raged outside the windows. "I could do with another bowl of chili."

"Me, too."

Before she hopped down the step to the floor, she went up on tiptoe and gave him a kiss on the forehead. It was nothing special, the kind of small affection a wife might regularly bestow on her husband. The utter simplicity blew him away.

Before she could turn her back and skip off into the dining room, he caught her hand and gave a tug. She was in his arms. When her body pressed against his, they were joined together the way they were supposed to be.

Then he kissed her.

D0928357

MOUNTAIN BLIZZARD

BY
CASSIE MILES

First Published in Great Britain 2017
By Mills & Boon, an imprint of HarperCollins*Publishers*
1 London Bridge Street, London, SE1 9GF

© 2017 Kay Bergstrom

ISBN: 978-0-263-92876-1

46-0417

Our policy is to use papers that are natural, renewable and recyclable products and made from wood grown in sustainable forests. The logging and manufacturing processes conform to the legal environmental regulations of the country of origin.

Printed and bound in Spain
by CPI, Barcelona

Cassie Miles, a *USA TODAY* bestselling author, lives in Colorado. After raising two daughters and cooking tons of macaroni and cheese for her family, Cassie is trying to be more adventurous in her culinary efforts. She's discovered that almost anything tastes better with wine. When she's not plotting Mills & Boon Intrigue books, Cassie likes to hang out at the Denver Botanical Gardens near her high-rise home.

For Nanna,
who will always be my screen saver and,
as always, to Rick.

Prologue

The double-deck luxury yacht rolled over a Pacific wave just outside San Francisco Bay as Emily Peterson wobbled down a nearly vertical staircase on her four-inch stilettos. Her short, tight, sparkly disguise gave her a new respect for the gaggle of party girls she'd hidden among to sneak on board. Somehow those ladies managed to walk on these stilts without falling and to keep their nipples covered in spite of ridiculously low-cut dresses.

Her plan for tonight was to locate James Wynter's private computer and load the data onto a flash drive. She'd slipped away from the gala birthday party for one of Wynter Corporation's top executives. The guests had been raucous as they guzzled champagne and admired their view of the Golden Gate Bridge against the night sky. Some had complained about having to surrender their cell phones, and Emily had agreed. It would have been useful to snap photos of high-ranking political types getting cozy with Wynter's thugs.

Belowdecks, she went to the second door on the right. She'd been told this was James Wynter's office. The polished brass knob turned easily in her hand. No need to pick the lock.

Pulse racing, she entered. The desk lamp was off, but moonlight through the porthole was enough to let her see the open laptop. In a matter of minutes, she could transfer Wynter's data to her flash drive, and she'd finally have the evidence she needed for her human trafficking article.

Before she reached the desk, she heard angry voices in the corridor. She backed away from the desk and ducked into a closet with a louvered door. Desperately, she prayed for them to pass by the office and go to a different room.

No such luck.

The office door crashed open. One of the men fell into the office on his hands and knees while others laughed. Another guy turned on the lamp. Light spread across the desktop and spilled onto the floor.

Her pulse thundered in her ears, but Emily stayed utterly silent. She dared not make a sound. If Wynter's men found her, she was terrified of what they'd do.

Carefully, she stepped out of her red stilettos and went into a crouch. Through the slats in the door, she could see the shoes and legs of four men. The man who had fallen kept apologizing again and again, begging the others to believe him.

She recognized the voice of one of his tormentors: Frankie Wynter, the youngest son of James Wynter. Though she couldn't exactly tell what was going on, she thought Frankie was pushing the man who was so very sorry while the others laughed.

There was a clunk as the man who was being pushed flopped into the swivel chair behind the desk. From this angle, she saw only the back sides of the three men. One of them rocked back on his heel, cracked his knuckles and then lunged forward. She heard the slap, flesh against flesh.

They hit him again. What could she do? How could she stop them? She hated being silent while someone else suffered. Each blow made her cringe. If her ex-husband had been here, he could have made a difference, would have done the right thing. But she was on her own and utterly without backup. Should she speak up? Did she dare?

The beating stopped.

"Shut up," Frankie roared at the man in the chair. "Crying like a little girl, you make me sick."

"Let me talk. Please. I need to see the kids."

"Don't beg."

Emily saw the gleam of silver as Frankie drew his gun. Terror gripped her heart. The other two men flanked him. They murmured something about waiting for his father.

Frankie opened the center drawer on the desk and took out a silencer. "I can do what needs to be done."

"But your father—"

"He's always telling me to step up." He finished attaching the silencer to his handgun. "That's what I'm going to do."

He fired point-blank, then fired again.

When Frankie stepped away, she saw the dead man in the chair. His suit jacket was thrown open. The front of his shirt was slick with blood.

Emily pinched her lips closed to keep from crying out. She should have done something. A man was dead, and she hadn't reached out, hadn't helped him.

"We're already out at sea," Frankie said. "International waters. A good place to dump a body."

"I'll get something to carry him in."

He glanced toward the closet…

Chapter One

Colorado
Six weeks later

He'd been down this road before. Though Sean Timmons was pretty sure that he'd never actually been to Hazelwood Ranch, there was something familiar about the long, snow-packed drive bordered on either side by wood fences. He parked his cherry-red Jeep Wrangler between a snow-covered pickup truck and a snowy white lump that was the size of a four-door sedan. Peering through his windshield, he saw a large two-story house with a wraparound porch. It looked like somebody had tried to shovel his or her way out, but the wind and new snow had all but erased the path leading to the front door.

Weather forecasters had been gleefully predicting the first blizzard of the Colorado ski season, and it looked like they were right for a change. Sean was glad he wouldn't have to make the drive back to Denver tonight. He hadn't formally accepted this assignment, but he didn't see why he wouldn't.

Hazel Hopkins from Hazelwood Ranch had called his office at TST Security yesterday and said she needed a bodyguard for at least a week, possibly longer. He wouldn't be protecting Hazel but a "friend" of hers.

She was vague about the threat, but he gathered that her "friend" had offended someone with a story she'd written. The situation didn't seem too dangerous. Panic words, such as *narcotics*, *crime lord* and *homicidal ax murderer*, had been absent from her conversation.

Hazel had refused to give her "friend's" name, which wasn't all that unusual. The wealthy folk who lived near Aspen were often cagey about their identities. That was okay with him. The money transfer for Hazel's retainer had cleared, and that was really all Sean needed to know. Still, he'd been curious enough to look up Hazelwood Ranch on the internet, where he'd learned that the ranch was a small operation with only twenty-five to fifty head of cattle. Hazel, the owner, was a small but healthy-looking woman with short silver hair. No clues about the identity of her "friend." If he had to guess, he'd say that the person he'd be guarding was an aging movie star who'd written one of those tell-all books and was now regretting her candor.

Soon enough he'd know the truth. He zipped his parka, slapped on a knit cap and put on heavy-duty gloves. It wasn't far to the front porch, but the snow was already higher than his ankles. Fat, wet flakes swirled around him as he left his Jeep and slogged along the remnants of a pathway to the front door.

On the porch, the Adirondack chairs and a hanging swing were covered with giant scoops of drifted snow. He stomped his boots and punched the bell under the porch lamp. Hazel Hopkins opened the door and ushered him into a warmly lighted foyer with a sweeping wrought-iron staircase and a matching chandelier with lights that glimmered like candles.

"Glad you made it, Sean." Her voice was husky. When he looked down into her lively turquoise eyes, he suspected that a lot of wild living had gone into creating her raspy tone. Though she wore jeans on the bottom, her top was kimono-style with a fire-breathing dragon embroidered on each shoulder. He had the impression that he'd met her before.

She stuck out her tiny hand. "I'm Hazel Hopkins."

Compared with hers, his hand looked as big as a grizzly bear's paw. Sean was six feet, three inches tall, and this little woman made him feel like a hulking giant.

"Hang your jacket on the rack and take off your wet boots," she said. "You're running late. It's almost dark."

"The snow slowed me down."

"I was worried."

Parallel lines creased her forehead, and he noticed that she glanced surreptitiously toward a shotgun in the corner of the entryway. Gently he asked, "Have there been threats?"

"I had a more practical concern. I was worried that you wouldn't be able to find the ranch and you couldn't reach us by phone. Something's wrong with my landline, and the blizzard is disrupting the cell phone signal."

He sat on a bench by the door to take off his wet boots.

Without pausing for breath, she continued. "You know how they always say that the weather doesn't affect your service on the cell phone or the Wi-Fi? Well, I'm here to tell you that's a lie, a bold-faced lie. Every time we have a serious snowstorm, I have a problem."

The heels on her pixie-size boots clicked on the terra-cotta floor between area rugs as she darted toward him, grabbed his boots and carried them to a drying mat under the coat hooks. She braced her fists on her hips and stared at him. "You're exactly how I remembered."

Aha, they had met before. He stood and adjusted the tail of his beige suede shirt to hide the holster he wore on his hip. "This may sound strange..." he said. "Have I ever been here?"

"I don't think so. But Hazelwood Ranch is the backdrop for many, many photos. The kids came here often."

Her explanation raised more questions. Backdrop for what? What kids? Why would he have seen the photos? "Maybe you could remind me—"

She reached up to pat his cheek. "I'm glad that you're still clean-shaven. I don't like the scruffy beard trend. I'll bet you picked up your grooming habits in the FBI."

"Plus, my mom was a good teacher."

"Not according to the photo on your TST Security website," she said. "Your brother, Dylan, has a ponytail."

"He's kind of a wild card. His specialties are electronics and cybersecurity."

"And your specialty is working with law enforcement and figuring out the crimes. I believe your third partner, Mason Steele, is what you boys call the 'muscle' in the group."

"I guess you checked me out."

"I have, indeed."

He took a long look at her, hoping to jog his brain. His mind was blank. Nothing came through. His gaze focused on her necklace, a long string of etched silver, black onyx and turquoise beads. He knew that necklace...and the matching bracelet coiled around her wrist.

Shaking his head, he inhaled deeply. A particular aroma came to him. The scent of roasted peppers, onions, chili and cinnamon mingled with honey and fresh corn bread. He couldn't explain this odor, but his lungs had been craving it. Nothing else was nearly as sweet or as spicy delicious. Nothing else would satisfy this newly awakened appetite.

His eyelids closed as a high-definition picture appeared in his mind. He saw a woman—young, fresh and beautiful. A blue jersey shift outlined her slender curves, and she'd covered the front with a ruffled white apron. Her long, sleek brown hair cascaded down her back, almost to her waist. She held a wooden spoon toward him, offering a taste of her homemade chili.

He had always wanted more than a taste. He wanted everything with her, the whole enchilada. But he couldn't have her. Their time was over.

He gazed down into her eyes...*her turquoise eyes!*

"You remember," Hazel said, "the wedding."

That Saturday in June, six and a half years ago, was a blur of color and taste and music and silence. His eyelids snapped open. "I recall the divorce a whole lot better."

These were dangerous memories, warning bells. He should run, get the hell out of there. Instead, he followed his nose down a shadowy hallway. Stiff-legged, he marched through the dining room into the bright, warm kitchen where the aroma of chili was thick.

Two pans of golden corn bread rested near the sink on the large center island with a dark marble countertop. She stood at the stove with her back toward him, stirring a heavy cast-iron pot. She wore jeans that outlined her long legs and tight, round bottom. On top, she had on a striped sweater. Over her shoulder, she said, "Hazel, did I hear the doorbell?"

The small, silver-haired woman beside him growled a warning. "You should turn around slowly, dear."

Sean gripped the edge of the marble countertop, unsure of how he was going to feel when he faced her. Every single day since their divorce five years ago—after only a year and a half of marriage—he had imagined her. Sometimes he remembered the sweet warmth of her body beside him in their bed. Other times he saw her from afar and reveled in coming closer and closer. Usually, he imagined her naked with her dark chestnut hair spilling across her olive skin.

Her hair! He stared at her back and shoulders. She'd chopped off her lush, silky hair.

"Emily," he said.

She whirled. Clearly surprised, she wielded her wooden spoon like a knife she might plunge into his chest. "Sean."

Her turquoise eyes were huge, outlined with thick, dark lashes. Her mouth was a thin, tight line. Her dark brows pulled down, and he immediately recognized her expression, a look he'd seen often while they were married. She was furious. What the hell did she have to be angry about? He was the one who had driven through a blizzard.

He stepped away from the counter, not needing the support. The anger surging through his veins gave him the strength of ten. "I don't know what kind of sick game you two ladies are playing, but it's not funny. I'm leaving."

"Good." She stuck out her jaw and took a step toward him. "I don't want you hanging around."

"Then why call me up here? I had a verbal contract, an agreement." TST had a strict no-refund policy, but this was a special circumstance. He'd pay back the retainer from his own pocket. "Forget it. I'll give your money back."

"What money?" Emily's upper lip curled in a sneer that she probably thought was terrifying. Yeah, right, as terrifying as a bunny wiggling its nose.

"You hired me."

"Not me." Emily threw her spoon back into the chili pot. "Aunt Hazel, what have you done?"

The silver-haired woman with dragons on her shoulders had maneuvered her way around so she was standing at the far end of the center island with both of them on the other side. "When you two got married, I always thought you were a perfect match."

"You were the only one," Emily said.

Unfortunately, that was true. Sean and Emily were both born and raised in Colorado, but they had met in San Francisco. She was a student at University of California in Berkeley, majoring in English and appearing at least once a week at local poetry slams. At one of these open-mike events, he saw her.

She'd been dancing around on a small stage wearing a long gypsy skirt. Her wild hair was snatched up on her head with dozens of ribbons. He'd been impressed when she rhymed "appetite" and "morning light" and "coprolite," which was a technical word for fossilized poop. He would have stayed and talked to her, but he'd been undercover, rooting out a drug dealer at the slam venue. Sean had been in the FBI.

When they told people they were getting married, their opposite lifestyles—Bohemian chick versus federal agent—were the first thing people pointed to as a reason it would never work. The next issue was an age difference. She was nineteen, and he was twenty-seven. Eight years wasn't really all that much, but her youthful immaturity stood in stark contrast to his orderly, responsible lifestyle.

"If you'd asked me at the time," Aunt Hazel said, "I'd have advised you to live together before marriage."

Sean hadn't wanted to take that chance. He had hoped the bonds of marriage would help him control his butterfly. "It was a mistake," he said.

Emily responded with a snort.

"You don't think so?" he asked.

"Are you still here? You were in such a rush to get away from me."

His contrary streak kicked in. He sure as hell wasn't going to let her think that she was chasing him out the door. Very slowly and deliberately, he pulled out a stool and took a seat at the center island opposite the stove top. He turned away from Emily.

"Aunt Hazel," he said, "you still haven't told us why you hired me as a bodyguard."

"You? A bodyguard?" Emily sputtered. "You're not a fed anymore?"

"Do you care?"

"Why should I?"

"What are you doing now?" he asked.

"Writing."

"Poetry?" He scoffed.

She exhaled an eager gasp as she tilted her head and leaned toward him. Her turquoise eyes flashed. Her face, framed by wisps of brown hair, was flushed beneath the natural olive tint. He remembered her spirit and her enthusiasm, and he knew that she wanted to tell him something. The words were poised at the tip of her tongue, straining to jump out.

And he wanted to hear them. He wanted to share with her, to listen to her stories and to feel the waves of excitement that radiated from her. Emily had always thrown herself wholeheartedly into whatever she was attempting to do. It was part of her charm. No doubt she had some project that was insanely ambitious.

With a scowl, she raised her hand, palm out, to hold him away from her. "Just go."

"Such drama," Aunt Hazel said. "The two of you are impossible. It's called communication, and it's not all that difficult. Sean, you're going to sit there and I'm going to tell you what our girl has been up to."

"I don't have to listen to this," Emily said.

"If I'm not explaining properly, feel free to jump in," Hazel said. "First of all, Emily doesn't write poems anymore. After the divorce, she changed her focus to journalism."

"Totally impractical," he muttered. "With all the newspapers going out of business, nobody makes a living as a journalist."

"I do all right."

Her voice was proud, and there was a strut in her step as she strolled from one end of the island to the other. Watching her long, slender legs and the way her hips swayed was a treat. He felt himself being drawn into her orbit. She'd always had the power to mesmerize him.

"Fine," he muttered. "Tell me about your big deal success in journalism."

"Right after the divorce, I got a job writing for the *Daily Californian*, Berkeley's student newspaper. I learned investigative techniques, and I blogged. And I started doing articles for online magazines. I have a regular bimonthly piece in a national publication, and they pay very nicely."

"For articles about eye shadow and shoes?"

"Hard-hitting news." She slammed her fist on the marble island. "I witnessed a murder."

"Which is why I called you," Aunt Hazel said. "Emily's life is in danger."

This was just crazy enough to be possible. "Have you received threats?"

"Death threats," she said.

His feet were rooted to the kitchen floor. He didn't want to stay…but he couldn't leave her here unprotected.

Chapter Two

Emily couldn't look away from him. Fascinated, she watched as a muscle in Sean's jaw twitched, his brow lowered and his eyes turned as black as polished obsidian. He was outrageously masculine.

With a nearly imperceptible shrug, his muscles tensed, but his frame didn't contract. He seemed to get bigger. His fingers coiled into fists, ready to lash out. He was prepared to defend her against anything and everything. His aggressive stance told her that he'd take on an army to keep her from harm.

When she thought about it, his new occupation as a bodyguard made sense. Sean had always been a protector, whether it was keeping a bully away from his sweet-but-nerdy brother or rescuing a stray dog by stopping four lanes of traffic on a busy highway. If Sean had been hiding in that louvered closet instead of her, he would have saved the man she now could identify as Roger Patrone.

Sean reached toward her. She yanked her arm away. She didn't dare allow him to get too close. No matter how much she wanted his embrace, that wasn't going to happen. This man had been the love of her life. Ending their marriage was the most difficult thing she'd ever done, and she couldn't bear going through that soul wrenching pain again.

"Did you report the murder to the police?" he asked.

"Of course," she said, "and to your former FBI bosses. Specifically, I had several chats with Special Agent Greg Levine. I'm surprised he didn't call and tell you."

"Levine is still stationed in San Francisco," he said. "Is that where the crime took place?"

"Yes."

"In the city?"

"Just beyond the Golden Gate Bridge."

"In open waters," he said. "A good place to dump a body."

It was a bit disturbing that his FBI-trained brain and Freddie Wynter's nefarious instincts drew exactly the same conclusion. *Maybe you need to think like a criminal to catch one.* "As it turned out, the ocean wasn't such a great dump site. The victim washed up on Baker Beach five days later."

"The waiting must have been rough on you," he said. "It's no fun to report a murder when the body goes missing."

Definitely not fun when the investigating officer was buddy-buddy with her ex-husband. She'd asked Greg not to blab to Sean, but she'd expected him to ignore her request. Those guys stuck together. The only time Sean had lied to her when they were married was when he was covering up for a fellow fed.

She wondered if Sean's departure from the FBI had been due to negative circumstances. Had Mr. Perfect screwed up? Gotten himself fired? "Why did you leave the FBI?"

"It was time."

"Cryptic," she snapped.

"It's true."

God forbid he give her a meaningful explanation! Leaving the FBI must have been traumatic for him. Sean was born to be a fed. He could have been a poster boy with his black hair neatly barbered and his chin clean-shaven and his beige chamois suede shirt looking like it had come fresh from the dry cleaner's. He'd been proud to be a special agent. Would he confide in her if they'd fired him? "You can be so damn annoying."

"Is that so?"

"I hate when you put off a perfectly rational query with a macho statement that doesn't really tell me anything, like a man's got to do what a man's got to do."

"I don't expect you to understand."

"Mission accomplished."

Hostility vibrated around him. A red flush climbed his throat. Oh yeah, he was angry. Hot and angry. They could have put him on the porch and melted the blizzard.

"I'll leave," he said.

"Not in this storm," Aunt Hazel said. "The two of you need to calm down. Have some chili. Try to be civil."

Emily stepped away from the stove, folded her arms at her waist and watched with a sidelong gaze as Sean and her aunt dished up bowls of chili and cut off slabs of corn bread. Sean managed to squash his anger and transform into a pleasant dinner guest. She could have matched his politeness with a cold veneer of her own, but she preferred to say nothing.

There had been a time—long ago when she and Sean were first dating—when she was known for her candor. Every word from her lips was truth. She had been 100 percent frank and open.

Those days were gone.

She'd glimpsed the ugliness, heard the cries of the hopeless, learned that life wasn't always good and people weren't always kind. She'd lost her innocence.

And Hazel was correct. She'd gotten herself into trouble from the Wynters. Though she didn't want to be, she was terrified. Almost anything could set off her fear…an unexpected phone call, the slam of a door, a car that followed too closely. She hadn't gotten a good night's sleep since that night in James Wynter's closet.

The only reason she hadn't disintegrated into a quivering mass of nerves was simple: Wynter and his men didn't know her identity. Her FBI contact had told her that they knew there was a witness to the murder, but didn't know who. It was only a matter of time before they found out who she was and came after her. *Tell him. Tell Sean. Let him be your bodyguard.*

Her aunt asked, "Emily, can I get you something to drink?"

Hazel and Sean had already sprinkled grated cheddar on top of their chili bowls and added a spoonful of sour cream. They were headed to the adjoining dining room.

What would it hurt to have dinner with him? The more she looked at him, the more she saw hints of his former self, her husband, the gentleman, the broad-shouldered man who had stolen her heart. She remembered the first time they were introduced when he'd tried to shake hands and she gave him a hug. They'd always been opposites and always attracted.

"I'm not hungry," Emily said.

"There's no reason to be so stubborn," Hazel scolded. "I've hired you a bodyguard. Let the man do his job."

"I don't want a bodyguard."

She glared at Sean, standing so straight and tall like a

knight in shining armor. She was drawn to his strength. At the same time, he ticked her off. She wanted to tip him over like an extra-large tin can.

Edging closer to the kitchen windows, she pushed aside the curtain and peered outside. Day had faded into dusk, and the snow was coming down hard and fast. The blizzard wasn't going to let up; he'd be here all night. She'd be spending the night under the same roof with him? *This could be a problem, a big one.*

"I've got a question for you," he said as he strolled past her and set his chili bowl on a woven place mat. "What kind of murder would trigger an FBI investigation?"

"The man who pulled the trigger is Frankie Wynter."

He startled. "The son of James Wynter?"

She'd said too much. The best move now was to retreat. She stretched and yawned. "I'm tired, Aunt Hazel. I think I'll go up to my room."

Without waiting for a response, she pivoted and ran from the kitchen. In the foyer, she paused to put Hazel's rifle in the closet. It was dangerous to leave that thing out. Then she charged up the staircase, taking two steps at a time. In her bedroom, she turned on the lamp and flopped onto her back on the queen-size bed with the handmade crazy quilt.

Memory showed her the picture of Roger Patrone sprawled back in the swivel chair with his necktie askew and his shirt covered in blood. When they came toward the closet, looking for something to wrap around poor Roger, she'd expected to be the next victim. She'd held tightly to the doorknob, hoping they'd think it was locked.

There had been no need to hold the knob. Frankie told them to get the plastic shower curtain from the bathroom. Blood wouldn't seep through. His quick orders had made her think that he might have pulled this stunt before. Other bodies might have gone over the railing of his daddy's double-decker yacht. Other murders might have been committed.

She stood, lurched toward the door, pivoted and went back to the bed. Trapped in her room like a child, she had no escape from memory. Her chest tightened. It felt like a giant fist was squeezing her lungs, and she couldn't get enough oxygen. She sat up straight. She was hot and cold at the same time. Her head was dizzy. Her breath came in frantic gasps.

With a moan, she leaned forward, put her head between her knees and told herself to inhale through her nose and exhale through her mouth. Breathe deeply and slowly. Wasn't working—her throat was too tight. Was she having a panic attack? She didn't know; she'd never had this feeling before.

The door to her bedroom opened. Sean stepped inside as though he didn't need to ask her permission and had every right to be there. She would have yelled at him, but she couldn't catch her breath. Her pulse fluttered madly.

He crossed the carpet and sat beside her on the bed. His arm wrapped around her shoulders. His masculine aroma, a combination of soap, cedar forest and sweat, permeated her senses as she leaned her head against his shoulder.

Her hands clutched in a knot against her breast, but she felt her heart rate beginning to slow down. She was regaining control of herself. Somehow she'd find a way to handle the fear. And she'd set things right.

Gently, he rocked back and forth. "Better?"

"Much." She took a huge gulp of air.

"Do you want to talk about what happened?"

"I already did. I told your buddy, Agent Levine."

"Number one, he's not my buddy. Number two, why didn't he offer to put you in witness protection?"

"I turned it down," she said.

"Emily, do you know how dangerous Frankie Wynter is?"

"I've been researching Wynter Corp for over a year," she said. "Their smuggling operations, gambling and money laundering are nasty crimes, but the real evil comes from human trafficking. Last year, the port authorities seized a boxcar container with over seventy women and children crammed inside. Twelve were dead."

"And Wynter Corp managed to wriggle out from under the charges."

"The paperwork vanished." That was one of the bits of evidence she'd hoped to get from James Wynter's computer. "There was no indication of the sender or the destination where these people were to be delivered. All they could say was that they were promised jobs."

"This kind of investigation is best left to the cops."

She separated from him and rose to her feet. "I know what I'm doing."

"I'm not discounting your ability," he said. "You might be the best investigative reporter of all time, but you don't have the contacts. Not like the FBI. They've got undercover people everywhere. Not to mention their access to advanced weaponry and surveillance equipment."

"I understand all that." He wasn't telling her anything she hadn't already figured out for herself.

"You're a witness to a crime. That's it—that's all she wrote."

She braced herself against the dresser and looked into the large mirror on the wall. Her reflection showed her fear in the tension around her eyes and her blanched complexion. Sean—ever the opposite—seemed calm and balanced.

"Can I tell you the truth?" she asked.

"That would be best."

She made eye contact with his reflection in the mirror. "I didn't actually witness the shooting. I saw Frankie with the gun in his hand. He screwed on a silencer. I heard the gunshot, and I saw the bullet holes… and the blood. But I didn't actually witness Frankie pointing the gun and pulling the trigger."

"Minor point," he said. "A good prosecutor can connect those dots."

"The body that washed ashore five days later was too badly nibbled by fishes for identification." She splayed her fingers on the dresser and stared down at them. "I was kind of hoping he was someone else, someone who jumped off the Golden Gate Bridge, but Agent Levine matched his DNA."

"To what?"

"I'd given a description to a sketch artist and identified the victim from a mug sheet photo. His name was Roger Patrone."

He shrugged. "I don't know him."

"He was thirty-five, only a couple of years older than you, and made his living with a small-time gambling operation in a cheesy strip joint. Convicted of fraud, he served three years."

"You've done your homework."

"Never married, no kids, he was orphaned when he was nine and grew up with a family in Chinatown. He speaks the language, eats the food, knows the customs and has a reputation as a negotiator for Wynter."

"Roger sounds like a useful individual," Sean said. "I'm guessing the old man wasn't too happy about this murder."

"Yeah, well, blood is still thicker than water. The FBI brought Frankie in for questioning, but one of the other guys in Wynter Corp confessed to killing Patrone and claimed self-defense. He took the fall for the boss's son."

Sean left the bed and came up behind her. His chest wasn't actually touching her back, but if she moved one step, she'd be in his arms.

In a measured tone, he said, "You're telling me that Frankie's not in custody."

"No, he's not."

"And he knows there's a witness."

"Yes."

"Did you write about the murder?"

"Agent Levine asked me not to." But she had written many articles about the evil-doing of Wynter Corporation.

"Does Frankie have your name?"

"No," she said. "I write under an alias, three different aliases, in fact. And I have two dummy blogs. Since my communication with these publications is via the internet, nobody even knows what I look like."

"Smart."

"Thank you." Her reflection smiled at his. *So far, so good.* She might make it through the night with no more explanation than that. There was more to tell, but she didn't want to get involved with Sean. Not again.

He continued. "And you're also smart to have left Frankie and the other thugs behind in San Francisco.

Hazelwood Ranch seems like a safe place to stay until this all dies down."

Unfortunately, she hadn't come to visit Aunt Hazel for safety reasons. Her gaze flickered across the surface of the mirror. She didn't want to tell him.

He leaned closer, whispered in her ear. "What is it, Emily? What do you want to say?"

The words came tumbling out. "Frankie is here in Colorado. The Wynter family has a gated compound over near Aspen. I didn't come here to give up on my investigation. I need to go deeper."

He grasped her upper arms. "Leave this to the police."

From downstairs, there was a scream.

Chapter Three

"Aunt Hazel!"

Though Emily's immediate reaction was to run toward the sound of the scream, Sean only allowed her to take two steps before he grabbed her around the middle and yanked her so hard that her feet left the floor. This was why he'd been hired.

He dragged her across the bedroom. There was only one thought in his mind: get her to safety. In the attached bathroom, he set her down beside a claw-foot tub.

"Stay here," he ordered as he drew his gun. "Keep quiet."

"The hell I will."

Though he hated to waste time with explanation, she needed to know what was going on. He spoke in a no-nonsense tone. "If there's been a break-in, they're after you. If you turn yourself in, we have no leverage. For your Aunt Hazel's safety, you need to avoid being taken captive."

"Okay, help her." Her face flushed red with fear and anger. Her eyes were wild. She pushed at his shoulder with both hands. "Hurry!"

Moving fast, he crossed to her closed bedroom door. He wished he was wearing boots instead of just socks.

If he had to go outside, his feet would turn to ice. He paused at the door and mentally ran through the layout of the house. From the upstairs landing, he could see the front door. He'd know if someone had broken in that way.

Sean was confident in his ability to handle one intruder, maybe two. But Frankie Wynter had a lot of thugs at his disposal, and they were loyal; one guy was willing to face a murder rap for the boss's son. One—or two or more—of them might be standing outside her bedroom door right now.

But he didn't hear anything. Outside, the snow rattled against the windows. The wind whistled. From downstairs, he heard shuffling noises. A heavy fist rapping at the door? A muffled shout. Sean turned the knob, pulled the door open and braced the gun in his hands, ready to shoot.

There was no one on the upstairs landing.

Emily dashed to his side. "Let me help. Please!"

He'd told her to stay back and she chose to ignore him. Emily was turning into a problem. "Is that tub in the bathroom made of cast iron?"

"It's antique. Now is not the time for a home tour."

"Get inside the tub and stay there." At least, she wouldn't be hit by a stray bullet.

"I'm coming with you."

Was she trying to drive him crazy or was this stubborn, infuriating behavior just a part of her natural personality? He couldn't exactly remember. He'd had damn good reasons for divorcing this woman. "No time to argue. Just accept the fact that I know what I'm doing."

"I need a gun."

"What you need is to listen to me."

"Please, Sean! You always carry two guns. Give one to me."

He pulled the Glock from his ankle holster and slapped it into her hand. "Do you remember how to use this?"

She recited the rules he'd taught her one golden afternoon six years ago in Big Sur. "Aim and don't close my eyes. No traditional safety on a Glock, so keep my finger off the trigger until I'm ready. Squeeze—don't yank."

"You've got the basics."

He'd treated their lessons like a game and had never insisted that she take his weapon from the combination safe when he was on assignment and she was alone at home. While he was working undercover, he'd worried about her safety, worried that she'd be hurt and it would be his fault. There was a strange irony in the fact that she'd put herself in ten times more danger than he could imagine.

He peered through the open bedroom door onto the upstairs landing where an overhead light shone down on the southwestern decor that dominated the house: a Navajo rug, a rugged side table and a cactus in an earthenware pot. A long hallway led to other bedrooms. The front edge of the landing was a graceful black wrought-iron staircase overlooking the foyer and chandelier by the front door.

Sean peered over the railing.

A menacing silence rose to greet him. He didn't like the way this was going. Emily's aunt wasn't the type of woman who cowered in silence. He gestured for Emily to stay upstairs while he descended.

At the foot of the staircase, he caught a glimpse of flying kimono dragons when Hazel raced across the foyer and skidded to a stop right in front of him.

She glared. "Where the heck is my rifle?"

Looking down from the landing, Emily said, "I moved it to the front closet."

"I had my gun right by the door," she said to Sean. "Emily shouldn't have moved it. Out of sight, out of mind."

The women in this family simply didn't grasp what it took to be cautious and safe. They needed ten bodyguards apiece. He rushed Hazel up the stairs, where she hugged Emily. The two of them commiserated as though the threat were over and done with. Had they forgotten that there might be an intruder?

"Hazel," he barked, "why did you scream?"

"I heard something outside and looked through the window. A fat lot of good it did, the snow's coming down so hard I couldn't see ten feet. But I caught a glimmer...headlights. I went toward the front door for a better look. At the exact same time, I heard somebody crashing against the back door like they were trying to bust it down. That's when I screamed."

Sean figured that five minutes had passed since they'd heard Hazel's cry for help. "After you screamed, what did you do?"

"I hid."

"Smart," he said. "You didn't reveal your hiding spot until you saw me."

She nodded, and her short silver hair bounced.

"Did you see the intruder? Did he make a noise? Was there more than one?"

"Well, my hearing isn't what it once was, but I'm pretty sure there was only one voice. And I guarantee that nobody made enough noise to tear down the back door."

As Sean herded Emily and her aunt into Emily's

bedroom, he tallied up the possible ways to break into the house. In addition to front and back door and many windows, there was likely an entrance to a root cellar or basement. The best way to limit access to the two women was to keep them upstairs. Unfortunately, it also meant they had no escape.

From Emily's bedroom, he peered through the window to the area where the cars were parked. He squinted. "I can see the outline of a truck."

"So?"

"Do you recognize it?" *Is that Frankie Wynter's truck?*

"We're in the mountains, Sean. Every other person drives a truck."

A coating of snow had already covered the truck bed; he couldn't tell if anybody had been riding in back. But the vehicle showed that someone else was on the property, even if there hadn't been other noises from downstairs.

He gave Emily a tight smile. "Stay here with Hazel. Take care of her."

"What are you going to do?"

"I'll check the doors and other points of access."

Her terse nod was a match for his smile. They were both putting on brave faces and tamping down the kind of tension that might cause your hand to tremble or your teeth to chatter. When she rested her hand against his chest, he was reminded of the early days in their marriage when she'd say goodbye before he left on assignment.

"Be careful, Sean."

He tore his gaze away from her turquoise eyes and her rose petal lips. Her trust made him feel strong and brave, even if he wasn't facing a real dragon. He was girding his loins, like a knight protecting his castle. In the old days, they would have kissed.

"I should come with you," Aunt Hazel said. "You need someone to watch your six."

"Stay here," he growled.

Emily hooked her arm around her aunt's waist. "We might as well do what he says. Sean can be a teensy bit rigid when it comes to obeying orders."

"My, my, my." Hazel adjusted the embroidered dragons on her shoulders. "Isn't that just like a fed?"

Hey, lady, you're the one who called me. And he was done playing their games. As far as he was concerned, they'd had their last warning. He refused to stand here and explain again why they shouldn't throw themselves into the line of fire when there was a possible intruder. He made a quick pivot and descended the staircase with the intention of searching the main floor.

The house was large but not so massive that he'd get lost. First, he would determine if an intruder was inside. The front door hadn't been opened. The door to a long, barrack-type wing where ranch hands might sleep during a busy season was locked, and the same was true for the basement door and the back door that opened onto a wide porch. Though it had a dead bolt, the back door lock was flimsy, easily blasted through with a couple of gunshots. As far as he could tell, no weapons had been fired.

When he pushed open the back door, a torrent of glistening snow swept inside. The area near the rear porch was trampled with many prints in the snow. Was it one person or several? He couldn't tell, but Hazel's story was true. She'd heard someone back here.

As he closed the rear door and relocked it, he heard Emily call his name. Her voice was steady, strong and unafraid. Weapon raised, he rushed toward the front of the house. The door was opening. A man in a brown parka with fur around the hood plodded inside.

Though he didn't look like much of a threat, Sean wasn't taking any chances. "Freeze."

"I sure as hell will if I don't close this door."

As the man in the parka turned to shut the front door, Hazel came down the staircase. "It's okay, Sean. This is my neighbor, Willis. He was a deputy sheriff until he retired a couple of years ago."

"I was worried, Hazel." As he shoved off his hood, unzipped the parka and stomped his snowmobile boots, puddles of melted snow appeared on the terra-cotta tile floor. "Couldn't reach you on the phone, so I decided to come over here and check before I went to bed. Hi, Emily."

"Hey, Willis."

"Take off those boots." Hazel pointed to the bench by the door. "Are you hungry? Emily made a big pot of chili."

He sat and grinned at Sean and Emily. His face was ruddy and wet. A few errant flakes of snow still clung to his thick mustache. "And who's this young fella with the Glock?"

"Sean Timmons of TST Security." He shook the older man's meaty hand. "I'm Emily's bodyguard."

Willis was clearly intrigued. Why did Emily need protection? What other kind of security work did Sean do? He pushed the strands of wet gray hair off his forehead and straightened his mustache before he asked, "You hiring?"

"Part time," Sean said. "I can always use a man with experience as a deputy sheriff."

"Seventeen years," Willis said. "And I still work

with the volunteer fire brigade and mountain search and rescue."

"Plus you've got your own little neighborhood watch." Sean had the feeling that Hazel got more attention from the retired deputy than the others in this area. "You have a key to the front door."

"That's right."

"Do you mind telling me why you banged on the back door and didn't let yourself in?"

"The back door is always unlocked, and it was a few less steps through the blizzard than the front. When I found it locked, I was pretty damn mad. I yanked at the handle to make sure it wasn't just stuck, and I might have let out a few choice swear words."

"Scared me half to death," Hazel said.

"I heard you scream." Willis looked down at the floor between his boots. He wore two pairs of wool socks. Both had seen better days. "And I felt like a jackass for scaring you."

She patted his cheek, halfway chiding and halfway flirting. "You're lucky I couldn't find my rifle."

While he explained that his keys were in the truck, and he had to tromp back out there to find the right ones, Hazel fussed over him. She was a touchy-feely person who hugged and patted and stroked. Sean noted her behavior and realized how similar it was to methods Emily used to calm him, mesmerize him and convince him to do whatever she wanted.

He glanced toward her. She sat on the fourth step, where she had a clear view of the others in the foyer. Her gaze flicked to the left, but he knew she'd been watching him. A hard woman to figure out. Was she angry or nervous? Independent or lonely?

Earlier tonight, she'd been on the verge of a panic

attack. Her eyes had been wide with fear. Her muscles were so tightly clenched that she couldn't move, couldn't breathe. Scared to death, and he didn't blame her. James Wynter and his associates were undeniably dangerous.

A muscle in his jaw clenched. Why had she chosen to go after these violent criminals? And how did Levine justify leaving this witness unprotected? The FBI had been chasing Wynter for years, way before Sean was stationed in San Francisco. A chance to lock up Frankie Wynter would be a coup.

"Then it's settled," Hazel said. "Willis is sticking around for some chili and a couple of beers. You kids come into the dining room and join us."

"In a minute," Emily promised as she rose to her feet and motioned for Sean to come toward her.

She stayed on the first step, and he stood below her. They were almost eye level.

He asked, "Did you have something you wanted to say?"

"You did good tonight. I know that Hazel and I can be a handful, but you managed us. You were organized, quick. And when we thought we needed you, there you were, charging around the corner and yelling for Willis to freeze. You were…" She exhaled a sigh. "Impressive."

Her compliment made him leery. "It's what I do."

"Not that we actually needed your bodyguard skills." She caught hold of his hand and gave a squeeze. "This was a simple misunderstanding because of the blizzard."

"You have plenty of reason to be worried," he reminded her. "You mentioned the Wynter family compound near Aspen. Tonight it was Willis at the door. Tomorrow it might be Frankie Wynter."

"Don't make this into a worst-case scenario." She continued to hold his hand, and he felt the tension in her grip. "Tonight a neighbor came to pay a visit. That's all. And the blizzard is just snow. It's harmless. Kids play in it. Ever build a snowman?"

"Ever get caught in an avalanche?" He was keeping the tone light, but there was something important he needed to say. "Seriously, Emily, you need a bodyguard."

"I agree, and the job is yours."

He'd expected an argument but was glad that she'd decided to be rational. He glanced toward the dining room. "I could do with another bowl of chili."

"Me, too."

Before she hopped down the stair step to the floor, she went up on tiptoe and gave him a kiss on the forehead. It was nothing special, the kind of small affection a wife might regularly bestow on her husband. The utter simplicity blew him away.

Before she could turn her back and skip off into the dining room, he caught her hand and gave a tug. She was in his arms. When her body pressed against his, they were joined together the way they were supposed to be.

Then he kissed her.

Chapter Four

Emily hadn't intended to seduce him. That little kiss on his forehead was meant to be friendly. If she'd known she was lighting the fuse to a passionate response, she never would have gotten within ten feet of him. *Not true. I'm lying to myself.* From the moment she'd seen him, sensual memories had been taunting from the back of her mind. It was only a matter of time before that undercurrent would become manifest.

Their marriage was over, but she never had stopped imagining Sean as her lover. Nobody kissed her the way he did. The pressure of his mouth against hers was familiar and perfect. *Will he do that thing with his tongue? The thing where he parts my lips gently, and then he deepens the kiss. His tongue swoops and swirls. And there's a growling noise from the back of his throat, a vibration.*

She'd never been able to fully describe what he did to her and what sensations he unleashed. But he was doing it right now, right in this moment. *Oh yes, kiss me again.*

She almost swooned. *Swoon? No way!* She'd changed. No more the lady poet, she was a hard-bitten journalist, not the type of woman who collapsed in a dead faint after one kiss, definitely not.

But her grip on consciousness was slipping fast. Her

knees began to buckle, and she clung to his shoulders to keep from slipping to the floor. Her hands slid down his chest. Even that move was sexy; through the smooth fabric of his beige chamois shirt, she fondled his hard but supple abs.

This out-of-control but very pleasurable attraction had to stop before she lost her willpower, her rationality…her very mind. Pushing with the flat of her palms against his chest, she forced a distance between them. "We can't do this."

"Sure we can." He slung his arm around her waist. "It's been a while, but I haven't forgotten how."

Tomorrow he'd thank her for not dissolving into a quivering blob of lust. Firmly, she said, "I can see that we're going to need ground rules."

He kissed the top of her head and took a step back. "You cut it."

"What?"

"Your hair, you cut it."

"Too much trouble." She fluffed her chin-length bob. "And getting rid of the Rapunzel curls makes me look more adult."

"Oh yeah, you're really grown up. How old are you now, twenty-one? Twenty-two?"

She didn't laugh at his lame attempt at humor. "I'm almost twenty-six."

Their eight-year age difference had always been an issue. When they first met, she'd just turned nineteen. They were married and divorced before she was twenty-one, and she'd always wondered if their relationship would have lasted longer if she'd been more mature. It was a familiar refrain. *If I knew then what I know now, things would be different.*

More likely, they never would have gotten together

in the first place. Older and wiser, she would have taken one look at him and realized that he wasn't the sort of man who should be married.

"I like your new haircut," he said. "And you're right. We need some ground rules."

She gestured toward the dining room. "Should we eat chili while we talk?"

"That depends on how much you want your aunt and former deputy Willis to know."

Of course, he was right. She didn't want to spill potentially dangerous information about Wynter Corp into a casual conversation. Until now the only thing she'd told Aunt Hazel was that she'd witnessed a murder in San Francisco. She hadn't named the killer or the victim and certainly hadn't mentioned that the Wynter family had a place near Aspen.

Regret trickled through her. She probably shouldn't have come here. Though she'd been ultracautious in keeping her identity secret and her connection to Hazel was hard to trace, somebody might find out and come after them. If anything happened to Hazel…

Emily shuddered at the thought. "I don't want my aunt to get stuck in the middle of this."

"Agreed."

"Come with me."

She led him across the foyer to a living room that reflected Hazel's eclectic personality with a combination of classy and rustic. The terra-cotta floor and soft southwestern colors blended with painted barn wood on the walls. The high ceiling was open beam. The rugged, moss rock fireplace reminded Emily that her aunt was an outdoorswoman who herded cattle and tamed wild mustangs. But Hazel also had a small art collec-

tion, including two Georgia O'Keeffe watercolor paint
ings of flowers that hung on either side of the fireplace.

While Emily went behind the wet bar at the far end
of the room, Sean studied the watercolor of a glowing
pink-and-gold hydrangea. "Is this an original?"

"A gift from the artist," Emily said. "Hazel spent
some time with O'Keeffe at Ghost Ranch in New Mexico."

"I keep forgetting how rich your family is. None of
you are showy. It's all casual and comfortable and then
I realize that you've got valuable artwork on the wall."
He made his way across the room to the wet bar. "When
I was driving up to this place, I had the feeling I'd seen
it before. Did we come here for a visit?"

"I don't think so. Hazel was in Europe for most of the
year and a half we were married." She peered through
the glass door of the wine cellar refrigerator. "White
wine or red?"

"How about beer?"

"You haven't changed." She opened the under-the-
counter refrigerator and selected two bottles of craft
beers with zombies on the labels. "You'll like this brand.
It's dark."

He didn't question her selection, just grabbed the
beer, tapped the neck against hers and took a swig. He
licked his lips. "Good."

A dab of foam glistened at the corner of his mouth,
and she was tempted to wipe the moisture off, better
yet, to lick it.

"Ground rules," she said, reminding herself as much
as him.

"First, I want to know why I have déjà vu about Hazelwood Ranch. Do you have any photo albums?"

She came out from behind the bar and shot him a

glare. "If you don't mind, I'd rather not take a side trip down memory lane. We have more urgent concerns."

"You're the one who introduced family into the picture," he said. "I want to understand a few things about Hazel. How long has she lived here?"

"The ranch doesn't belong to our family. Hazel's late husband was the owner of this and many other properties near Aspen. He renamed this small ranch Hazelwood in honor of her. They always seemed so happy. Never had kids, though. He was older, in his fifties, when they got married."

She scanned the spines of books in a built-in shelf until she found a couple of photo albums. As she took them down and carried them to the coffee table in front of the sofa, she realized that she hadn't downloaded her own photos in months. Digital albums were nice, but she really preferred the old-fashioned way.

"I knew there'd be pictures," he said.

"Do you remember those journals I used to make? I'd take an old book with an interesting cover and replace the pages with my own sketches and poetry and photos."

"I remember." His voice was as soft as a caress. "The Engagement Journal was the best present you ever gave me."

"What about the watch, the super-expensive, engraved wristwatch?"

"Also treasured."

She went back to the bar, snatched up her beer and returned to sit on the sofa beside him. "I'm an excellent present giver. It's a family trait."

"How are they, the Peterson family?"

"My oldest sister had a baby girl, which means I'm an aunt, and the other two are in grad school. Mom and Dad moved to Arizona, which they love." She took a taste of the zombie beer, which was, as she'd expected, excellent, and gave him a rueful smile. "I don't suppose Aunt Hazel told my mom that she was calling you."

"Your mom hated me."

Emily made a halfhearted attempt to downplay her mother's opinion. "You weren't their favorite."

Her parents had begged her to stay in college and wait to get married until she was older. Emily was her mom's baby, the youngest of four girls, the artistic one. When Emily's divorce came, Mom couldn't wait to say "I told you so."

"Toward the end," he said, "I thought she was beginning to come around."

"It was never about you personally," she said. "I was too young, and you were too old. And Mom didn't really like that you did dangerous undercover work in the FBI."

"And what does she think of your current profession?"

She took a long swallow of the dark beer. "Hates it."

"Does she know about the murder?"

"Oh God, no." She cringed. If her mother suspected that she was actually in danger, she'd have a fit.

Emily opened the older of the two albums. The photographs were arranged in chronological order with Emily and her sisters starting out small and getting bigger as they aged. Nostalgia welled up inside her. The Petersons were a good-looking family, wholesome and happy. In spite of what Sean thought, they weren't really rich. Sure, they had enough money to live well and take vacations and pay for school tuitions. But they weren't big spenders, and their home in an upscale urban neighborhood in Denver wasn't ostentatious.

Like her older sisters, she had tried to be what her

parents wanted. They valued education, and when she told them she was considering becoming a teacher, they were thrilled. But Emily went to UC Berkeley and strayed from the path. She was a poet, a performance artist, an activist and a photographer. Her marriage and divorce to Sean had been just one more detour from the straight and narrow.

Aunt Hazel was more indulgent of Emily's free-spirited choices. Hazel approved of Sean. She'd invited him to be a bodyguard. Maybe she knew something Emily hadn't yet learned.

He stopped her hand as she was about to turn a page in the album. He pointed to a wintertime photo of her, wearing a white knit hat with a pom-pom and standing at the gate that separated Hazelwood Ranch from public lands. She couldn't have been more than five or six. Bundled up in her parka and jeans and boots, she appeared to be dancing with both hands in the air.

"This picture," he said. "You put a copy of this in the journal you gave me. I must have looked at it a hundred times. I never really noticed the outline of the hills and the curve in the road, but my subconscious must have absorbed the details. Seeing that photo is like being here."

His déjà vu was explained.

She asked, "What are we going to do to protect Hazel?"

"How does she feel about Willis? Do they have a little something going on?"

She and her aunt hadn't directly talked about who Hazel was dating, but Emily couldn't help noticing that Willis had stopped by for a visit every day. Sometimes twice a day. "Why do you ask?"

"We could hire Willis to be a bodyguard for Hazel.

They might enjoy an excuse to spend more time together."

"That's not a bad idea," she said. "His performance tonight—tromping around in the snow looking for a house key—wasn't typical. Usually he's competent."

"I wouldn't want to throw him up against an army of thugs with automatic pistols," he said, "but that shouldn't be necessary. If you settle here and keep a low profile, there's no reason for Wynter to track you down. You're sure he doesn't know you're the witness?"

"I was careful, bought my plane tickets under a fake name, blocked and locked everything on my computer, threw away my phone so I couldn't be tracked."

"How did you learn to do all that?"

"Internet," she said. "I read a couple of how-to articles on disappearing yourself. Plus, I might have picked up a couple of hints when we were married."

"But you didn't like my undercover work." He leaned back against the sofa pillows and sipped his beer. "You said when I took on a new identity, it was a lie."

At the time, she hadn't considered her criticism to be unreasonable. Any new bride would be upset if her husband said he was going to be out of touch for a week or two and couldn't tell her where he was going or what he was doing. She jabbed an accusing finger in his direction. "I had every right to interrogate you, every right to be angry when you wouldn't tell me what was going on."

His dark eyes narrowed, but he didn't look menacing. He was too handsome. "You could have just trusted me."

"Trust you? I hardly knew you."

"You were my wife."

It hadn't taken long for them to jump into old argu-

months. Was he purposely trying to provoke her? First he mentioned the age thing. Now he was playing the "trust me" card. Damn it, she didn't want to open old wounds. "Could we keep our focus on the present? Please?"

"Fine with me." He stretched out his long legs and rested his stocking feet on the coffee table. "You claim to have covered your tracks when you traveled and when you masked your identity."

"Claimed?" Her anger sparked.

"Can you prove that you're untraceable? Can anybody vouch for you?"

"Certainly not. The point of hiding my identity is to eliminate contacts."

"Just to be sure," he said, "I'll ask Dylan to do a computer search. If anybody can hack your identity or files, he can."

"It's not necessary, but go ahead." She was totally confident in her abilities. "I've always liked your brother. How's he doing?"

"We keep him busy at TST doing computer stuff. You'll be shocked to hear that he's finally found a girlfriend who's as smart as he is. She's a neurosurgeon."

"I'm not surprised." The two brothers made a complementary pairing: Dylan was a genius, and Sean had street smarts.

"I'll use my FBI contacts, namely, Levine, to keep tabs on their investigation." He drained his beer and stood. "That should just about cover it."

"Cover what?"

"Ground rules," Sean said as he crossed the room toward the wet bar. "You and Hazel will be safe if you stay here and don't communicate with anybody. I'll need to take your cell phone."

"Not necessary," she said. "I'm aware that cell

phones can be hacked and tracked. I only use untraceable burner phones."

"What about your computer?"

She swallowed hard. In the back of her mind, she knew her computer could be hacked long distance and used to track her down. There was no way she'd give up her computer. "All my documents are copied onto a flash drive."

"I need to disable the computer. No calling except on burner phones. No texting. No email. No meetings."

Anger and frustration bubbled up inside her. Though she hadn't finished her beer and didn't need a replacement, she followed him to the bar. She climbed up on a stool and peered down at him while he looked into the under-the-counter fridge. When he stood, she glared until he met her gaze.

To his credit, Sean didn't back down, even though she felt like she was shooting lightning bolts through her eye sockets. When she opened her mouth to speak, she was angry enough to breathe fire. "Your ground rules don't work for me."

He opened another zombie beer. "What's the problem?"

"If I can't use the internet, how can I work?"

"Dylan can probably hook up some kind of secure channel to communicate with your employer."

"What if I don't want to stay here?"

"I suppose I could move you to a safe house or hotel." He came around the bar and faced her. "What's really going on?"

"Nothing."

"You always said you hated lying and liars, but you're not leveling with me. If you don't tell me everything, I can't do my job."

The real, honest to God problem was simple: she hadn't given up on the Wynter investigation. One of the specific reasons she'd come to Colorado was to dig up evidence against Frankie. She swiveled around on the bar stool so she was facing away from him. "I don't want to bury my head in the sand."

"Explain."

"I want to know why Roger Patrone was murdered. And I want to stop the human trafficking from Asia."

He nodded. "We all want that."

"But I have leads to track down. If I could hook up with people from the Wynter compound and question them, I might get answers. Or I could break in and download the information on their computers. I might find evidence that would be useful to the FBI."

"Seriously?" He was skeptical. "You want to keep digging up dirt, poking the dragon?"

She shot back. "Well, that's what an investigative reporter does."

"This isn't a joke, Emily. You saw what happens to people who cross Frankie Wynter."

"They get shot and dumped."

Wynter's men could toss her body into a mountain cave, and she wouldn't be found for years. When she voiced her plan out loud, it sounded ridiculous. How could she expect to succeed in her investigation when the FBI had failed?

"If you want to take that kind of risk," he said, "that's your choice. But don't put Hazel in danger."

He was right. She shouldn't have come here, and she definitely shouldn't have talked to him. *Trust me? Fat chance.*

Their connection had already begun to unravel, which was probably for the best. He irritated her more than a mohair sweater on a sunny day. Her unwarranted attraction to him was a huge distraction from her work. She should tell him to go. She didn't need a bodyguard.

But Sean was strong and quick, well trained in assault and protection. He knew things about investigating and undercover work that she could only guess about. Her gut instincts told her she really did need him.

"Come with me," she said. "Back to San Francisco."

Chapter Five

At five o'clock the next morning, Sean stood at the window in the kitchen and opened the blinds so he could see outside while he was waiting for the coffeemaker to do its thing. He'd turned off the overhead light, and the cool blue shadows in the kitchen melted into the shimmer of moonlight off the unbroken snow. The blizzard had ended.

Soon the phones would be working. Lines of communication would be open. There would be nothing to block Emily's return trip to San Francisco. She'd decided that she needed to go back and dig into her investigation, and it didn't look like she was going to budge.

It was up to him whether he'd go with her as her bodyguard or not. His first reaction was to refuse. She had neither the resources nor the experience to delve into the criminal depths of Wynter Corp, and she was going to get into trouble, possibly lethal trouble. He needed to make her understand her limitations without insulting her skills.

Outside, the bare branches of aspen and fir trees bent and wavered in the wind. So cold. So lonely. A shiver went through him. Their divorce had been five years ago. He should be over it. But no. He missed her every single day. Seeing her again and hearing her voice, even if she was arguing with him most of the time, touched a part of him that he kept buried.

He still cared about Emily. Damn it, he couldn't let her go to California by herself. She needed protection, and nobody could keep her safe the way he could. He would die for her…but he preferred not to.

After she'd made her announcement in the living room, she outlined the plan. "Tomorrow morning, we'll catch a plane and be in San Francisco before late afternoon. There'll be time for you to have a little chat with Agent Levine and the other guys in that office. We'll talk to my contacts on the day after that."

He'd objected, as any sane person would, but she'd already made up her mind. She flounced into the dining room and ate chili with Hazel and Willis. The prime topic of their conversation being big snowstorms and their aftermath. The chat ended with Emily's announcement that she'd be going back to San Francisco as soon as the snow stopped because she had to get back to work.

During the night, he'd gone into her room to try talking sense into her. Before he could speak, she asked if he would accompany her. When he said no, she told him to leave.

Stubborn! How could a woman who looked so soft and gentle be so obstinate? She was like a rosebush with roots planted deep—so strong and deep that she could halt the forward progress of a tank. How could he make her see reason? What sort of story could he tell her?

Finally, the coffeemaker was done. He poured a cup, straight black, for himself and one for her with a dash of milk, no sugar. Up the staircase, he was careful not to spill over the edge of the mugs. Twisting the doorknob on her bedroom took some maneuvering, but he got it open and slipped inside.

For a long moment, he stood there, watching her sleep in the dim light that penetrated around the edges of the blinds. A pale blue comforter was tucked up to her chin. Wisps of dark hair swept across on her forehead. Her eyelashes made thick, dark crescents above her cheekbones, and her lips parted slightly. She was even more beautiful now than when they were married.

She claimed that she'd changed, and he recognized the difference in some ways. She was tougher, more direct. When he thought about her rationale for investigating, he understood that she was asserting herself and building her career. Those practical concerns were in addition to the moral issues, like that need to get justice for the guy who was murdered and to right the wrongs committed by Wynter Corp. He crossed the room, placed the mugs on the bedside table and sat on the edge of her bed.

Slowly, she opened her eyes. "Has it stopped snowing?"

He nodded.

"Have you changed your mind?"

"Have you?"

She wiggled around until she was sitting up, still keeping the comforter wrapped around her like a droopy cocoon. Fumbling in the nearly dark room, she turned on her bedside lamp and reached for the coffee. "I'd like a nip of caffeine before we start arguing again."

"No need to argue. I want to help with your investigation."

"I'd be a fool to turn you down."

Damn right, you would. His qualifications were outstanding. In addition to the FBI training at Quantico, he'd taken several workshops and classes on profiling. When he first signed on, his goal was to join the Behavioral Analysis Unit. But that was not to be. His psych tests showed that his traits were better suited to a different position. He was a natural for undercover work; namely, he had an innate ability to lie convincingly.

"Plus, I'm offering the services of my brother, the computer genius and hacker."

Suspicion flickered in her greenish-blue eyes. "I appreciate the offer, but what's the quid pro quo?"

"Listen to you." He grinned. "Awake for only a couple of minutes and already speaking Latin."

She turned to look at the clock and then groaned. "Five-fifteen in the morning. Why so early?"

"Couldn't sleep."

"So you thought you'd just march in here and make sure I didn't get a full eight hours."

"As if you need that much."

The way he remembered, she seldom got more than five hours. He often woke up to find her in the middle of some project or another. Emily was one of those people who bounced out of bed and was fully functional before she brushed her teeth.

"It's going to be a long day." She drank her coffee and dramatically rolled her eyes. "Plane rides can be so very exhausting."

"Here's the deal," he said. "There aren't any direct flights from Aspen to San Francisco. You'll be routed through Denver first."

Watching him over the rim of her mug, she nodded agreement.

"Since we're already there, let's make a scheduled stop in Denver, spend the night and talk to Dylan. We'll still be investigating. Didn't you say you were looking for documents about imports and exports? He could hack in to Wynter Corp."

"Information obtained through illegal hacking can't be used for evidence."

"But you're not a cop," he said. "You don't have to follow legal protocols."

"True, and a hack could point me in the right direction. Dylan could also check company memos mentioning the murder victim. And, oh my God, accounting records." She came to an abrupt halt, set down her coffee and stared at him. "Why are you making this offer?"

"I want to help you with your new career."

Though he truly wished her well, helping her investigation wasn't the primary reason he'd suggested a stop in Denver. Sean wanted to derail her trip to San Francisco and keep her out of danger. As far as he was concerned, the world had enough investigative journalists. But there was only one Emily Peterson.

Her gaze narrowed. "Are you lying?"

He scoffed. "Why would I lie?"

"Turning my question into a different question isn't an answer." A slow smile lifted one corner of her mouth. "It's a technique that liars use."

"Believe whatever you want." He rose from her bed and placed his half-empty coffee mug on the bedside table. "I'm suggesting that you use Dylan because he's skilled, he has high-level contacts and he won't get caught."

She threw off the covers and went up on her knees. An overlarge plaid flannel top fell from her shoulders and hung all the way to her knees. The shirt looked familiar. He reached over and stroked the sleeve that she'd rolled up to the elbow. "Is this mine?"

"The top?" Unlike him, she was a terrible liar. "Why would I wear your jammies?"

"Supersoft flannel, gray Stewart plaid from L.L.Bean," he said. "I'm glad you kept it."

"I hardly ever wear flannel. But I was coming to Colorado and figured I might want something warm." She tossed her head, flipping her hair. "I forgot this belonged to you."

Another lie. He wondered if she'd been thinking of him when she packed her suitcase for this trip. Did she miss him? When she wore his clothing to bed, did she imagine his embrace?

He stepped up close to the bed and glided his arms around her, feeling the softness of the flannel plaid and her natural, sweet warmth. She'd been cozy in bed, wrapped in his pajamas that were way too big for her.

She cleared her throat. "What are you doing?"

"I'm holding you so you won't get cold."

He stroked her back, following the curve of her spine and the flare of her hips. With his hands still on the outside of the fabric, he cupped her full, round ass. Her body was incredible. She hadn't changed in the years they'd been apart. If anything, she was better, more firm and toned. He lifted her toward him, and she collapsed against his chest, gasping as though she'd been holding her breath.

"Ground rules," she choked out. "This is where we really need rules."

He lifted her chin, gazed into her face and waited until she opened her eyes. "You're supposed to be the spontaneous one, Emily. Let yourself go—follow your desires."

"I can't."

The note of desperation in her voice held him back. Though he longed to peel off the flannel top and drag her under the covers, he didn't want to hurt her. If she wanted a more controlled approach, he would comply.

"One kiss," he said, "on the mouth."

"Only one."

"And another on the neck, and another on your breast, and one more on…"

"Forget it! I should know better than to negotiate with you. There will be no kissing." She wriggled to get away from his grasp, but he wasn't letting go. "No touching. No hugging. No physical intimacy at all."

"You promised one," he reminded her.

"Fine."

She squinted her eyes closed and turned her face up to his. Her lips were stiff. And she was probably gritting her teeth. He'd still take the kiss. He knew what was behind her barriers. She still had feelings for him.

His kiss was slow and tender, almost chaste, until he began to nibble and suck on the fullness of her lower lip. His fingers unbuttoned the pajama top, and his hand slid inside. He traced a winding path across her torso with his fingertips, and when he reached the underside of her breast, she moaned.

"Oh, Sean." A shudder went through her. "I can't."

His hand stilled, but his mouth took full advantage of her parted lips. His tongue plunged into the hot, slick interior of her mouth.

She spoke again. "Don't stop."

She kissed him back. Her hand guided his to her nipples, inviting him to fondle. Her longing was fierce, unstoppable. Her body pressed hard against his.

And then it was over. She fell backward on the bed and buried herself, even her face, under the covers. He loved the way he affected her. As for the way she affected him? He couldn't ignore his palpitating heart and his rock-hard erection. But his attraction was more than that.

"About these ground rules," he said. "Don't tell me there's no physical intimacy allowed. If I'm going to be around you and not allowed to touch, I'll explode."

"You scare me," she said as she crawled out from under the covers. "I don't want to fall in love with you again."

Would it really be so bad? She kept talking about how she had changed, but he was different, too. Not the same undercover agent that he was five years ago, he had learned tolerance, patience and respect.

Much of this shift in attitude came from his developing relationship with his brother; he was learning how to be a team player. Sean still teased—that was a big brother's prerogative—but he also could brush the small irritations away. At TST Security, he didn't insist on being the lead with every single job. He'd be nuts to interfere with Dylan's computer expertise, and their other partner, Mason Steele, was good at stepping in and taking charge.

His relationship with Emily was different. When they had been married, he might have been impatient. The way she kept prodding him about his work had been truly annoying. Why hadn't she been able to understand that undercover work meant he had to be secretive? If he kissed another woman while he was undercover, it didn't mean anything. How could it? In his mind, she was the perfect lover.

"First ground rule." He had to lay out parameters that allowed them to be together without hurting each other. "No falling in love."

"That's a good one," she said. "Write it down."

He sat at the small desk, found a sheet of notebook

paper and a pen to jot down the first rule. "What about touching, kissing, licking, nibbling, sucking…" His voice trailed off as he visualized these activities. "I can't even say the words without needing to do it."

"I feel it, too, you know. We've always been amazing in bed, sexually compatible."

"Always."

In unison, they exhaled a regretful sigh.

"How about this?" she said. "No PDA."

Public display of affection? He wrote it down. "I can live with that."

She sat up on the bed and reached for her coffee mug again. After a sip, she proposed, "No physical contact unless I'm the one who initiates it."

He didn't like the way that sounded. "I need to have some kind of voice."

"You mean talking dirty?"

"Not necessarily. I might say something like I want to touch your cheek." Illustrating, he glided his hand along the line of her jaw, and then he leaned closer. "I want to kiss your forehead."

When he kissed her lightly, she pushed his face away. "You can ask, but I have veto power. At any time, I can say no."

"So you have veto power and you can also initiate."

"Yes."

"What does that leave for me?" he asked as he returned to sit at the desk.

She cast him an evil smile. "Begging?"

"I'm not writing that down."

As far as he was concerned, their negotiation was taking a negative turn. The way she described it, she controlled all physical contact. She had all the power.

No way would he be reduced to begging. There had to be another way to work it out.

As he doodled with the pen on the paper, he heard the ringtone from the cell phone in his pocket. "Finally we have communication from the outside world."

"Who is it?"

"The caller ID says Zebra929. So it has to be my brother. Dylan likes to play with the codes."

As soon as he answered, his brother said, "This is a secured call, bouncing the signal. It needs to be short."

"Shoot."

"I got a call from FBI Special Agent Levine out of San Francisco. Guess who he's trying to contact?"

"Emily Peterson," Sean said. A chill slithered down his spine. This was bad news.

"Whoa, are you psychic?"

"I'm looking right at her."

"Emily Peterson Timmons?"

Sean heard the amazement in his brother's tone.

"Emily the poet? Emily with the long hair? Your ex-wife?"

"What was the message from Levine?"

"He wanted to warn her. There's a leak in SFPD. Wynter might know her identity."

"Why did Levine call me?"

"He's grasping at straws," Dylan said. "None of her San Francisco contacts know where she went."

"What about her parents?"

"I asked the same question. The Petersons are out of the country."

Actually, that was good news. A threat to Emily could mean other people in her family might become targets for Wynter. Sean asked, "Did Levine mention an aunt in the mountains? A woman named Hazel?"

"Is that the Hazel Hopkins you took a contract with?"

Sean's pulse quickened. Not only had he received phone calls from Hazel, but he'd looked her up on the internet. It had taken nothing but a phone call for Levine to track him down. If Frankie Wynter figured out that connection, he might hack in to TST Security phones or computers. They could find Hazel. "How secure are our computers?"

"Very safe," Dylan said. "But anything can be hacked."

"Wipe any history concerning Hazel Hopkins."

"Okay. We should wrap up this call."

"Thanks, Zebra. I'll be flying back to Denver today with Emily. We need your skills."

He ended the call and looked toward her. No more fun and games. She was in serious danger.

Chapter Six

Emily watched Sean transformed from a sexy ex to the hard-core FBI agent she remembered from their marriage. His devilish grin became tight-lipped. Twin worry lines appeared between his eyebrows. His posture stiffened.

She didn't like the direction his phone call was taking. As soon as he ended the call, she asked, "Why were you talking to your brother about Hazel?"

"If you're in danger, so is your family."

"Not Hazel. Our last names aren't the same. Nobody knows we're related."

"Can you be one hundred percent sure of that?"

"Not really."

When she'd first started writing articles that might be controversial, she disguised her identity behind a couple of pseudonyms. She didn't want to accidentally embarrass her mom and dad or her sister in law school, and she liked being a lone crusader. Anonymous and brave, she dug behind the headlines to expose corruption.

One of her best articles dealt with a cheating handyman who overcharged and didn't do the work. Another exposed a phone scam that entrapped the unwary. This story about Wynter Corp was her first attempt to investigate serious crime.

She should have known better. A personal threat was bad enough, but she'd brought danger to her family. Her spirits crumbled as she sat on the bed listening to Sean's recap of the phone call with his brother. This was her fault, all her fault.

Moments ago, she'd been kissing her gorgeous ex-husband and had been almost happy. Now she felt like weeping or hiding under the covers and never coming out. Why couldn't the blizzard have lasted forever? The snow would have hidden her.

Trying to soothe herself, she rubbed the soft fabric of her sleeve between her thumb and forefinger. Despite what she'd told him, she hadn't worn this top by accident; she knew very well that it belonged to Sean. Cuddling up in his pajamas always gave her a feeling of warmth and safety. Sometimes she closed her eyes and pretended that she could still smell his scent even though the pajamas had been laundered a hundred times.

He sat beside her and took her hand. "Are you okay?"

"Not at all." She heard the vulnerability in her voice and hated it. "You probably want to tell me that I never should have done this article, that I'm a girlie girl and should stick with poetry."

He squeezed her hand. "As I recall, your poetry wasn't all lollipops and sparkles. There was something about a fire giver and vultures that ate his liver."

"Prometheus," she remembered. "He started out trying to do the right thing, just like me. And then he was eternally damned by the gods. Is that my fate?"

"You made some mistakes, had some bad luck."

"I'm being a drama queen." She was well aware of that tendency and tried to tamp the over-the-top histrionics before she threw herself into full-on crazy mode. "Tell me I'm exaggerating."

"It's safe to say you're not really cursed by the gods," he said, "but don't underestimate the seriousness of this threat."

"I won't." Her lower lip trembled. She fought the tears that sloshed behind her eyelids. "Oh God, what should I do?"

"No crying." He held her chin and turned her face so they were eye to eye. "You told me you were an investigative journalist. Well, you need to start acting like somebody who stands behind her words and takes responsibility for her actions."

His dark gaze caught and held her attention. His calm demeanor steadied her. Still, she was confused. "I don't know how."

"You're not Prometheus, and you're not little Miss Sunshine the poetry girl. Think of yourself as a reporter who got into trouble. What should we do next?"

"Make sure my family is safe."

Her parents were currently out of the country, visiting friends in the South of France. She didn't need to worry about Mom and Dad. Her three sisters were back east, and the two who were still in school lived alone. It seemed unlikely that Wynter would hunt them down. Nonetheless, they should be warned. "I should call my sisters."

"I'm going to ask you to wait until we get to Denver," he said. "The signal from your phone might be traced, and Dylan has equipment that's extremely secure."

"What about you?" She pointed to his cell phone. "What about that call?"

"It originated from the TST Security offices behind strong, thick firewalls."

She sat beside him, struggling to think in spite of the static waves that sizzled and shivered inside her head. From outside her bedroom door, she heard her aunt chattering to Willis as they went downstairs. It was early, a little after six o'clock and not yet dawn, but they were both already awake. Did they sleep together last night? Emily smiled to herself. *Ironic!* The senior citizens were getting it on while she and Sean stayed in separate bedrooms.

"I need to talk to Hazel." She looked toward him for guidance. "How much should I tell her?"

"She already knows you've witnessed a murder, so it won't come as a big shock that she's in danger. Until this is over, I'd advise her to leave Hazelwood, maybe stay in a hotel in Aspen."

"I'm guessing that Willis might have an extra bedroom," she said. "And he would probably be a good protector."

"A former deputy," Sean said. "I'd trust him."

And she didn't think it would take much to convince Hazel to spend more time with Willis. Emily's eccentric aunt had never remarried after her husband had died fifteen years ago, but she had taken several live-in lovers. Willis had always been a friend. Maybe it was time for him to be something more.

She picked up her coffee mug from the bedside table and drained it in a few gulps. Today was going to be intense, and she'd need all the energy she could muster. "After taking care of the family, what do I do?"

"It's up to you."

"The first thing that comes to mind is run and hide." That was exactly what the old Emily would have done. She would have hidden behind her big, strong husband.

But that wasn't her style, not anymore. "I want to take responsibility. I'll go after the story."

He shrugged. "San Francisco, here we come."

With Sean at her side, she could handle the threat. She could take down James Wynter and his son. What she couldn't do was…forget. The blood spreading across Roger Patrone's white shirt flashed in her mind. The sounds of a beating and fading cries for help echoed in her ears. She could never erase the memory of murder.

OVER COFFEE IN the kitchen, Emily convinced Hazel that there was a real potential for danger and she ought to move in with Willis. It didn't take much persuasion. Hazel agreed almost immediately, and she was happy, as perky as a chipmunk. Her energy and the afterglow of excitement confirmed Emily's suspicion that her aunt and Willis were more than friends.

Hazel dashed upstairs to her bedroom to pack a few essentials, and Willis swaggered around the kitchen, talking to Sean about how he should make sure Hazel was safe and secure. Though Emily had a hard time imagining Willis the kindhearted former deputy facing off with Wynter's thugs, she believed he was competent. Plus, he had the advantage of experience. He knew how to handle the dangers of the mountains and to use the elements to his advantage. His plan was to take Hazel to a ski hut he'd built on the other side of Aspen. The hut was accessible only by snowmobile or cross-country skis.

"What about the blizzard?" she asked.

Willis squinted out the kitchen window at a brilliant splash of sunlight reflecting off a pristine snowbank. "The big storm gave up during the night. We only got twenty or so inches, probably not even enough to close down the airport in Aspen."

She'd lived in San Francisco for so long that she'd forgotten how dramatically Colorado weather could change. Yesterday was a blizzard. Today she could get sunburned from taking a walk outside.

The timer on the oven buzzed. Emily opened the door, and the scent of sweet baked goods rushed toward her. Hazel had popped in a frozen almond-flavored coffee cake to thaw. Not as good as fresh made but decent enough for a rushed breakfast.

Willis went upstairs to help Hazel, and Emily turned toward Sean. "We need plane reservations to Denver," she said. "I'll go ahead and make them."

"You shouldn't." He pointed out the obvious. "Just in case the bad guys have a way to track airline tickets, you ought to avoid using your real name."

"No problem." Her solution was sort of embarrassing, and she really didn't want to tell him. She placed the pan of coffee cake on a trivet on the counter and cut off a slab. With this breakfast in hand, she headed toward the exit from the kitchen. "I'm going to get packed, and then I'll call the airlines."

He blocked the exit. "I hope you aren't thinking about buying plane tickets with a fake ID and credit card. That kind of ploy can get you on the no-fly list."

"It's not exactly fake," she muttered. "Just out of date by about five and a half years."

As realization dawned, his eyes darkened. "The way I remember, you changed your name back to Peterson after the divorce."

"I did."

"Please don't tell me you're using your married name."

"The identity was just sitting there. I doctored an old driver's license and applied for a credit card as Emily Timmons, using my own Social Security number and my address in San Francisco. It works just fine."

"The no-fly list and fraud." Still blocking her way so she couldn't run, he glared at her. A muscle in his jaw twitched. "Anything else you want to tell me?"

"If I confess everything, we'll have nothing to discuss on the flight." She patted his cheek and slipped around him. "You can make the reservations."

"For today, you'll be Mrs. Timmons. And then no more."

"Don't count on it."

"What's that supposed to mean? Are you planning some kind of strange reconciliation that I don't know about?"

"This has nothing to do with you," she said coolly. "But I might need your name for fake identification."

With her almond cake in one hand and coffee in the other, she climbed the staircase and went to her bedroom. She sat at the small desk and activated one of her disposable phones. She couldn't wait until they got to Denver to contact her sisters. If Sean didn't like it, too bad. She really didn't think Wynter would go after them, but they deserved a heads-up. Michelle, who was in law school, asked how she could get in touch with Emily if she heard anything.

"You can't call me back."

"I know," Michelle said. "The phone you're using right now doesn't show up on my caller ID listing."

"Contact me through TST Security in Denver. I hired a bodyguard." Emily hoped to avoid mentioning her ex-husband. "They can get me a message."

"TST Security," Michelle repeated. "I'm looking

them up on the Internet right now. Found the website. Well, damn it, sis, here's an interesting coincidence. One of the owners of the aforementioned security firm happens to be Sean Timmons."

"I didn't call him."

"Really?" Michelle's tone dripped with sarcasm. "Do you want me to believe that he magically appeared when you were in trouble? Was he wearing a suit of armor and riding a white steed?"

"Aunt Hazel called him." Emily wanted to keep this conversation short. "And I don't have to justify my decisions to you or anybody else in the family."

"But justice will be served," said the future lawyer. "To tell the truth, Emily, I always liked Sean. I'm glad he's watching over you."

Emily avoided mentioning Sean to her other two sisters. Those calls ended quickly, and she jumped in the shower. Though she had time to wash and blow-dry her hair, she decided against it. Going out in the snow meant she'd be wearing a hat and squashing any cute styling.

She lathered up while her mind filled with speculation. No doubt, Michelle would blab to the rest of the family. And the questions would begin. *Would she get back together with him?* That seemed to be the query of the day. A few moments ago, Sean had asked about reconciliation.

Never going to happen. And her sisters should understand. Didn't they remember how devastated she'd been when she'd filed for divorce?

Their attitude about Sean had always been odd. When she first married him, the three sisters talked about how he was too old for her and his job was too dangerous for a stable relationship. In the divorce, however, the sister witches took Sean's side. They blamed her for being fickle and undependable when she should have been supportive. They told her to grow up. She couldn't always have things her own way.

Maybe true. Maybe she hadn't been the most understanding wife in the world. But he brought his own problems to the table: Being inflexible. Not taking her seriously. Concentrating too much on his work and not enough on his wife.

Wrapped in a towel after her shower, she padded into the bedroom and pulled out her luggage from under the bed. Since they were headed back to San Francisco, where she had clothes and toiletries at her apartment, she packed light. She tucked her three disposable cell phones in her carry-on. All data had already been downloaded off her de-activated computer.

She hid the flash drive in a specially designed black-and-silver pendant, which she wore on a heavy silver chain. A black cashmere sweater and designer jeans completed her outfit. Her practical boots and her parka were in the downstairs closet.

Before she left the bedroom, she checked her reflection in the mirror. *Not bad.* She didn't look as frazzled as she felt. Her hair was combed. Her lipstick properly applied. Her cheeks were flushed with nervous heat, but the high color might be attributed to too much blush.

Returning to San Francisco was the right thing to do, but she was sorely tempted to take off for a quickie Bahamas vacation with Sean. He owed her a trip. On their Paris honeymoon, he had held her hand in a sidewalk café and promised that every anniversary he would take her somewhere exciting. Their first anniversary rolled around and no trip. They couldn't get their schedules coordinated. And they argued about where to go. And when she told him to just forget it, he did.

What a brat she'd been! But at the time, she was too furious to make sense. She'd counted on Sean to be rational. That was his job. Somehow he should have known that even though she told him to forget it, he was supposed to lavish her with kisses and gifts until she changed her mind.

Their marriage had crumbled under the weight of hundreds of similar misunderstandings. Underneath it all, she wondered if they might actually be compatible. Certainly, there was nothing wrong with their sexual rapport. But could they talk? Was he too conservative? Were their worldviews similar? Was there any way, after the divorce, that she'd be willing to put her heart on the line and trust him? *I guess I'll find out.* While he was being her bodyguard and they were forced to be together, she had a second chance.

Chapter Seven

Clearing the runway in Aspen took longer than expected, and their flight as Mr. and Mrs. Timmons didn't land at DIA until after four o'clock in the afternoon. Sean rented a car and drove toward the TST office, where Dylan had promised to meet them.

In the passenger seat, Emily shed her parka and changed from snow boots to a pair of ballet flats. She peeked out the window at the undeveloped fields near the airport. "It's crazy. The snow's already melted."

"Denver only got a couple of inches."

"And the sky is blue, and the sun is shining. Every time I come back to Colorado, I wonder why I ever left."

"You don't have family in Denver, anymore."

"Nope." She gave him a warm smile. "But you do. I'm looking forward to seeing Dylan."

When Emily was being cordial, there was no one more charming. Her voice was as sweet as the sound of a meadowlark. Her intense blue-green eyes sparkled. Every movement she made was sheer grace. It was hard to keep his hands off her.

Sitting close beside her on the plane, inhaling her scent and watching her in glimpses, had affected him. He was going to need more than a flimsy set of relationship "ground rules" to maintain control.

Following the road signs, he merged onto I-70. His real problem would come tonight. Their flight to San Francisco was scheduled for tomorrow morning at about ten o'clock, which meant they'd be sleeping in the same place tonight. After the stop at TST, he intended to take her to his home, where the security was high and he could keep an eye on her. He had an extra bedroom. What he didn't have was willpower. When she was in bed, just down the hall, he would be tempted.

"Sean?"

He realized that she'd been talking while he wasn't listening. "Sorry, what did you say?"

"How did you name your company? I get that TST stands for your initials, Timmons, Timmons and your other partner, Mason Steele. But your logo is a four-leaf clover with three green leaves and one a faded red."

"At one time, there were four of us." Sean had told this story dozens of times, but his chest still tightened. Some scars never heal. This deep sadness would never go away. "We grew up together. Me and Dylan lived down the block from Mason and Matt Steele. Matt was my best friend. We were close in age, went to the same school, played on the same teams and went on double dates. When we were kids we pretended to be crime fighters."

"And when you grew up, you decided to fight crime for real."

"Not at first," he said. "We went to different colleges, followed our own separate ways. Matt joined the marines, and he liked the military life. That was why he couldn't be our best man. He was deployed, working his way up the chain of command."

There must have been a hint of doom in his tone, because Emily went very still. She listened intently.

He cleared his throat and continued. "About five years ago, Matt was killed in Afghanistan. His heroic actions rescued three other platoons, and he received a posthumous Purple Heart."

"I'm so sorry," she whispered.

"His death came right about the time our divorce was final. And I'd finished a sleazy undercover job where a good lawyer got the bad guys off with a slap on the wrist."

Remembering those dark days left a sour taste in his mouth. He'd just about given up. Life was a joke, not worth living. He went on an all-out binge, drugs and alcohol. Thanks to his undercover work, he was familiar with the filthy underbelly of the city, and he went there. He found rock bottom while seeking poisonous thrills that could wipe away his sorrow and regret and the senseless guilt that he was still alive while his friend was not. His judgment was off. He took stupid risks, landing in the hospital more than once. His path was leading straight to hell.

She reached across the console and touched his arm. "If I had known…"

"There was nothing you—or anybody else—could do. I didn't ask for help, didn't want anybody holding my hand."

"How did you get better?"

"I came back to Colorado and got on a physical schedule of weight lifting and running ten miles a day. I visited places where Matt and I used to go." He paused. "This sounds cheesy, but I found peace. I quit mourning Matt's death and celebrated his life."

"Not cheesy at all," she said.

"Weak?"

"That's the last word I'd use to describe you."

"Anyway, I did a lot of wilderness camping. One morning, I crawled out of my tent, stared up into a clear blue sky and decided I wanted a future."

"TST Security?"

"I quit the FBI, contacted my two buds and set up the business. I'd like to think that Matt would approve. We don't take cases that we don't like. And there are times like now when we can actually do some good."

"Is that how you think of my investigation into Wynter Corp?" She brightened. "As something that could make a difference?"

"I guess I do feel that way."

He hadn't realized until this moment that he wanted Frankie Wynter to pay the price for murder. Plus, they might take down members of a powerful crime family, and that felt good.

Exiting the interstate, they were close enough to downtown Denver for him to point out changes in the city where she'd lived for so many years. Giant cranes loomed over new skyscrapers—tall office buildings and hotels to accommodate the tourists. New apartment buildings and condos had popped up on street corners, filling in spaces that seemed too small. Denver was thriving.

Sean applauded the growth. More people meant more business and more opportunity. But he missed the odd, eclectic neighborhoods that were being swallowed by gentrification. Like most Denver natives, he was stubbornly protective of his city.

He parked the rental car in a small six-car lot behind a three-story brick mansion near downtown. "We're here."

"Your office is in a renovated mansion." She beamed. "I can't believe you chose such a unique place."

"It's not unusual. This entire block is mansions that have been redone for businesses. We have the right half of the first floor. On the left side, there are three little offices—a life coach, a web designer and a woman who reads horoscopes. We all share the kitchen and the conference rooms upstairs."

"About the horoscope lady, what kind of conference meetings does she have?"

"Séances."

He opened the back door for her and held it while she entered an enclosed porch that was attached to the very modern kitchen with stainless steel appliances and a double-door refrigerator. It smelled like somebody had just microwaved a bag of popcorn.

"I love it," Emily said. "When you worked for the FBI, you never would have gone for a place like this."

"I've changed."

They went down the hallway to the spacious foyer with a grand staircase of carved oak and high ceilings. To the right, he stopped beside a door with an opaque glass window decorated with old-fashioned lettering for TST Security and their four-leaf clover logo. Using a keypad, Sean plugged in a code to open the door. Before he followed Emily inside, he touched the red leaf that represented Matt, as he always did.

Dylan greeted his former sister-in-law with enthusiasm, throwing his long arms around her for a big hug. He and Sean were the same height, but Dylan seemed taller because he was skinny. During his early years, Dylan was the epitome of a ninety-eight-pound weakling with oversize glasses and a permanent slouch. Sean had taken his little brother under his wing and got him working out. Under his baggy jeans and plaid flannel shirt, Dylan was ripped now.

They had two desks in the huge front office, but that wasn't where Dylan wanted to sit. He dragged her over to a brown leather sofa. On the coffee table in front of the sofa were snacks: popcorn, crackers and bottles of water.

She reached up to tuck a hank of brownish-blond hair behind his ear. "Almost as long as mine. I like the ponytail."

"I remember your super-long hair," he said.

"It was always such a mess."

"Not to me. It was beautiful. But I like this new look."

"Sorry to interrupt," Sean said, "but whenever you're done comparing stylists, there are some very bad men after Emily, and we need to take them out of the picture."

"Impatient," Dylan said as he pushed his horn-rimmed glasses up on his nose. He turned to Emily. "There's no need to be nervous in the TST office. It's one of the most secure spots in Denver. We've got bulletproof glass in the windows, sensors, surveillance cameras all around and sound-disabling technology so nobody can electronically eavesdrop."

"That's very reassuring." She opened a bottle of water and took a sip. "Can you make my computer un-hackable?"

"I can make it real hard to get in." Dylan pushed his glasses up again. "I've got an update."

"Another call from Agent Levine?" Sean guessed as he sat on the opposite end of the sofa from Emily.

"Levine isn't comment-worthy." Dylan plunked himself into a high-back swivel chair on wheels and paddled from a desk to the sofa. "I'm not insulting you, but the feds aren't real efficient."

"No offense taken," Sean said.

"This call was a few hours ago, a man's voice. He claimed to be an old friend from San Francisco. He identified himself as Jack Baxter. Sound familiar?"

"Not a bit," Sean responded. "Emily, do you know the name?"

"I don't think so."

Sitting on the big leather sofa with her hands in her lap and her ankles crossed, she looked nervous and somewhat overwhelmed. Dylan could be a lot to take; he tended to bounce around like an overeager puppy.

Also, Sean reminded himself, she was aware of the threat, the potential for danger. He directed his brother. "We need to focus here. What did Baxter want?"

"Supposedly, he was just thinking of you, his old pal. It seemed too coincidental for you to be contacted by a supposed friend on the same day Levine called." He shot a look at Emily. "He kept asking about you. Suspicious, right?"

Sean remained focused. "Did you track the call?"

"He claimed to be in San Francisco, and his cell phone had the 414 area code. But I triangulated the microwave signal." Dylan paused for effect. "He was calling from DIA."

Emily shot to her feet. "He's here? At the Denver airport?"

Dylan winced. "It gets worse. I ran a reverse lookup on the cell phone. It belongs to John Morelli."

"I know him," she said. "He works for Wynter."

"Bingo," Dylan said. "I've been doing a bit of preliminary hacking on Wynter. And Morelli is vice president in charge of communication."

"That's right," Emily said. "I interviewed him for

my first article on Wynter Corp. He's the only person I spoke to in person."

"Which might be why he was sent to Denver to find you," Sean said. "When you met with him, did you use the Timmons alias?"

She shook her head. "Timmons is only for travel and the one credit card. I use another alias for my articles and interviews."

"How did Wynter make the connection between us?"

Dylan rolled toward him on the swivel chair. "Remember how I said the feds were idiots? Well, I think Wynter had their phones tapped. When Levine called here, looking for you, I told him you weren't involved with Emily. But the contact must have sent up a red flag to Wynter."

His deduction made sense. "I want you to dig deeper into Wynter Corp. Check into their bank accounts and expenses."

"Forensic accounting." Dylan nodded. "Will do."

"How much can you find out?" Emily asked. "That information belongs to Wynter Corp. It's protected."

"I've got skills," Dylan said, "and I can hack practically anything. Unlike the feds, I don't have to worry about obtaining the evidence through illegal means because I don't plan to use the data in court. This is purely a fact-finding mission."

She accepted him at his word. "Concentrate on the import-export business. Check inventories against shipping manifests—look for warehouse information."

"I took a peek earlier," Dylan said. "They also handle real estate, restaurants and small businesses."

"For now I'm looking for evidence of smuggling and human trafficking." She bounced to her feet. "I have information that will give you a starting point."

"Cool," Dylan said. "If you give me the flash drive you've got hidden in your necklace, I'll get started."

"How did you know?" She touched her black-and-silver pendant. "Is it obvious?"

"Only to me," he said as he held out his flat palm.

Although Sean didn't speak up and steal his brother's thunder, he had also figured out where she was hiding her flash drive. *Simple logic.* All day long, she'd been touching her pendant, guarding it. What would she want to protect? Her most precious possession was her work; therefore, he guessed she had her documents on a flash drive. And she'd hidden it in chunky jewelry that wasn't her usual style.

Dylan rolled his chair to a computer station with four display screens and three keyboards. Emily followed behind him, eager to learn the magic techniques that allowed Sean's brother to dance across the World Wide Web like a spider with a ponytail and horn-rimmed glasses.

Long ago Sean had given up trying to understand how Dylan did what he did. The technical aspects of security and investigative work had never interested Sean. He learned more from observing, questioning the people involved and creating a profile of the criminals and the victims. When he'd gone undercover for the FBI, he had to rely on instinct to separate the good guys from the bad. And his gut was good. He was seldom wrong.

He left the sofa and sauntered across the large, open room with high ceilings to the window. It bothered him that John Morelli was in Denver. Dylan's theory of how Wynter got his name had the ring of truth. Tapping the FBI phones was depressingly obvious.

His brother and Emily stared at the screens as though answers would materialize before their eyes. Sean hardly remembered a time when computers weren't a part of life, but he'd never fallen in love with the technology and he hated the way people stumbled around staring at their cell phones. His brother called him a Luddite, and maybe he was. Or maybe he'd made the decision, when they were kids, that computers would be Dylan's thing. Whatever the case, it appeared that Dylan and Emily would be occupied for a while.

Sean announced, "I'm going out to pick up some dinner. Is Chinese okay?"

Barely looking away from the screens, they both murmured agreement.

"Any special requests?"

The response was another mumble.

He went to a file cabinet near the door, unlocked it and took out a Glock 17. He had to pack both of his handguns on the plane and take out the bullets. For the moment, it was quicker to grab the semiautomatic pistol and insert a fresh magazine into the grip. He was almost out the door when Emily ran up behind him and grasped his arm.

"You shouldn't go out there," she said. "Mr. Morelli could be waiting in ambush."

"Mr.?"

"That's what I called him in the interview. He's older, in his forties."

"If he was sneaking around, close enough to show up on Dylan's surveillance, we'd be hearing a buzzer alarm."

She kissed his cheek. "Be careful."

It had been a long time since anybody was worried about his safety. He kind of liked being fussed over.

At the back door, he paused to peer into the trees that bordered the parking lot. There were garages and

Dumpsters in the alley behind their office, lots of hiding places if Morelli had staked out the office.

He went down the stairs and got into the rental car to pick up food from Happy Food Chinese restaurant. Then, he backed out into the alley. In less than a mile, he noticed a black sedan following him. Wynter's men had found him. And he'd made it easy. *Damn it, I should have ordered delivery.*

Chapter Eight

Emily watched the numbers unfurling across two screens while Dylan used a third screen to enter the forbidden area of the dark web where you could buy or sell anything. Pornographers, killers, perverts and all types of scum hung out on those mysterious, ugly sites.

She looked away. "What's a nice guy like you doing in a place like that?"

"If you want to get the dirt, you can't keep your hands clean."

Even though her investigation was for a worthy cause, she didn't like spying. Hacking broke one of the ethical rules of journalism that said you needed at least two sources for every statement before you could call it a fact. And they had to be credible sources. Some bloggers just fabricated their stories from lies and rumors. She wasn't like that. Not irresponsible. The thought jolted her. *Wow, have I changed!* When she was married to Sean, he'd complained about her lack of responsibility. Now she was saying the same about other people.

She strolled across the room to a window and looked out at the fading glow of sunset reflected on the marble lions outside the renovated mansion across the street. "We shouldn't have let Sean go without backup."

"He can take care of himself," Dylan said. "He took a gun."

And that worried her, too. If he wasn't expecting trouble, why did he make sure he was armed? "We should go after him."

"Call him." Dylan gestured to the old-fashioned-looking phone on the other desk. "Press the button for extension two. That rings through to his cell phone."

"Are you extension number one?"

"No way." He glanced over his shoulder at her. "That number is, and always will be, Mom."

"Sean told me that your parents are still in Denver."

"And my mother would lo-o-o-ve to see you and Sean get back together. Her dream is grandbabies."

"I heard you're dating someone."

"Her name is Jayne. It's a serious relationship." His eyes lit up. "But we aren't talking about babies."

From the sneaky smile on his face, she could tell that the topic of marriage had come up. Little brother Dylan had found a woman who would put up with his computers. She was happy for him.

As she tapped the extension on the office phone, she hoped that she was worrying about nothing. Sean would pick up and tell her he was fine.

From the other side of the desk, she heard his ring-tone. Then she saw his cell phone next to the computer screen. He hadn't taken the phone with him.

"Dylan, we have to go." She hung up the phone. "We have to help Sean."

He lifted his hands off the keys and looked up at her. "Is there something about this Morelli person that I don't know about? Is he particularly dangerous?"

Her impression of the man she'd interviewed was that he was a standard midlevel management guy. He'd worn a nice suit without a necktie. His shoes were polished loafers. His best feature was his thick black hair, which was slicked back with a heavy dose of styling gel. When he spoke he did a lot of hemming and hawing, and she had the sense that he wasn't telling her much more than she could learn from reading about Wynter Corp on the internet.

"Not dangerous," she said. "He was the contrary. Quiet, secretive. Morelli is the kind of guy who fades into the woodwork."

"I'm guessing my brother can handle him."

"I hate to say this." But she remembered those horrible moments on the boat when Patrone was killed. "What if Morelli's not alone?"

That possibility lit a fire under Dylan's tail. He was up and out of his computer chair in a few seconds. He motioned for her to follow, and she ran after him. They raced out the front door and onto the wide veranda to an SUV parked at the curb.

SEAN WOULD HAVE known right away that he was being followed if it hadn't been the middle of rush hour with the downtown streets clogged and lane changing nearly impossible. He first caught sight of a black sedan when he was only three blocks away from the office. After he doubled back twice, he was dead certain that the innocent-looking compact sedan, probably a rental from the airport, was on his tail.

Weaving through the other cars on Colfax Avenue, his pursuer had to stay close or risk losing Sean in the stop-and-go traffic. A couple of times, the sedan was directly behind Sean's car. At a stoplight, he studied the rearview mirror, trying to figure out if Morelli was by himself or with a partner.

He appeared to be alone.

Emily had described him as being in his forties. That was the only information Sean had. He should have asked for more details, but he didn't want to alarm her. Leaving the office without a plan had been an unnecessary risk. He knew that. So why had he done it? Was he feeling left out while Dylan did his thing with the computers? Jealous of his little brother?

Envy might account for 5 percent of his decision, but mostly he'd wanted time alone to refresh his mind. Ever since he saw Emily, he'd been tense. And when they kissed...

He checked his side mirror. The black sedan was one car back, still following. Dusk was rapidly approaching. Some vehicles had already turned on their headlights. If he was going to confront the man in the sedan, he should make his move. Darkness would limit his options.

Sean didn't necessarily want to hurt Morelli. He wanted to talk to the guy, to have him send a message back to James Wynter that Sean wasn't somebody to mess around with, and he was protecting Emily. The bad guys needed to realize that she wasn't helpless, and—in his role as her bodyguard—he wouldn't hesitate to kick ass.

He set a simple trap. Accelerating and making a few swerving turns, he sped into a large, mostly empty parking lot at the west end of Cherry Creek Mall. Sean fishtailed behind a building, parked and jumped out of the car before the black sedan came around the corner.

His original plan had been to hide behind his car, but a better possibility appeared. Though the parking lot was bare asphalt right now, there had been snow that morning. The plows had cleared the large lot and left the snow in a waist-high pile near a streetlight. Sean dove behind it.

Holding his gun ready, he watched and waited while the black sedan cautiously inched closer and closer. It circled his car, keeping a distance. The sedan parked behind his car, and a man got out. He braced a semi-automatic pistol with both hands.

"Sean Timmons," he shouted. "Get out of the car. I'm not going to hurt you."

"You got that right." Sean came out from behind the snow barrier. His position was excellent, in back of the driver of the sedan. "Drop the gun and raise your arms."

If it came to a shoot-out, he wouldn't hesitate to drop this guy. But he wouldn't take the first shot. The man set his gun on the asphalt, raised his hands and turned. "We need to talk."

Since they were standing in view of a busy street with rush hour traffic streaming past, Sean lowered his gun as he approached the other man. In spite of the gun, this guy didn't seem real threatening. Dressed in a conservative blue sweater with khaki trousers, he wore his hair slicked back. His pale complexion hinted that he spent most of his time indoors.

Sean asked, "Is your name Morelli?"

"John Morelli."

"Are you a hit man, John?"

"Of course not."

"What do you want to say?"

"It's about your ex-wife." He took a step forward and Sean raised his gun, keeping him back. "If you'll let me talk to her, I can explain everything."

He sounded rational, but Sean wasn't convinced. "You could have called her," he pointed out.

"I tried," Morelli said. "I left messages on her an-

swering machine. She's a hard woman to reach, especially since she gave me a fake name."

That much was true. "How did you find out her real
name?"

Morelli didn't answer immediately. He exhibited the
classic signs of nerves: furrowed brow, the flicker of
an eyelid, the thinning of the lips and the clearing of
his throat. All these tics and twitches were extremely
subtle. Most people wouldn't notice.

But Sean was a pro when it came to questioning
scumbags. He knew that whatever Morelli said next
was bound to be a lie.

"It's like this," Morelli said. "I saw her on the street
and followed her to her house."

"You stalked her?"

Quickly Morelli said, "No, no, it wasn't creepy. I
guessed her neighborhood from something she said at
our interview."

"Not buying that story."

"Okay, you got me." He tried a self-deprecating gesture that didn't quite work. "I got her fingerprint at our
interview and ran it through identification software."

Sean had enough. "Here's what I think. Your boss,
James Wynter, used an illegal wiretap, overheard her
name. When he pulled up her photo, you recognized
the reporter who interviewed you."

Morelli was breathing harder. A dull red color
climbed his throat. "I don't know anything about illegal wiretaps, and I'm insulted that you think I would
be that sort of person."

As if being a stalker was more reputable? "This is
your last chance to be honest, Morelli. Otherwise, I'll
turn you in to the feds. They keep an open file on Wynter, and they'll be interested in you."

"Wait!" He lowered his hands and waved them frantically. "There's no need for law enforcement."

"Don't tell me another lie."

"Truth, only truth, I swear."

Sean tested that promise by asking, "Did Wynter send you to Denver?"

"Yes."

"What were you supposed to do?"

"Find your ex-wife. When he said her name was Emily Peterson, I didn't know who he was talking about. I knew her as Sylvia Plath."

Sean stifled a chuckle. Emily's obviously phony alias referenced a famous poet. "What made you think she might come looking for me? Did you miss the 'ex' in front of husband?"

"After I learned that she'd gone on the run, I checked her background on the internet. Your name popped up, and I knew. The first person the girl would look to for help was her macho, ex-FBI husband who runs a security firm."

His story sounded legit. Or maybe Sean just enjoyed being called macho. He liked that he was the guy to call when danger struck. Or was he being conned?

Morelli was turning out to be a puzzle. He readily admitted that he worked for Wynter and he carried a gun, but he looked like a middle-aged man who had just finished a game of billiards in a sunless pool hall. He was less intimidating than a sock puppet.

Sean made a guess. "You don't get out of the office much, do you?"

"Not for a long time." He gave a self-deprecating smile. "I've had both knees replaced."

Scenes from old gangster movies where some poor shmuck was getting his kneecaps broken with a baseball bat flashed through Sean's mind. But he didn't go there. This was the twenty-first century, and criminals were more corporate…more like the man standing before him.

"There's something bothering me," Sean said. "When you called the TST office, you used your own phone."

"So? I wasn't giving anything away. My number's unlisted."

"An easy hack," Sean said. "I might even be able to do it."

"I should've used a burner." The corners of his mouth pulled down. He seemed honestly surprised and upset. *What is going on with this guy?* If Wynter hadn't sent him to wipe out the witness to his son's crime, why was Morelli here?

Sean said, "What were you supposed to do when you found my ex-wife?"

"To warn her."

"About what?"

"If she prints her article from information I gave her, it's going to have several errors. Wynter Corp is planning a significant move in regard to our real estate holdings."

As he spoke, his face showed signs that he was lying. His lip quivered. He even did the classic signal of looking up and to the right. For a thug, Morelli was a terrible liar.

"Seriously," Sean said. "You want me to believe that you rushed out to Denver, tailed my car through rush-hour traffic and pulled a gun so you could talk real estate?"

"Doesn't make sense, does it?"

"Last chance. Tell me the real reason. What do you want from Emily?"

"I want to find out what she knows."

His statement seemed sincere. "Why would you think Emily has information that you don't?"

"She's been researching Wynter Corp for quite a while, and it's possible she stumbled over some internal operations data that would be embarrassing to Mr. Wynter."

"Lose the corporate baloney. What's the problem?"

"Somebody's stealing from us, and we want to know who."

"Now you're talking." Sean believed him. Wynter wouldn't be happy about somebody dipping into his inventories. "Do you really think Emily might have information you missed? Is she that good an investigator?"

"Her first article on Wynter Corp was right on target."

It occurred to Sean that if he pretended that Emily had valuable information, the hit men wouldn't hurt her. Luckily, he was an excellent liar. "I shouldn't tell you, but she's come up with a working hypothesis. She's figured out what's happening on the inside. If she gets hurt, it all goes public."

"I knew it was an insider." Morelli cleared his throat. "And there's that other matter I need to discuss."

"The murder?"

"She might have imagined seeing something that did not, in fact, happen."

Sean shook his head. "She's sure of what she saw, and she won't be convinced otherwise."

"How much would it take to unconvince her?"

And now Sean had full comprehension. Morelli wasn't here to kill her. He'd come to Denver to seduce her into working for Wynter Corp with cash payoffs and assurances that she was brilliant. Clearly, he didn't know Emily.

It was time to wrap up this encounter. If Sean had still been a fed, he would've taken Morelli into custody and gone through a mountain of paperwork to come up with charges that would be dismissed as soon as Wynter's lawyers got involved. As a bodyguard, he didn't have those responsibilities. His job was to keep Emily safe.

He made a threat assessment. "Are there other Wynter operatives in Denver?"

"No."

But a quick twitch at the corner of his eye told Sean the opposite. "How many?"

For a moment, Morelli sputtered and prevaricated, trying to avoid the truth. Then he admitted, "One other person. He does things differently than I do."

Sean translated. "He's more of a 'shoot-first' type."

"You could say that."

He needed to get Emily out of town before the less subtle hit man caught up with them. He picked up Morelli's pistol, removed the ammo and returned it to him. At the same time, Morelli handed him a business card.

"It's got all my numbers," Morelli said.

"I'll get your message to Emily. If she agrees to talk to you, she'll call. Don't approach her or me again."

They walked away from each other, each returning to his separate rental car. As Sean slid behind the wheel, he wished that he could trust Morelli. It would've been handy to have an inside man at Wynter Corp.

As he drove to the homely, little Chinese restaurant where they always ordered carryout, he checked his rearview mirrors and scanned the traffic. There was no sign of Morelli. He didn't know what the other hit man—the more dangerous thug—would be driving.

At the restaurant, he spotted Dylan and Emily sitting at one of the small tables near the kitchen. He would have been annoyed that she'd left the security of the office and put herself in danger, but this happenstance worked for him.

She stood and faced him. "Next time," she said, "take your damn phone. I was worried."

"Ready to go?" he asked.

Dylan held up a large brown paper bag with streaky grease stains on the side. "It's our usual order."

"Bring it. I get hungry on plane rides."

Emily gaped. "Plane?"

Sean wasn't going to hang around in Denver, waiting for the second hit man to find them. For all he knew, Morelli had already contacted his partner-in-crime. Sean and Emily had to escape. The sooner, the better.

Chapter Nine

Emily had no idea how Sean accomplished so much in so little time. It seemed to be a combination of knowing the right people and calling in favors; she couldn't say for sure. Maybe he was magic. In any case, he'd told her that Denver was too dangerous, and within an hour she was on a private jet, ready to take off for San Francisco.

After she'd been whisked to a small airfield south of town, Sean rushed her into an open hangar and got her on board a Gulfstream G200. Her only other experience with private aircraft was a ski trip on a rickety little Cessna, which was no comparison to this posh eight-passenger jet. Sean left her with instructions not to disembark.

She strolled down the strip of russet-brown carpet that bisected the length of the cabin. Closest to the cockpit were four plush taupe leather chairs facing one another. Behind that was a long sofa below the porthole windows on one side and two more chairs on the other. The galley—a half-size refrigerator, cabinet, sink and microwave—was tucked into the rear.

Her stomach growled, and she made a quick search of the kitchenette. There were three different kinds of water in the fridge and the liquor cabinet was well stocked, but the cupboards were almost bare.

At the front of the cabin, she sank into one of the chairs. The cushioned seat and back cradled her, elevating her to a level of comfort that was practically a massage. Still, she didn't relax. A persistent adrenaline rush stoked her nervous energy.

Bouncing to her feet, she paced the length of the aircraft, all the way to the bathroom behind the galley to the closed door that separated the cockpit from the cabin. Sean had left her suitcase, and she wondered if she should change out of the black sweater she'd been wearing since before dawn this morning. A fresh outfit might give her a new perspective, and she needed something to lighten her spirits and ease her tension.

Not that she was complaining about the way Sean had handled the threat from Morelli. He'd done a good job, but she wished that she'd been there. Somehow it felt like the situation was slipping through her fingers. She was losing control.

Or was she overreacting? The trip to San Francisco had originally been her idea, not his. But she had new information and needed to reconsider. Sean should have consulted with her before charging into the breach and arranging for a private jet. She had opinions. This was her investigation. He wasn't the boss. When push came to shove, he was actually her employee.

A sense of dread rose inside her. She'd felt this way before. Frustrated and voiceless, she was reminded of the final, ugly days of their marriage. Until the bitter end, Sean had tried to make all the decisions. He wanted to be the captain who set their course while she was left to swab the decks and polish the hardware. Her only option had been mutiny.

In the past when she'd tried to stop him, she failed more than she succeeded. He was so implacable. And she didn't want to fight. *Make love, not war.* She'd changed. No longer a nineteen-year-old free spirit who tumbled whichever way the wind was blowing, the new Emily was solid, determined and responsible. As soon as she could get Sean alone, she meant to set the record straight.

Dylan stuck his head through the entry hatch. His long hair was out of the ponytail and hanging around his face, making him look like a teenager. "I brought you a brand-new, super-secure computer."

He sat and wiggled his butt. "Nice chair."

"Very." She sat opposite.

Obviously he'd been in this jet before. He knew exactly how to pull out a table from the wall. When it stretched out between them, he set a laptop on it, opened the lid and spun it toward her. "As I've said before, about a hundred times, anything can be hacked. This system has extreme firewalls, but when you're not using it, log off with this code."

He typed in numbers and letters that ran together: 14U24Me.

"One for you two for me," she read.

"Easy to remember." He reached into his backpack. "And here's your new cell phone, complete with camera and large screen. It's loaded with everything that was on your old phone, but this baby is also secure. It bounces your signal all around the world."

She stroked the smooth plastic cover. "I've missed having a phone."

"Yeah, well, don't get tempted to play with this. Keep texting to the bare minimum and don't add a bunch of apps. In the interest of security, keep your calls short. And when you aren't using the phone, log off."

"I thought cell phones could be tracked even when they were off."

"Not this one. Not unless somebody hacks my most recent software innovation, and that's not going to happen for a couple of weeks at least." Digging into his pocket, he produced her flash drive. "You can slip this back into your necklace. I've got a copy."

"While we're gone, will you keep hacking Wynter?"

"You bet."

"You might run comparisons between shipping manifests and inventory, plus sales figures."

He pushed the glasses up on his nose. "Morelli seemed convinced that there was theft. That gives me another angle."

In her research, she hadn't uncovered any evidence that someone was stealing from Wynter. But she hadn't been using the sophisticated hacking tools that Dylan so deftly employed. Part of her wanted to have him teach her; the more ethical part of her conscience held her back. Hacking wasn't a fair way to investigate.

Dylan stood. Before leaving, he gave her a brotherly kiss on the cheek. "I know Sean is supposed to be taking care of you. But keep an eye on him, okay? Don't let him do anything crazy dangerous."

"I'll try."

When Dylan left, she was alone in the cabin. Still seated, she peered through a porthole. Through the open door to her hangar, she could see one of the lighted runways, part of another hangar and several small planes tethered to the tarmac. The control tower was a four-story building with a 360-degree view that reminded her of some of the lighthouses up the coast in Oregon. As she watched, a midsize Cessna taxied to the far end of the airstrip, wheeled around and halted. With a burst of speed, the white jet sped forward and gracefully lifted off. Silhouetted against the night sky, the Cessna's lights soared to the right, toward the dark shadow of the mountains west of the city.

Sean came through the hatch and sat in the chair opposite her, where Dylan had been sitting. As easily as Dylan had pulled down the table, Sean removed that barrier between them. He leaned forward with his elbows resting on his knees.

"Are you okay?" he asked.

His gentleness threw her off guard. She noticed that he hadn't shaved, and dark stubble outlined his jaw. By asking how she was, he'd given her an opening to rationally discuss how she should be kept in the loop. Right now she should assert her needs and desires, let him know she was in charge. *Right now! This moment!*

Instead she stared dumbly at his face, distracted by the perfect symmetry of his features. Why did he have to be so gorgeous?

"Emily?" His eyebrows lifted as though her name were a question. "Emily, tell me."

"When did you find time to change?" He'd discarded his turtleneck for a cotton shirt and a light suede bomber jacket. She couldn't say he looked fresh as a daisy. Sean was much too rugged to be compared to a flower.

"Only took a minute," he said. "Are you—"

"You asked if I was okay." She stumbled over the words. "Okay about what?"

"Going to San Francisco," he said. "We're set to leave in ten minutes. A flight plan has been filed, but this is a private jet. You can change your mind and go anywhere."

She wasn't following. "What do you mean?"

"San Francisco is dangerous. There are alternative

destinations, like Washington State or heading south to Mexico. We could even go to Hawaii."

Irritated, she pushed herself out of the cozy chair and stalked toward the rear. "I'm not afraid."

"I didn't say you were." He followed her down the aisle.

"But you think I might want to run away." She pivoted to face him. "Maybe I'd like to take a vacation in Hawaii and lie on the beach. Is that what you want? For me to hide in a safe place while Wynter runs his human trafficking ring and his son gets away with murder."

"It's not about what I want."

"I'm glad you understand." But she almost wished he'd be unreasonable. Making her point was easier when he argued against her. His rational approach meant she had to also be thoughtful.

"You don't have to step into the line of fire," he said. "You could keep researching the crimes on computer. Work with Dylan. There's no need for you to confront Wynter in his lair."

"I've considered that." There were threads of evidence that she needed to be in San Francisco to follow. With Sean to accompany her, she had more access.

"I need an answer on our destination."

"I've got a question for you," she said. "How do you rate a private jet?"

"Don't worry about it."

"I sincerely hope you're not charging my aunt some exorbitant fee."

"This trip is a favor, and it's free," he said. "You'll recognize the pilot from our wedding. David Henley."

She knew the name. "The guy who plays the banjo?"

"Flying planes is his real job."

"Good for him. He couldn't have made much of a living as a banjo picker."

"In addition to this sweet little Gulfstream, he has a Cessna, an old Sabreliner and two helicopters. He freelances for half a dozen or so companies, flying top execs around the country."

The aforementioned David Henley swung through the entry hatch and marched down the aisle toward them. "Emily, my princess. It's been a while."

Though David was an average-looking guy with wavy blond hair, she most certainly remembered him from the wedding. He'd hit on each of her sisters and ended up going home with her former roommate. He tapped Sean on the shoulder. "May I give this princess a hug?"

"Don't ask me," Sean said. "She can speak for herself."

He held his arms wide. "Hug?"

"Don't get too snuggly," she said. "I see that wedding band on your finger."

His arms wrapped around her. "I like to tease the princesses, but that's as far as it goes. My heart belongs to my queen, my wife."

"My former roommate." She remembered the announcement from a few years ago. "Please give Ginger a hug from me."

"She'll be bummed that she didn't have a chance to get together with you."

She preferred this mature version of David to the horny banjo player. "Thanks for the plane ride."

"I'm sorry you're in so much trouble." He held her by the shoulders and looked into her eyes. "Are we going to San Francisco?"

"Yes, so be sure to wear some flowers in your hair."

"Still cute." He turned toward Sean. "I won't be using

you as copilot. This flight is a good opportunity to train the new guy I hired. Now, I've got to run some equipment checks before we take off. Ciao, you two."

While David went forward to the cockpit, she asked Sean, "You know how to fly a plane?"

"David's been teaching me. The helo is more fun." He gestured toward the seats across the aisle from the sofa bench. "Get comfortable. I'll see if he's got any food back here."

In the rush to get to the airfield, they'd forgotten the Chinese food. She couldn't honestly say she had regrets. Fast food from Denver didn't compare with San Francisco's Chinatown, but the remembered aroma tantalized her. Her stomach rumbled again. No doubt, Dylan would munch the chicken fried rice, chop suey, broccoli beef and General Tso's for dinner. With an effort, she managed to pull out the table between the two seats.

Sean didn't have much to put on it: Two small bags of chips and two sparkling waters. "This will have to do."

Not enough to appease her hunger, but it was probably good that she wouldn't be settling down and getting comfortable. Other than being starving, things seemed to be going her way. She wanted to go to San Francisco, and that was where they were headed. If she was smart, this would be a good time to stay quiet. But she wanted to lay down the basics of a plan for *her* investigation, with emphasis on *her*.

She cleared her throat. "I want to talk about what we're going to do when we land."

"Right," he agreed. "I need to make hotel reservations."

"We can stay in my apartment."

"You're joking."

"Not really."

He regarded her with a disbelieving gaze. "Morelli came all the way to Denver to find you. I'm guessing that Wynter's men have found your apartment."

"But they think I'm in Denver."

"These aren't the sort of guys to play cat and mouse with. As soon as they figure out where you really are, they'll be knocking at your door or busting a hole with a battering ram."

She deferred to his expertise. "Make the reservations."

"I like the Pendragon Hotel," he said. "It's near the trolley line and close to Chinatown."

"We're not going on a sightseeing trip."

The copilot boarded the jet, bringing cold cuts and bread for sandwiches. *Food!* She almost kissed him.

While she and Sean slapped together sandwiches, they dropped their discussion of anything important. The sight and smell of fresh-sliced ham and turkey and baby Swiss made her giddy. And the copilot hadn't stinted on condiments, providing an array of mustard, mayo, horseradish and extra-virgin olive oil. Her mouth was watering. Tomatoes, cucumbers, baby bib lettuce and coleslaw.

She sliced a tomato thin and placed it carefully on the ciabatta bread between the mustard and the lettuce. "I suppose we should make something for David and the copilot."

"We should." He glanced in her direction. "But you really don't look like you can wait for one more minute."

"I'm ravenous."

"Get started without me. I'll take food to the cockpit."

"Best offer I've had all day."

The sandwich she'd assembled was almost too big for her mouth, but she tore off a chunk and chomped down on it. The explosion of flavor in her mouth was total ecstasy. As the sandwich slid down her throat, she relished texture, the taste and the nourishment. She took another bite and another.

The last food she'd had was that morning in the mountains, and that felt like a lifetime ago. While she continued to eat, her eyelids closed. She groaned with pleasure.

After a few more bites, she opened her eyes to reach for her water and saw Sean standing behind his chair, looking down at her. He grinned and said, "Sounds like you're enjoying the sandwich. Either that or you've decided to join the Mile High Club all by yourself."

She swallowed a gulp of water. "How do you know I'm not already a member?"

"Are you?"

"No way," she said. "I'm pretty sure it takes two."

"I'd be happy to volunteer."

Standing there, he was devilish handsome with his wide shoulders, his tousled hair, his stubble and his hands, his rugged hands. Too easily, she imagined his gentle caress across her shoulders and down her back. His eyes, when they'd made love, turned the color of dark chocolate, and his gaze could make her melt inside.

She shoved those urges aside and returned her attention to the sandwich. She needed refueling. Before she was full, the Gulfstream taxied onto the runway.

"Don't bite my arm off," Sean said as he scooped up the remains of her sandwich. "The food has to move before takeoff. Or you'll be wearing it."

David opened the door from the cockpit. "Fasten your seat belts."

She buckled up, gripped the arms of her seat and braced herself as the whine of the engines accelerated

and a tremor went through the jet. Though she'd actually never been afraid of flying or of heights, she suffered an instinctive twinge in her gut and a shimmer of
vertigo when a plane took off or when she stood at the
edge of a cliff. Again, she closed her eyes.

Her mind ran through various streams of evidence
they'd investigate in San Francisco, ranging from a
meeting with the feds to a possible reconnaissance on
Wynter's luxury double-decker yacht.

In moments, they were airborne.

Her eyelids opened. She looked at Sean and said
the first thing on her mind, "Don't let me forget Paco
the Pimp."

"I'm hoping that's a nickname for something else."

"He's a real guy. I met him about a year ago when
I was doing an article on preteen hookers." She shuddered. "That was a painful experience, one horrifying
story after another. I almost decided to quit journalism
and go back to soothing poetry or lyric writing. Paco
changed my mind."

"By offering you a job?"

"Oh, he did that…several times. Not that either of us
took his offers seriously. Anyway, he reminded me of
my obligation to shine a light on the ugly truth in the
hope that people would pay attention. And the horror
would stop…or at least slow down."

He lowered himself into the seat opposite her and
pulled out the table. Instead of returning the last few
bites of her sandwich, he placed a bottle of red wine
and two plastic glasses on the flat surface. "And why
do you need to remember Paco?"

"He's got an ear to the street. He hears all the gossip.
And I want to find out if he remembered anything from
that night." She hesitated. Maybe she was bringing up

a volatile topic. She didn't want Sean to be mad at her. "He might have seen something I missed."

He used a corkscrew to open the wine. "Are you talking about the night of the murder?"

Averting her gaze, she looked through the porthole window. The lights of Denver glittered below them. Ahead was the pitch-dark of the Rocky Mountains. She didn't want to answer.

Chapter Ten

Sean was familiar with most of Emily's tactics when it came to arguments. When she didn't answer him back right away, her silence meant she was hiding something. He sank into the plush chair opposite hers. He didn't want to fight. They were on a private jet headed toward one of the most romantic cities in the world, and he hadn't completely ruled out the possibility of inducting her into the Mile High Club.

But he couldn't leave Paco the Pimp hanging. Apparently this Paco had been a passenger on Wynter's deluxe yacht. "You've told me about the night of the murder. You claimed you were at a yacht party. True or false?"

"True."

He poured the wine, a half glass for her and the same for himself. "But you never told me how you got an invite to this insider party. I'm guessing it had something to do with Paco the Pimp. True or false?"

"I don't want to talk about this."

"And I know why," he said. "Your pal Paco was invited to provide a bunch of party girls for the guys on the yacht. And you convinced him to take you along. You went undercover."

"Fine," she snapped. "You're right. I was all dolled

up in a sparkly skintight dress, four-inch heels and gobs of heavy makeup."

"A hooker disguise."

"Sleazy except for my long hair. I had it pinned up on top of my head when I went there. I thought it was sophisticated." She sipped her wine. "Paco said I should wear it down. He thought the men would like it."

Imagining her being ogled in a sexy dress made his blood boil. Of course they liked her long, beautiful hair. "What the hell, Emily? You used to believe that hiding your identity was dishonest and unfair."

"You've got no room to talk," she said. "You used to go undercover all the time."

"And you never approved."

"Maybe not."

"And I was trained for it. I have certain traits and abilities that lend themselves to undercover work, namely, I'm good at deception." He downed his wine in two glugs. "You're not like that. You're a lousy liar."

"I've changed. I know when to keep my mouth shut instead of blurting out the truth. I can be circumspect."

"You can't change your basic nature," he said as he poured more wine. "Undercover work is not your thing."

"I pulled it off on Wynter's yacht."

He glared at her. "Not a shining example of a successful mission."

"I made mistakes," she admitted. "Okay, all right, it was gross. Witnessing the murder was the worst, but being pawed by sleazeballs was bad. One of them grabbed me by my hair and kissed me. Another patted my hair like I was a dog. The very next day, I went to the beauty shop and told them to cut it off."

"You're never going to go undercover again, understand?"

"Don't tell me what I can and can't do."

Through clenched teeth, he said, "I'm sorry."

She looked at him as though he'd sprouted petunias from the top of his head. "Did I hear you correctly?"

"You're right. I can't tell you what to do. However, if you decide to go undercover again, I want to know. Give me a chance to show you how to do it without getting yourself killed."

"My turn to apologize," she said. "You're also right. I had no business waltzing onto that yacht without the proper training. The only reason I got out of there in one piece was dumb luck."

He held up his plastic glass to salute her. The wine he'd already inhaled was taking the sharp edge off, but he was still alert enough to realize that something significant had occurred: they hadn't gotten into a fight.

Both of them had been ticked off. They'd danced around the volcano, but neither had erupted. Instead, they'd talked like adults and settled their differences. Maybe she'd matured. Maybe he'd gotten more sensitive. *Whatever!* He'd gladly settle for this fragile truce instead of gut-wrenching hostility.

He didn't want to discuss their successful handling of the problem for fear that he'd jinx the positive mood. What had they been talking about before takeoff? Oh yeah, the agenda for their time in San Francisco. He wanted to take her to dinner at the Italian restaurant where he proposed.

He gazed toward her. She looked youthful but not too young. Had she changed in the past five years? If he looked closely, he could see fine lines at the corners of her turquoise eyes, and her features seemed sharper, more honed. With her black sweater covering her torso, he could only guess how her body had changed. A vision of her nicely proportioned shoulders, round breasts and slender waist was easy to recall. He hadn't forgotten the constellation of freckles across her back or the tattoo of a cute little rodent above her left breast that she referred to as a "titmouse."

Since he wasn't allowed to touch her without disobeying half a dozen of their weird ground rules, he had to stop thinking like this. Her unapproachable nearness would drive him mad. Back to business, back to the investigation, he said, "Tomorrow, our first appointment should be a meeting with Levine to see if the FBI has any new info."

"But not at the fed office," she reminded him. "Dylan thinks their phones are bugged."

He considered it unlikely that Levine was working with Wynter, but Sean didn't want to take any chances. "I'd rather not let him know where we're staying. We'll meet him for breakfast."

"After that," she said, "we should go to Chinatown. I had a couple of leads there, and I'd like to talk to Doris Liu again. She's the woman who took in Roger Patrone and raised him."

He'd almost forgotten that Patrone was an orphan who had been taken in by a family in Chinatown. "There must have been something remarkable about Patrone when he was a kid. Most residents in Chinatown aren't welcoming to strangers."

"It's been hard for me to ask around," she said. "Patrone's gambling operation—last I heard it was a stud poker game, Texas Hold'em and two blackjack tables—is in the rear of a strip club in the Tenderloin. Even with the attempts at gentrification, I don't blend in."

The Tenderloin had earned its reputation as a high-crime district. He was deeply grateful that she hadn't tried an undercover stunt as a stripper. "I'll go there, no problem."

"And I wouldn't mind sneaking onto Wynter's yacht and looking around."

Breaking and entering didn't appeal to him, but he definitely liked the idea of getting out on the water in the bay. San Francisco had many charms, ranging from unique architecture to culture to amazing restaurants. The best, he thought, were the piers and the ocean…the scent of salt water…the whisper of the surf.

She yawned. "Maybe we should go to the docks. I only tried to get in there once, and it didn't go well. The guys who work with shipping containers ignored me, and the supervisors were overly polite, thinking I was sent by management to check up on them."

"What can we learn there?"

"I'm not sure," she said. "It's another avenue."

They were going to be busy. "Tired?"

"A bit," she said.

"You can take off your seat belt and lie on the sofa. It folds out into a bed."

She peeked out the porthole. "How long before we're in San Francisco?"

"A couple of hours." The flight time on commercial airlines was two and a half hours. The Gulfstream took a little longer.

"I wouldn't mind a catnap," she said.

He moved their wineglasses to cup holders beside the chairs, picked up the nearly empty wine bottle and tucked away the table. Before he transformed the sofa into a bed, he opened a storage compartment and took out a thermal blanket and a pillow. Then he dimmed the lights.

After fluffing the pillow, she stood and fidgeted beside the sofa bed. "I feel selfish, taking the only bed. You're as tired as I am."

"Is that an invitation to join you?"

"No," she said softly. "Sorry, I didn't mean to give you that idea."

Her tone sounded regretful. If he pushed, he might be able to change her mind. But now wasn't the right time. He didn't want to rock the boat while they were in a fairly good place. At least they weren't fighting. It was best not to complicate things with sex. *Great sex*, he reminded himself. They'd always had great sex.

"Not tonight," he said, as much to himself as to her. "Lie down. I'm going up to the cockpit."

"With the other cocks?"

"You might say that." He wouldn't, but she would.

No matter how much she claimed to be a responsible, sober adult, there was a goofball just below the surface. That was the Emily that drove him crazy, the Emily he loved.

WHILE SHE SLEPT, Sean spent time with his buddy David and the copilot. He loved the night view from the cockpit with stars scattered across the sky. He felt like they were part of the galaxies.

They talked, and he made coffee to counteract the slight inebriation he'd felt. A professional bodyguard shouldn't be drinking on the job, but he couldn't pretend that this was a standard assignment.

If she'd been anyone else, he would have advised them to leave the investigating to the police. And if they refused, he would have terminated the contract. Not a detective, he was well aware that he didn't have the resources that were available to him when he was in the

FBI. On the other hand, he had the hacking skills of his brother and none of those pesky restrictions.

Finally, he was peering through the clouds and wispy curtains of fog to see the lights of San Francisco, and he felt a surge. His pulse sped up. His blood pumped harder. This city was the setting for the best time in his life and the absolute, rock-bottom worst. Emily was intrinsic to both.

He went back to the cabin and found her lying on her side, spooning the pillow. As soon as he touched her shoulder, she wakened.

"I'm up," she said, throwing off the blanket.

"Almost there. You need to put on a seat belt."

"Do I have time to splash water on my face?"

"Okay, if you hurry."

While she darted into the bathroom, he verified their arrangements on his phone. They had a suite reserved at the Pendragon Hotel and there should be a rental car waiting at the private airfield. Sean wanted to believe they'd be safe, at least for tonight, but his gut told him to watch for trouble. He put in a call to Dylan at the TST office.

"We're here," Sean announced, purposely not naming the city in case somebody was listening. "Anything to report?"

"Wynter must be taking advantage of his location near Silicon Valley and hiring top-notch programmers. His security is state-of-the-art, truly hard to hack."

Oddly, Dylan sounded happy. Sean asked, "You like the challenge?"

"Oh yeah. Getting through these firewalls will be an accomplishment."

"I'll leave you to it."

"Hang on a sec. I had a phone call from your new

BFF, Morelli. He wanted to make an information exchange."

"What did you tell him?"

"I said you'd call him back."

"Thanks, bro."

He disconnected the call. Morelli's business card with all his numbers was burning a hole in his pocket. Though Sean was tempted to make the call, he'd warned Morelli not to contact him. It might seem weak to call back. But it was possible that Morelli had useful information.

Sean set the scrambler on his phone so he couldn't be traced and punched in the numbers for Morelli's cell phone. As soon as the other man answered, he said, "What do you want?"

"Let me talk to Emily."

"You're wasting my time," Sean said. "Talk."

"Tell her that she's not going to be able to sell her articles to the *BP Reporter* anymore. That's one of the places she published her last article on Wynter."

"Why can't she sell there?"

"A terrible accident happened in their office. The police are saying a leak in the gas main resulted in the fiery explosion that destroyed the building."

"Any deaths or injuries?"

"The editor is in the hospital." Morelli paused for a moment. "It's fortunate that Emily wasn't there."

Chapter Eleven

Any complacency Emily had been feeling vanished when Sean told her of the explosion. *BP Reporter* was a giveaway newspaper filled with shopping specials and coupons, and the pay for articles was next to nothing. Most writers saw *BP*, which stood for Blog/Print, as a stepping-stone to actual paying assignments. The editor, Jerome Strauss, wasn't a close friend, but she knew him and she felt guilty about his injuries. She was to blame. There wasn't a doubt in her mind that Wynter was behind the supposed "gas leak" detonation.

Refreshed from her catnap and energized by righteous rage, she found it difficult to wait until they got to the Pendragon Hotel to start her inquiries. They'd gained an hour traveling to the West Coast. It was after two o'clock in the morning when they entered the suite.

She set up her laptop on a desk in the living room and watched while Sean prowled through the suite with his gun held ready. The floor plan for the suite was open space with the kitchen delineated by a counter and the bedroom separated by a half wall and an arch. Sean was thorough, peering into closets and looking under the bed. When he was apparently satisfied that there were no bad guys lurking, he unpacked some strange equipment. One piece looked like an extension rod for selfies.

"What's that?" she asked.

"An all-purpose sweeper to locate bugs, hidden cameras and the like."

Though she appreciated his attention to detail, she didn't understand why it was needed. "How would anybody know we were coming to this hotel and were assigned to this room?"

"I've stayed here before. And I asked for this room. It's on the top floor, the sixth. Since this is the tallest building on the block, it's hard for anybody with a telescope or a sniper rifle to take aim. There's a nice view when the fog lifts."

"It's a nice hotel," she agreed. The exterior was classic San Francisco architecture, and the furnishings were clean lined, Asian inspired. "Why would there be bugs?"

"I want to be sure we're safe." He started waving his long camera thingy, scanning the room for electronic devices. "Get used to this, Emily. From now on, I'm hyperprotective."

Tempted to make a snarky comment about how vigilance sometimes crossed the line into obsessive-compulsive disorder, she kept her lip zipped. He was the expert, and she needed to rely on his judgment. She sauntered across the room to the counter that separated the kitchenette and climbed onto a stool. "I need to start making phone calls. Which phone should I use?"

"It depends on who you're calling."

"How so?"

He explained, "If you're talking to somebody suspicious who might try to track your location, use the secure phone Dylan gave you. If it's somebody you feel safe with, use a burner. We can load up a burner and pitch it."

He seemed to be thinking of all contingencies. "I want to track down Strauss by calling hospitals."

"Burner," he said as he continued to sweep the room.

She called four hospitals before she found the right one. The only information the on-duty nurse would give her was that Strauss was in "fair" condition, but not allowed to have visitors, especially not visitors from the press.

Relieved but not completely satisfied, she wished she had the type of access the FBI and SFPD had. It didn't seem fair. Law enforcement officers wouldn't be barred from the room, but the press—the very people Strauss worked with every day—had to take a step back.

If Strauss was awake, she'd bet he was planning his coverage on the explosion. The story had fallen into his lap. Would he let her be the one to write about it?

She wasn't his favorite reporter. He knew her as Emily, and she submitted only puff pieces, but the explosion might be a way to integrate her real identity with her secret pseudonym. Strauss already did business with her fake persona; the article about Wynter had been published first by an online news journal that paid for her investigative skills. Strauss had permission for a reprint that cost him nothing.

Maybe she could get Sean to use his influence with Agent Levine to sneak her into the hospital room. She went into the bedroom area behind Japanese-style screens to ask.

There were two full-size beds, and he had taken the one nearer to the archway connecting bedroom and living room. He'd pulled back the spread and collapsed onto the sheets. His shoes were off, but he still wore his jeans and T-shirt. In repose, his features relaxed, and he seemed almost innocent. She crept up beside him and turned off the globe-shaped lamp on the bedside table.

Before she could tiptoe out of the room, his hand shot out and grasped her wrist. His movement was unexpected. She gasped loudly and struggled to pull away from him. He held on more tightly. "Turn it back on."

"I wanted to make it dark so you could sleep."

"Can't see an intruder." He hadn't opened his eyes. "Leave the light on."

She flicked the switch, he released his grasp and she scuttled into the front room with her heart beating fast. He'd startled her, and her fear was close to the surface. If he could spook her so easily, how was she going to fall asleep?

If she stayed up, what could she do? It was too early to make phone calls, and she wanted to talk to Dylan before she used the laptop so she wouldn't accidentally trigger any alarms.

A sigh pushed through her lips. Lying down on the bed was probably a good idea. Getting herself cleaned up was next best.

The huge bathroom was mostly white marble with caramel streaks. Fluffy white towels in varying sizes sat on open shelving that went floor to ceiling. She wasn't really a bathtub person, and the glassed-in shower enticed her.

For a full half hour, Emily indulged herself. Steaming hot water from four different jets sluiced over her body. The sandalwood fragrance of the soap permeated her skin, and she washed her hair with floral-scented shampoo while humming the song about San Francisco and flowers in her hair.

She toweled dry, styled her hair with a blow-dryer and slipped into a sleeveless nightshirt that fell to her knees Before leaving the bathroom, she turned out the light so she wouldn't disturb Sean.

After she pulled down her covers, she glanced over at his sleeping form. Under the sheets, he stretched out the full length of the bed on his back with his arms folded on his chest. His eyes were closed. He'd stripped off his clothes and appeared to be naked, which had always been his preferred way to sleep.

When they were married, she'd always looked forward to those nights when she was already in bed, not quite asleep and waiting for him. He'd enter the room quietly and slip under the covers, and she'd realize that he was completely naked. She remembered the heat radiating from his big, hard, masculine body, and when he'd pulled her into his arms, she was warmed to the marrow of her bones.

The pattern of hair on his chest reminded her of those days, long ago. Her fingers itched to touch him. She sat on the edge of her bed, silently hoping that he'd open his eyes and ask her to come closer.

Their ground rules started with the obvious: no falling in love, followed by no public display of affection. The complicated part was initiating contact. If he went first, he had to ask. But she was free to pounce on him at any time. *What am I waiting for?*

She shifted position, sitting lightly on his bed and watching him for any sign that he was awake. The steady rise and fall of his chest indicated that he hadn't noticed her nearness. Maybe she'd steal a kiss and return to her own bed.

She leaned down closer. Her heart thumped faster. Her entire body trembled with anticipation. Falling in love with her ex-husband was completely out of the question. If anything happened between them, she couldn't expect it to mean anything. *Really? Am I capable of having sex without love?*

A couple of times in the past, she'd engaged in meaningless sex. The result was never good, hardly worth the effort. Maybe that type of sex would be blah with Sean, but she doubted it. He was too skillful, and he knew exactly which buttons to punch with her. The real question was: Did she dare to open herself up to him, knowing that he'd broken her heart and fearing that he might do it again?

A scary possibility, too scary. She was too much of a coward to take the risk. Exhaling a sigh of sad regret, she pulled away from him, turned her head and stood.

"Emily?"

"Yes."

He was out of the bed, standing beside her. She glided into his embrace, and he positioned her against his naked body. They fit together like yin and yang, like spaghetti and meatballs, like Tarzan and Jane. *Take me, Lord of the Jungle!* She was becoming hysterical. If she was going to avoid sex, she'd better stop him now.

His kiss sent her reeling. With very little effort, he'd caught her.

All logic vanished. The pleasure of his touch erased conscious thought. All she wanted was to savor each sensation. He pressed more firmly against her. She couldn't fight him, didn't want to. *If this is what sex without love feels like, sign me up.*

He gathered the hem of her nightshirt in his hands. Looking down, he read the message on the front. "Promote Literacy. Kiss a Poet."

"I'm just doing my bit to promote education."

"Noble," he said.

In a single gesture, he lifted the nightshirt up and

over her head. Underneath, she was as nude as he. By the light of the bedside lamp, her gaze slid appreciatively downward, from his shoulders to the dusting of chest hair to his muscular abs and lower. He was even more flawless than she remembered.

"Hey, lady." He lifted her chin. "My eyes are up here."

"And they're very nice eyes, very dark chocolate and hot. At the moment, however—" she gave him a wicked smile "—I'm more interested in a different part of your body."

He scooped her off her feet and dove with her onto the bed. With great energy, he flung off the covers, plumped pillows and settled her in place before he straddled her hips.

For a moment, she lay motionless below him. She just stared at her magnificent ex-husband. Sex always brought out the poet in her. *He was her knight errant, her Lancelot, a conquering hero who would plunder and ravage her.* Which made her…what? Surely not a helpless maiden; she drove her own destiny. And she most certainly would not lie passively while he had all the fun.

Struggling, she sat up enough to grab his arms and pull him toward her. *A futile effort.* He was in control, and he let her know it by pinning her wrists on either side of her head. He was too strong. She couldn't fight him.

"Relax, Emily." His baritone rumbled through her. "Let me take care of you."

She wriggled. "Maybe you could speed it up."

"I've thought about this for a long time." He dropped a kiss on her forehead. "I want it to last for a very long time."

He hovered over her, balancing on his elbows and

his knees. In contrast to his flurry of activity, he slowly lowered himself, seeming to float inches above her. Their lips touched. His chest grazed the tips of her breasts.

She arched her back, desperate to join her flesh with his. He wrestled her down, forcing her to experience each feather touch separately. Shivers of pleasure shot through her, setting off a mad, convulsive reaction that rattled from the ends of her hair to the soles of her feet. She threw her head back against the pillow. Her toes curled.

"Now, Sean. I want you, please."

"Good things are...worth the wait."

His seduction was slow and deliberate, driving her crazy. Her lungs throbbed. She breathed hoarsely, panting and gasping as a wave of pleasure rolled over her. Oh God, she'd missed this! The way he handled her, manipulating her so she felt deeply and passionately. Transformed, she was aware of her own sexuality.

"You're a goddess," he whispered.

And she felt like some kind of superior being who was beautiful, brilliant and powerful. If she could be like this in everyday life, Emily would rule the world.

Somehow, magically, they changed positions and she was on top. She kissed his neck, inhaling his musky scent and tasting the salty flavor of his flesh. She bit down. He was yummy, a full meal.

He nudged her away from his throat. "Did you turn into a vampire or are you just giving me a hickey?"

"I'll be a sultry vampire." She raked her fingers through the hair on his chest. "And you can be a wolf man."

"I like it."

"Me, too."

Sex with Sean was a full contact sport, engaging mind and body, mostly body, though. He teased and cajoled and fondled and kissed and nibbled.

She'd missed the great sex that only Sean could give her. Not that it was all his doing. She played her part—the role of a goddess—in their crazy, wild affection. And when she reached her earth-shaking climax, she came completely undone, disassembled. It felt like she'd actually left her body and soared to the stratosphere. When she came back to earth, she couldn't wait to do it again.

So they did. Twice more that night.

Chapter Twelve

The next morning, Sean lifted his eyelids and scanned the open-space suite at the Pendragon Hotel. Yesterday might have been the longest day of his life with more ups and downs than a roller coaster, but he wasn't complaining. The day had turned out great. Sex with Emily was even better than he'd remembered. Their chemistry was incredible. No other woman came close.

He gazed at her, sleeping beside him. She was on her stomach, and the sheet had slipped down, revealing a partial view of her smooth, creamy white bottom. He wanted to see more. Carefully, so he wouldn't wake her, he caught the sheet between two fingers and tugged.

Immediately, she reached back to swat his hand away. She peered through a tangle of hair as she rolled to her side and rearranged the sheet to cover her lovely round breasts. *A bit late for modesty*, he thought, but he said nothing. He wanted another bout of sex, and he was fairly sure she was ready for more of the same.

"Time?" she asked.

He stretched his neck so he could see the decorative clock on the bedside table. The combination of chrome circles and squares showed the time in the upper-left corner.

"Eight forty-six." He looked past the archway into the living room, where faint light appeared around the shades. "The sun's up."

"I thought we were going to run out the door early and have breakfast with Levine."

"It'll have to be brunch. Maybe even lunch." He made a grab for her, but she evaded him. "About last night…"

"Enough said." She climbed out of bed with the sheet wrapped around her. "I'm glad we got that out of the way."

She made wonderful sex sound like a distasteful chore. Surely he'd heard her wrong. "Are you talking about us? You and me? About what happened last night?"

"It was just sex."

"Sure, and Everest is just a mountain. The Lamborghini is just a car."

"The tension was building between us, and we had to relieve it. That's what last night was about." With one hand, she clutched the sheet while the other rubbed the sleep out of her eyes. "I promise you—it's never going to happen again."

She pivoted, squared her shoulders and marched into the bathroom while he sat on the bed, gaping as he watched her hasty retreat. *Never going to happen again?* He'd be damned if he believed her. She might as well tell the birds not to sing and the fish not to swim. He could not deny his nature, and his inner voice told him to have sex with her as soon and as often as possible.

His number one job, however, was keeping her safe, and meeting with Special Agent Greg Levine was a good place to start. Sean decided not to make the phone call to set the time and the place until he and Emily were near the restaurant; he didn't want Levine to have time to plan ahead.

After they were dressed, he gave her a glance, pretending not to notice how tiny her waist looked in the bolted slacks that hugged her bottom. He stared pointedly at her flat ballet shoes. "Do you have sneakers?"

"They don't exactly go with this outfit." She slipped on the matching gray jacket to the pantsuit. "I want to look professional to meet with Levine, and my suitcase is packed with outdoorsy stuff for Colorado."

"You need to wear running shoes. Obvious reasons."

"Okay." She exhaled a little sigh. "Anything else?"

"A hooded sweatshirt?"

"Don't have one with me. I've got several at my apartment. Can we swing past there?"

She wasn't actually disagreeing with him, but her reluctance to follow his instructions was annoying. "Don't you get it? These guys want to kill you. If they recognize you, you're dead."

Her full lips pinched together. "If we can figure out a way to go to my apartment, I have a couple of already-made disguises to go with my pseudonyms. There's a really good one that makes me look like a guy."

Impossible!

He turned away from her and went to the kitchenette to fill his coffee mug again. "Try to find something that makes you look anonymous. Wynter's men might be following Levine."

When she emerged from the bedroom, she threw her arms wide and announced her presence. "Ta-da! Do I look like a punk kid from the city streets?"

Without makeup, her face looked about fourteen. But her jeans were too well fitted. And her Berkeley sweatshirt looked almost new. "Not a street kid," he said. "You look more like a cheerleader."

"Is that anonymous enough?"

"Still too cute. Men will notice you." He motioned for her to come closer. "Give me the sweatshirt."

In one of the kitchen drawers, he found a pair of heavy scissors, which he used to whack off the arms on the sweatshirt and to make a long slit down from the collar. He turned it inside out and tossed it back to her.

"You ruined my sweatshirt," she said as she pulled it over her head. Underneath, she wore a blue blouse with long sleeves. "How's this?"

"Better, but I still can't erase your prettiness." He tilted his head to the side for a different perspective. "Maybe we should cut off the jeans."

"I'd rather not. These cost almost two hundred bucks."

He stalked into the bedroom, dug around in his backpack and took out two baseball caps. The one that was worse for wear, he gave to her. "Whenever you go outside, wear this. It won't change your appearance, but it hides your face."

His clothes were more nondescript than hers; people tended not to notice a guy in jeans, T-shirt and plaid flannel overshirt. If he stooped his shoulders a bit to disguise his height, he'd fade into almost any background.

They left the hotel shortly after ten o'clock, late enough that the morning fog had lifted. When he'd been living in San Francisco, he had a hard time adjusting to fog. Sunny days in Denver numbered about 245 a year, and when it was sunny the sky was open and blue. Sean came to think of the morning fog as the day waking slowly, reticent to leave nighttime dreams behind.

This was the city where he first fell in love with Emily, and he saw the buildings, neighborhoods and streets through rose-colored glasses. If last night's sensuality had been allowed to grow and flourish, he would have felt the same today, but she'd squashed his mood.

Behind the wheel of his rental car, he asked, "Is that North Beach café with the great coffee still there?"

"You mean Henny's," she said. "It's there and the coffee is still yummy."

The location wasn't particularly convenient to the FBI offices near Golden Gate Park, but Sean wasn't planning to go easy on his former coworker. The best explanation for how Wynter found out about Emily was that Levine was incompetent enough to get his phone tapped and not know it. At worst, he was working with Wynter.

There was street parking outside Henny's Café, a corner eatery with a fat red hen for a logo. He found a place halfway down the block and parallel parked. He ordered her to stay in the car while he did swift reconnaissance inside the café, which was only half-full and had a good view of the street and an exit into the alley.

Back in the car, he called Levine. The trick to this phone call would be to keep from mentioning Emily or Wynter or the possibility that the FBI phones were tapped.

After the initial hello, Sean said, "Long time no see, buddy. Do you remember that case we worked? With the twins who kept spying on each other?"

"Uh-huh, I remember." Levine sounded confused.

"The big thing in that case has been getting more and more common." Sean's reference was to wiretapping, which had been the key to solving the twin case. "Have you ever had a problem like that?"

"What are you getting at?"

"It's probably nothing. I just hope you aren't in- fected…" *With a bug on your phone.* "Know what I mean?"

"Damn right I do." His confusion was replaced with

anger. As a rule, feds don't like having somebody outside the agency tell them that their phones aren't secure. "What about that other matter? The problem with—"

"The Em agenda," Sean said. "Meet me, within the hour, and we'll talk."

After he rattled off the name of the restaurant and the address, he ended the call and turned to Emily, who had been patiently, quietly waiting.

"He'll be here," he said. "We'll wait in the car until he shows up."

"Did you refer to me as the Em agenda?"

"To avoid saying your name."

"Cool, like a code name." She was off and running, chattering on about how she could be a spy. "Just call me Agent Em."

She needed to understand that they weren't playing a fantasy espionage game. The danger was real. But when Emily followed one of her tangents, she was bright and charming and impossible to resist.

When they were married, it was one of the things he had loved about her. He could sit back and listen to her riff about some oddball topic. She called it free verse; he called it adorable.

"Hold on," he said. "I'm still mad."

"About what?"

"You gave me the brush-off this morning."

"Didn't mean to upset you," she said. "We had an agreement, ground rules. I'm just making sure I don't fall in love with you again."

"There's a difference between sex and love."

"Well, listen to you." Her eyebrows lifted. "Aren't you surprisingly sensitive?"

"I told you I've changed."

"You hardly seem like the same guy who took me

to a Forty-Niners game at Levi's Stadium and got in a shouting match that almost came to blows."

"They insulted my Broncos," he said.

"Heaven forbid."

The near fistfight at the football game hadn't been his finest hour, but the undercover work had been eating away at him. He'd needed to let off steam. "I know there were times when I was hard to live with."

"Me, too," she said. "Let's keep it in the past. And never fall in love again."

"As long as we agree that not falling in love doesn't mean we can't have sex."

"That's a deal."

When she held out her hand to shake on the agreement, he yanked her closer and gave her a kiss. He caught her in the middle of a gasp, but her mouth was pliant. Soon she was kissing him back. Emily's recently logical brain might be opposed to sex, but her body hadn't gotten the message. She wanted him as much as he wanted her.

When he turned away and looked out the windshield, he spied Special Agent Greg Levine crossing the street and heading toward Henny's. Walking fast and staring down at the cell phone in his hand, Levine gave off the vibe of a stressed-out businessman and had the wardrobe to match: dark gray suit, blue shirt and necktie tugged loose. His dark blond hair was trimmed in much the same style as Sean's but wasn't as thick. The strands across the front were working hard to cover his forehead.

As Sean escorted Emily up the sidewalk to the café, she asked, "Is there anything I should be careful of saying or not saying? You know, in case Levine isn't on our side."

"Don't mention Hazel. Definitely don't mention that Dylan might hack in to his system." Until they knew otherwise, Sean would treat Levine like an ally instead of an enemy. "First I'm going to pump him to find out how Wynter learned there was a witness. And then how he knew the witness was you."

"I want to ask him what the FBI knows about Patrone's family in Chinatown, the people who took him in when he was a kid."

He nodded. "Anything else?"

"It goes without saying that I want to see if Levine can get me into the hospital to see Strauss."

Inside Henny's, they joined Levine in a cantaloupe-orange leatherette booth at the back. Henny's specialized mostly in breakfast and lunch. The decor was chipper with sunlight filtering through the storefront windows, dozens of cutouts and pictures of chickens and a counter surrounded by swivel stools. A cozy place to wake up, and yet they served alcohol.

Sean did a handshake and half hug with Levine. They'd worked together but never had been close. Since Sean worked undercover, he was seldom in the office; the only agent he cared about was his handler/supervisor, and he knew she'd returned to Quantico. He listened while Levine updated him on other people they knew in common.

The waitress returned to their table with a Bloody Mary for Levine. He must have ordered when he walked in the door. Vodka before noon; not a good sign. Remembering her preference, Sean ordered a cappuccino for Emily. He wanted a double espresso.

"You and Emily," Levine said with a knowing grin. "I always thought you two would get back together."

"We're not together." Emily said. "I hired Sean to act as my bodyguard."

"You're his boss? The one who cracks the whip?" His grin turned into a full-on smirk. "I underestimated you, girl."

"Don't call her girl," Sean said coldly. "And yeah, you didn't give her enough credit. I haven't seen your files, but she's got enough on Wynter for an arrest."

"I'm working on it." Levine swizzled the celery in his glass before he raised it to his lips. "I've got a snitch on the inside."

Sean hadn't expected him to be so forthcoming. As long as Levine was being talkative, he asked, "How did Wynter find out there was a witness to Patrone's murder?"

"The murder was investigated by the SFPD. Patrone was a known associate of Wynter, which put suspicion off Wynter. At first, they investigated Wynter's rivals."

Sean didn't need a history of the crime. "But they came around to the real story. How did that happen?"

Levine couldn't meet his gaze. Dark smudges under his eyes made Sean think he wasn't sleeping well. His chin quivered as he attempted to change the direction of their conversation. "Why do you think my phone is bugged?"

"Simple logic. There's no reason for anybody to connect Emily to me. We haven't seen or talked to each other since the divorce. But you called my office in Denver—"

"I told you," Levine said. "I always thought the two of you would get back together. Hell, you're the reason Emily showed up on our doorstep instead of going to the police. She knew us because of you."

He looked to Emily for confirmation. "Is that true?"

"I thought the FBI would be more careful about keeping my identity secret."

Anger heated Sean's blood. She should have been able to trust the feds, but they'd been sloppy. He glared at Levine. "Did you tell them about Emily?"

"I had to give them something. The cops were off base, asking questions that riled other gangs." His voice held a note of believable desperation. "I said there was a witness and leaked her account of the murder. But I didn't give her name."

Assessing his behavioral cues, Sean deduced that Levine was honestly sorry about the way things had turned out. He'd never meant to put Emily in danger. "I believe you."

"Damn right you do." Levine nodded vigorously. His relief was palpable. "You would have done the same thing."

"I don't think so." Sean didn't allow him to get comfortable. "There are other ways to play a witness, but I'm not here to give you a lesson. You asked why I suspected a wiretap on your phone."

"Right."

"After you called my office, one of Wynter's men made the same contact. How would they know about me if they weren't monitoring your phone?"

Levine took another drink. His Bloody Mary was almost gone, and he ordered another when the waitress brought their coffee drinks. Sean and Emily also ordered breakfast. Levine didn't want food.

While the waitress bustled back to the kitchen, Levine leaned across the table on his elbows and asked, "Did you talk to the guy Wynter sent?"

Sean nodded. "John Morelli."

Levine bolted upright in the booth. It looked like he'd been poked by a cattle prod. "Morelli is my snitch."

Chapter Thirteen

Emily twisted her hands together in her lap as though she could somehow physically hold things together. Nothing made sense anymore. Morelli was her contact but also a snitch, and then he'd pulled a gun on Sean, which made him an enemy. The more Levine talked, the more confounded she felt. Had Morelli been lying to Sean when he said he only wanted to talk to her? He'd said she had information about who was stealing from Wynter. It might be important to go through her notes and figure out what he meant.

While Sean and Levine talked about Morelli, trying to figure out if he could be trusted, she pulled her cap lower on her forehead and slouched down in the booth. How was she ever going to make sense of this tangled mess? Maybe Sean had been right when he suggested leaving town and forgetting all about Wynter and human trafficking. She could retract her witness statement and start her life over.

But she couldn't ignore her conscience, and, somewhere in the back of her mind, she imagined the ghost of the murdered man haunting her. She owed it to him to bring his killer to justice.

She spoke up, "It seems like everybody knows I'm the witness. I should just go to the SFPD."

"Makes sense," Sean said. "And that's ultimately what you'll have to do. But right now we're flying under the radar. Let's take advantage of the moment."

"Where do we start?"

"If we figure out why Patrone was murdered, it takes the focus off you."

Similar ideas had been spinning through her mind, but he pulled it together and made perfect sense. Why was Patrone killed? What was the motive?

After the waitress delivered their breakfast, Emily took a bite of her omelet and looked over at Levine. "You might be able to help us."

"What do you need?"

"More background data on Roger Patrone. I know about the gambling operation in the strip club. And I know the woman who took him into her home is Doris Liu." Emily had visited her once and gotten a big, fat, "No comment" in hostile Cantonese. "Patrone must have had other friends and associates outside Wynter's operation."

"He almost married a woman who owns a tourist shop in Chinatown on Grant. Her name is Liane Zhou. Nobody bothers her because her brother, Mikey Zhou, is said to be a snakehead."

Emily shuddered. The snakeheads were notorious gangsters who smuggled people into the country. "Does Mikey Zhou work with Wynter's people?"

"Their businesses overlap."

"If you can call crime a business," she said.

"Hell, yes, it's a business."

"A filthy business."

Her own fears and doubts seemed minor in comparison to these larger crimes. Tearing people away from their homes and forcing them into a life of prostitu-

tion or slave labor horrified her. According to her research, parents in poverty-stricken villages sometimes
sold their children to the snakeheads, thinking their
kids might achieve a better life in a different country.
Others signed up with the snakeheads to escape per-
secution at home.

"Human smuggling is a complex job," Levine said as
he carefully smoothed the thinning hair across his forehead. "They need ledgers and accounting methods to
track how many have been taken and how they're trans-
ported. Most often, it's in shipping containers. Then
they have to determine how many arrived, how they'll
be dispersed and the final payout for delivery. But you
know that—don't you, Emily? Isn't that why you were
on Wynter's yacht in the first place? You intended to
steal his computer records and ledgers."

"So what?" She hadn't actually told him about her
plan to download Wynter's personal computer, but it
wasn't a stretch for him to figure it out.

"Did you get the download you were looking for?"

She'd failed. After Frankie and the boys had cleared
out of the office, she had spent the rest of the night
running and hiding. But she didn't want to share that
information with Levine. There was something about
him that she didn't trust. "The only thing that matters
is stopping Wynter. How can we disrupt his business?"

"Cut into his profit," Sean said. "But that won't work
as long as there's a market for what he's selling."

"It's slavery," she said. "Twenty-first-century slavery. And it's wrong. How can people justify the buying
and selling of human beings?"

"Don't be naive," Levine said. "People argue that
prostitutes are a necessary vice. And slave labor keeps

production costs down. The freaking founding fathers owned slaves. It took a civil war to change our ideas."

She glanced between Levine and Sean. The FBI agent thought she was a wide-eyed innocent who had no clue about the real world. Her ex-husband had told her dozens of times that she was unrealistic and immature. But those complaints were years ago. Sean was different now.

Looking him straight in the eye, she said, "It's our responsibility as decent human beings to expose these crimes and disrupt this network of evil and depravity."

Levine chuckled. "That sounds like a good lead for one of your articles."

"Sounds like the truth," Sean said.

"Do you really think so?" she asked.

"I've always tried to be a responsible man."

A man she could love. She bit her lower lip. *Don't say it, don't.* After the divorce, she'd wondered how two people who were so unlike each other could be attracted. What had she ever seen in him?

This was her answer. At his core, Sean was decent, trustworthy and, yes, responsible. He was a good man.

She straightened her posture and dug into her breakfast. If she was going to save the world, she needed fuel in her system. Listening with half an ear, she heard Sean and Levine discussing lines of communication that wouldn't compromise Sean's location and would make Wynter think his wiretap at the FBI was still operational.

"Then there's Morelli," Sean said. "Can you use your snitch to feed bad information to Wynter?"

"He wasn't always lying to me," Levine said. He fussed with his hair and finished his second Bloody

Mary. "I made a couple of arrests based on intel he gave me."

"You can't trust him," Sean said firmly. "Get that through your head. Morelli isn't your pal."

Emily felt Sean's temperature rising. He was getting angry, and she didn't blame him. Levine was beginning to slur, and his eyelids drooped to half-mast.

Before Sean blew his top, she needed information from Levine. "What can you tell me about Jerome Strauss?"

"The editor of *BP*? He's fine, already out of the hospital."

Good news, finally! She waved her hands. "Yay."

"Strauss is one lucky bastard. He'd fallen asleep at the office and just happened to wake up a few minutes before the bomb—which was on a timer—went off. Strauss was in the bathroom when it exploded. The EMTs found him wandering around with no pants."

"So he wasn't badly hurt?"

"If he'd been in the office near the window, he'd be dead. All he had were some bruises and a minor concussion. Lucky, lucky, lucky."

Or not. Emily enjoyed fairy tales about pots of gold at the end of the rainbow and genies in lamps who granted three wishes, but life wasn't like that. There were few real coincidences. Strauss had escaped, and she was glad but…but also suspicious. He might have been complicit in blowing up his own office.

While she and Sean dug into their food, Levine scooted to the edge of the booth. "I should get back to work," he said. "I can't say it's been great to see you."

"Same here," Sean said.

"If I can be of help, let me know." He gave a wave

and whipped out the door, obviously glad to be leaving them behind.

She watched him lurch down the street. He stumbled at the curb. "He's about three months away from getting a toupee."

"I didn't remember him as being so nervous." Sean sopped up the last bit of syrup with his pancake. "The FBI in SF has gone downhill since I left."

She nudged his shoulder. "I'll bet you were the best fed since…who's a famous FBI agent?"

"Eliot Ness."

"The best since him," she said. "Tell me, Nessie, what do we do next?"

"I already talked to Dylan this morning," he said, "but I need to call him again and make sure he's hacking in to Wynter's personal computer, the one he had on the yacht. Levine seemed way too interested in whether you'd managed a download."

She was pleased that she'd picked up the same nosy, untrustworthy attitude. "Something told me I shouldn't share information with him."

"Good instinct, Emily."

"Thanks."

He didn't allow her time to revel in his compliment. "We also need to talk to your friend Jerome Strauss. I'm not buying that coincidental escape from the bomb."

"Me, neither," she said. "But if he knew about the bomb, why would he stay close enough to be injured?"

"His injury makes a good alibi."

So true. The bomb almost killed him; therefore, he didn't set the bomb. She wanted to ask him why. What was his motivation for risking his life? "First we need disguises. Can we please go by my apartment? I'll only take a minute."

"We had this conversation last night."

"And I agreed that we shouldn't stay there. But a quick visit won't be a problem."

"Unless Wynter has men stationed on the street outside, watching to see if you return to your nest."

"They'd never notice me. I have a secret entrance."

HER APARTMENT WAS on the second floor of a three-story building that mimicked the style of the Victorian "painted ladies" with gingerbread trim in bright blue and dark purple and salmon pink. Following her directions, Sean drove the rental car up the street outside her home.

"Nice," he said. "You've got to be paying a fortune for this place."

"Not as much as you'd think," she said. "One of my former professors at Berkeley owns the property and makes special deals for people she wants to encourage, artists and writers."

"Wouldn't she rather have you writing poetry?"

"She likes that I do investigative journalism. It's her opinion that more women should be involved in hard-boiled reportage." She shrugged. "Otherwise, how will idealism survive?"

"Hard-boiled and idealistic? Those two things seem to contradict, but you make them fit together." He glanced over at her. "You're a dewy-eyed innocent… but edgy. That's what makes you so amazing."

Another compliment? He'd already noticed the cleverness of her gut instincts, and now he liked her attitude. He'd called her amazing. "Turn at the corner and circle around the block so we'll be behind my building."

"Your secret entrance isn't something as simple as a back door, is it?"

"Wait and see."

The secret wasn't all that spectacular. It had been discovered by one of the other women who lived in the building, an artist. She'd been trying to evade a guy who'd given her a ride home. He wanted to come up to her place and wouldn't take no for an answer. She said goodbye and disappeared through the secret entrance.

On the block behind Emily's apartment, she told him to park anywhere on the street. She hadn't noticed anybody hanging around, watching her building. But it was better to be cautious.

As soon as she got inside, she intended to grab as many clothes and shoes as she could. Living out of one suitcase that had been packed for snow country didn't work for her.

She led him along a narrow path between a house and another apartment building. The backyards were strips of green dotted with rock gardens, gazebos and pergolas. People who lived here landscaped like crazy, needing to bring nature into their environment.

Her building had three floors going up and a garden level below. A wide center staircase opened onto the first floor. Underneath, behind a decorative iron fence, was a sidewalk that stretched the length of the building. She hopped over the fence, lowered herself to the sidewalk and ducked so she couldn't be seen from the street. There were three doors on each side for the garden-level apartments. She opened an unmarked seventh door in the middle, directly below and hidden by the staircase leading upward.

She and Sean entered a dark room where rakes and paint cans and outdoor supplies were stored. She turned on the bare lightbulb dangling from the ceiling. "In case somebody saw us, you might want to drag something over to block the door."

He did as she said. "And how do we get out?"

"Over here." She'd found a flashlight, which she turned on when she clicked off the bulb. They went from the outdoor storage room to an indoor janitor's closet with a door that opened onto a hallway in the garden level. She turned off the flashlight and put it back.

The sneaking around had pumped up her excitement. She ran lightly down the hall and up two staircases to her floor. Her apartment was on the northeastern end of the building. She wasn't an artist and therefore didn't care if she had the southern or western light.

As she fitted her key in the lock, she realized that she was excited for Sean to see her place. When they were married, they had enjoyed furnishing their home, choosing colors and styles. For her place, she'd chosen an eclectic style with Scandinavian furniture and an antique lamp and a chandelier. Her office was perfectly, almost obsessively, organized.

The moment she opened the door, she knew something was wrong. Her apartment had been tidy before she left for Colorado. Now it was a total disaster.

Ransacked!

The sofa and coffee table were overturned. Pillows were slashed open and the stuffing pulled out. The television screen was cracked. All the shelves had been emptied.

"No," she whispered.

In her office, the chaos was worse. Papers were wadded up and strewn all across the floor and desktop. Every drawer hung open. All her articles were reduced to rubble. *Why?* What were they doing in here? Were they searching?

Barely conscious of where she was going, she stumbled into the bedroom. If they were searching, there was no need for them to go through her clothing. But her closet had been emptied and the contents of her drawers dumped onto the carpet.

Numbly, she stumbled back to the living room. On the floor at her feet was a framed photo that had hung on the wall, a wedding picture of her and Sean. She was so pretty in her long white gown with her hair spilling down her back all the way to her waist. And he was so handsome and strong. She had always thought the photo captured the true sense of romance. Their marriage didn't work, but they had experienced a great love.

The glass on the front of the photo was shattered.

Sean waved to her, signaled her. "Emily, hurry—we need to get out of here."

She heard heavy footsteps climbing the staircase outside her apartment. Her door crashed open, and she gave a yelp.

It was one of the men she'd seen with Frankie on the yacht when the murder was committed. She knew him from mug shots she'd studied when trying to identify Patrone.

"Barclay."

She knew he was a thug, convicted of assault and acquitted of murder. Not a person she'd want to meet in a dark alley.

Chapter Fourteen

The man who stormed into her apartment didn't turn around. He had his back to Sean, and he paused, staring at Emily.

This would have been an excellent occasion to use a stun gun. Sean didn't want to kill the guy, but Barclay—Emily had called him Barclay—had to be stopped.

"How do you know me?" Barclay demanded.

"I'm a reporter. I know lots of stuff." Emily hurled the framed photo at him. "Get away from me."

When Barclay put up an arm to block the frame, Sean saw the gun in his right hand. In a skilled move, he grasped Barclay's gun hand and applied pressure to the wrist, causing him to drop his weapon.

Barclay, who was quite a bit heavier and at least eight inches shorter than Sean, swung wildly with his left hand. Sean ducked the blow but caught Barclay's left arm, spun him around and tossed him onto the floor on his back. He flipped Barclay to his belly and squatted on the man's back.

Sean glanced up at Emily. "I really need to start carrying handcuffs. This is the second time in as many days that a pair of cuffs would have been useful."

Barclay squirmed below him. "Let me up, damn it. You don't know who you're dealing with."

"I know exactly who you are," Emily said. Her face was red with anger. "You were with Frankie when he shot Patrone."

"How the hell would you know about that?"

"I was there."

"No way." Though Sean had immobilized him, Barclay twisted around, struggling to get free. "Nobody was anywhere near. Nobody saw what happened."

She kept her distance but went down on her knees so she could stare into his eyes. "Three of you dragged Patrone into the office. You took turns slapping him around and calling him a coward, a term that more accurately should have been applied to you three bullies. You threw him in the chair behind the desk. Frankie screwed a silencer onto his gun and shot Patrone in the chest, twice."

Barclay mumbled a string of curses. "This is impossible. We were alone. I swore there was no witness."

"You misspoke," she said.

"Don't matter," he growled. "It's your word against ours."

From his years in the FBI, Sean knew Barclay's assessment was true. A hotshot lawyer could turn everything around and make Emily look like a crackpot. Still, he wished she hadn't blurted out the whole story and confirmed that she was a witness. She would have been safer if there had been doubt. "Emily, pick up his gun please."

Barclay twisted his head to look up at her. "You cut your hair. I wouldn't have recognized you."

But now he would. Now he'd tell the others and they'd know exactly what to look for. Sean bent Barclay's right arm at an unnatural angle. "Why are you coming after her? What do you want from her?"

"You're hurting me."

"That's the idea." But he loosened his hold. If he hoped to get any useful information from this moron, he needed to get him talking, answering simple questions. "Have you got a first name?"

"I don't have to tell you."

Sean cranked up the pressure on his arm. "I like to know who I'm talking to."

"They call me Bulldog."

Sean could see the resemblance in the droopy eyes and jowls. "Do you know Morelli?"

"Yeah, I know him."

"Do you have a partner?"

"I work alone."

Bulldog hesitated just long enough for Sean to doubt him. He twisted the arm. "Your partner, is he waiting in the car?"

"I'm alone, damn you."

Sean decided to take advantage of this moment of cooperation. "You were told to be on the lookout for Ms. Peterson, is that right?"

"Yeah, yeah. Let go of my arm."

Sean wanted to know if Bulldog was responding to an alert that might have come from Levine or if he'd seen them sneak through her secret entrance. "Why did you come into the apartment?"

"I saw you."

"Outside?"

"No," Bulldog said. "There are two cameras in here."

Surely someone else was watching, and Bulldog would have reinforcements in a matter of minutes. They needed to get the hell out of there.

Sean should have guessed. Dylan would have figured out the camera surveillance and also would have known how to disarm the electronics. But Dylan wasn't here. Sean needed to step up his game.

"They told you to look for her," Sean said. "When you found her, what were you supposed to do?"

"Not supposed to kill her. Just to grab her, bring her to Morelli or to Wynter."

"What do they want from her?"

"How the hell would I know?"

Sean thought back to his conversation with Morelli, who had also denied that he meant to hurt Emily. Morelli wanted information about a theft. Why did these guys think she knew something about treachery among smugglers?

Using cord from the blinds, he tied Bulldog's wrists and ankles. He could have called the FBI, but he didn't trust Levine. And they couldn't wait around for the cops; Bulldog's backup would get here first. When he pulled Emily out the door, he was surprised to see that she was dragging an extra-large suitcase.

"What's in there?" he asked.

"I'm not sure. I just grabbed clothes and shoes."

Behind the building, she struggled to push the suitcase through the grass. He took it from her and zipped across the backyards to the sidewalk to their rental car.

Using every evasive driving technique he'd been taught and some he'd invented himself, he maneuvered the rental car through the neighborhoods, up and down the hills of San Francisco on their way back to the Pendragon. Sean was good at getting rid of anyone who might be following. Sometimes he pretended he was being tailed just for the practice.

He seemed to be dusting off many of the skills he'd learned at Quantico and in the field. The martial arts techniques he'd used to take down Bulldog came naturally. And he had a natural talent for interrogation.

Still, he didn't have the answer to several questions: Why did Wynter's men think Emily knew who was stealing from them? Were they being robbed? Was it a rival gang?

It was clear to him that he and Emily needed a different approach to their situation. A strong defense was the first priority, protecting her from thugs like Bulldog who wanted to hurt her. But they also ought to develop an offensive effort, tracking down the details of the crime. He couldn't help thinking that Patrone's murder was somehow connected to the smuggling.

"I don't get it," she said. Her rage had begun to abate, but her color was still high and her eyes flashed like angry beacons. "Why did they tear my home apart? What were they looking for?"

"Evidence," he said. "The research and interviews that went into your articles about Wynter must have hit too close to home. Morelli said he wanted information from you."

"What does that have to do with my personal belongings?"

"Flash drives," he said.

"What about them?"

Her outrage about having her apartment wrecked and her things violated seemed to be clouding her brain function. "Think about it," he said. "You'd store evidence on a flash drive, right?"

"And they were searching for those." She did an eye roll that made her look like a teenager. "As if I'm that stupid? I'd never leave valuable info lying around."

She leaned back against the passenger seat and cast a dark, moody gaze through the windshield. He doubted that she even noticed that they were driving along the Embarcadero where they used to go jogging past the Ferry Building clock tower. They'd stop by the fat palm trees out in front and kiss. She'd have her long hair tamed in braids and would be dressed in layers of many colors with tights and socks and shorts and sweats. He'd called her Raggedy Ann.

Long ago, when they'd been falling in love, the scenery had felt more beautiful. The Bay Bridge spanning to Yerba Buena Island seemed majestic. He came to think of that bridge as the gateway separating him from her apartment in Oakland. When he drove across, he'd tried to leave his FBI undercover identity behind.

After swinging through a few more illogical turns, he doubled back toward Ghirardelli Square. "Do you want to stop for chocolate?"

"No," she said glumly. "Wait a minute. Yes, I want to stop." She threw her hands up. "I don't know."

"Still upset," he said. "You were pretty mad back at your apartment."

"I was."

"It showed in the way you threw that picture at Bulldog. For a minute, I thought I'd need to protect him from you."

She chuckled, but her amusement faded fast. Her tone was completely serious as she said, "I need to be able to protect myself."

"I've been thinking the same thing, but I'd rather not give you a firearm."

"Why not?" She immediately took offense. "I know how to handle a gun."

"Too well," he said. "I'd rather not leave a trail of dead bodies in our wake like a Quentin Tarantino film. I think you should have a stun gun."

"Yes, please."

At the hotel, he used the parking structure to hide their vehicle. In their suite, he ran another sweep for bugs and found nothing alarming. He might be overcautious, but it was better to be too safe than to be too sorry.

He sank down on the sofa. "I wish I'd caught the

mini-cameras at your apartment. As soon as we walked in the door and saw the place ransacked, I should have known. Electronics are an easier way to do surveillance than a stakeout."

"No harm done." She flopped down beside him, stretched out her legs and propped her heels against the coffee table.

"Now they know what we look like. You heard what Bulldog said. He must have been working off an old photo of you, didn't even know you'd cut your hair."

"And they have a video of you." She smiled up at him. "Not that it matters. They already had photos of you from our wedding pictures."

"You don't keep those lying around, do you?"

"The picture I threw was from our wedding. We were outside my parents' house by the Russian olive tree."

He was surprised that she'd had their photo matted and framed and hanging on the wall. He'd stuffed his copies of their wedding photos into the bottom of a drawer. He didn't want to be reminded of how happy they'd been. "Why did you keep it?"

"Sentimental reasons," she said. "I like to remember the good stuff, like when you kissed me in the middle of the ceremony, even though you weren't supposed to."

"Couldn't help it," he mumbled. "You were too beautiful."

"What woman doesn't want a memento of the sweetest, loveliest day of her life?"

"I guess men see things differently." He slipped his arm around her shoulders and pulled her closer until she was leaning against him.

"How different?"

"If it's over, move on," he said. "Better to forget when you've lost that loving feeling and it's gone, gone, gone. Whoa, whoa, whoa."

Her chin tilted upward. The shimmer in her lovely eyes was just like their wedding when he couldn't hold back. Sean had to kiss her. He had to taste those warm pink lips and feel the silky softness of her hair as the strands sifted through his fingers.

When he brought her back to the Pendragon, he hadn't planned to sweep her off her feet and into the bedroom, but he couldn't help himself. And she didn't appear to be objecting.

After the kiss subsided, her arms twined around his neck. She burrowed against his chest, and she purred like a feminine, feline motorboat. He rose from the sofa, lifting her, and carried her toward the bed with covers still askew after last night's tryst.

The other bed had barely been touched. The geometrically patterned spread in shades of black, white and gray was tucked under the pillows. He placed her on that bed. Her curvy body made an interesting artistic contrast with the sleek design. He could have studied her for hours in many different poses.

But she wouldn't hold still for that. "Don't we have a lot of other things to do?"

He stretched out beside her. "Nothing that can't wait."

"You haven't forgotten the murder, have you? And our investigation?"

The only detective work he wanted to do was finding out whether she preferred kisses on her neck or love bites on her earlobe. He pinned her on the bed with his leg straddling her lower body and his arm reaching across to hold her wrist. Taking his time, he kissed her thoroughly and deeply.

When he gazed once again into her eyes, her pupils were unfocused. The corners of her mouth lifted in a contented smile. But she didn't offer words of encouragement.

"This is not surrender," she said.

"We're not at war. We both want the same thing."

"Later," she whispered. "I promise."

"Don't say ground rules."

He stole a quick kiss and sprang off the bed. It took a ton of willpower to walk away from her when he so desperately wanted to fall at her knees and beg for her attention. But he managed to reach the kitchenette, where he filled a glass with water and helped himself to an apple from the complimentary fruit basket on the counter.

He was ready to get this crime solved. As soon as he did, she'd promised to give him what he wanted. That was an effective motivation.

She appeared in the archway between the living room and bedroom. "We should start in Chinatown. And don't forget that I want to talk to Jerome Strauss."

They could launch themselves onto the city streets, trying not to be spotted by Wynter's men and hoping they'd stumble over the truth. Or they could take a few minutes to reflect and create a plan. He could use the skills he'd learned at Quantico.

"It'll save time," he said, "if we build profiles. That way, we'll know what we're looking for."

"Profiles? Like you used to do in the FBI?"

"That's right."

She'd always hated his work, and he braced for a storm of hostility. Instead of sneering, she beamed. "Let me get my computer. I want to take notes."

Her reaction was uncharacteristic. He'd expected her to object, to tell him that the feds didn't know how to do anything but lie convincingly. Instead, she hopped onto a stool and set up her laptop on the counter separating the kitchenette from the living room.

When she was plugged in and turned on, she looked up at him. "Go ahead," she said brightly. "I'm ready."

Who are you, and what have you done with my cranky, know-it-all ex-wife? The words were on the tip of his tongue, but he knew better than to blurt them out.

She hated the FBI. While they were married, she'd told him dozens of times that he shouldn't be putting himself in danger, shouldn't be assuming undercover identities and lying to people, shouldn't be taking orders from the heartless feds. On one particularly dismal occasion, she'd told him to choose between her and his work. She would have easily won that contest, but he didn't want her to think she could make demands like that.

Her opinion had changed. And he was glad. "We need two profiles," he said, "one for the victim, Roger Patrone, and another for the person or persons who are stealing from Wynter."

"Frankie Wynter killed Patrone," she said. "What will we learn from the victim's profile?"

"We know *who* killed Patrone, but we don't know *why*. Was Frankie acting alone? Following orders from his father? It could be useful to have the victimology."

"One of the last things Patrone said before he was shot was 'I want to see the kids.' Is that important?"

He nodded. "Who are the kids, and why is he looking for them? It's all important."

While she talked, her fingers danced across the keyboard. "You mentioned profiling the person or persons who might be stealing from Wynter. Why?"

"Once we've identified them, we can use that information as leverage with Morelli and Wynter."

"Got it," she said. "Leverage."

He enjoyed the give-and-take between them. "Solving the crime against the criminals gives us something else to pass on to the FBI."

"If this all works out, we could put Wynter out of business and the person or persons who are stealing from him. We could take down two big, bad birds with one investigation." She hesitated. "It's funny, isn't it? When I look at it this way, I'm not really in danger."

"How do you figure?"

"If I tell Wynter's men what they want to know, they'll owe me a favor. At the very least, they'll call off the chase."

Her starry-eyed, poetic attitude had returned full force. Sean knew this version of Emily; he'd married her. He remembered how she'd tell him—with a completely straight face—that all people were essentially good. She was sweet, innocent and completely misguided.

He gently stroked her cheek. "I guess it's safe to say that investigative reporting hasn't tarnished your sunny outlook."

"But it has," she said. "I'm aware of a dark side. Wynter and his crew have committed heinous crimes. They're terrible people."

"Not people you can trust," he pointed out.

"Oh."

"And what do you think these heinous people will do when they find out what you know? They'll have no further use for Emily Peterson."

"And they'll let me go," she said hopefully.

"They'll kill you."

Chapter Fifteen

Perched on a high stool, Emily folded her arms on the countertop that separated the kitchenette from the living room. She rested her forehead on her arms and stared down her nose at the flecks of silver in the polished black marble surface. She tried to sort through the options. Every logical path led to the same place: her death. There had to be another way. But what? According to Sean, Wynter's men would consider her expendable after she named the person who was stealing from them, which was information she didn't have.

"If I ever figure out who's messing with Wynter," she said, "I can't tell."

"True," Sean said. "But we've got to pretend that you know, starting now."

Crazy complicated! "Why?"

"Information is power. Wynter won't hurt us as long as we have something he wants, either intelligence or, better yet, evidence."

"But I don't," she said.

"It's okay, as long as he doesn't know that you don't know what he wants to know."

Groaning, she lifted her head and rubbed her forehead as though she could erase the confusion. "I don't get it."

"Think of a poker game," he said. "I know you're familiar with five-card stud because I vividly remember the night you hustled me and three other FBI agents."

She remembered, too. "I won fifty-two dollars and forty-five cents."

"Cute," he said.

"I know."

"Anyway, when it comes to Wynter and the info he wants, we're playing a bluff…until we have the whole thing figured out."

"And then what happens?"

"We pull in the feds, and you go into protective custody."

"Or to Paris," she said. That was another solution. *Why not?* They could forget the whole damn thing and soar off into the sunset. "We could have a nice, long trip. Just you and me."

He still hadn't shaved off his stubble, and his black hair was tousled. He looked rather rakish, like a pirate. She wouldn't mind being looted and plundered by Sean. It wouldn't be like they were married or anything…just a fling.

"Havana," he said, "the trade winds, the tropical heat, the waves lapping against the seawall."

"Let's go right now. I could do articles about Cuba and see Hemingway's house. We'd lie in the sun and sip mojitos."

But she knew it wasn't possible to toss aside her responsibilities. She needed to take care of the threat from Wynter before he went after her family. Or her friends, she thought of the explosion at *BP Reporter*. She'd tried to call Jerome Strauss, but he didn't answer and she really couldn't leave a text or a number that could be backtracked to her.

"It might take a long time to neutralize the threat," he said. "What if it's never safe for you in San Francisco?"

"I wouldn't mind traveling the world." Living the life of a Gypsy held a certain romantic appeal. "Or I could settle down and live in the mountains with Aunt Hazel. The great thing about freelance writing is that I can do it anywhere. I might even move back to Denver."

"The city's booming," he said.

"I know. You showed me."

Looking up at him, she saw the invitation in his eyes. If she came to Denver, that would be all right with him. And she wouldn't mind, not a bit. She wanted to spend more time with him. Nothing serious, of course.

"Before I forget…" Sean went to his bag. He tucked away the device he'd used to sweep the room and took out a small, metallic flashlight. "This is for you."

"Not sure why I need a flashlight."

"This baby puts out forty-five million volts."

He held it up to illustrate. With the flashlight beam directed at the ceiling, he hit the button. There was a loud crack and a ferocious buzz. Jagged blue electricity arced between two poles at the end. A stun gun!

Eagerly, she reached for it. "I can't imagine why I haven't gotten one of these before."

"When you're testing, only zap for one second or it'll wear itself out. When you're using it for protection, hold the electric end against the subject for four or five seconds while pushing down on the button. That ought to be enough to slow them down."

"What if I wanted to disable an attacker?" Hopping down from the stool, she held the flashlight like a fencing sword and lunged forward. "How long do I press down to do serious damage?"

"Kind of missing the point," he said. "A stun gun

or, in this case, a stun flashlight is supposed to momentarily incapacitate an attacker. Much like pepper spray or Mace."

"Does it hurt the attacker more if I press longer?"

"That's right," he said. "And the place on the body where you hit him makes a difference. The chin or the cheek has more impact."

"Or the groin." That was her target. A five-second zap in the groin might be worse than a bullet.

She released the safety, aimed the flashlight beam at the coffeemaker and hit the button for one second. The loud zap and sizzle were extremely satisfying. She glanced at him over her shoulder. "I'd love to try it out on a real live subject."

"Forget it."

She hadn't really thought he'd let her zap him, and she didn't want to hurt him. She hooked the flashlight onto her belt where she could easily detach it if necessary. "Have you got other weapons for me?"

"A canister of pepper spray."

"I'll take it. Then I can attack two-handed. Zap with the flashlight and spritz with the pepper spray."

"A spritz?" He placed a small container on the counter beside her computer. "Enough with the equipment. We can get started by profiling Patrone."

She climbed back up on the stool. "I've already done research on him."

"You told me," he said. "He was thirty-five, never married, lost both parents when he was nine and was raised by a family in Chinatown. Convicted of fraud, he spent three years in jail, which wasn't enough to make him go straight. He runs a small, illegal gambling operation at a strip club near Chinatown. Do you have a picture of him?"

She plugged a flash drive into her laptop and scanned the files until she located Roger Patrone. The photo she had was his booking picture from when he was recently arrested. A pleasant-looking man with wide-set eyes and a flat nose, he had on a suit with the tie neatly in place. His brown hair was combed. Smiling, he looked like he was posing for a corporate ID photo.

"For a guy who's going to spend the night in the slammer, he doesn't seem too upset," she said. "Does that attitude come from cockiness? Thinking he's smarter than the cops?"

"Maybe," Sean said as he squinted at the picture. "Does he strike you as being narcissistic?"

"Not really. To tell the truth, I feel sorry for him. He's kind of a lonely guy. Doesn't have much social life and never married. Apart from Liane Zhou, I couldn't find a girlfriend. I only talked to one woman at the strip club, and she said he was a nice guy, always willing to help her out. In other words, Patrone was a pushover."

"Characteristic of low self-esteem, he's easily manipulated," Sean said. "But why is he smiling in his booking photo?"

"It's a mask," she said. "When life is too awful to bear, Patrone puts on a mask and pretends that everything is fine."

When she looked over at Sean, he nodded. "Keep going."

"He ignored trouble while it got closer and closer. When he finally took a stand, it got him killed."

"That's a possible scenario," he said. "You're good at reading below the surface."

A thrill went through her. It was comparable to the excitement she experienced when she'd written a fierce and beautiful line of poetry. "Is this profiling?"

"Basically."

"I like it."

"We're using broad strokes," he said. "Our purpose is to create a sketch. Then we'll have an idea of what we should be looking for to fill in the picture."

"Can I try another direction?" she asked.

"Go for it."

"Abandonment issues." She pounced on the words. "His parents left him when he was only nine. And he probably didn't fit in very well with the kids in Chinatown. He didn't know the customs, didn't even speak the language."

"Feelings of abandonment might explain why he joined Wynter. Patrone needed a place to belong, a surrogate family."

"Frankie was like a brother. Patrone trusted him, believed in him," she said. "And Frankie shot him dead."

What had Patrone done to deserve that cruel fate? The Wynter organization was his family, and yet there was something so important that he betrayed them.

Sean echoed her thought. "What motivated Patrone to go against people he considered family?"

"He mentioned seeing the children, which makes me think of human trafficking."

"No doubt," he said. "The theft Morelli mentioned might be about smuggling. Wynter's best profits come from shipping people, mostly women and children, in containers from Asia."

"Someone is stealing these poor souls who have already been stolen." Disgust left a rotten taste in the back of her mouth. "There's got to be a special place in hell for those who traffic in slavery."

"You're passionate about this. I could feel it when I read the series of articles you wrote on the topic."

She was pleased that he'd read the articles, but she wished he hadn't noticed her opinion. "Those were supposed to be straightforward journalism, not opinion pieces."

"You successfully walked that line," he said. "Because I know you, I could hear the rage in your voice that you were trying so hard to suppress. Most people feel the way you do."

"Which is still not an excuse to rant or editorialize," she said. "Anyway, I think we know what was stolen…people."

"Bringing us to our second profile, namely, figuring out who's stealing from Wynter. What are the important points from your research?"

She didn't need to refer to a computer file to remember. "Trafficking is a thirty-two-billion—that's billion with a *b*—dollar business. It's global. Over twelve million people are used in forced labor. Prostitution is over eight times that many. Those are big numbers, right?"

He nodded.

"Less than two thousand cases of human trafficking ended in convictions last year."

She could go on and on, quoting statistics and repeating stories of sorrow and tragedy about twelve-year-old girls turned out on the street to solicit and seven-year-old children working sixteen-hour days in factories.

After a resigned shake of her head, she continued. "Here's the bottom line. Wynter probably imports around a thousand people a year and scoops up three times that many off the streets. His organization has never once been successfully prosecuted for human trafficking. Mostly, this is because the victims are afraid to accuse or testify."

He sat on a stool beside her at the counter. "Much as

I hate to be the optimistic one, I'm thinking it's possible that the person who stole from Wynter had a noble motive."

"Free the victims?" She gave a short, humorless laugh. "That's unrealistic, painfully so. The trafficking business runs on fear and brutality. These people are too terrified to escape. They've seen what happens to those who disobey."

When she first dug into the research on Wynter, she'd considered breaking the first rule of journalism about not getting involved with your subject. She'd wanted to sneak down to the piers, wait for a container to arrive and free the people inside. Her fantasy ended there because she didn't know what she'd do with these frightened people. They'd been stolen and dumped in a land where they knew no one and nothing.

"Impossible," she muttered.

"Not really."

"Even with noble motives, it'd be extremely hard to do the right thing."

"Rescuing the victims couldn't be a one-person operation. You'd need transportation, translators, lawyers and more. The FBI would coordinate." He paused to put the pieces together. "I'm sure they aren't involved in anything like this at present. If they had a rescue strategy under way, you can bet that Levine would have bragged to us about it."

Another thought occurred to her. "What if it wasn't a hundred people being stolen from Wynter? What if it was only a handful of kids?"

He jumped on her bandwagon. "A few kids could be separated from the others by an inside man, someone like Patrone."

She built on the theme. "He could have been helping

someone else, maybe doing a favor for the woman who raised him. Or it could have been Liane."

She wanted to believe this was what had happened. Patrone had been trying to do a good thing. He didn't die in vain. He was a hero.

"More likely," Sean said, "the human cargo was stolen by a rival gang."

"Who'd dare?" From the little she knew about the gangs in San Francisco, they focused on local crime, small scale. "Wynter is big business, international business."

"So are the snakeheads."

And they were lethal. "Liane's brother is a snakehead."

"Her brother might have used Patrone to get access to the shipments. He could have told them arrival times and locations."

"And Frankie found out."

She shuddered, imagining a terrible scenario with Patrone caught between the brutal thugs who worked for Wynter and the hissing snakeheads.

Which way would he go? Being shot in the chest was a kinder death than what the snakeheads would do to him. She hoped that was a decision she never had to make.

Chapter Sixteen

While tracking down Jerome Strauss, Emily insisted on taking the lead. She was driving when they went down the street where the *BP Reporter*'s offices had been. The storefront windows were blown out, and yellow crime scene tape crossed off the door. The devastation worried her. "If Jerome had been in there, he would have been fried."

In the passenger seat, Sean held up his phone and snapped photos. "I'll send these pictures to Dylan. He might be able to give us a better idea of what kind of bomb was used."

"I'll circle the block again."

She wasn't sure how the attack on Jerome connected to her. He knew her as Emily, a poet who he occasionally published in the *Reporter*. Her journalism was done under a pseudonym. She'd engineered the publication of the Wynter material by Jerome, making sure he got it for free. And they'd discussed the content. But she never claimed authorship.

She thought of Jerome as a friend. Not a close friend or someone she'd trust with deep secrets but somebody she could have a drink with or talk to. She'd hate if anything bad happened to him, and it would be horrible if the bomb had been her fault.

On this leg of their investigation, she and Sean were more prepared for violence. She had her pepper spray spritzer and stun gun. He was packing two handguns, two knives, handcuffs, plastic ties to use as handcuffs, mini-cameras and other electronic devices. Sean was a walking arsenal, not that he looked unusual, not in the least. His equipment fit neatly to his body, like a sexy Mr. Gadget. Under his olive cargo pants and the denim jacket lined with bulletproof material, he wore holsters and sheaths and utility belts.

Her outfit was simple: sneakers and skinny jeans with a loose-fitting blouse under a beige vest with pockets that reminded her of the kind of gear her dad used to wear when he went fishing in the mountains. This vest, however, was constructed of some kind of bulletproof Kevlar. She also wore cat's eye sunglasses and a short, fluffy blond wig to conceal her identity.

Sean's only nod to disguise was slumping and pulling a red John Deere baseball cap low on his forehead. Surprisingly, his change of appearance was effective. The slouchy posture made his toned, muscular body seem loose, sloppy and several inches shorter. He'd assumed this stance immediately; it was a look he'd developed in his years working undercover.

Years ago, she'd hated when he left on one of those assignments. The danger was 24/7. If he made one little slip, he'd be found out. While the life-threatening aspect of his work had been her number one objection, she'd also hated that he was out of communication with her or anybody else. She'd missed him desperately. He'd been her husband, damn it. His place had been at home, standing by her side. To top it off, when he finally came home, he couldn't tell her what he'd done.

Given those circumstances, she was amazed that their marriage had lasted even as long as it did.

At the crest of a steep hill, she cranked the steering wheel and whipped a sharp left turn while Sean crouched in the passenger seat beside her, watching for a tail.

"Are we okay?" she asked.

"I think so. Are you sure you don't want me to drive?"

"I've got this."

Actually, she wasn't so sure that she could find Jerome's apartment. The only time she'd visited him had been at night, and she'd been angry. She wasn't sure of the location. And she didn't have an address because he was subleasing, and there was somebody else's name above his doorbell.

Also, it was entirely possible that he hadn't returned home after leaving the hospital. "I hope he's all right," she said.

"The docs wouldn't have released him if he wasn't."

It was difficult to imagine Jerome in a hospital bed with his thick beard and uncombed red hair that always made her think of a Viking. "I'm guessing that he wasn't a good patient."

"Are we near his apartment?"

"I think so."

Jerome liked to present himself as a starving author with a hip little publication. Not true. He had a beer belly, and his beard hid a double chin. Not only was he well fed but he lived in a pricey section of Russian Hill with a view of Coit Tower from his bedroom. The word *bedroom* echoed in her mind. She never should have gone into his bedroom.

In her one and only visit, she'd been naive, and he'd had way too much to drink. While showing her the view, he lunged at her. She sidestepped and he collapsed across his bed, unconscious. She left angry. Neither of them had spoken of it.

She recognized the tavern on the corner, a cute little place called the Moscow Mule. "Almost there, it's one block down."

As they approached, Sean scanned the street. "I don't see anybody on stakeout, but I'm not making the same mistake twice. Go ahead and park."

In one of the multitude of pockets in his cargo pants, he found a gray plastic rectangular device about the size of a deck of playing cards. He pulled two antennae from the top.

She parallel parked at the curb. "What's that?"

"It's a jammer. It disrupts electronic signals within a hundred yards."

"Inside Jerome's apartment," she said, "hidden cameras and bugs will be disabled."

He handed her a tiny clear plastic earpiece. "It's a two-way communicator. You can hear me and vice versa."

"But won't this little doohickey be disrupted as well?"

"Yeah," he said with a nod, "but I'll only use the jammer for three minutes while I enter Jerome's place. I'll get him out of there, and deactivate the jammer while I bring him down to the car."

Compared to dodging through the broom closet at her place, this was a high-tech operation. She popped the device in her ear. "I'm ready."

He slipped out the door, barely making a sound.

Turning around in the driver's seat, she watched him as he strode toward the walk-up apartment building, staying in shadows. Though Sean was still doing his slouch and his poorly fitted denim jacket gave him extra girth, he looked good from the back with his wide shoulders and long legs. She was glad to be with him, so glad.

As he entered Jerome's building across the street from where she'd parked, she heard his voice through the ear device. "I'm in," he said. "Which floor?"

"Wow, your voice is crystal clear. Can you hear me?"

"I can hear. Which floor?"

"Jerome is three floors up, high enough to have a view, and his apartment is to the right of the staircase. I can't remember the number, but it's toward the front of the house and—"

A burst of static ended her communication. *Jammer on!*

She looked over her shoulder at the apartment building. If it had been after dark instead of midafternoon, Jerome would have turned his lights on. They would have known right away if he was home or not.

Had three minutes passed? She should have set a timer so she'd know when he'd been gone too long. Not that they'd discussed what she should do if Sean didn't return when he said he would. Her fingers coiled around the flashlight/stun gun. If thugs were hiding out in Jerome's apartment, she might actually have a chance to use it.

The static in her ear abruptly ended. She heard Sean's voice, "Jerome's not here. I'm sure it's his place. He's got stacks of *BP Reporter* lying around."

"What a jerk," she muttered. "He promised to distribute these all over town. They're freebies, after all."

"Great apartment, though. Excellent view."

She saw Sean leave the building and jog to the car. He'd barely closed the door when she offered a suggestion. "We should try the tavern down the block. Jerome goes there a lot."

"No need for an earpiece." He held out his hand, and she gave him the plastic listening device. "Let's go to the Mule."

Sean took over the driving duties and chose his parking place so that if they ran out the back door from the Mule, the rental car would be close at hand for a speedy getaway. He wasn't sure what to expect when they entered through the front door. A tavern named Moscow Mule in the Russian Hill district was a little too cutesy for his taste, and he was glad the Mule turned out to be a regular-looking bar, decorated with neon beer signs on the wall and an array of bottles. Stools lined up in a long row in front of the long, dark wood bar. The only Moscow Mule reference came from the rows of traditional copper mugs on shelves.

Jerome Strauss sat at the bar, finishing off a beer and a plate of French fries. He didn't seem to notice them, and Sean led Emily to a table near the back.

She sat and leaned toward him. "I can't believe he didn't recognize me. This blond wig isn't a great disguise."

"Maybe your friend Jerome isn't that bright."

When she chuckled, he noticed Jerome's reaction. His back stiffened, and he tilted his head as though that would sharpen his hearing. Sean wasn't surprised. You can change the tone of your voice, but it's nearly impossible to disguise a laugh.

Whatever the reason, Jerome spun around on his bar stool and stared at Emily. His big red beard parted in a grin as he picked up his beer and came toward them.

He squinted at her. "Is that you, Emily?"

"Join us," she said.

He wheeled toward Sean. "And who's this dude? Is he supposed to be your bodyguard?"

"That's right," Sean said as he rose to his full height, towering over Jerome. In case the editor wasn't completely intimidated, Sean brushed his hand against his hip to show his holstered gun. "Ms. Peterson asked you to join us."

"Sure." Jerome toppled into a chair at the table.

Emily gave Sean an amused smile. "Would you like to try a Moscow Mule?"

"Not now," he said for Jerome's benefit. "I'm on duty."

"They're really yummy, made with vodka, ginger beer and lime juice and served in one of those cute copper mugs."

Obviously she'd tasted the drink before. It was a somewhat unusual cocktail, probably not available in many places. Sean had to wonder if she'd spent much time with Jerome in this tavern. The newspaper editor had a definite crush on her.

"I like the blond hair," Jerome said.

Sean suspected that he'd like her whether she was blonde, brunette or bald. But they hadn't come here to encourage their friendship. "You don't seem curious, Mr. Strauss, about why Emily is in disguise and why she needs a bodyguard."

"I can guess." When he leaned forward, Sean noticed his eyes were unfocused. Jerome was half in the bag. He whispered, "To protect you from Wynter."

She fluttered her eyelashes. In the fluffy wig, she managed to pull off an attitude of hapless confusion. "Whatever do you mean? I'm a poet. Why would I have anything to do with a murderous thug like Wynter?"

"You can drop the act," Jerome said, "I've known for a long time that you're Terry Greene, the journalist."

She didn't bother to deny it. "How did you guess?"

"I'm an editor, a wordsmith. I noticed similarities in style. Even your poetic voice reminded me of Greene's prose. You have a way of writing that keeps the passion bubbling just under the surface."

"Uh-huh." Disbelief was written all over her face. The fluffy blonde had been replaced by cynical Emily. "Tell me how you really figured it out."

"I wasn't spying on you. It was an accident." He drained the last of his beer. "I noticed some of the Wynter research on your computer, but don't worry."

Jerome waved to the bartender, pointed to his empty bottle and held up three fingers.

"Don't worry about what?" Emily asked.

"I never told those guys, never, ever." The alcohol was catching up with him. Jerome had trouble balancing on his chair and rested his palms on the table as an anchor.

"What guys?" Emily asked. Her disbelief had turned into concern. "Did someone threaten you? Did they blow up your office?"

"Shhhhh." He waited until three beers were delivered and the bartender returned to his other customers. It was too early for the after-work crowd, but there were a half dozen other people at the bar and at tables.

Emily grasped Jerome's hand. "Tell me."

He raised her fingers to his lips and kissed her knuckles. "A guy came to talk to me. Middle-aged, expensive suit, slicked-back hair, he showed me a business card from Wynter Corp, like it was a regular legit business."

"Morelli," she said. "What did he want?"

"He asked for Terry Greene, and I told him that the

Wynter article was just a reprint. He'd have to go to her original publisher." Jerome winced. "I knew it was you that he was after, and that's why I blew up my office."

"What!" She spoke so loudly that everybody in the bar paused to stare. Emily waved to them. "It's okay—nothing to worry about."

"You've got to believe me," Jerome begged. "I'd never tell."

When the murmur of conversation resumed, she glared at him. "You blew up your own office. What the hell were you thinking?"

"I was afraid I might accidentally spill something incriminating, and I didn't want to risk exposing you. Don't you see, Emily? I did it for you."

She surged to her feet and took a long glug of beer. "Please don't do me any more favors."

Sean believed that Jerome was telling the truth, but it wasn't the whole story. Something had scared him enough to make him blow up his office. He was in this bar because he was afraid to go home. And Morelli wasn't all that frightening.

"Who else?" Sean asked. "After Morelli left, who else paid you a visit?"

"I don't know what you're talking about." He lifted the beer bottle to his lips but didn't drink. "I'd never, ever tell. What makes you think there was somebody else?"

His fingers trembled so much he couldn't manage another swig of beer. Though he was half-drunk, Jerome's eyes flickered. He was lying. Sean figured that someone else had been following Morelli, wanting to know what he knew. And the second someone was menacing. "Who was it?"

"Frankie," Emily said. "Was it Frankie Wynter? I

feel terrible for putting you in this position. Did he threaten you?"

"I'm the one who should feel bad."

Sean agreed. He figured that Jerome had let vital information slip to the other visitor. It was probably an accident, but Jerome had been terror stricken, numb, and in that state, he'd revealed Emily's true identity. "Was it Frankie? Or someone else?"

"A Chinese guy." Jerome stared down at the table-top. "A snakehead."

Chapter Seventeen

Sean had been hoping to avoid confrontation with the snakeheads. They descended from gangs in Asia that had roots going back hundreds of years. He'd heard that the word *thug* had been invented to describe the snakeheads that, in ancient days, preyed on caravans. Now they specialized in grabbing people from Asian countries and transporting them around the world to North America, Australia and Europe.

After warning Jerome that he was damn right to be scared if he'd crossed the snakehead, Sean told the half-drunk editor that hiding out in the corner bar wasn't going to save him. He needed to go to the police…even if he'd been stupid enough to blow up his own office.

Then Sean swept Emily away from the bar and into their rental car. The answers to their investigation would be found in Chinatown. Sean was certain of it. But he wasn't sure how to proceed.

Taking extra care to avoid being followed, he made a couple of detours to grab something to eat. San Francisco truly was a town for food lovers. The array of fast food included sushi, fresh chowder, meat from a Brazilian steak house and the best hamburgers on earth. He stocked up and then drove back to the hotel.

As soon as she entered their room, Emily yanked the

blond wig off her head and took the carryout bags from
him. "I'll set up the food while you do your searching-
for-bugs thing."

He placed the jammer on the small round table,
pulled up the antennae and turned it on. Sean wasn't
taking the smallest chance that they might be overheard.
"After we eat, we're going to plan the rest of our time
in San Francisco. Then we're out of here."

The corner of her mouth twisted into a scowl. "Do
you mind if I ask where?"

"I'm not sure. We're going far, far away from the
thugs and Wynter and all the many people who want
to kill you."

"I don't understand. I'm such a nice person."

"Speaking of not-so-nice people," he said, "I'd advise you to keep your distance from Jerome. Not only
is he crazy enough to set a bomb in his own office but
he's a coward."

"What do you mean?"

"I think we have Jerome to thank for making the
link between Emily Peterson and your pseudonym."

"But he said…" She paused. "Wasn't he telling the
truth?"

"He protested too much about how he'd never tell. I
call that a sure sign of a liar."

He swept the room, still finding nothing. Thus far,
the hotel had been safe. But how much longer was this
luck going to hold? After turning off the jammer, he sat
at the table and gazed across at the fine-looking lady
who had once been his wife. She liked to set a table,
even if they were only eating fast food on paper plates.

Using the chopsticks that came with their order, he
picked up a tidbit of sushi. In addition to the California
rolls and *sashimi*, he'd ordered fried eel, *unagi*, because

it was supposed to increase potency and virility. Not that he believed in that kind of magic…but it couldn't hurt.

"This meal almost makes sense," she said. "We start with the colorful orange-and-green sushi appetizer, then the hamburger and fries main course and finally the doughnuts for dessert."

"Perfect." He wasn't exaggerating. It was an unproven fact that eight out of ten American men would choose burgers and doughnuts for any given meal.

"And what do we do with the lovely hula Hawaiian pizza? And the meat and salad from the steak house?"

"We might not have another chance to eat for the rest of the day. I say we fill up."

She gave an angry huff. "I've told you a million times about how you can't eat once and expect it to last for hours. It's like fuel—you have to keep burning at a steady level."

"Spicy," he said as he assembled a piece of ginger, *wasabi* and *unagi*. "Eat what you want, and we'll take the rest with us."

"Fine." She raised the burger to her mouth. "Tell me about our next plan."

"First we make a phone call to Dylan and find out how much he's learned from hacking. After that, we go to Chinatown."

"After dark?"

He nodded. "At night, we don't stand out as much. Well, I do because I'm tall, but you can blend right in if you keep your head down. While we're there, we need to visit Doris Liu and Liane Zhou, the girlfriend."

"Whose brother is a snakehead," she reminded him. "Do you think Mikey Zhou was the guy who frightened Jerome?"

"It'd be neat and tidy if he was the one," he said.

"Otherwise, we need to start working another angle."

"I don't think so. If this scenario doesn't pan out, we've got to move on. I'd like to resolve the motive for the murder, but it's too dangerous and too complex for us to solve."

"Is it really? Look at how much I got figured out all by myself."

"That's because you're a skilled and talented investigative journalist."

For a moment, they ate in silence. He enjoyed the stillness of late afternoon when work assignments were winding down and evening plans had not yet gotten under way. The sunlight faded and softened. The streets were calm before rush hour. It was a time for relaxing and reflecting. Though he'd seldom worked at a desk job with nine-to-five hours, his natural rhythm made a shift from work time to evening.

His gaze met hers across the table. She was alert but not too eager. In spite of her mini-lecture about his poor eating habits, she wasn't pushing that agenda. Not like when they were married, and she felt like she had to change him, to whip him into shape.

He didn't miss the nagging, but he wondered why she stopped. It must be that she'd given up on him and decided he wasn't worth all that fuss. He was just a guy she was hanging out with. Technically, he was her employee, not that he planned to charge her or Aunt Hazel for his services. He wouldn't know how to itemize a bill like that. For intimate services, should he charge by the hour or by the client's satisfaction?

"You're smiling," she said. "What are you thinking?"

"I'm imagining you in a waterfall. You're covered in

body paint, wild orchids and orange blossoms, and the spray from the waterfall gradually washes you clean."

Her voice was a whisper. "Hey, mister, I'm supposed to be the poetic one."

"We've changed, both of us."

When they'd been married, she never sat still. Nor was she ever silent. He liked this new version of Emily who could be comfortable and relaxed and didn't need to fill the air with chatter.

He wiped his mouth with one of the paper napkins, came around the table and took her hands. "There's one more part to my plan that I didn't mention."

"Let me guess," she said as she stood. "It's the part that takes place in the bedroom."

Hand in hand, they walked into the adjoining room where both beds were messy. He'd hung the "Do Not Disturb" on the door and also requested no maid service at the front desk. He paused at the foot of one of the beds and turned her toward him.

He lifted her chin, gazed into her face. "Nobody ever said it had to be in the bedroom."

"That's a spa shower in the bathroom." A sly smile curled the ends of her mouth. "I haven't figured out how to use all the spray jets."

"We can learn together."

The bathroom also used an Asian-influenced decorating theme with white tile and black accents. On the double-sink counter, there were three delicate orchids in black vases. The tub was simple and small. The shower was Godzilla. A huge space, enclosed in glass with stripes of frosted glass, the shower had an overhead nozzle the size of a dinner plate. Eight jets protruded from the wall at various heights, and there was a handheld sprayer.

He peeled off his Mr. Gadget outfit and dropped the clothes in a pile with his Glock on top for easy access. Earlier, he'd noticed a special feature in the bathroom: dimmer dials for the lights. Playing around with the overhead and four sconces around the mirrors, he set a cool, sexy mood.

"Do you like this?" he asked.

"It's almost as good as candlelight."

She didn't have nearly as many clothes as he did, but it was taking her longer to get out of them. He was happy to help, reaching behind her back to unhook her bra as she wiggled out of her skinny jeans.

He entered the shower. "I'll get the water started."

As she neatly folded her jeans, she said, "Quite a coincidence, Sean. You have a fantasy about waterfalls, and here we are, stepping into a shower."

"Swear to God, I didn't plan this. But it's not altogether a coincidence. The thought of you, wet and naked, is real good motivation to find a shower."

With the overhead rainfall shower drizzling, he opened the door and took her hand, leading her into the glass enclosure. Her step was delicate, graceful. The dim light shone on her dusky olive skin and created wonderful, secretive shadows on her inner thighs and beneath her breasts.

When she moved under the spray and tilted her head up, he was captivated. She was everything a woman should be. How had he ever let her slip away from him?

With her back pressed into his chest, he encircled her with his arms and held her while her slick, supple body rubbed against him. The intake and exhale of their breathing mingled with the spatter of droplets in a powerful song without words or tune. Swirling clouds of steam filled the shower.

She turned on the jets and edged closer, letting the water pummel her. "That feels great, like a wet massage."

She moved him around, positioning him so he'd be hit at exactly the right place near the base of his spine. He groaned with pleasure.

They took turns soaping each other, paying particular attention to the sensitive areas and rinsing the fragrant sandalwood lather away. She massaged shampoo into her hair.

"Let me," he said, taking over the job. "I remember when we'd wash your long hair. It hung all the way down to your butt."

"A lot of work," she said.

"I like it better this way. No muss, no fuss."

"Like wham, bam, thank you, ma'am."

"Hey, there, if you're implying that I don't want to take my time, you're dead wrong. With all that hair out of the way, I can devote my attention to other parts of you."

He started by nibbling on her throat and worked his way down her body. Though he wasn't usually a fan of electronic aids, he started using the pulsating, handheld sprayer about halfway down.

The way she shimmied and twitched when aroused drove him crazy. Her excitement fed into his, building and building. One thing was clear: he wasn't going to be able to hold back much longer. On the verge of eruption, he had to get her into the bedroom. In the shower, he wasn't able to manage a condom. For half a second, he wondered if using prevention was necessary. Would it be a mistake to have a kid with Emily? He shook his head, sending droplets flying. Now was not the time for such life-changing decisions.

He brought her from the shower to the bed, tangling them both in towels. Condom in place, he entered her. Her body was ready for him, tight and trembling. She was everything to him.

An irresistible surge ripped through him. He felt something more than physical release. More than pleasure, he felt the beginning of something he'd once called love. *Not the same.* He couldn't be in love with her. Those days were over.

He collapsed on the bed beside her. They lay next to each other, staring up at the ceiling, thinking their own private thoughts. Did he love her? He'd give his life for her without a second thought. Was that love? She delighted him in so many ways. *Love?* He was proud of her, of the woman she'd become.

Does it matter? He should let those feelings go. Taking on the biggest gang in the city and the snakeheads, they'd probably be dead before the night was over.

He cleared his throat. "After Chinatown, we've done all the investigating that we can hope to do. Then we leave. We need to put distance between us and the people who want us dead."

"Right."

Reluctantly, he hauled himself up and out of the bed. "I need to make that call to my brother."

Swaddled in the white terrycloth robe provided by the hotel, he went to the desk in the living room and set up his computer equipment to have a face-to-face conversation with Dylan. Through the windows, he noticed that dusk had taken hold and the streetlights were beginning to glow. By the time he was prepared to make contact, Emily had blow-dried her hair and slipped on a nightshirt that left most of her slender, well-toned legs exposed.

She sprawled on the sofa. "Put it on speakerphone."

He took out the earbuds and turned up the volume. Though it was after eight o'clock in Denver, Dylan answered the number that rang through to the office immediately.

"Are you still at work?" Sean asked.

"Of course not. I transferred everything to a laptop, and I'm at my place."

"Turn on your screen and let me see."

"Just a sec."

Sean heard the unmistakable sound of a female voice, and he asked his brother, "Am I interrupting something?"

A slightly breathless female answered, "Hello, Sean. How's San Francisco? It's one of my favorite places. With the cable cars and the fog. Did I mention? This is me, Jayne Shackleford."

She was the neurosurgeon his brother had been dating and was crazy in love with. Sean envied the newness of their relationship. He and Emily would never have that again; they were older and wiser.

"It's a great city." He liked it better when nobody wanted to kill him and Emily. "Put Dylan on."

After a bit of fumbling around, his brother was back on the line. He turned on his screen so Sean could see into his house and also catch a glimpse of Jayne in a pretty black negligee before she flitted from the room.

"Here's the thing," Dylan said. "I've done a massive hack in to Wynter's accounts, both personal and professional. It took some special, super-complicated skills that I'm not going to explain. I'll take pity on your Luddite soul that barely comprehends email."

"Thanks."

"Is that Emily I see behind you?" Dylan leaned close to the screen and waved. "Hi, Emily."

From her position on the sofa, she waved back, "Right back at you, Dylan."

"You did good. You gathered a ton of info with the research tools at your disposal. But you were missing the key ingredient, namely, James Wynter's personal computer."

"I knew it." She straightened up. "The personal documents are what I was going after on his yacht."

"That's where he kept the real records that didn't synch up with income."

"What does it prove?" Sean asked.

"Somebody's stealing from Wynter," Dylan said. "If I have the codes figured correctly, and I'm sure I do, he lost twelve people last month. They disappeared."

"And there's no way to track them?"

On-screen, Dylan shook his head and rolled his eyes. "What part of disappeared don't you understand? These people—referred to as human cargo—were supposed to arrive at Wynter's warehouse facility. They just didn't show."

Sean took a guess. "Did they come from Asia? Arriving in shipping containers?"

"There was a container. It came up three children short, five-year-olds. All the adult females were accounted for."

And the women would never rat out the kids if they'd somehow found a way to escape. Could those be the children whom Patrone was concerned about?

Sean asked, "What about the other nine?"

"They came on a regular boat. One way Wynter smuggles from Asia is taking his yacht out to sea, picking up the cargo and returning to shore north of San

Francisco where he off-loads. Morelli was in charge of the last delivery, which was over six weeks ago."

"When Patrone was killed," Emily said.

"You guessed it," Dylan said. "No human trafficking since then. There's got to be a connection."

"What happened to the nine?" Dylan asked.

"Morelli swore they got onto a truck."

"But they disappeared," Sean said. "You don't happen to know where the yacht off-loads?"

"Medusa Rock, a little town up the coast."

Sean offered his usual brotherly, laconic compliments for a job well done. In contrast, Emily was over the moon, couldn't stop cheering.

"Enough," Dylan told her. "Sean'll get jealous. It's not good to have big brother ticked off."

"He most certainly can be a bear."

Sean growled. "If you two are done, I've got one more question for Dylan. Is Wynter connected with the snakeheads?"

"He's refusing to pay the snakeheads until he gets his hands on the missing twelve. The local gangs are up in arms, inches away from gang warfare."

And Sean and Emily were right in the middle.

Chapter Eighteen

Emily decided against the blond wig for their trip to Chinatown. Instead she tucked her hair behind her ears and put on a baseball cap. She wore high-top sneakers, jeans and a sweatshirt because it was supposed to be chilly tonight. All her curves were hidden. She looked like a boy, especially when she added the khaki bulletproof vest.

Sean regarded her critically. "Do you have a beret?"

"Not with me. I have a knit cap in cranberry red that I packed for the mountains."

"Put it on," he said.

"Really? But the baseball cap is better. I'm trying to pass for a boy."

He slung an arm around her waist, pulled her close and gave her a kiss. "There's too much of the feminine about you. You look like a girl pretending to be a boy, and that attracts attention."

She dug through her suitcase until she found the cap. It covered her ears, smashed her hair down and had a jaunty tassel on top.

"Better," he said.

"Yeah, great. Now I look like a deranged girl."

"When we're on the street," he said, "keep your head

down. Don't make eye contact. If they don't notice you, they can't recognize you."

He was more intense than earlier today, and that worried her. "Who do you expect to run into?"

"We're walking into the tiger's maw."

"Very poetic."

"I stole it from you," he said, "from a poem you wrote a long time ago. The description applies. Chinatown is home base for the snakeheads and a familiar place for Wynter's men. I bet they even have a favorite restaurant."

"The Empress Pearl."

When she first started her research, she'd gone there several times to watch Wynter's men and try to overhear what they were talking about. She'd often seen Morelli, but when they finally met for his interview, he didn't recognize her, which made her think that Sean was right about being anonymous and, therefore, forgettable.

She asked, "Are we coming back to the hotel?"

"Sadly no, our suitcases are packed."

"I want to make a phone call from here to Morelli. If he tries a trace, it doesn't matter."

Thoughtfully, he rubbed his hand along his still unshaven jawline. "Why talk to him?"

"At one time, we had a rapport, and maybe that counts for something. I have a question I hope he'll answer."

"You're aware, aren't you, that Morelli is the most likely person to be stealing from Wynter? He has inside information, and he signed off on the nine that went missing."

"I think he's being framed," she said.

"We never did a profile on Morelli," he said. "I see him as a corporate climber, a yes-man scrambling to got ahead He wouldn't take the initiative in stealing from Wynter, but he might support the double-crosser who took off with the nine."

All this crossing and double-crossing still didn't explain why they were coming after her. Like Bulldog said at her apartment, Wynter wasn't worried about her eyewitness testimony. His expensive attorneys were clever enough to make her look like the crook. If she was about to be framed, she wanted to know why.

She took her last burner phone from her pocket. "I'm making the call."

"And leave the phone behind," he said.

It took a moment to find Morelli's number. He answered quickly, and his voice had a nervous tremor. When she identified herself, he sounded like he was on the verge of tears.

"Emily, I have to meet with you, please. Name the place."

"Actually, John…" She used his given name to put them on a more equal footing. "I was looking for some information. If you help me, I might help you."

"Always the reporter," he said. "Ask me anything."

"According to you and also to Mr. Barclay, aka Bulldog, there's a rumor floating around that I know something about human cargo going missing on shipments from Asia."

"Do you?" He was overeager. If he'd been a puppy, his tail would be wagging to beat the band.

She said, "You first."

"Based on detailed information in your articles about Wynter, I suspected that you had an inside edge. When you talked about our warehouses and distribution, you knew about the supposed warehouse where we stored our human cargo."

"What do you mean 'supposed' warehouse?"

"Don't play dumb with me, Emily. You know it's just a house with mattresses in the basement."

He had it wrong. She had the number of warehouses but not all the addresses. If she'd known where they were keeping the kidnapped people, she would have informed the police.

Morelli continued. "I thought you had inside information, and Bulldog confirmed it."

"Do you always listen to Bulldog?"

"If you didn't want him to talk, you shouldn't have left him tied up in your apartment. It only took ten minutes for somebody to show up and let him go."

"Should we have killed him?"

"Not the point," Morelli said. "He told me that you witnessed the murder from inside the closet in the office."

"That's right." She wasn't sure where this was going but wanted him to keep talking.

"You were in the private office on the yacht…alone with James Wynter's private computer. You were the one who made changes on the deliveries and receipts, trying to cover up the theft."

"I hate to burst your bubble, but everybody on that ship had access."

"Not true. The office was unlocked for a short time only. Only Frankie had a key."

And she'd been unlucky enough to stumble onto the one time when she could get herself in deep trouble. She was done with this conversation. "Here's what I have for you, Morelli. I'm leaving San Francisco and never coming back. I'm gone, so you can quit chasing me. No more threats. Bye-bye."

When she ended the call, she felt an absurd burst of

confidence. She dropped the cell phone like a rock star with a microphone. *Emily out.*

AFTER DARK, CHINATOWN overflowed with activity. Sean parked downhill a few blocks, avoiding the well-lit entrance through the Dragon's Gate. They hiked toward the glaring lights, the noise of many people talking in many dialects and the explosion of color. Lucky red predominated. Gold lit up the signs, some written in English and others in Chinese characters. Some of the pagoda rooftops were blue, others neon green.

Sean wasn't a fan of this sensory overload. He ducked under a fringed red lantern as he followed Emily toward the shop owned by Liane Zhou. His gut tensed. This wasn't a good place for them, wasn't safe. He wanted to take care of business and get out of town as quick as possible.

Emily stepped into an alcove beside a postcard kiosk and pulled him closer. "It's at the end of this block. I think the name of the shop is Laughing Duck, something like that. There isn't an English translation, but guess what's in the window."

"Laughing ducks."

"I think you should do the talking. I've already met Liane, and she was tight-lipped with me. You might encourage her to open up."

The only thing he wanted to ask Liane was if her snakehead brother intended to kill them. If so, Sean meant to retreat. "What did you talk to her about before?"

"I didn't know about the missing human cargo, so I concentrated on Patrone. At that time, he was only missing, and I didn't tell her about the murder."

"And what did she say?" he asked.

"Not much." She scowled. "She might open up if you spoke Chinese. Do you know the language?"

"A little." He'd picked up a few phrases when he was working undercover. Needless to say, the people who taught him weren't Sunday school teachers. In addition to "hello" and "goodbye," he knew dozens of obscene ways to say "jerk," "dumb-ass" and "you suck."

"Liane is easy to recognize. She's five-nine and obviously likes being taller than the people who work for her because she wears high heels."

Glumly, he stared through the window into the fish market next door. A pyramid arrangement went from crabs to eels to prawns to a slithering array of fish. He hunched his shoulders and marched past the ferocious stink that spilled from the shop to the sidewalk. They entered the Laughing Duck, a colorful storefront for tourists with lots of smiling Buddhas, fans painted with cherry blossoms, parasols, pouches and statuettes for every sign of the Chinese zodiac. Since his zodiac animal was the pig, he pretty much disregarded that superstition. Emily was a sheep.

A young woman met them at the front with a wide smile. "Can I help you find anything?"

"Liane Zhou," he said as he entered the shop.

The narrow storefront was misleading. Inside, the shop extended a long way back and displayed more items. He knew from experience that Liane very likely sold illegal knockoffs of purses and shoes and other merchandise that was not meant to be seen by the general public.

Most of these shops had a dark, narrow staircase at the rear that led to second and third floor housing. An entire family, including mom, dad, kids and grandmas, might live in a two-bedroom flat. All sorts of business were conducted from these shady little cubbyholes, ranging from legitimate cleaning and repair services to selling drugs.

Emily's description of Liane was accurate. The tall, slender woman stood behind the glass-top counter near a cash register. She wore a bright blue jacket with a Mandarin collar over silky black pants and stiletto heels. Her sleek black hair was pulled up in a ponytail and fell past her shoulders. Her lips pursed. Her eyes were shuttered.

Hanging on the wall behind her were several very well-made replicas of ancient Chinese swords and shields. He knew enough of history to recognize that the Zhou dynasty was one of the most powerful, long-lived and militaristic. Liane was the daughter of warriors, a warrior herself.

It seemed real unlikely that she'd open up to him… or to anybody else. He decided to start off with a bombshell and see if he could provoke a reaction.

He met her gaze. Sean had been told, more than once, that his eyes were as black as ebony. Hers were darker. In a voice so quiet that not even Emily would overhear, he asked, "Do you want revenge for the murder of Roger Patrone?"

She blinked once. "Yes."

Chapter Nineteen

A fierce hatred was etched into the beautiful features of Liane Zhou. Looking at her across the counter, Sean was convinced that the lady not only wanted revenge but was willing to rip the replica antique Chinese swords off the wall and do the killing herself.

Instinctively, he lifted his hand to his neck, protecting his throat from a fatal slash. He nodded toward the rear of the shop. "We should go somewhere quiet to talk."

Without hesitation, she shouted in Chinese to the young woman running the shop, and then she strode toward the back. When Liane Zhou made up her mind, she took action. It was an admirable trait...and a little bit scary.

Emily had fallen into line, walking behind him, and he wondered if Liane had noticed her. Behind the hanging curtain that separated the front from the back of the shop, Liane rested her hand on the newel post at the foot of a poorly lit staircase and looked directly at Emily. "Good evening, Terry Greene."

"Good evening to you," Emily said. "That's not my real name, you know."

"You are Emily Peterson. You were married to this man."

"I'm sorry I lied to you," Emily said as she pulled the cranberry knit cap off her head. "I thought an investigative reporter needed to go undercover and use an alias. I was wrong."

"How so?"

"There's never a valid reason to lie."

Liane Zhou turned her attention toward him. Her gaze went slowly from head to toe. "You," she said. "You are very...big."

Unsure that was a compliment, he said, "Thank you."

Liane took them to the second floor and unlocked the door to her private sitting room. Compared with the musty clutter in the rest of the building, her rooms were comfortable, warm and spotlessly clean.

When Liane clapped her hands, a heavily made-up woman who was skinny enough to be a fashion model appeared in an archway. Liane gave the order in Chinese, and the wannabe model scurried off.

Liane said, "We will have tea and discuss my revenge."

They sat opposite each other. Liane perched on a rattan throne while the two of them crowded onto a love seat. On the slatted coffee table between them were two magazines and a purple orchid.

Sean said, "You knew Roger Patrone for a long time."

"We arrived in Chinatown at the same time. Roger's parents sold him to Doris Liu."

Sean had never heard this version of the story. He knew the parents were out of the picture, but he didn't know why. They sold him? Sean mentally underlined abandonment issues in their profile analysis of Patrone.

"He was a boy with special talent," Sean said, taking care not to phrase conversation in questions. He wanted Liane to see him as an equal.

"He was smart." Her voice resonated on a wistful note. "But not always wise."

"A typical male," Emily muttered. "Why did Doris want him so much that she'd pay for him?"

"His English was very good. Written and spoken. And he picked up Chinese quickly, many dialects. He took care of her correspondence."

"It's a little odd," Emily said, "to trust a nine-year-old with that kind of sensitive work."

"Doris preferred using a child. She wanted him to depend on her for his food and shelter. She owned him, and he had no choice but to obey."

"How much?" Emily asked. "I'm curious."

"A thousand dollars. Doris didn't pay. Her boyfriend bought Patrone as a gift. How could that ugly old hag have a man?" She scowled. "Must be witchcraft, *wugu* magic."

The wannabe model brought their tea on a dark blue tray with a mosaic design in gold and silver. She gave a slight bow and left the apartment.

Though they appeared to be alone, Sean didn't trust Liane. Until he felt safer with her, he'd keep the conversation in the past, going over information that wasn't secret and held no current threat. "You didn't live with Doris Liu."

"Only when I chose to," she said. "My parents would never sell me. They were brave and good. In China, we were poor. Life was difficult. But they would not abandon me. They were killed by snakeheads who stole me and my brother."

"I'm sorry," Emily said.

"As am I."

Sean wished he could warn Emily not to blurt the truth.

If she confirmed that she'd seen Frankie kill Patrone, there would be little reason for Liane to talk with them.

He sipped his tea and complimented her on the taste and the scent. "You mentioned your brother, Mikey Zhou."

"Do you know him?"

Why would he? Again Sean struggled to remain impassive. "I'm aware of him, but we've never met."

"Agent Levine said you were a good friend. Yet he has not introduced you."

Shocked and amazed, Sean swallowed his tea in a gulp. Levine had told them he had a snitch, and he'd identified that snitch as Morelli. Mikey Zhou, too? Sean's estimation of Special Agent Levine rose significantly. No wonder the guy had been slugging back vodka at breakfast. Levine was playing a dangerous game.

While he sat silently, too surprised to speak, Emily filled the empty air space.

"Greg Levine is an old friend," she said. "He came to our wedding, and we went our separate ways. You know how it is. And then Sean moved back to Colorado after the divorce."

"You made a mistake," Liane said. "You should never have let Sean go."

"Right," Emily said. "Because he's so…big."

Liane inclined her head and leaned forward. "Is it true?"

Emily looked confused. "Is what?"

"Did you witness the murder?"

Sean jumped back into the conversation with both feet. "Your brother is a snakehead. But you said the snakeheads killed your parents and abducted both of you."

"The last wish of my father was for Mikey to protect me. He did what he had to do." She exhaled a weary breath. "I was twelve, and my brother was eight. When the snakeheads took us, I knew my fate. As a virgin, I would fetch a good price for my first time. They would make me a sex worker."

Emily reached across the table and took her hand. "How did Mikey stop them?"

"He sacrificed himself. A handsome child, he could have been adopted. He might have worked as a servant. But he refused. Instead he disfigured himself. He made a long scar across his face. He was damaged goods."

"Did they hurt him?" Emily asked.

"He was beaten but not defeated. He did their bidding with the understanding that I would come to no harm. Mikey labored until he collapsed. He took on every challenge. Ultimately, the snakeheads came to respect him."

"And what happened to you?"

"The expected," she said darkly. "My flower was sold for many thousands but not enough to set me and my brother free. I wore pretty things and worked as a party girl until I was treated badly, ruined. Luckily, I had a head for numbers and learned to help Doris and others in Chinatown with accounts and contracts."

"You and Patrone worked together," Sean said.

"Patrone, my dearest friend, translated and negotiated deals with smugglers, local gangs, Wynter Corp and snakeheads. He helped me save until I could open Laughing Duck."

While he was learning to profile, Sean had heard a lot of traumatic life stories. Few were as twisted as the childhood of Liane and Mikey…and Patrone, for that matter. No wonder Mikey Zhou had become a snakehead. And Patrone had been murdered. No doubt, Liane had secrets and crimes of her own.

"I have told my story," she said. "Now Emily must tell me. Who killed my dearest friend?"

Emily glanced at Sean. When he gave her the nod, she cleared her throat and said, "I saw Frankie Wynter and two others drag Patrone into an office on the yacht. Frankie shot him. They threw his body overboard."

Liane bolted to her feet. Her slender fingers clenched into fists at her side, and she spewed an impressive stream of Cantonese curses that Sean recognized from his undercover days.

"I promise," he said as he stood. "We'll bring Frankie Wynter to justice."

"Your justice is not punishment enough. He must die."

Sean was going to pretend that he never heard her threaten Frankie's life. The world would be a better place without the little jerk, but it wasn't his decision. And he wouldn't encourage Liane to take the law into her own hands.

"You're right, Liane." Emily also stood. "It's not fair, and it's not enough pain. But we want to get the person who is truly responsible."

"What do you mean?"

"Frankie pulled the trigger, but he isn't very clever and certainly not much of a leader. He was probably following orders from someone higher up."

"True." Liane spat the word. "Morelli?"

"Or James Wynter himself."

"Wait!" Sean said. "We've got to investigate. We need proof that it's Morelli or Wynter or somebody else."

He glanced from one woman to the other. They couldn't have been more different. Emily had had a

charmed childhood and grew up to be a poet and journalist who loved the truth. Liane had suffered; she had
to fight to survive. And yet each woman burned with
a similar flame. Both were outraged by the murder of
Roger Patrone.

"One week," Liane said. "Then I will take my revenge against Frankie Wynter."

Sean couldn't let that happen. He feared that Liane's
attack against Wynter would end in gang warfare with
the snakeheads.

"We need more information," he said. "What do you
know about the human cargo that's gone missing from
Wynter's shipments?"

"I help these people," she said simply. "So does
Mikey. If you want to speak to him, he is at the club
where Patrone worked."

"How do you help them?" Sean asked.

She pivoted and stalked down a narrow hallway.
Carefully, she opened the door. Light from the hall
spilled across the bed where three beautiful children
were sound asleep.

Liane tucked the covers snugly around them and
kissed each forehead.

Chapter Twenty

On the sidewalk outside the strip club where Patrone had run an illegal poker game in the back room, Emily stared at the vertical banner that read, "Girls, Nude, Girls." The evening fog had rolled in, and the neon outlines of shapely women seemed to undulate beside the banner. A barker called out a rapid chatter about how beautiful and how naked these "girls" would be.

"Not exactly subtle," she said as she nudged Sean. "At least it's honest."

"That depends on your definition of beauty. And I'd guess that some of these ladies left girlhood behind many years ago."

"How did you get to be an expert?"

"When I was undercover, I spent a lot of time in dives like this, the places where dreams come to die." He gave her arm a squeeze. "You always wanted to know what I did on my assignments. You pushed, but I couldn't say a damn word. The information I uncovered was FBI classified. And I felt filthy after spending a day at one of these places."

She knew his undercover work had been stressful. One of the reasons she'd pushed was so he could unburden himself. "If you'd explained to me, I would have understood. It had to be hard spending your day with addicts, strippers, pimps and criminals."

"They weren't the worst," he said. "I was. I lied to them. I knew better and didn't try to help."

"I never thought of your work that way."

"But you understand." He gazed down at her, and the glow from the pink neon reflected in his eyes. "You told Liane that you were wrong to lie when you were investigating."

"Maybe we're not so different." Why was she having this relationship epiphany on a sidewalk outside a strip club? "Let's get in there, talk to Mikey and go on our way."

He nodded. "There's not much more we can learn. I'll report to the FBI, sit back and let them do their duty."

She watched the patrons, who shuffled through the door with their heads down, looking neither to the right nor to the left. With her dopey cranberry hat pulled over her ears, she fit right in with this slightly weird, mostly anonymous herd...except for her gender. The few women on this street looked like hookers.

Inside the strip club, she pulled her arms close to her sides and jammed her hands into her pockets. The dim lighting masked the filth. The only other time she'd been here was in daylight, and she'd been appalled by the grime and grit that had accumulated in layers, creating a harsh, dull patina. Years of cigarette smoke and spilled liquor created a stench that mingled with a disgusting human odor. The music for the nude—except for G-string and pasties—girls on the runway blared through tinny speakers. Emily didn't want to think about the germs clinging to the four brass stripper poles.

Long ago, this district, the Tenderloin, had been home to speakeasies, burlesque houses and music clubs.

Unlike most of the rest of the city, the Tenderloin had resisted gentrification and remained foul and sleazy.

Fear poked around the edges of her consciousness. Nothing good could happen in a place like this. She moved her stun gun from a clip on her belt to her front pocket so it would be more accessible. And she stuck to Sean like a nervous barnacle as she tried to think of something less squalid than her immediate surroundings.

Liane's life story had touched her. The woman had gone through so much tragedy, from witnessing the murder of her parents to the loss of her "dearest friend." Though she hadn't admitted that Patrone was her lover, it was obvious that she cared deeply about him. And he must have felt the same way about her. He had stolen the three children for her.

After Liane kissed the children, she explained. Patrone had been part of the crew unloading the shipping container. He'd arrived before anyone else because he was supposed to conclude negotiation with the snakeheads. When Patrone saw the kids, his heart had gone out to them. He'd unloaded them from the container and moved them to the trunk of his car. The poor little five-year-olds had been starving and dehydrated, barely able to move. Patrone had taken them to Liane.

This wasn't the first time she'd rescued stolen children and their mothers, protecting them from a life of servitude to women like Doris Liu. Liane fed them and nursed them. The plight of these kids wakened instincts she never thought she had. Though she was unable to bear children, she felt deep maternal stirrings.

Emily hoped that these three children would be Liane's happy ending. According to Emily's calculations, the children arrived shortly before Patrone was murdered. Only six weeks, but Liane loved them as though she'd raised them from birth.

Emily was content to let the story end there. She tugged Sean's sleeve and whispered, "We should go."

"After we check out the poker game," he said. "If Mikey isn't there, we're gone."

"Did Liane call him?"

"She said he'd know we were coming."

Behind a beaded curtain and a closed door, they were escorted into the poker game by the bartender, whom Sean had bribed with a couple of one-hundred-dollar bills. Emily didn't know Chinese, but she could tell from the bartender's tone as he introduced them that she and Sean were being described as rich and stupid, exactly the people you'd want to play poker with.

There were four tables: three for stud poker and one for Texas Hold'em. Emily narrowed her eyes to peer through the thick miasma of cigar and cigarette smoke. Almost every chair at the tables was filled. Most of the patrons were Asian, and there was only one other woman.

Sean guided her to a table and sat her down. He spoke to the others in Chinese, and they laughed. He whispered in her ear, "I said you were my little sister. They should be nice to you, but not too nice because you like to win."

"Are you leaving me here alone?"

"I'll be close. Don't eat or drink anything."

"Don't worry."

When she felt him move away from her, it took an effort for her to stay in the chair and not chase after him. The dealer looked at her and said something in Chinese. She nodded. Since she knew how the game was played, she could follow the moves of the other players without getting into trouble.

The player sitting directly to her right was an older man with thinning hair and boozy blue eyes. He spoke English and directed one condescending remark after another to her. If she hadn't been so scared, she would have told him off.

Her plan was to be as anonymous as possible. Then she was dealt a beautiful hand: a full house with kings high. Her self-preservation instinct told her to fold the hand and not attract attention to herself. But she really did like to win. She bid carefully, taking advantage of how the others at the table paid her very little regard.

While she was raking in her winnings, she looked around for Sean and spotted him by the far wall, talking to an Asian man with a shaved head. He gave her a little wave, and she felt reassured. He was keeping an eye on her.

She quickly folded the next two hands and then tried a bluff that succeeded. *Really?* Was she really holding her own with these guys? The condescending man on her right gave his seat to another, and she turned to nod. His thick black hair grew in a long Mohawk and hung down his back in a braid. His arms and what she could see of his chest were covered in tattoos. The scar that slashed across his face told her this was Mikey Zhou.

He leaned closer to her. His left hand grazed her right side, and she felt the blade he was holding. "Fold this hand and come with me."

"Yes," she said under her breath. Frantic, she scanned the room. Where had Sean disappeared to? How could he leave her here unprotected?

Though terrified, she managed to keep focus on the game. Lost it but played okay. She rose from the table, picked up her chips and allowed Mikey to escort her toward a dark door at the back of the room. His grip on her arm was tight.

He whispered, "Don't be scared."

Though she wanted to snap a response, her throat was swollen shut by fear. She could barely breathe. The fact that she was moving surprised her because her entire body was numb. She was only aware of one thing: the stun gun in her pocket. Somehow she got her fingers wrapped around it. She got the gun out of her pocket without Mikey noticing.

When he shoved her into a small room filled with boxes and lit by a single overhead bulb, she whirled. Lunging forward, she pressed the gun against his belly. She heard the electricity and felt the vibration.

Mikey shuddered. His eyes bulged, and he went down on his hands and knees.

Before she could move in to zap him again, another man appeared from the shadows and grabbed her arms from behind. He knocked the gun from her hand.

She kept struggling, but couldn't break free. When she tried to kick backward with her legs, he swept her feet out from under her, and she was on her knees with her arms twisted back painfully. She tried to inhale enough air to scream. Could she summon help? Who would come to her aid? Nobody in this club was going to cross Mikey Zhou.

He stood before her and leaned down. His long braid fell over his shoulder. Roughly, he yanked her chin upward so she had to look into his dark eyes. Even with the tattoos and the scar, she saw a resemblance to Liane in the firm set of the jaw.

"Emily," he said. "Special Agent Levine said you would cause trouble."

"Let me go," she said. "I'll leave and you'll never see me again, I promise."

"I will not harm you."

He said something in Chinese to the man who was holding her arms, and he released her. She sat back on her heels. What was going to happen to her? *And where is Sean?*

If Mikey didn't intend to hurt her, why did he grab her? She wasn't out of danger, not by a long shot. "What do you want from me?"

"Wynter has an arrangement with snakeheads. It has been thus for many years. There is disruption. Why?"

"Do you want me to find out?"

Mikey rubbed at the spot where she'd zapped him. "The disruption must end."

Slowly she got to her feet. Common sense told her that only a fool picked a fight with the snakeheads, but she didn't want to lie. The whole reason she was in trouble could be traced to her lies when she'd used an alias and posed as a hooker.

If she told Mikey that she'd help him by finding out who was messing up the smooth-running business of human trafficking, that wouldn't be the truth. She hated that the snakeheads were buying and stealing helpless people from Asia, and she also hated that Wynter Corp distributed the human cargo. Couldn't Mikey see that? After what happened to him and Liane, couldn't he understand?

She inhaled a deep breath, preparing to make her statement. These might be the last words she ever spoke. She wanted to choose them carefully.

The door whipped open, and Sean entered the room. As soon as she recognized him, he was at her side, holding her protectively.

"Are you all right?" he asked her. "Did he hurt you?"

Mikey laughed as he returned her stun gun. "Other way around."

She looked up at Sean. "He wants me to help him. I can't do that. I'm against human trafficking, and if it's interrupted, I'm glad."

"I want peace," Mikey said. "I do not hurt my own people. Explain to her, Sean."

"That might take a while."

She didn't understand what they were talking about, but it was obvious that they'd had prior contact. Did Sean know that Mikey was going to grab her and scare her out of her mind?

Mikey said, "You go now."

Sean whisked her toward the exit door from the small room. When he opened it, she saw the foggy night blowing down an alley.

"Hold on," she said, jamming her heels down. "I need to cash in my chips."

"Not tonight."

As if she'd ever return to this place? Reality hit her over the head, and she realized that she was lucky to be walking out this door with no major physical injuries.

She went along with Sean as he propelled her around the corner and down two streets to where he'd parked. A misty rain was falling, and she was wet by the time they got to the rental car. As soon as they were inside the car, he started the engine.

"We need to hurry," he said.

"Why?"

"There's another shipment coming in tonight."

She snapped on her seat belt. She had to do whatever she could, anything that would help.

Chapter Twenty-One

Mikey the snakehead would not be getting any pats on the back from Sean. After Emily told him how Mikey had mishandled her, Sean was glad she'd zapped him with her stun gun.

"He wasn't supposed to scare you," he said.

"Well, he wasn't Mr. Friendly. When he got close to me, I felt the knife in his hand."

"His comb." Mikey's long braid didn't just happen. He worked on that hair. "A metal comb."

"How was I supposed to know?" she grumbled. "All he had to do was tell me you were waiting for me. And his friend grabbed me. He twisted my arm and forced me down on my knees."

"After you zapped Mikey with a stun gun?"

"Okay, maybe I was aggressive."

"You shot forty-five million volts through him."

She huffed and frowned. "What did he mean about wanting peace?"

"I'll explain."

The fog parted as he drove toward the private marina where the Wynter yacht was moored. It was after midnight. The city wasn't silent but had quieted. Misty rain shrouded the streets.

Though Mikey was a member of the notoriously

cruel and violent snakeheads, Sean was inclined to believe him. In his experience, the guys who were the most dangerous were also the most honest, flip sides of the same coin. Besides, Mikey had nothing to gain from lying to Sean.

"Mikey says he's not involved in the actual business of human trafficking. His hands aren't clean, far from it. His job is to take care of snakehead business in San Francisco, buying and selling and extracting payments. His sister's dearest friend, Patrone, helped him negotiate."

"And that's why he knows Levine," she said.

"Right. Mikey's not a snitch. He's more like a local enforcer. He knows that if the snakeheads and Wynter keep losing money, there's going to be a war."

"And we're supposed to stop it?" The tone of her voice underlined her disbelief. "I didn't sign up for this job."

It wasn't fair to drag her any deeper into this quagmire. Until now, she'd been ready to go. Mikey must have scared her, made her realize that she was in actual danger. "You're right."

"Am I?"

"I can turn this car around, hop onto I-80, and we'll be back in Colorado in two days. You'd be safer with your aunt. Better yet, TST Security has a couple of safe house arrangements."

She sat quietly, considering his offer. With a quick swipe, she pulled off the knitted cap, fluffed her hair and tucked it behind her ears. She'd been through a lot in the past few days, and Sean wouldn't blame her if she opted to turn her back on this insanity.

In a small voice, she said, "I started investigating Wynter Corp six months ago, and I've learned a lot. I want to see this through. I want justice for Patrono. And I want the bad guys punished."

Damn, he was proud of her. She'd grown into a fine woman, a fine human being. He was glad she'd chosen to stay involved. If they dragged the FBI into the picture too soon, the investigation could turn messy. Liane might lose the kids and Mikey could be in trouble. If Sean handled the things, the case would be gift wrapped and tied up with a pretty red bow.

At the marina, he parked behind a chain-link fence, grabbed a pair of binoculars and went toward the gate. Security cameras were everywhere. "We can't get much closer. Do you remember where Wynter's yacht was moored?"

"I remember every detail of that night. My red dress and the shoes I could hardly walk in. I remember the other girls, several blondes, a couple of brunettes and some Asian. And I remember Paco the Pimp. He was incredibly helpful. Sure, he charged me a hefty bribe, but he was efficient and kind. Do you think we should talk to him?"

"Save Paco for another story," he said. "Do you remember where you boarded the yacht?"

"Near the end of the pier." When she squinted through the fog, he handed over the binoculars. She fiddled with the adjustments and then lowered the glasses. "I don't see it."

"I was hoping we could catch them before they took off," he said, "but it was a long shot."

"The cargo might be arriving via container ship. We'd have to go to the docks in Oakland to check it out."

A chilly breeze swept across the bay and coiled the fog around them. He wrapped his arm around her shoulder, welcoming the gentle pressure of her body as she leaned against him. She turned, her arm circled his torso and she looked up at him.

Her cheeks were ruddy from the cold. Her eyes sparkled. Before he could stop himself, he said, "I love you."

Her lips parted to respond, but he didn't want words. He kissed her thoroughly, savoring the heat from her mouth and the warmth of her body. She felt good in his embrace, even with several layers of clothes between them.

Saying "I love you" might have been one of the biggest mistakes in his life. He might have sent her reeling backward, frantically trying to get away from his cloying touch. But he wasn't going to take back his statement. He loved her, and that was all there was to it. He'd never really stopped loving her from the first day he saw her.

When he ended the kiss, he didn't give her a chance to speak. "We need to hustle."

"Where are we going?"

"Medusa Rock."

In the car, he immediately called his brother to get the coordinates for the place where Wynter off-loaded cargo. As usual, Dylan was awake. Sean was fairly sure that his genius brother never slept. They discussed a few other electronic devices before Sean ended the call and silence flooded into the car.

After a few miles, she pointed to the device fastened to the dashboard. "Is this the GPS location?"

"That's right."

"Medusa Rock," she said. "Do you think there are a lot of snakes?"

"I don't know. It's a good distance up the coast."

Again, silence.

With a burst of energy, she turned toward him. "We

had ground rules, Sean. There's no way you can tell me you love me, no way at all. We had our chance, we had a marriage. When it fell apart, my heart shattered into a million little pieces. I can't go through that again."

"I apologize," he said. "I couldn't stop myself."

"I never thought I'd say this." When she paused, he heard a hiccup that sounded as though she was crying. "You're going to have to practice more self-control."

"Never would have believed it." He tried to put a good face on a bad move. "This time I'm the one who can't keep himself in check. I couldn't stop myself from blurting. What's the deal? Am I turning into a chick?"

"Not possible." She reached across the console and patted his upper thigh. "You're too...big."

WHEN HE TOLD her he loved her, she thought she'd explode. The longing she'd been holding inside threatened to erupt in a sky-high burst of lava. And then, to make it worse, he kissed her with one of those perfect, wonderful kisses.

They had both changed massively since the divorce, but she still wasn't ready to risk her heart in another try with Sean. Maybe she'd never be ready. Maybe they were the sort of couple who was meant to meet up every ten years, have great sex and go on their merry way.

While he drove, she kept track of their route on the GPS map. Soon this would be over, and she'd be able to use her phone again. Right now she really wanted to know about the possibility of snakes at Medusa Rock. According to the map, this place was a speck about a hundred miles north along the Pacific Coast Highway from San Francisco.

At their current speed, which was faster than she liked, they'd be there in about an hour. There was almost zero traffic on this road. In daylight when the fog burned off, the view along this highway was spectacular.

"There's a blanket in the backseat," he said. "It might be good for you to get some sleep. If we catch Wynter's men in the act, we'll need to follow them. And probably will switch off driving."

She didn't need much convincing. The spike of adrenaline from her encounter with Mikey had faded, leaving her drained of energy. She snuggled under the blanket. An hour of sleep was better than none.

It seemed like she'd barely closed her eyes when the car jolted to a stop. She sat up in the seat, blinking madly. She grasped Sean's arm. "Are we safe?"

"You're always safe with me." His voice was low and calm with just a touch of humor to let her know he was joking...kind of joking. "We're here."

"I see it." Medusa Rock sat about a hundred yards offshore. Shaped like a skull, it had shrubs and trees across the top that might have resembled snaky hair. "Looks more like Chia pet to me."

The heavy fog from San Francisco had faded to little more than a mist. The car was parked up on a hill overlooking a small marina where Wynter's party boat was moored. Sean placed the high-power binoculars in her hand, and she held them to her eyes. The running lights on the yacht were off, but there was still enough light to see four men leaning over the railing at the bow and smoking.

"How long have we been here?" she asked.

"Just a few minutes."

"They're waiting for something."

"If they take delivery from another boat," he said,

"there's nothing more we can do. But if it's a truck, we'll follow."

She sat up a bit straighter in the passenger seat and fine-tuned the binoculars. The resolution with these glasses was incredible. She could make out faces and features. "Guess who's here."

"I'm pretty sure it's not big daddy James," he said. "Frankie boy?"

"The next best thing." She made a woofing noise. "It's Barclay the Bulldog, the guy who wrecked my apartment."

"It's good to know he doesn't specialize in ransacking."

"The Bulldog is an all-purpose thug." She chuckled as she continued to watch the yacht. "If they drive, we'll be able to see where they make the drop-off."

"We'll coordinate with Levine," he said. "It's not really fair. We do all the work, and that jerk gets all the glory."

"Not necessarily," she said.

She passed the binoculars to him. A fifth man had joined the other four on deck. She'd recognized him right away from his nervous gestures. It was Special Agent Greg Levine.

Chapter Twenty-Two

Outraged, Sean stared down the hill at the fancy yacht with four thugs and a rat aboard. Levine was a double-crossing bastard who might precipitate a gang war that would tear San Francisco apart. Why hadn't Sean seen the problem before? It should have been obvious to him when he heard that Levine was using both Morelli and Mikey. *Quite a juggling act!* Levine wasn't a charmer and had nothing to offer. Neither of those men had a reason to work with him.

"Maybe," Emily said, "this is a sting."

Sean calmed enough to consider that scenario. On a scale of one to ten, he'd give it a three. Levine wasn't clever enough to set up a sting like this. And Sean hadn't noticed FBI backup in the area. Still, he conceded, "It's possible."

"But not likely," she said.

"Not at all."

They watched for another half hour. The night was beginning to thin as the time neared four o'clock, less than two hours before sunrise. Would Levine dare to drive into San Francisco during morning rush hour? Either he was massively stupid or had balls the size of watermelons.

A midsize orange shipping truck with a green "Trail

Blazer" logo rumbled down to the pier. The driver jumped out and trotted around to the back. As soon as he rolled up the rear door, the armed men on the boat herded a ragged group of people who had been belowdecks, waiting in the dark. Sean counted seventeen. Only two men; the rest were women and children. He was glad to see that they also loaded bottles of water and boxes he hoped were food.

"Now what?" she asked.

"We follow," Sean said. "As soon as we figure out his plan, we'll call for backup."

"Why wait?"

"I don't want to waste this opportunity." He was thinking like a cop, not a bodyguard, which probably wasn't a good thing. Undercover cops took risks, while bodyguards played it safe. He promised himself to back down before it got dangerous. "Their destination might lead to another illegal operation."

"Like a sweatshop," she said. "We might be able to track the distribution network for the sex workers."

The orange truck pulled away from the pier with Levine behind the wheel and two armed men in the cab beside him. Staying a careful distance behind so they wouldn't be noticed, Sean followed in the rental car.

The roads leading away from Medusa Rock were pretty much empty before dawn. As soon as possible, Sean turned off the headlights, figuring that their nondescript sedan would be almost invisible in the predawn light.

The orange truck wasn't headed toward San Francisco. Levine was taking them east. *Where the hell is he going?*

With his assistance, Emily set up a conference call with his brother, who was—surprise, surprise—asleep.

It was worth waking him up. If anybody could figure out how to track a moving vehicle, it was Dylan.

"Big orange truck?" His yawn resonated through the phone. "What do you want me to do with it?"

"We're trying to track it," Sean said. "When the sun comes up, in a couple of minutes, the driver of the truck might notice that we're tailing him. I want to drop back…way back."

"That sounds right," Dylan said. "What should I do? Turn you invisible?"

"Wake up, baby brother. I need you to be sharp now—right now."

"I have an idea," Emily said. "Satellite surveillance."

"It's hard to pull off," Dylan said. "If there are any clouds, it blocks the view."

"You could use a drone," she suggested.

"The only drones in the area are probably operated out of Fort Bragg, and I'm not going to hack in to the Department of Defense computers. Stuff like that could get me sent away for a long time."

"There must be something," she said.

"An idea," Dylan said. "Sean, do you have any of those tracking devices I put together a while back?"

"I have the big ones and the teeny-tiny ones."

"Slap a couple of each on the truck when he stops for gas. Turn them on right now, and I'll see if I can activate from here."

While they continued to follow, Sean told Emily where he kept the tracking devices in his luggage. Following his instructions, she checked batteries and made sure they were all working. She activated each.

"Good," Dylan said. "I've got four signals."

Emily chuckled. "You're amazing, Dylan. You can track us all the way from Denver?"

"And I kind of wish I could see what was going on. In the next generation of trackers, I'm adding cameras."

"Where are we?"

"On the road to Sacramento," Dylan said. "According to my maps, there aren't any major intersections on your route."

"But he might be stopping here," Sean said as he dropped back, slowing the rental car and allowing the truck to get almost out of sight. He stretched the tense muscles in his shoulders. He didn't like keeping surveillance in crowded traffic, but these empty roads were equally difficult.

After rummaging around in his backpack, Emily found energy bars and a bottle of water. Both food and drink were welcome. He hadn't slept last night, and the sun was rising.

The orange truck rumbled through Sacramento, still heading east.

Dylan called them back with an alert. "Make sure your car has enough gas. It looks like the route he's taking is Highway 50, otherwise known as the loneliest road in America."

"That's right," Emily said. "I'm reading the road signs. It's Highway 50, and it goes to Ely, Nevada."

"The road's quiet," Sean said, "but not that lonely."

He'd actually driven Highway 50 on one of his trips between San Francisco and his parents' house in Denver. On the stretch across Nevada, there were maybe fifteen towns, some with populations under one hundred.

The good thing about the desolate road was that it wouldn't be difficult to keep track of the orange truck. The negative was that there was nowhere to hide. If he didn't stick the trackers onto the truck soon, he'd never be able to sneak up and do it.

Finally, just outside Ely, the truck made a rest stop. If Levine and the other guards had been decent human beings, they would have made sure the people in the back of the truck were okay. That didn't appear to be part of their plan.

Sean drove up a gravel road behind the gas station and parked on a hillside behind a thicket of juniper and scrub oak. With the tracking devices in his pocket, he started down the hill. Emily caught his arm.

"One kiss," she said.

They made it a quick one.

EMILY PACED BEHIND the car, stretching her legs after too many hours sitting. She needed to take her turn behind the wheel. Sean was exhausted, and she wanted to help.

Looking for a vantage point, she moved along the edge where the hill dropped off. Behind a clump of sagebrush, she crouched down and lifted the binoculars to watch Sean. He'd found a hiding place behind the gas station, not far from the orange truck.

Her heart beat faster as she realized he was in danger. He had to stay safe, had to stay in one piece. She couldn't bear to lose him again. But that was exactly what was going to happen.

She saw him dart forward and place the tracking devices, and then she lowered the binoculars. Their investigation was wrapping up. Soon, it would be over, and Sean would leave her. If they couldn't be in love, they couldn't be together. He'd be gone.

Behind her right shoulder, she heard the sound of a footstep. Someone was approaching the rental car and being none too subtle about it. She couldn't see him but as soon as she heard him wheezing from the hike up the hill, she knew it was Bulldog.

He whispered her name. "Emily. Are you here, Emily?"

What kind of game is he playing? She still had her stun gun in her pocket and wouldn't hesitate to zap him. But that meant getting close, and she preferred to keep her distance.

Again he called to her. "Come out, Emily. I have a surprise for you."

She ducked down, making sure he couldn't see her.

"Forget you," he said. "I'm outta here."

She heard him walking away and knew he'd take the gravel road rather than scrambling up and down the hillside. She scooted around the shrubs and sagebrush to get a peek at Bulldog and see what he was doing. He jogged down the hill toward the truck. Before reaching the gas station, he paused and looked back toward the rental car.

Incongruously, he held a cell phone in his hand. With his chubby fingers, he punched in a number. The answering ring came from the rental car. That innocent sound was the trigger.

The car exploded in a fierce red-hot ball of fire.

The impact knocked her backward and she sat down hard. Her ears were ringing, and she fell back, lying flat on the dusty earth, staring up at a hazy sky streaked with black smoke from the explosion and licked with flames. The earth below her seemed to tremble with the force of a second explosion. Vaguely she thought it must be the gas tank.

Sprawled out on the ground, she was comfortable in spite of the heat from the flames and the stench of the smoke. Moving to another place might be wise. There was a lot of dry foliage. If it all caught fire, there would be a major blaze. Her grip on consciousness diminished. A soft, peaceful blackness filled her mind.

Sean was with her. He scooped her up and carried her down the hill to the gas station. The orange truck was gone.

In the gas station office, he sat her in a chair and leaned close. "Emily, can you hear me?"

"A little."

"Do you hurt anywhere?"

She stretched and wiggled her arms and legs. Nothing was broken, but she was as stiff and sore as though she'd run a marathon. "I do hurt a little."

"Where?"

"All over." Though wobbly in the knees, she rose to her feet. She grabbed the lapels of his jacket and stared into his face. "I. Love. You."

She wasn't supposed to say that, but she meant it. If he said it back, they'd be on the same page. It would mean they should be married, again. *Say it, Sean.*

"Emily." He kissed the tip of her nose. "You need to sit down."

He guided her back into the chair, brought her cold water and a damp washrag from the restroom. Her hearing was starting to return as she watched the volunteer fire brigade charge past the gas station windows and attack the blaze.

"It was Bulldog," she said to Sean. "He set off a bomb."

"I know."

"How did he know I was with the car?"

He shrugged. "He must have spotted you through binoculars. I was worried that they'd notice us following."

"Did you take care of the plants?"

"Mission accomplished." He ran his thumb across her lips. "You're going to be okay. I want you to stay here. I'll come back for you."

Not a chance. "This is my investigation. You're not going to leave me behind."

He didn't argue with her. As she drank her water and nibbled a sandwich the gas station owner had given her, she was aware of Sean striding around, yakking into his cell phone and making plans. If he had figured out some way to follow Levine, she was coming with him, and she told him so after he loaded her into the back of the local sheriff's car, and they went for a short ride. Had she really said, "I love you"?

As they sat in a pleasant lounge in the Ely airport, Emily's mind began to clear. She was picking up every third or fourth word as Sean buzzed around the room, talking on two phones at once. She figured, from what Sean was saying, that Dylan was able to track the orange truck. Levine wasn't getting away; he was driving into a trap.

The local sheriff and some of his deputies were in the lounge with her. Law enforcement was involved, and she was glad. She and Sean had taken enough risks. *Like saying I love you?* It was time for somebody else to step up.

Sean sat beside her. "It's almost over."

With all the excitement and confusion swirling around them, she had only one cogent thought. She loved him.

"I can't take it back," she said. "I can't lie."

"You love me," he said.

Not to be outdone, she said, "And you love me right back."

He gently kissed her, and she drifted off into a lovely semiconscious state. Still clinging to her bliss, she boarded a private plane flown by none other than their buddy David Henley. This Cessna wasn't as big or as fancy as the Gulfstream they'd taken to San Francisco, but she liked the ride.

"Sean, where are we going?"

"Aspen."

"Of course."

It made total sense. They'd gone from intense danger in San Francisco—crooked FBI agents, the crime boss's thugs and Chinese snakeheads—to the peaceful, snow-laced Rocky Mountains. She smiled. "I think we should live in Colorado."

"As you wish," he said.

"I also think I'm awake," she said. "Can you give me an explanation?"

"Dylan's tracker worked. Levine and the two idiots drove the truck on Highway 50. The feds and law enforcement are keeping tabs on them. I thought we could join in the chase at Aspen."

"Why Aspen?"

"The timing seemed right," he said. "Ely is about eight hours from Aspen."

It occurred to her that the orange truck could keep rolling all the way across the country, leading a parade of FBI agents and police officers to the Atlantic shoreline.

But that was not to be.

By the time they landed in Aspen, Sean received word that the orange truck had stopped at a ranch in a secluded clearing. The FBI was already closing in.

He turned to her. "Do you want to stay here? I could arrange for your aunt to pick you up."

"I'm coming with you. I won't let you face danger all by yourself…"

"Half the law enforcement in the western United States will be there to protect me."

"But you need me, and I need you."

"I love you, Emily."

"And I'm a reporter." She gave him a hug. "I'm not going to miss out on this exclusive story."

Sean and Emily arrived at the scene in time to see the people in the orange truck go free, as well as dozens of other women and children who had been assembling electronics at this secluded mountain sweatshop.

Greg Levine was arrested, along with the rest of the men working at the ranch and their leader. The big boss was none other than Frankie Wynter himself.

THREE WEEKS LATER, when Emily's four-part article was published, she was able to say that Frankie had been charged with the murder of Roger Patrone. Though she knew Patrone was killed because he had saved three children and thwarted Frankie's operation, she managed to write her story without mentioning the kids. Liane Zhou deserved her family.

And so did Emily. Resettling in Denver was easy. She fit very nicely into Sean's house.

On the wall by the fireplace, there were two wedding photos: one from the original wedding and another from the mountain ceremony at Hazelwood.

* * * * *

"I will find the baby." And he'd put away whoever had taken the child.

He escorted her through the back to a holding cell. Ryder scanned the space as he followed. Two cells. The other was empty.

At least she wasn't being thrown in with some dangerous derelict.

The cell door closed with a clang. Tia looked small and helpless inside that cell, yet he'd seen the fight in her when she'd confronted her ex.

"Please find Jordie," she whispered in a raw, pained voice. "He's just a few days old. He…needs me."

Yes, he did.

But Ryder had seen the worst of society on that last case. The head of the ring had seemed like an upstanding citizen. But evil had lurked beneath the surface.

Did Tia deserve to have her son back?

For the life of him, he wanted to believe her. Maybe because no kid should grow up thinking his mother had gotten rid of him, like he had.

THE LAST
MCCULLEN

BY
RITA HERRON

MILLS
BOON
&

First Published in Great Britain 2017
By Mills & Boon, an imprint of HarperCollins*Publishers*
1 London Bridge Street, London, SE1 9GF

© 2017 Rita B. Herron

ISBN: 978-0-263-92876-1

46-0417

Our policy is to use papers that are natural, renewable and recyclable products and made from wood grown in sustainable forests. The logging and manufacturing processes conform to the legal environmental regulations of the country of origin.

Printed and bound in Spain
by CPI, Barcelona

USA TODAY bestselling author **Rita Herron** wrote her first book when she was twelve but didn't think real people grew up to be writers. Now she writes so she doesn't have to get a real job. A former kindergarten teacher and workshop leader, she traded storytelling to kids for writing romance, and now she writes romantic comedies and romantic suspense. Rita lives in Georgia with her family. She loves to hear from readers, so please visit her website, www.ritaherron.com.

This one is for all the fans of
The Heroes of Horseshoe Creek series
who wrote asking for the twins' stories!

Chapter One

Ryder Banks needed a shower, a cold beer and some serious shut-eye.

Three months of deep undercover work had paid off, though. He'd caught the son-of-a-bitch ringleader of a human trafficking group who'd been kidnapping and selling teenage girls as sex slaves.

Sick bastard.

He scrubbed a hand over his bleary eyes as he let himself inside his cabin. The musty odor and the dust motes floating in the stale air testified to the fact that he hadn't seen this place in months.

Tired but still wired from the arrest, he grabbed a beer from the fridge, kicked off his shoes and flipped on the news.

"This is Sheriff Maddox McCullen of Pistol Whip, Wyoming." The newscaster gestured toward a tall, broad-shouldered man with dark hair. "Sheriff McCullen has just arrested the person responsible for three-year-old Tyler Elmore's abduction and for the murder of the boy's mother, Sondra Elmore. Sheriff?"

"The man we arrested was Jim Jasper, a sheriff himself," Sheriff McCullen said. "He confessed to the homicide."

"What about the man who was originally charged with

the murder?" The news anchor consulted his notes. "Cash Koker, wasn't that his name?"

McCullen nodded. "Sheriff Jasper also admitted that he framed Koker, so Koker has been cleared of all charges." Sheriff McCullen offered a smile. "On a more personal note, my brothers and I learned that Mr. Koker—Cash— is our brother. He and his twin were kidnapped at birth from our family."

"That explains the reason his last name isn't McCullen?"

"Yes, he was given the name of the foster parent who first took him in." McCullen paused. "We're delighted to reconnect with him. We're also searching for Cash's twin. We hope he'll come forward if he's watching."

A photo of Cash Koker flashed onto the screen.

Ryder swallowed hard. Dammit, the man not only re- sembled the other McCullen brothers with his dark hair, square jaw, big broad shoulders and rugged build, but he looked just like *him*.

The number for the sheriff's office flashed onto the screen and Ryder cursed, then hit the off button for the TV.

Maddox McCullen was a damn good actor. The emo- tions on his face seemed real.

He wanted the world to believe that his twin brothers had been stolen from his family.

But that was a lie.

Ryder knew the truth.

The McCullens had sold those babies.

All for the money to expand their ranch, Horseshoe Creek.

Sure, on the surface, the McCullens looked like model citizens, like a loving family. But that family had dirty little secrets.

Although he'd always known he was adopted, and that his adopted parents, Myra and Troy Banks, loved him, four years ago after Troy died, he'd had a bug to find his birth parents. A little research had led him to the McCullens.

He'd confronted his mother, and she'd broken down and admitted that she'd gotten him through a private adoption. That his birth parents had needed money at the time. She and Troy had wanted a child so badly they'd paid to get custody of Ryder.

A hundred thousand dollars. That's what he'd been worth.

The Bankses had sacrificed their entire life savings to take him in while the McCullens used the cash to buy more cattle and horses.

But they hadn't told him about Cash. Did his parents know he had a twin?

If so, why hadn't they adopted both of them?

Because they couldn't afford it...

So where had Cash been all these years?

His phone buzzed, and he glanced at the number. His boss, Connor Statham, assistant director of the FBI's criminal investigative division.

He pressed Connect. "Ryder."

"Listen, Banks, I know you just came off a major case, but I need you on another one."

The shower beckoned. So did a bottle of bourbon to stave off the anger eating at him over that news report.

"It's a missing baby and possible homicide—mother insists someone kidnapped her infant. Soon-to-be ex-husband suggested the mother did something with the child. She thinks *he* did something to the baby."

Ryder's stomach knotted. "She thinks he killed his own child?"

A tense heartbeat passed. "Either that or he sold him."

Statham's statement echoed in Ryder's head as if someone had hit him in the skull with a sledgehammer. The situation hit too close to home. "You think she's telling the truth?"

"He said, she said. Local deputy who took her statement thinks she's unstable. He issued an Amber Alert, but so far nothing's come of it."

Anger slammed into Ryder. What kind of world was it that people sold their children?

"I want you to investigate, watch her," Statham said. "If she's lying and gave the baby to someone or hurt the child, she'll slip up."

Ryder downed another sip of his beer. "Text me her name and where she lives." A second later, the name Tia Jeffries appeared on his screen along with an address.

He hurried to the shower. The bourbon would have to wait. So would the sleep.

If this woman had hurt her baby, she wouldn't get away with it. And if the father was at fault, he'd throw him in jail and make sure he never saw the light of day again.

TIA JEFFRIES SLIPPED the Saturday night special from her purse as she parked her minivan outside her ex-husband's apartment. A low light burned in the bedroom, the outline of a man—Darren—appearing in front of the window.

A woman sidled up behind him, hands reaching around Darren's naked midriff, her fingers trailing lower to stroke his erection.

Bile rose to Tia's throat. How many times had she fallen prey to the man's charms and jumped into bed with him?

Only she'd believed he was marriage material at the time. Father material for the child she'd always wanted.

A baby that would be the beginning of the big family she'd dreamed about having.

The one that would replace the family she'd lost years ago.

Her mother, father and brother were all wiped out in a plane crash when they were on the way to her college graduation.

Her fault.

She would never forgive herself.

If she hadn't insisted on them attending, they would still be alive.

But the loss of her baby boy, Jordan, was even worse.

Only Jordan wasn't dead. At least, she didn't believe he was.

Someone had stolen him from her bedroom while she'd been sleeping. The police had questioned her as if she'd done something with him.

Guilt made her throat clog with tears. She certainly hadn't hurt Jordan. But she was supposed to protect him. Keep him safe.

Instead she'd been sleeping while he disappeared.

She'd begged the police to find her baby. Had told them that she suspected Darren.

But they hadn't believed her. Darren was a good old boy. Tight with the mayor's wife, because he could charm the pants off anyone.

But Darren had lied.

And Tia was going to find out the reason.

Her hands shook as she gripped the handle of the .33. Sweat beaded on her neck and forehead.

The bedroom excitement heated up, Darren and the woman moving together in a frenzied, harried coupling. Sickened at the sight, she closed her eyes to shut out the images.

Anger and bitterness welled inside her. How dare he move on to another woman when he'd left her empty and hollow inside?

When their son was gone?

She forced even, deep breaths in and out to steady the racing of her heart. She hadn't slept since Jordan had gone missing two days ago.

Damn Darren for not caring about his own son.

Letting her fury drive her, she whipped open her car door, clenched the gun inside the pocket of her black hooded sweatshirt and scanned the area to make sure no one was watching. Except for Darren's truck and the shiny BMW that must belong to his long-legged lover girl, the parking lot was empty.

Well, hell, except there was a black SUV parked at the corner by some bushes. She studied it for a second, nerves clawing at her.

Thankfully it was empty.

She glanced back at the apartment and saw Darren padding naked to the bathroom. Uncaring that anyone could see them through the window, the woman dressed slowly, drawing out her movements as if she was performing.

If that was the kind of woman Darren wanted, why had he connected with her? Why had he gone to the trouble to act like he cared instead of just leaving their relationship at a one-night stand?

The answer hit her swift and hard. Because he'd wanted access to the money in her charity.

Tia inched up the sidewalk, taking cover in the over-grown bushes as the woman sashayed back through the apartment. Seconds later, Darren's lover opened the door, wobbling on heels that made Tia dizzy as she hurried to her fancy car and slipped inside.

Adrenaline shot through Tia as the car sped from the parking lot.

The bastard was alone.

She couldn't survive one more sleepless night without

knowing what had happened to her son. At night, she heard his cries, saw his tiny little face looking at her with trust.

Trust she didn't deserve.

The wind picked up, rattling trees and sending leaves raining down. A cat darted out from behind a cottonwood, startling her, but she bit back a yelp.

She inched her way up the sidewalk to Darren's apartment door. His was the end unit, shrouded in bushes.

She scanned the parking lot and surrounding area again as she reached for the door. Satisfied no one was watching, she turned the doorknob.

Shocking that the sleazy girl had actually locked it.

She bit her lip, then pulled the lock-picking tool she'd bought at the pawnshop from her pocket and jimmied the door. It squeaked as she opened it, and she paused, listening for Darren's footsteps or his voice.

The sound of the shower running soothed her nerves slightly.

A quick glance at the living room confirmed that Darren still hadn't mastered the art of picking up or cleaning. Dirty dishes filled a sink and clothes littered the sofa. A red bra hung from the end of a chair. The woman who'd just left or another lover?

Not that she cared who he screwed.

She just wanted to know where her son was.

Gripping the gun with both hands, she crept toward the bedroom. The low light burning accentuated the unmade, rumpled bed.

Her legs were trembling, so she sank into the wing chair by the dresser facing the bathroom door, then laid the gun in her lap and wiped her sweaty palms on her jeans.

Seconds dragged into minutes. Tension coiled inside her. Anger made her stomach churn.

But a calmness swept over her as the water kicked off. Tonight she would get some answers.

The shower door slammed in the bathroom. Footsteps sounded. Darren was humming.

A nervous giggle bubbled in her throat.

Darren stepped from the bathroom, wrapping a towel around his waist. His chest and hair were damp, and he was smiling.

When he spotted her, his smile faded.

She lifted the gun and aimed it at his chest. He was going to tell her the truth or she'd kill him.

RYDER LIFTED HIS binoculars and focused on Darren Hoyt's apartment, his instincts on full alert as Tia Jeffries confronted the man.

When Ryder first arrived at Tia's house, she'd been running to her car like she was on a mission. Then she'd tucked that gun inside her purse and his instincts had kicked in.

Dread had knotted his stomach as he'd followed her to Hoyt's apartment. For a while, she'd sat perusing the parking lot, and he'd thought she might abandon whatever plan she had tonight.

No such luck.

She'd watched Darren screw some woman, waiting patiently as if the scene didn't disturb her.

Then she'd slid from the car and slunk up to the apartment.

A movement inside Hoyt's apartment snagged his eye.

The lights flickered in the bedroom. Movement as Darren, wearing nothing but a towel, stalked toward Tia.

Maybe they'd gotten rid of the baby together and this was rendezvous time.

A shadow moved. Tia standing now.

The silhouette of her body revealed an outstretched hand.

No, not outstretched. An arm extended, hand closed around a gun.

He jerked the door to his SUV open and ran toward the apartment.

Just as he reached the apartment, a gunshot rang out.

Chapter Two

Tia's hand trembled as she fired a shot at Darren's feet. "Tell me what you did with Jordan."

Darren jumped back, his eyes blazing with fear and shock. "What the hell are you doing, Tia?"

She lifted the gun and aimed it at his chest. "I want the truth, Darren. Where is my baby?"

"I told you I don't know." He took a step backward. "Now put down that damn gun. You don't want to hurt me."

Oh, but she did. "Maybe I do," she said, allowing her anger at his betrayal to harden her voice. "You cheated on me, emptied my bank account, then left me pregnant and alone." Thank God she'd had the good sense to protect her charity so he couldn't touch those funds.

The eyes that Tia had once thought were alluring darkened to a menacing scowl. "I wouldn't have cheated if you'd satisfied me, baby."

Oh, my God. He was a total jerk. "I don't care who you sleep with or how many women you have. All I want is my son."

His eyes narrowed. "You're the one who lost him," Darren said sharply. "So tell me what *you* did with him, Tia?"

Rage boiled inside Tia. "I was exhausted from labor and the night feedings. I went to sleep." Still, the guilt clawed at her. "That's when you snuck in and stole him, didn't you? You were mad that I wouldn't give you more money, so you decided to get revenge. Did you hurt him or leave him with someone?"

"You're crazy," Darren shouted. "I can't believe the cops haven't already locked you up."

She was terrified they would. Then she couldn't find her baby.

He reached for his cell phone on the bed. "I'm calling them now—"

Panicked, she fired the gun again. The bullet zinged by his hand. He pulled it back and cursed. She started toward him, but a low voice from behind her made her pause.

"Put down the weapon, Tia."

A chill swept through her at the gruff male voice. She clenched the gun with a white-knuckled grip and pivoted slightly to see who'd entered the room.

"Put it down, Tia," a big, broad-shouldered man with dark brown hair said. "No one needs to get hurt here."

"She's insane. She tried to kill me," Darren screeched.

Tia inhaled a deep breath at the sight of the man's Glock aimed at her.

"He stole my baby," Tia cried. "I just want him to tell me where Jordan is." She swung the gun back toward Darren. She'd come too far to stop now. If this man worked for Darren, she didn't intend to turn over her weapon. Then she'd never convince Darren to talk.

Suddenly the big man lunged toward her. She screamed as he knocked her arm upward, twisted the other one behind her back and growled in her ear, "I said drop it."

"Who are you?" Tia said on a moan. It felt as if he was tearing her arm out of the socket.

"Special Agent Ryder Banks. FBI."

Shock robbed her of breath. Or maybe it was his strong hold.

A second later, he whipped the Saturday night special

from her hand. She cried out as he pushed her up against the wall, and yanked her other arm behind her.

The sound of metal clicking together sent despair through her as he handcuffed her and guided her to a chair.

"You saw her. She tried to kill me," Darren shouted.

Tears blurred Tia's eyes. If she went to jail, she'd never find her son.

RYDER NEVER LIKED being rough with a woman. But he had no choice. This one was about to shoot a man.

Whether the guy deserved it, he didn't know.

He wished to hell he'd had more time to do a background check on both of these two.

"Thanks, man." Darren released an exaggerated breath and gestured toward Tia. "She's a total nut job. She was going to kill me."

"I was not." Tia shot him a rage-filled look. "I just want to know what you did with our baby."

"You fired at me," Darren shouted.

Ryder jerked a thumb toward Darren. "Sit down and shut up."

Darren sputtered an oath. "I didn't do anything. She broke in and pulled a gun on me."

Unfortunately she had done that—Ryder had witnessed it himself.

Perspiration beaded on Darren's forehead. "Arrest her and take her to jail."

Tia started to argue, but Ryder threw up a warning hand, then addressed Darren. "Do you know where the baby is?"

A vein throbbed in the man's neck. "No." He tightened the towel around his waist.

"Put on some damn clothes," Ryder said, annoyed that the man hadn't asked to get dressed.

Darren sauntered to the closet, yanked out a shirt and jeans, then disappeared into the bathroom.

Tia cleared her throat. "I wasn't going to kill him," she said again. "I just wanted to scare him into talking."

Ryder's gaze met hers. His boss had failed to mention that Tia Jeffries was gorgeous. Petite in height, but curvy with big, bright blue eyes that made her look innocent and sexy at the same time.

An intoxicating combination.

"You should have let the police handle it," he said, forcing a hardness into his statement. He had to do his job, find the truth, ignore the fact that when he'd handcuffed her, he'd felt a shiver ripple through her. That she felt fragile— well, except for that gun.

Still, she wasn't experienced with it. Her hand had been shaking so badly he'd had to wrestle the gun from her before she hurt her ex or shot herself.

"I tried," she said, anger mingling with desperation in her voice. "But that sheriff treated me like I'd hurt my own baby. He believed Darren instead."

"That's because Tia is unstable," Darren said as he stepped into the bedroom. "She did something to Jordan and now she's trying to blame me."

"That's not true." Tia's voice broke. "I would never hurt my son. I...love him."

She said *love* in the present tense. A sign that she might be telling the truth. Sometimes when people were questioned about the suspicious disappearance of a loved one, they used past tense, which meant they already knew their loved one was dead.

"She has emotional problems," Darren said. "Just check her history. She had a breakdown a few years ago."

Ryder raised a brow. "Yet you married her?"

The man's eye twitched. "Hell, I didn't know it at the

time. But then she started acting weird and depressed and erratic. I encouraged her to get help, but she refused."

Hurt flickered in Tia's eyes. "That's not true."

"Yes, it is. When we met, she was all over me. Later, I realized that was just because she wanted a baby." His voice grew bolder. "I guess she thought she could trap me into staying with her. And I fell for it. But she was obsessed with the pregnancy. She stockpiled baby clothes and toys and furniture for months."

Tia's eyes glistened with tears. "It's true I wanted a baby, but I wasn't obsessed."

Ryder folded his arms. Some women did that to trap a man. Then again, if Darren hadn't wanted a child, he had motive to do something to the infant.

"You must have been angry when you discovered you were going to be a father," he said, scrutinizing Darren for a reaction.

"He was," Tia said. "But I didn't get pregnant on purpose."

"Yes, she did." Darren's eyes flickered with anger. "And, yeah, sure, I was mad, but I took responsibility."

The bastard made it sound as if he'd done Tia a favor, not as if he actually cared about his own offspring.

Darren pasted on a smile that looked as phony as a three-dollar bill. "I stayed with her for a couple of months, but she's impossible to live with." Another exaggerated sigh, as if he was a victim of a crazy woman. "She pushed me away, told me she wanted me gone. That she'd just used me to get the child and she didn't need me anymore."

Pain streaked Tia's face as she shook her head in denial. "That's not the way it happened at all. He started cheating on me, dipping into my money."

Ryder studied Darren then Tia. No wonder the local sheriff had asked for help.

Both stories were plausible.

Although Darren's attitude rubbed him the wrong way. The man seemed too slick, as if lying came easy.

The anguish in Tia's eyes seemed real.

Although her anguish could stem from guilt.

He steeled himself against the tears in her deep blue eyes.

He would find out the truth.

No child should have to suffer at the hands of the very people who were supposed to love and protect him.

THE COLD METAL felt heavy on Tia's wrists.

She could go to prison for attempted murder.

God…where had this federal agent come from? Had he been following her?

And why? Because the local sheriff had passed her case to the feds and thought she was guilty of doing something to Jordan?

Pain made her stomach clench. How could anyone think that?

She gulped back a sob. What was going to happen now?

She had to convince Agent Banks that she was telling the truth.

Darren strode across the room as if he owned the world and grabbed his belt. "Are you going to take her in?"

"You intend to press charges?" the agent asked.

Darren paused, his mouth forming a scowl. "I should. She would have killed me if you hadn't shown up."

"Don't do this, Darren. You know I'm not crazy or violent." Her voice cracked. "I just want my little boy back."

The agent crossed his arms. Darren walked over and stared into Tia's eyes with a coldness that chilled Tia to the bone. "Then tell the cops what you did with him and maybe they'll find him. And stop trying to make me sound like the guilty one."

Tia jutted up her chin, battling a sob. Her arms were beginning to ache from being bound behind her. "He's your son, Darren. But you really don't care about him, do you? If you did, you'd be asking the police to search for him, too."

"How do I even know he's mine?" Darren asked sarcastically. "Maybe you lied so I'd hang around."

Hurt robbed her of speech. How could he be so cruel?

Giving her one last icy look, he turned to the agent. "Lock her up so I don't have to worry about her shooting me tonight in my sleep."

"Darren, please," Tia whispered, desperate. "If you know who took Jordan, tell me. I won't even press charges. I just want him back."

Instead of answering, his jaw hardened. "Agent Banks, I told you to get her out of here. I have things to do."

A hopeless feeling engulfed Tia as the agent helped her stand.

"You need to come to the sheriff's office to file an official police report," the agent told Darren.

Darren gave a quick nod and muttered that he would.

Tia searched the agent's face for some hope that he believed her story, that he would help her.

But hope faded as he guided her outside to his car.

Dark storm clouds rolled in, obliterating the few stars that had shined earlier.

He opened the back door and gestured for her to get in. Emotions overwhelmed her as she sank into the backseat and he drove toward the jail.

Chapter Three

Tia hunched in the backseat of the agent's car, her nerves raw.

She was going to jail. She'd never see her baby again. If Darren had given Jordan to someone else, little Jordan would grow up without ever knowing her.

He might never know she'd looked for him, that she loved him.

A hollow emptiness welled in her chest. Hands still cuffed behind her, she leaned forward. She couldn't breathe.

Tears trickled down her cheeks, but she was helpless to wipe them away.

She closed her eyes, willing herself to be strong. An image of her son's tiny body nestled in the baby blue blanket and cap she'd knitted taunted her.

Even if she never got him back, she had to know he was safe.

But how could she do that locked in a cell?

The car bounced over a rut in the road, and she lifted her head and looked out the window. Rugged farm and ranch land passed by. Trees swayed in the wind, leaves raining down. Dark shadows hovered along the deserted stretch of land, signaling that night had set in.

Another night away from her baby boy.

Minutes crawled by, turning into half an hour.

She gulped back a sob and cleared her throat. "Where are you taking me?"

Agent Banks met her gaze in the rearview mirror. "The sheriff's office in Sagebrush."

Despair threatened again. The sheriff, Dan Gaines, had been less than sympathetic when she'd asked for help. He'd practically accused her of killing her child so she could be single, footloose and fancy-free.

He had no idea that footloose and fancy-free was the last thing she wanted.

Or that she'd spent her adult life missing the family she'd lost. That all she wanted was someone to love to fill the hole in her aching heart.

That she spent her days working with kids and families in need, helping them find housing and counseling so they could patch their lives back together. That the money she'd received from her parents' life insurance had gone toward a charity she'd started called Crossroads.

Agent Banks drove through the small, quaint town of Sagebrush, then parked at the sheriff's office. Dread made her stomach roil.

She had to find someone who'd believe her. Sheriff Gaines certainly hadn't.

Maybe Agent Banks would.

Somehow she had to convince him she wasn't the lunatic Darren had painted her to be.

RYDER CLENCHED THE steering wheel with a white-knuckled grip. Tia Jeffries looked tiny and frightened, and so damn vulnerable that he felt like a jerk for handcuffing her.

She had a damn gun and shot at a man.

Whether she'd been provoked made no difference. The law was the law. He was a by-the-book man.

Except sometimes there were grays…

Where did this woman fall on the spectrum?

He parked at the sheriff's office, killed the engine, then walked to the back of the car and opened the door. Tia looked up at him with the saddest expression he'd ever seen.

Eyes that could suck a man in with that sparkling color and innocence.

Except the innocence was yet to be proven.

He had to keep his head clear, his emotions out of the picture.

Only her lower lip quivered as he took her arm and helped her from the vehicle, making his gut tighten.

"I don't care what you do to me," she said with a stubborn lift to her chin. "But please find my baby."

What could he say to that? She wasn't pleading for him to release her, but she was worried about her child.

Wasn't the sheriff looking for the baby?

His gaze met hers. "I'll find him," he said. And if she was lying, he'd make sure she stayed locked up.

But…if there was any truth to her story, he'd find that out, too.

She inhaled sharply as he led her to the door of the sheriff's office. When they entered, a husky man in a deputy's uniform sat at the desk. He looked up with a raised brow.

"Where's the sheriff?" Ryder asked.

"On a call." The man stood and extended his hand. "Deputy Hawthorne." He gave Tia a once-over. "What's going on?"

"Miss Jeffries needs to cool down awhile. Pulled a gun on her ex." He didn't add that she'd fired that weapon.

The deputy grabbed a set of keys, jiggling them in his hand. "I'll put her in a holding cell."

Ryder nodded, although the terrified look on Tia's face twisted his insides. Dammit, he didn't have a choice.

"Can I have my phone call?" Tia asked.

"In time," Deputy Hawthorne said.

"Let her make the call," Ryder said. For some reason, he didn't trust how quickly the deputy planned to follow through.

Deputy Hawthorne shrugged and gestured toward the phone. "Is it local?"

Tia nodded, and he handed her the handset. The handcuffs jangled as she punched in a number.

Ryder gestured for the deputy to step to the side. "Miss Jeffries claims her baby was kidnapped from her home. Has the sheriff been investigating?"

The man shrugged. "He thinks she got rid of the kid. No proof yet, though."

"Anything on the Amber Alert?"

"So far nothing."

"He talked to the baby's father, Darren Hoyt?"

Deputy Hawthorne nodded. "Man had an alibi."

Ryder wondered how solid it was. "Did the sheriff tape his interview with Miss Jeffries?"

The deputy narrowed his eyes. "Not when he got the call and went to her house. But she came in and he recorded that conversation."

"I'd like to watch the tape."

Hawthorne worked his mouth side to side. "Maybe you should wait on the sheriff to return."

"I can look at it here or get a warrant and take the tape with me, so why not make it easy on both of us?"

The deputy seemed to think it over, then muttered agreement. Tia hung up the phone, her hands trembling as she placed them back on her lap. Hawthorne wasted no time. He escorted her through the back to a holding cell. Ryder scanned the space as he followed. Two cells. The other was empty.

At least she wasn't being thrown in with some dangerous derelict. He removed the handcuffs before he motioned her inside.

The cell door closed with a clang. Tia looked small and helpless behind those bars, yet he'd seen the fight in her when she'd confronted her ex.

"Please find Jordie," she whispered in a pained voice. "He's just a few weeks old. He…needs me."

Yes, he did.

But Ryder had seen the worst of society on that last case. The head of the damn ring had seemed like an upstanding citizen. But evil had lurked beneath the surface.

Did Tia deserve to have her son back?

For the life of him, he wanted to believe her. Maybe because no kid should grow up thinking his mother had gotten rid of him like Ryder had.

"I will find the baby." And he'd put away whoever had taken the child.

He gestured to the deputy. "The video?"

The man frowned but led him to a small office across the hall from the cells. Another room was designated for interrogations.

Ryder took a seat. Seconds later, Hawthorne started the video feed of his initial interview at his office with Tia after her son disappeared.

Ryder knotted his hands in his lap as he watched the recording.

Tia paced the interrogation room. "Sheriff, you have to find my baby. I think my ex did something to him." She looked haggard in a worn T-shirt and jeans, her hair yanked back in a ponytail and her eyes swollen from crying.

Sheriff Gaines, a robust man with a scar above his left eye, pointed to a chair. "Sit down. Then tell me what happened again."

"I don't want to sit down," Tia cried. "I want you to find Jordan."

Sheriff Gaines jerked a thumb toward the chair, his voice brusque. "I said sit down."

Tia heaved a breath and sank into the chair in front of the rickety wooden table. She fidgeted with a tissue, wiping her eyes then shredding it into pieces. "I think Darren is responsible."

Sheriff Gaines folded his beefy arms on the table. "Start at the beginning and tell me what happened."

"For God's sake, we went through this when I first called you yesterday." Tia ran a hand through the front of her tangled hair. "Jordie is only six weeks old." She pressed a hand over her chest. "I fed him at midnight the night before, and he fell asleep in my arms." A smile curved her mouth as if she was remembering. "He's so little, and he eats every three hours, so I was exhausted from being up at night." She looked down at her hands. "I shouldn't have, but I laid him in the crib, then went to my room and crawled on my bed. I was only going to close my eyes for a minute, but I must have fallen into a deep sleep."

Instead of reassuring her that it was okay to rest while her baby slept, the sheriff grunted. "Go on."

Guilt streaked her face. "Anyway, a little while later, a noise woke me up."

"A noise?" the sheriff asked. "The baby crying?"

"No." Tia closed her eyes and rubbed her temple as if she was trying to remember. When she opened her eyes again, she exhaled a shaky breath. "It sounded like a gunshot, but then I realized it was a car. Backfiring. I looked out the window and saw taillights racing away." She rubbed her arms now as she paced. "Then I went to check on Jordan, but...his crib was empty."

A heartbeat passed, the silence thick with tension. "You

believe that someone broke into your house and stole your baby while you were asleep?"

Tia nodded miserably. "I told you that already. I usually put him in the cradle by my bed, but I'd been rocking him in the nursery so I left him alone in there. I...thought I'd hear him if he woke up."

The fact that she'd varied her routine must have struck the sheriff as suspicious, because a scowl darkened his face. "So the one night you put him in the other room, he disappears?"

Tia nodded. "It's all my fault. I should have put him in the cradle, but I'd barely slept since he was born and I wasn't thinking."

"I see. You were exhausted and tired of dealing with a fussy baby, so you left the baby where you couldn't hear him," Sheriff Gaines said.

"No." Tia stopped pacing long enough to throw up her hands. "That's not what I meant! But I thought he'd be safe in his nursery and I was only going to take a nap, and we were alone." Her voice cracked and she dropped into the chair again. "But someone came in and stole him."

The sheriff leaned forward, arms still folded. "Don't you mean that you were sick of taking care of a crying infant so you wanted to get rid of him? Maybe you lost it and smothered him, then you panicked and buried him in the yard or put him in the trash."

"No, God, no!" Horror turned Tia's skin a pale color. "That's not what happened. I love my baby—"

"It happens, Miss Jeffries. Mothers are exhausted, suffering from postpartum depression. They can't take it anymore and they snap. They shake the baby to get it to be quiet or they put it in the bed a little too hard or—"

"No!" Tia shouted. "I love my son. I came here for your help, not for you to accuse me of hurting my son." She launched herself at the man and grabbed his shirt. "You have to do something. Look for him!"

The sheriff gripped her hands and pried them from his shirt. "Listen, Miss Jeffries, it'll be easier on you if you co-operate. Tell me what you did with your baby. Maybe he's still alive and we can save him."

Tia sucked in a sharp breath. "I didn't do anything with him except feed him and put him to bed. I think my ex took him."

"Why would he do that?" Gaines asked.

"Because he didn't want a baby in the first place."

"But you got pregnant anyway," the sheriff said in a voice laced with accusations. "You thought if you got pregnant he wouldn't leave you, didn't you?" Sheriff Gaines growled. "Then you had the baby and he left anyway, so you did something to the kid and are trying to get revenge by blaming him."

Tia shook her head vehemently. "No," she cried. "Please believe me."

The sheriff set her away from him. "I will investigate, Miss Jeffries. In fact, my deputy and I are going to search your place again now."

Ryder chewed the inside of his cheek. Gaines was playing tough cop, pushing Tia, just as he might have done.

But had he ignored the possibility that Tia might be telling the truth?

Had he even checked into Tia's ex or canvassed the neighbors to see if anyone had heard that car backfire or seen someone snooping around Tia's place?

Ryder's phone buzzed. He checked the number.

McCullen.

Dammit. He hadn't planned on ever talking to the family. But one of them had obviously found him.

What the hell was he going to do about it?

Chapter Four

Ryder checked the video where the sheriff interviewed Darren.

Hoyt seemed cocky, self-assured. He insisted he hadn't been in Tia's house and that he hadn't taken the baby. He also accused Tia of trying to trap him into marriage, just as he'd told Ryder.

Had the bastard practiced his story?

For some reason, the sheriff didn't push Hoyt. Didn't pursue his past or the financial angle.

Because he'd decided that Tia was the guilty party.

"Hell, Tia was jealous that I was moving on with my life," Darren said. "She probably faked the kidnapping to get my attention, hoping I'd come back to her."

Damn. The federal agent in him agreed that Darren's story was plausible.

But Tia didn't appear to be in love with Darren—she was only concerned about the baby.

Although it was true that the parents were always suspects in a child's kidnapping, disappearance or death. He couldn't clear her just yet.

But what if she was telling the truth?

Just because his parents had sold him didn't mean this woman had done the same thing. But if she had, he'd make sure she paid.

He didn't give a damn if her hair looked like sunshine and her blue eyes poured tears as big as a waterfall.

Or if she looked terrified and pale. That could be explained from guilt. Criminals or people who committed crimes in a fit of passion often experienced guilt.

Sometimes they imploded on themselves.

Unless they were pathological liars or sociopaths.

But she didn't fit that profile.

He had to run background checks on both of them, look at their computers, phone records, talk to neighbors and friends.

He scrubbed a hand over his bleary eyes, a good night's sleep beckoning. But the image of Tia in that cell made him decide to put bed on hold for a while, at least until he did some work.

He shut off the tapes, phoned his boss and requested warrants, then stepped back into the front office. The deputy was leaning back in his desk chair, feet propped on the desk, a grin on his face.

"Yeah, Martha, I should be there in about an hour."

Ryder folded his arms and stared at the man, sending him the silent message to get off the phone.

The deputy scowled, tilted his head sideways so Ryder couldn't hear his conversation, then ended the call.

The idea of Tia sitting alone in a dark cell all night rubbed Ryder the wrong way. "You're leaving the woman alone in here tonight?"

Hawthorne frowned. "The night shift deputy is coming in. Why? That woman probably killed her kid. She deserves to rot in prison."

Anger shot through Ryder. "Have you ever heard the phrase *innocent until proven guilty*?"

Hawthorne barked a laugh. "Yeah, but don't let those blue eyes fool you."

"What makes you so sure she's the culprit? Why not the baby's father? He didn't want a child in the first place."

Hawthorne cut his gaze to the side. "I know women, that's why."

Ryder leaned forward, hands on the desk, body coiled with tension. "Just make sure she's safe in there," he said in a low growl.

A muscle ticked in the deputy's jaw. "I know how to do my job."

Ryder gritted his teeth. Small-town sheriffs and deputies disliked the feds encroaching on their territory.

"Did you need something else?" Hawthorne asked.

Ryder met his gaze with a stony look. "Darren Hoyt is supposed to come in and file an official report. Let me know if he shows up."

Hawthorne gave a clipped nod.

"Do you have Miss Jeffries and Hoyt's computers?"

"The sheriff already looked at them but didn't find anything."

"Phone records?"

Hawthorne shrugged. "Have to ask Sheriff Gaines."

"I will." But he'd prefer to look at them himself anyway, especially since the deputy and sheriff had already made their decision about Tia's guilt.

Ryder tossed his business card on the desk. "Let me know if you hear anything." He didn't wait for a response.

Even if the sheriff had investigated thoroughly, which it didn't appear he had, Ryder would conduct his own inquiry.

If Jordan had been kidnapped for money, Tia would have received a ransom call.

Which meant whoever took him had a different motive.

Worse—every day this baby was missing meant the chance of finding him diminished.

TIA SHIVERED AS she hunched on the only piece of furniture

In the cell— a tiny cot. The low lights in the small hallway barely lit the inside of the tiny barred room. A threadbare blanket lay on top of a single mattress that was so thin you could feel the metal springs beneath it.

Tia curled her arms around her waist, clenching her fingers into her palms so tightly she felt the pain of her fingernails stabbing her skin.

She deserved the pain. She was a terrible mother. If she hadn't fallen asleep, her baby wouldn't have been taken.

How could she have been so deep in sleep that she hadn't heard someone break into the house?

The sheriff said there were no signs of a break-in.

But there had to be.

Unless she'd been so exhausted she'd forgotten to lock the door.

No…she always locked the door. She was compulsive about it and checked it at least three times a night.

A squeaking noise alerted her to the fact that someone had opened the door between the cells and the front office. Footsteps echoed on the concrete floor.

Her stomach knotted. Had Sheriff Gaines returned to make more accusations? To taunt her?

A big, hulking shadow moved across the dimly lit hall. More footsteps. A breath rattled in the quiet.

She tightened her hands again in an attempt to hold herself together and braced herself for whatever Gaines or his deputy dished out.

"Tia?"

She jerked her head up. Not Gaines's snide voice. Special Agent Ryder Banks.

God, had he come back to rescue her from this nightmare?

He stopped in front of the cell, his big body taking up so much air that she could barely breathe. Then he shoved a notepad and pen through the bars. "I need you to write down all your contacts. The people you work with, your friends, neighbors, anyone you can think of who might vouch for you or who had access to your house."

Hope warred with despair. What if it was too late?

"Tia?" This time his voice was gruff. Commanding. "If you want my help, take the pad and start writing."

She pulled herself from her stupor, stood on shaking legs and crossed the small space. Her hand trembled as she grabbed the pad and pen. "You're going to help me?"

Silence stretched for a full minute while he stared at her. She felt his scrutiny as if he was dissecting her.

"I'll find your son. Then I'll make whoever kidnapped him pay."

The coldness in his tone suggested he hadn't decided on her innocence yet.

But at least he was going to investigate. That was a lot more than Gaines had done.

She sighed, then walked back to the cot, sank onto the mattress and began the list.

Her coworkers and the volunteers at the shelter came first. Two of her neighbors next.

"Don't leave anyone out," he said.

She ignored the distrust in his tone. As long as he looked for her son, she could put up with anything. "I won't. Are you going to have Darren do this, too?"

"Absolutely." He paused, then cleared his throat. "You said you run a charity for families in need. Is this for abused women and children?"

Tia shrugged. "Yes. But it's also open to anyone who needs help. Sometimes mothers come to us when their husbands or children's fathers abandon them. They need help finding housing and food and jobs. We've also had families in crisis—it could be drug or alcohol related, one of them has lost his job, even a long-term illness where the parent has to go into a hospital for treatment. We work through social services, but we also find temporary foster homes through local churches and provide counseling to help them get back on their feet. Our goal is to keep the family intact or to reunite them if there's a separation period."

"Admirable." His dark eyes narrowed. "Can you think of anyone you've angered? Maybe a father or mother who lost their kids to the system, someone who'd want revenge against you."

Tia's pulse jumped. There were a couple of names.

"Write them down," he said as if he'd read her mind.

Tia nodded, then scribbled every name she could think of, including the hospital staff and attendants as well as Amy, a young delivery nurse, who'd befriended her.

Finally she handed the agent the list. Her fingers brushed his big hands, and a tingle of something dangerously like attraction shot through her.

She yanked her hand back quickly. She'd never be foolish enough to fall for another man.

When she got Jordan back, he would be the only one in her life.

RYDER LEFT TIA, shaken by the spark of electricity he'd felt when she'd touched his hand. Then she'd looked up at him with those damn sea-like blue eyes and he'd thought he would drown in them.

She had some kind of pull on him.

A pull he had to ignore.

He was a loner. Always had been. Always would be. There was no place for a woman or family in his line of work.

It was still odd, since he wasn't usually drawn to gun-carrying women who shot at their husbands or to suspects in his cases.

His reaction had to be due to lack of sleep. He wasn't thinking clearly.

He needed that beer and a bed. Although an image of Tia sprawled naked on the sheets with her hair fanned out taunted him.

He shook the image away.

The list of names in his hand meant he had work to do. Sleep would have to wait.

He just prayed Tia would be safe in that cell. At least she couldn't get herself in any more trouble by killing her ex.

He bypassed Hawthorne, who was on the telephone again, strode outside to his SUV and headed toward Crossroads. Although it was getting late in the evening, hopefully someone would still be awake.

The old Victorian house was nestled on an acre of land literally at the crossroads of the town limits and the countryside. The porch light and lights inside were on, indicating someone was there.

Ryder swung down the drive, surprised at the wildflowers growing in patches along the drive. A cheery-looking sign in blue and white boasted its name, and underneath, etchings of children and parents linking hands in a circle as if united had been carved into the wood.

He passed a barn and spotted two horses galloping on a hill to the east.

Rocking chairs and porch swings filled the wraparound porch, making the place look homey and inviting.

He climbed the porch, wiped his feet on the welcome mat, and banged the door knocker, which was shaped like the sun. Through the window, he noted a kitchen with a large round oak table and a woman at the sink washing dishes.

A second later, a twentysomething blonde with pale green eyes opened the door. She couldn't be more than five feet tall and couldn't weigh a hundred pounds. Her eyes widened as her gaze traveled from his face down to his size-thirteen boots and back to his face.

He flashed his identification. "Special Agent Ryder Banks, FBI. I need to ask you some questions about Tia Jeffries."

She blinked, a wariness in her expression. "Yes, Tia told me you'd probably be coming. I'm Elle Grist, Tia's assistant."

"When did she tell you I was coming?"

"When she called after you arrested her," the woman said, disapproval lacing her tone.

So she'd used her one phone call to call the charity. Why? To request they cover for her?

"Before you even ask, no, Tia would never do anything to hurt her baby or anyone else. She's the most loving, caring person on this planet."

"You're loyal to her. I get that."

"Yes, I am, but with good reason," Elle said. "Tia lost her family—every one of them—on the day of her college graduation. They were flying to the ceremony when the plane went down." Her voice cracked with emotion. "She still blames herself. More than anything in the world, she values family. That's why she started this place. She's helped so many people over the past five years that she deserves a medal."

Elle dabbed at her eyes. "Tia also took me in when I lost my mother two years ago. She let me live with her until I could get a job. She saved me from…"

Ryder arched a brow. "From what?"

Elle rubbed a finger over a scar on her wrist. "I wouldn't be alive if it weren't for her." Footsteps sounded, and the heavyset woman he'd seen through the window washing dishes appeared, drying her hands on a checked cloth.

"Miss Elle speaks the gospel. Everyone loves Miss Tia." She planted her beefy hands on her hips. "You gonna find the evil one that took her baby?"

Ryder swallowed, choosing his words carefully. From Tia's list, he guessed this woman must be Ina, the cook and housekeeper. "I'm certainly going to try. But I need your help."

"We'll do anything for Tia," Ina said.

He gestured to the notepad. "Then let me come in. I want you to look over this list Tia made and tell me about the people on it."

The women exchanged questioning looks, then a silent agreement passed between them, and they motioned for him to enter.

"Just be quiet now," Ina said. "We have two families here with little ones. Took their mamas forever to get them to sleep tonight."

Ryder glanced at the stairs and nodded. It certainly appeared that Tia was some kind of saint to these people. If that was the case, who had stolen her son?

And what had they done with the little boy?

Chapter Five

Ryder studied the photos on the wall of Tia's office. She and the staff had taken pictures of several families who'd come through Crossroads and displayed them on the wall to showcase that their efforts were working.

Personalized thank-you notes and cards were interspersed, creating a collage that triggered Ryder's admiration.

"Darren Hoyt claims Tia is unstable, that she suffered from depression," Ryder said.

Elle's mouth grew pinched. "She is not unstable and she certainly doesn't suffer from depression."

"That girl had it rough a while back," Ina interjected. "Losing her mama and daddy and brother all at once. Anyone would have been grief stricken. On top of that, she blamed herself 'cause they were on their way to see her."

That would have been tough.

"She was only twenty-one at the time," Elle said. "She was suddenly alone and didn't know what to do. But one of her friends convinced her to go to an in-house therapy program. So she did. No shame in that."

No, he supposed not.

"I admire her," Elle continued. "She took her own personal tragedy and used it to make her stronger and to help others by building this place."

That was admirable. Ryder addressed Ina. "What did you think about Darren Hoyt?"

Ina folded her arms. "He was a con man. He knew Tia had money from her folks and married her to get hold of it. But that girl was smart and set up the charity so no one could touch it."

A wise move. "She didn't trust Darren from the beginning?" Ryder asked.

Elle shrugged. "It wasn't that. She just wanted to protect her family's money and for their deaths to stand for something."

"She barely paid herself a salary," Ina said. "But she gave openly to others."

"When Darren realized he would never get her inheritance, he left her," Elle said. "That man was a manipulative SOB—he never loved her."

"She loved him?" Ryder asked, wondering why that thought bothered him.

Elle blew out a breath. "At first I think she did."

"She was young, vulnerable, lonely and naive," Ina said. "Darren Hoyt took advantage of that."

Ryder gritted his teeth. "Do you think she was jealous that he moved on? She wouldn't have done something to get Darren's attention and win him back?"

"Heavens, no," Ina murmured.

Elle shook her head. "Tia had never seemed happier than during that pregnancy."

Ina smiled softly. "She wanted that baby more than anything."

Ryder rubbed his chin. "Can you think of anyone who'd want to hurt her? Maybe someone whose family came through Crossroads?"

Both women shook their heads no.

He consulted the notepad. "Tell me about Bennett Jones."

"He was furious when his wife left him and took their son," Ina said.

"Do you think he kidnapped Tia's little boy for revenge?" Elle asked.

Ryder shifted on the balls of his feet. "I don't know—do *you* think he did?"

Elle chewed her bottom lip. "It's hard to say how far he'd go. Tia suggested he attend anger-management classes."

"He did have a mean streak," Ina agreed, her cheeks puffing out.

Ryder checked the list again. "What about Wanda Hanson?"

Ina fanned herself. "Lord help, that woman had her issues."

"What do you mean?" Ryder asked.

"She had back problems and became addicted to pain meds, then escalated to harder stuff," Elle said. "Husband found her passed out while their baby was left unattended. They lived on a lake, and their toddler was outside alone."

Ina tsked and shook her head. "It's a wonder the little fellow didn't drown."

Ryder arched a brow. "What happened?"

"Father tried everything to convince her to get help. He finally divorced her and moved with the boy to Texas to be close to his folks."

Ryder thanked Elle and Ina, then extended his business card. "Please call me if you think of anything else that could be helpful."

Ina caught his arm. "Agent Banks, you gonna help our Tia?"

Ryder cleared his throat. These women had sung Tia's praises. If everything they said was true, she was a victim. "I'm going to find Jordan," he said.

Both women nodded, and he headed out the door.

If Bennett and Wanda had lost custody of their children, they might blame Tia.

It was a place to start.

TIA COUNTED THE scratches on the wall of the cell beside the cot. Foul language mingled with crude sketches and another area where someone had drawn lines counting the days.

She wondered if she should start her own calendar.

A cold chill washed over her at the thought. Knowing Sheriff Gaines, he'd keep her locked up until he finished making his case against her for hurting her baby and she went to trial. Now, he'd probably add attempted murder for threatening Darren.

The blasted man. If he'd done his job and found her son, she wouldn't have been forced to take matters into her own hands.

She stretched her fingers, shocked at herself for firing that gun. She'd never believed she had it in her to hurt another human.

Not until she'd held her baby. The very second she'd looked into his little face, she'd known she'd do anything to protect him.

Yet she'd failed.

Tears blurred her vision. She blinked in an attempt to hold them back, but it was futile. The enormity of her loss struck her again and she walked over to the bars of the cell and curled her fingers around them.

She had no idea what time it was, but the windowless cell and the dim light made it feel like it was the middle of the night.

She wrapped her arms around her waist, and rocked herself back and forth. She felt empty inside and ached to hold her little boy again.

Where was he now? Was he safe?

He ate every few hours. Was he hungry?

Just the thought of feeding him made her breasts throb. They'd shared a tender bond when she'd nursed him.

The tears broke through as she realized she might never get to hold him again. No one would ever love him as much as she did.

She just prayed that whoever had kidnapped him takes care of him and keeps him safe until she finds him.

And she *would* find him, no matter how long it took or what she had to do.

RYDER'S STOMACH GROWLED. He hadn't eaten all day. And he'd never gotten any sleep.

He would take care of the food, though, while he did a little research on Darren Hoyt.

He parked at the Sagebrush Diner, a place that reminded him of an old Western saloon. The log cabin sported rails outside to tie up horses. Considering the closest stable was twenty miles away, he doubted it was used much, but it was a nice touch.

Several cars filled the parking lot, and a group of teens had parked in the back corner and were sitting on the hoods of their cars hanging out. The flicker of a lighter lit the air, and smoke curled upward. Cigarettes or weed—he didn't know which.

Not that he cared at the moment. He had more important things to do—like finding Jordie Jeffries.

Country music blared from an old-fashioned jukebox in one corner, chatter and laughter buzzed through the room, and burgers sizzled on a griddle in the kitchen area. He claimed a seat at a booth just as a twentysomething waitress approached.

She gave him a once-over, then a big smile. "Hey, tall, dark and handsome, what can I get you?"

He bit back a chuckle at her attempt to flirt. He wasn't interested and didn't take the bait. "Burger, chili and a beer." He set his laptop on the table. "You have Wi-Fi?"

She nodded. "Finally. Password is Sagebrush."

The name of the diner—original.

He thanked her, then booted up his machine, ending the conversation. He quickly connected to the internet, then the FBI's database and plugged in Darren Hoyt's name.

A preliminary background check revealed the man had been born in Houston to a preacher and his wife, who'd died when Darren was in college. Had he used that fact to bond with Tia?

His work history showed that he'd dabbled in real estate and had touted himself as an entrepreneur. He'd lived in Montana and Colorado and had been single until he'd married Tia.

A couple of speeding tickets, but no charges filed against him. No rap sheet.

The waitress returned with his beer and food and he muttered thanks. Hoyt was no saint. If Elle and Ina were correct and he was a con man, there had to be something in his history that was suspicious.

He sipped his beer, then dug into the food. By the time he'd finished, he'd found a photo of Darren online from a charity fund-raiser Tia had organized the year before and plugged it into facial recognition software.

Seconds later, he had a hit. Only the man in the photograph wasn't Darren Hoyt. His name was Bill Koontz.

Bill Koontz was born in a small town in Texas. His mother was Renee Koontz, who had a record for solicitation and had served prison time for drug dealing when her son was fifteen. He'd been in and out of foster homes for a few months, then lived on the streets. At eighteen, he'd disappeared for a while.

Around twenty-five, he resurfaced in Montana, where he'd worked odd jobs, then had become a groomer at a country club stable.

Several women at the club had reported that he'd swindled them out of their savings. Eventually the guy had served three years in prison. When he was released, he moved to Wyoming, where he eased his way back into another country club and resorted to his old tricks.

At first, life must have been good. But then reports of him trying to con members out of their savings cropped up, and he was fired.

Two years later, Darren Hoyt had been born. The name was new, but Ryder would bet his life that the con game had continued.

Tia had simply been a mark.

The waitress appeared, the flirtatious smile joined by a gleaming in her eyes. "Another beer, sugar?"

"Just the check." Another beer and she might take it as a sign that he was interested.

Her smile dipped into a frown and she handed him the bill. He tossed some cash the table to cover it, then dug around another minute for more information on Hoyt. Nothing again on that name.

Curious, he ran a search on country clubs in the area and found one about five miles from Crossroads.

His pulse jumped. Maybe Tia had approached members to donate to her charity.

He found the number and left a message identifying himself and asking for a return call from the director.

Exhaustion knotted his muscles, and he finally stood and

left the diner. The waitress waved to him as he left, but he ignored her. He didn't have time for women.

Not when a baby needed him.

A HALF HOUR LATER, Ryder pulled down the drive to his cabin. An image of Tia alone in that prison cell sleeping on that cot taunted him.

From what he'd learned, she didn't deserve to be in jail. While she was locked up, her son's kidnapper was getting farther and farther away.

He had to do something.

Tomorrow he'd confront Darren about his past. Then maybe he'd persuade the man to talk.

Woods backed up to his cabin, trees swaying in the wind. He'd chosen the place because it was virtually deserted, a retreat after working undercover or dealing with criminals.

He tucked his laptop beneath his arm, then climbed from the SUV, scanning the area for trouble as he always did. Once a detective, always a detective.

Satisfied the area was clear, he let himself into the cabin. He flipped on the light switch, then headed straight toward the shower. Before he could undress, a knock sounded at the door.

Startled, he gripped his gun and eased into the living room. He'd made too many enemies on the job to trust anyone.

He inched to the side window in front, eased the curtain aside and checked the yard. A beat-up pickup truck sat in the drive.

Hmm.

Holding his gun to his side, he stepped over to the front door and opened it.

Shock stole his breath at the sight of the man standing on his porch.

A man who looked like him.

It had to be his twin brother, Cash Koker.

Chapter Six

Ryder blinked to clear his vision. It was almost eerie, seeing himself yet knowing the man in front of him wasn't him. Same dark brown eyes, wide jaw, broad shoulders.

Except Cash looked freshly shaven where Ryder was scruffy, with three-day-old beard stubble on his jaw and hair that needed a wash and a trim.

Cash shoved his hands in the pockets of his denim jacket. "Damn," Cash muttered. "They told me I had a twin, but I couldn't believe it."

Words tangled on Ryder's tongue. He swallowed to make his voice work. "You knew about me?"

Cash shook his head. "Not until recently." His gaze traveled up and down Ryder as if he too couldn't believe what he was seeing. "You knew about me?"

Ryder shook his head. "Not until I saw that news report where Sheriff McCullen was interviewed."

"That's Maddox." Cash glanced inside the cabin. "Uh, can I come in?"

Ryder squared his shoulders. Was he ready for this conversation? Hell, no.

But he had questions and couldn't turn this man away, not when he looked so much like him it was shocking. They *were* brothers, twins.

And none of this was Cash's fault. Judging from Maddox's statement, Cash had only recently learned about the McCullens, too.

"Sure." He stepped aside and gestured for Cash to enter, then led him to the small den. "Sorry this place is a wreck. I haven't been here for a while."

Cash studied him, arms folded. "You're with the FBI, aren't you?"

"Yes." Ryder clenched his jaw. "How did you know that? And how did you find me?"

Cash shrugged. "My—our—brothers have been looking for you awhile. Ray's a private investigator and Maddox used his connections in the sheriff's department to expedite the search."

Ryder gritted his teeth. What did you say to a brother you didn't know you had? "Do you want a beer or something?"

A small grin tugged at Cash's mouth. "Yeah. Thanks."

Ryder grabbed two cold ones from the refrigerator just to have something to do. He knew how to handle hardened criminals, but he had no idea how to handle this situation.

When he turned back, Cash was watching him. "Sorry for just showing up here." He popped the top of the beer and took a sip. "But once Ray found you, I…had to see for myself."

Ryder gave a nod of understanding, then gestured toward the back deck. It offered a great view of the woods and was his favorite spot to think and unwind after a case.

He and Cash stepped outside, a breeze stirring the warm air. Ryder claimed the rocker and Cash settled on the porch swing. It creaked back and forth as he pushed it with his feet, the silence between them thick with questions and the revelation that they were identical twins but also strangers who knew nothing about each other.

He sipped his beer, stalling.

"So how did you grow up?" Cash finally asked.

Ryder heaved a wary breath. "I was adopted by a couple named Troy and Myra Banks. They told me I was adopted when I was little, but not about my birth family."

Cash's jaw tightened.

"You weren't adopted?"

Cash shook his head. "Nope, I was sickly. Bounced from foster home to foster home."

Guilt gnawed at Ryder. "That must have been rough."

"I survived," Cash said, although the gruffness of his voice hinted that it had been tough.

No wonder Cash had welcomed the McCullen brothers.

"So how did you find out about the McCullens?" Ryder asked.

A sardonic chuckle escaped Cash and he swallowed another sip of beer. "A few months ago I got arrested. Maddox and Brett and Ray showed up at my bail hearing. Took me home with them and paid for my defense."

Ryder narrowed his eyes. "Just like that? No strings attached?"

Cash frowned. "Well, Maddox made it clear that if I was guilty he wouldn't cover for me. But they investigated and helped me clear my name."

Ryder stared at the sliver of moon trying to peek through the trees.

"Your turn," Cash said. "How did you find out about the McCullens?"

Ryder silently cursed. "After my dad died, I became curious and did some digging. Finally I asked my mom."

"You mean your adopted mother?"

"Same thing," Ryder said, his loyalty to the woman who'd raised him kicking in. "She told me what happened."

Cash narrowed his eyes. "She told you that you were kidnapped, that your real mother died trying to find you?"

Ryder locked his jaw and debated what to say. But he refused to lie. "Not exactly."

"Then what did she tell you?"

Ryder leaned forward, arms braced on his thighs as he studied Cash. "That the McCullens needed money to expand their ranch, so they made a deal with a lawyer and sold me."

A startled look passed across Cash's face. "What? Damn, that's not the way it happened."

"How do you know?" Ryder asked. "We were both babies at the time."

Cash scraped a hand over his face, drawing Ryder's gaze to the long scar on his forehead. Ryder's gut pinched. How had he gotten that?

Cash settled his Stetson on his lap. "That's right, but once the McCullens found me, they explained everything. It's a long story. The doctor who delivered us made a mistake with another delivery, a mistake that cost another couple their child. That baby's father stole us from the hospital to replace the child he lost, and the doctor covered out of guilt. He told our parents that we were stillborn."

Shock rolled through Ryder. "That's the story the McCullens told you?" Ryder said, well aware his comment sounded like an accusation. "How do you know it's true?"

Cash sucked in a sharp breath. "Because Maddox investigated. That doctor remained friends with the McCullens, especially Joe, our father. He finally admitted what happened—that Mom was murdered because she didn't believe we'd died and because she was searching for us. Dunn, the man who'd taken us, killed her to cover up the truth."

Ryder's mind raced. "If that's true, why didn't the man who kidnapped us raise us?"

Cash grunted. "Apparently his wife figured out what he'd done and insisted he take us back to the McCullens.

The man was afraid of being arrested, so he dropped us off at a church instead."

Ryder swallowed hard. But Myra and Troy Banks claimed they'd gotten him from an attorney and led him to believe the McCullens orchestrated the deal. They hadn't mentioned anything about a church.

Ryder stood and walked to the edge of the deck. A wild animal growled from the woods. He could almost see its predator eyes glowing in the dark.

"Last year, our father, Joe, realized what had happened. He started looking for us, too. Then he was murdered."

Ryder drained his beer. "Listen, Cash, it sounds like you had a rough childhood. I'm sure it feels good to think the McCullens want you." He balled his hand into a fist and pressed it over his chest. "But I have a family—a mother, at least. And I don't want or need the McCullens in my life."

Emotions wrestled in Cash's eyes. He'd obviously thought Ryder would be thrilled to learn about his roots.

Ryder might—if he didn't already know the real story. Of course the McCullen brothers wouldn't admit that their parents had been greedy enough to trade two of their children for money.

Cash removed a manila envelope from the inside of his jacket. He laid it on the coffee table. "Inside are letters and cards our mother wrote to you. I have an envelope just like it."

Ryder raised a brow in question.

"She—our mother, Grace—wrote to us after we went missing. She bought cards for Christmases and birthdays. Read them and you'll see I'm telling the truth."

Without another word, Cash set his empty beer bottle on the table with a thud, then strode back through the house and outside. Ryder stared at the envelope, his heart pounding, until he heard Cash's truck spring to life and chug away.

Anger and resentment mingled with doubt. He squashed the doubt. His mother loved him. She wouldn't have lied to him.

He didn't need any letters or cards or for his life to be disrupted by the McCullens.

He was fine on his own. He always had been. He always would be.

THE HOURS DRAGGED BY. Tia had felt alone when her family had died, but she'd never felt more alone than she did now, without her baby in her arms.

Her eyes felt gritty from staring at the ceiling of the jail cell, and her body ached from fatigue. But that discomfort was nothing compared to the emptiness inside her.

She might never see Jordie again.

She'd read stories about children who went missing and were never recovered. There were other accounts where the child was located years later but had bonded with whoever had raised them.

Jordie was only an infant. Babies changed every day. What if it took months or years to find him and she didn't even recognize him?

She paced the cell for the millionth time, mentally retracing the events of the past couple of days.

Darren had moved out months ago. But he'd contacted her two weeks before she was due, offering to set up a fund for the baby—with her money. He wanted to invest in a surefire project that would double the money in a week's time.

She had refused. At that point, she didn't trust him. He'd already cleaned out her savings account and most of her checking account.

He could have kidnapped Jordan for revenge. Maybe he was even working with someone else.

Although if he'd taken Jordan because of the money, why hadn't he asked for a ransom?

Everything was normal. He was eating and gaining weight. Although the doctor insisted he was too young to smile, he had smiled at her as she'd hugged him on the way back to the car.

Of course he'd had a fit when she put him in the car seat. Apparently he didn't like to be confined.

The bars on the cell mocked her. Neither did she.

She closed her eyes and saw his little face again. So trusting. So sweet and innocent. He'd smelled like baby wash. He had her blue eyes and a full head of light-colored hair.

At the doctor's office, two other mothers had commented on how beautiful he was. The nurse who'd delivered him, Amy Yost, had phoned to see how the checkup went. Tia had invited the young woman over for coffee the next day. They'd chatted and become friends. Amy suggested she and her three-year-old daughter, Linnie, get together more often.

After Amy left, Tia's neighbor Judy Kinley had dropped by with brownies and a basket of goodies for Jordie—diaper wipes, baby washcloths, onesies and a blanket she'd crocheted herself.

Tia had enjoyed the visit but finally admitted that she needed a nap, that she'd been up half the night and maybe they could visit another day.

But none of those memories were helpful. She hadn't seen anyone lurking around the house watching her. No strangers had come to the door. She hadn't seen any cars following her. And she hadn't received any odd phone calls.

She closed her eyes and flopped back on the cot, her

head spinning. Just as she was about to drift to sleep, the sound of a baby crying echoed in her ears.

She jerked upright in search of Jordie and realized she was still in jail. Emotions racked her body.

She was no closer to finding her son than she had been the day before.

JUST AFTER DAWN, Ryder crawled from bed, irritated that he'd let thoughts of his conversation with Cash keep him awake. When he'd finally gotten the McCullens off his mind, Tia's big blue eyes had haunted him.

He showered and shaved, then dressed and strapped on his holster. He called Darren Hoyt on his way out the door.

"Meet me at the Sagebrush jail in half an hour. If you aren't there to file a report, I'll assume you're dropping the charges and I'll release Miss Jeffries."

He'd also fill Sheriff Gaines in on what he'd learned about Hoyt.

Then he wanted to search Tia's house himself. Maybe the sheriff had missed a clue.

Storm clouds hovered in the sky, painting the woods a bleak gray and making the deserted land between his cabin and town look desolate. As he drove into town, he noted that the diner was already filling up with the breakfast crowd and several young mothers strolled their babies on the sidewalk and at the park while their toddlers and pre-schoolers ran and squealed on the playground.

He parked at the jail and went inside, his stomach clenching at the sight of another deputy at the desk. The old-timer had gray hair and a gut, and was slumped back in the chair, snoring like a bear.

Had he even checked on Tia?

Ryder rapped on the wooden desk. The man jumped,

sending the chair backward with a thud as the edge hit the wall.

"Wha-what's going on?" The man fumbled with his wire-rimmed glasses.

Ryder identified himself. "I need to talk to Sheriff Gaines."

The man's face grew pinched as he adjusted his glasses. "This about the prisoner?"

"Yes," Ryder said between clenched teeth. "That and her missing child."

The man yawned. "Sheriff'll be in here soon. You can wait."

Ryder opened his mouth to ask him what he knew about the missing baby case, but the door swung open and Darren Hoyt barreled in. His clothes were disheveled, his eyes bloodshot and he reeked of whiskey.

"I'm here," Hoyt snapped. "Now let me sign those damn papers. I've got stuff to do."

Ryder grabbed the man by the collar and led him to the corner.

"Listen to me, you jerk. I did some digging on you last night and I know about your past."

"What are you talking about?" Hoyt growled. "I don't have a record."

"Not as Darren Hoyt, but you do under your real name."

Panic flared on Hoyt's face.

"Now, I suggest you tell me where Jordie Jeffries is."

"I told you last night, I don't know." He flung his hand toward the door leading to the cells. "Go ask my ex. She's the one that took the runt to her house."

Ryder jammed his face into the man's and gave him a warning look. "Because I don't believe she did anything but love that baby. You, on the other hand are a dirtbag of a father, a con man and a criminal."

Hoyt shook his head in denial. "That's not true—"

"Yes, it is," Ryder said coldly. "But if you confess and tell me where to find the baby, I'll go to bat for you with the judge."

"I don't know where he is," Darren screeched. "I swear I don't."

Ryder studied him for a long, frustrating minute. He wanted to beat the bastard until he confessed, but he couldn't do that here, not with that deputy watching.

"If that's true, prove it and drop the charges against Tia. The best way to find your son is for me to work with her."

Hoyt's breath rasped out. "You gonna watch her, see if she leads you to the baby?"

Ryder's gut tightened, but the lie came easy. "Exactly. You do want your son found unharmed, don't you?"

Hoyt's eyes darted toward the deputy, then the door opened and Sheriff Gaines strode in.

"What's going on?" the sheriff asked.

Ryder reluctantly released Hoyt. "Hoyt and I were just making a deal. He wants us to find his baby real bad."

The sheriff's eyebrows climbed his forehead as he jerked his head toward Hoyt. "That so?"

Hoyt nodded. Ryder patted his arm. "And you're dropping the charges against Miss Jeffries, right?"

Hoyt hissed a curse word, then gave another nod. "Just tell that crazy bitch not to come near me again."

Ryder barely resisted slugging the jerk. But he would keep Tia away from Hoyt for her own protection.

He gestured toward the deputy. "Please bring Miss Jeffries to the front."

The older man ambled through the door, and Ryder turned to Gaines. "I need everything you have on this missing child case."

"Wait just a damn minute," Gaines said. "This is my jurisdiction."

"Kidnapping is a federal offense. I'm officially taking over the case now."

If he didn't, Gaines would probably railroad Tia to prison and they'd never find her son.

Chapter Seven

Ryder watched as Hoyt stormed out the door. If the bastard cared about his baby, he'd be pushing him and the sheriff to find him.

Instead, Hoyt was more concerned with himself.

"Sheriff Gaines, did you search Tia's house after she reported her child missing?"

Gaines shifted, his chin set stubbornly. "Of course."

"What did you find?"

"Like I put in my report, the window was unlocked. No prints. No sign of foul play or that anyone had been in the house except Miss Jeffries."

"Can I see that report?"

Gaines shoved a file folder from his desk toward Ryder. Ryder quickly skimmed the notes on Tia's interview and photos of the empty crib and nursery.

"Did you take pictures when you searched the outer premises?"

Sheriff Gaines shook his head. "Wasn't nothing to photograph."

Ryder frowned. If an intruder had broken in, he would have expected to find something. Maybe footprints, brush disturbed.

He wanted to conduct his own search. "You can release her now."

The sheriff glared at him. "You sure that's a good idea?"

Ryder nodded. "Keep an open mind, Gaines. If Tia is innocent, whoever abducted her baby could be getting away."

FOOTSTEPS ON THE concrete floor startled Tia. What was going to happen now? Was the sheriff or that agent taking her to court for a bail hearing?

Had one of them found Jordie?

An older deputy appeared, his scowl menacing. Keys jangled as he unlocked the cell.

She rubbed her wrists. Even though the agent had removed the handcuffs, she could still feel the weight of the cold metal. Was he going to handcuff her again?

"Let's go," the deputy barked.

Tia inhaled a deep breath, stood and crossed the floor to the cell door. The deputy gestured for her to follow him, but he surprised her by not cuffing her. Exhaustion pulled at her, but she held her head high.

Darren had depleted her checking and savings. If she needed bail money, she could ask her assistant at Crossroads to dip into their funds to bail her out.

But that was a last resort.

Except for paying herself a small salary, she *never* used the charity's money for personal reasons.

But if her parents had been alive, they'd agree that she should do anything to find her baby.

When the deputy opened the door to the front office, she blinked at how bright it seemed, a reminder that life in prison meant missing fresh air and sunshine.

A shadow caught her eye, then the figure came into focus. Agent Banks.

Her lungs squeezed for air. If he hadn't arrested her, she might find him attractive.

He *was* attractive. Tall, dark and handsome.

But he'd locked her up the night before and left her alone in jail when she should have been out looking for her baby.

RYDER SCRUTINIZED TIA to make certain she was okay. Leaving a woman alone in a jail with a male-only staff, especially with men he didn't know, always worried him.

She looked exhausted and frightened, but there were no visible signs that she'd been abused or manhandled.

"What's going on?" she asked.

"Hoyt decided to drop the charges," Ryder said.

She glanced at the sheriff for confirmation.

"Guess it's your lucky day," the sheriff said in a voice harsh with displeasure. "But I suggest you stay away from your ex or you'll be right back here."

Tia gave a nod. "Do you have new information on my son?"

Gaines cut his eyes toward Ryder. "You'll have to ask him. It's his case now."

Another surprised look flitted across Tia's face, then relief. She obviously didn't trust Gaines to do his job.

Ryder gestured toward the door leading outside. "I'll drive you home."

Tia rubbed her hands up and down her arms as if she was trying to hold herself together as they crossed the room to the door.

"Don't leave town, Miss Jeffries," Gaines muttered.

She paused, animosity streaking her face. "I'm going to find my little boy," she said sharply.

Gaines started to say something else, but Ryder coaxed Tia out the door before they shared another exchange.

He placed his hand to Tia's back as they stepped onto the sidewalk and felt a shiver run through her.

"Are you all right?" he asked gruffly.

She shook her head. "I won't be all right until I'm holding Jordie again."

He understood that. "Let's talk at your house. I'm sure you want a shower and some food."

She didn't comment. She simply slid into the passenger seat of his SUV.

"I don't know how you convinced Darren to drop the charges, but I appreciate that."

He started the engine. "I don't like him," he said bluntly.

A small smile tugged at her mouth, making him wish he could permanently wipe the anguish from her face. "You mean you saw through his act. Sheriff Gaines certainly seems to believe whatever Darren says."

"I know. I don't understand that." He gripped the steering wheel tighter, then veered onto the road leading to Tia's house.

She angled her head, her eyes narrowed. "How do you know where I live?"

He winced. "It's my job, Tia."

She heaved a breath. "You were watching me, weren't you? That's the reason you were at Darren's when I confronted him."

Confronted was putting it mildly. "Yes," he said, deciding to be straightforward. "Kidnapping and a missing baby warrant the feds' attention."

He pulled into the drive of the small bungalow. Flowers danced in the window boxes, the house was painted a soothing gray blue and a screened porch made it look homey—and totally at odds with Tia's current situation.

"Do you own or rent?" Ryder asked.

"I own it," Tia said. "I was living in an apartment before, but I wanted Jordie to have a real home with a yard to play in." Her voice broke. "I thought when he got older, we'd get a dog."

Ryder swallowed hard. There was no way this woman had hurt her child.

"I know Sheriff Gaines searched the house and property, but I intend to conduct my own search."

Ryder grabbed his kit from the trunk then followed Tia up to the front porch. She opened the door, and he followed her in.

Just as he'd expected, signs of a new baby were everywhere—a basket of baby clothes from the laundry. An infant bouncy seat. Toys scattered on a dinosaur blanket on the floor.

"The nursery is this way." Tia picked up a stuffed bear from the couch and hugged it to her as if she needed something in her arms to fill the void of her missing baby.

She led him across the den into a small hallway. A bathroom was situated between two bedrooms.

"Jordie's room is in here."

The moment he stepped inside the nursery, the love Tia had put into decorating the room engulfed him.

"Has anyone been inside the house since Jordie was born?" Ryder asked.

Tia rubbed her temple. "Elle and Ina dropped by and brought dinner and a basket of baby things."

"I spoke with them. They sang your praises." He paused, mentally eliminating them from his suspect list. He needed to look into the two people they'd suggested might hold a grudge against Tia.

"They're both wonderful and are godsends with the women and families who come through. I wish I could afford to pay them more, but they don't seem to mind."

"Who else?"

"A neighbor dropped by to bring me some treats and a gift for Jordie."

"Which neighbor?"

"Judy Kinley, the lady who lives behind me."

Ryder made a mental note to check her out. "Anyone else?"

She scrunched her mouth in thought. "Darren stopped by to drop off the finalized divorce decree."

He bit back a curse. "What a guy."

"I know. I was an idiot to ever believe he cared."

Ryder didn't comment. Men like Darren Hoyt were predators. He saw it all the time.

"I'm going to look around the room and check outside," he said instead.

Hopefully he'd find a clue that the sheriff had missed.

TIA DESPERATELY WANTED a shower, but she felt uncomfortable with the federal agent in the house, so she watched as he combed through the nursery.

"What are you looking for?" she asked.

"Fingerprints. Forensics that would prove someone broke in."

He dusted the crib and the windowsill for prints.

"Did you find anything?"

He shook his head. "Not yet. But the kidnapper could have worn gloves."

Because he'd planned this. But who would do such a thing? Darren was the only one who knew about her inheritance. And he hadn't asked for money. He'd denied knowing anything about the kidnapping, when in private he could have blackmailed her into paying.

Ryder examined the window lock, then knelt to check the floor below, then the wall. He removed a camera from his kit and took a picture.

"What do you see?" she asked.

"Scuff marks. It's not enough to cast, but it might be important."

He examined the lock again. "This definitely wasn't jimmied. Did someone else come in the house that day? Someone who might have unlocked the window without you being aware?"

Tia pressed two fingers to her temple as she mentally retraced her movements that day. "Judy came by and a friend I made at the hospital, my delivery nurse, Amy, stopped in with her little girl. We had coffee. Elle and Ina came later. They dropped off a casserole and saw Jordie for a minute. But none of them would have unlocked the window."

"I asked Elle and Ina about two people on your list, Wanda Hanson and a man, Bennett Jones. They mentioned they might hold a grudge against you."

"They were both angry," Tia said. "But I can't imagine either one of them kidnapping Jordie to get back at me."

"I want to talk to them anyway," Ryder said. "Sometimes people crack and do unexpected things."

She followed him outside to the back of the house, to the nursery window.

"Stay put," he said bluntly. "If there is something here, you don't want to contaminate it."

Tia wrung her hands together and hoped that he found something that would lead them to her baby.

RYDER CIRCLED THE house outside, searching the patches of grass and weeds. An area near the window looked as if the foliage had been mashed—as in footprints.

It could have happened when Gaines conducted his search, although the man obviously hadn't been very thorough. If he had, he would have photographed the window and surrounding area.

He snapped photos of his own, capturing the disturbed bushes and dirt. A partial shoe print was embedded in the ground, which at least suggested someone—a man?—had been outside the room.

That lent credence to Tia's story.

Of course, Gaines could argue that Tia had paid someone to take the baby.

He texted the tech team at the Bureau, instructing them to check Tia's financials for anything suspicious, and also to look into Wanda Hanson and Bennett Jones.

He peered closer and discovered smudges on the wood beneath the window frame. Another partial boot print where the intruder had climbed onto the ledge and slipped through the window. He snapped pictures of the ledge, noting broken splinters around the edge and smudges on the windowpane.

He studied it for a print, but the kidnapper must have worn gloves, as there was no clear print.

Something caught his eye below, wedged into the weeds, and he stooped and combed through the area.

A pack of matches, with a logo for the Big Mug.

He hadn't seen ashtrays or any evidence that Tia was a smoker in her house.

His pulse kicked up. The matches could have belonged to the person who'd taken her son.

Chapter Eight

Still grungy from the jail cell, Tia stepped onto the porch for air. When she'd first bought the house, she'd imagined rocking Jordan out here on cool spring and fall nights, doing artwork with him as he grew older and adding a swing set to the backyard.

She blinked back more tears, then spotted Judy, the neighbor whose house backed up to Tia's, standing on her deck. She was peering at Tia's house through binoculars.

Ryder stepped onto the porch, his phone in hand. "Who's the woman with the binoculars?"

"That's Judy Kinley."

"Tell me about her."

Tia bit her lower lip. "She seems friendly, although she's a little nosy. She works at home doing accounting for a couple of small businesses."

"Married? Kids?"

"No." Tia shook her head. "At first I thought it was comforting to have a neighbor close by, in case of an emergency, one who'd watch out for my property, but she tends to just drop by. I guess she's lonely."

Agent Banks arched a brow. "She comes by a lot?"

Tia shrugged. "A few times. Once she brought cookies and another time a pie. Apparently she likes to bake."

"Did she know your ex?"

"No," Tia said. "I wanted a fresh start, so I moved here after he and I split up."

He nodded. "Is she always peering at the neighbors?"

Tia tucked a strand of hair behind her ear. "She started a community watch program."

"Was she home the night Jordie disappeared?"

"Yes," Tia said. "When I found his crib empty, I called the sheriff. A few minutes after he arrived, Judy rushed over to see what was wrong and what she could do to help."

An odd expression flickered in Ryder's eyes. "I'm going to talk to her. I also want to speak to some of your other neighbors. Maybe one of them saw something."

Although if so, why hadn't he or she come forward?

RYAN CROSSED TIA'S BACKYARD, then strode toward the neighbor's back deck. He waved his identification. "Ma'am, my name is Special Agent Ryder Banks. I'd like to ask you some questions."

She lowered the binoculars and stepped back as if startled. Ryder paused at the bottom of the steps, studying her. She was probably in her early forties, with a face already weathered from too much sun. A few strands of gray hair mingled with the muddy brown, and she wore a drab T-shirt and jeans that hung on her thin frame.

"Tia said your name is Judy. Is that right?"

"Yes. I assume you're investigating the disappearance of her baby."

Ryder nodded. "Yes, ma'am. May I come up and talk to you for a few minutes?"

She clenched the binoculars by her side. "I don't know how I can help, but sure, come on up."

Ryder wasn't buying the innocent act. Anyone who

watched their neighbors through binoculars knew what was going on in the neighborhood.

His footsteps pounded the wooden steps as he climbed them.

"Can I get you some lemonade or tea?" Judy asked.

"No, thanks." He gestured toward Tia's house and saw her watching. "How well do you know Tia Jeffries?"

Judy shrugged and leaned against the deck railing. "We've chatted a few times."

"You were living here when she moved in?"

"No, I moved in after her. My husband passed away and I wanted to downsize."

"Tell me what you know about Tia."

Judy fluttered her fingers through her short hair. "Tia seems like a nice young woman. She was alone, too, so I introduced myself."

"Did you meet her ex-husband?"

Judy pursed her lips. "No, I can't say I wanted to, either. Any man who'd abandon his pregnant wife is pretty low in my book."

He agreed. "Tia said you started a neighborhood watch program. You were also home the night her baby disappeared. Did you notice any strangers lurking around? A car that was out of place?"

She shook her head no. "Although Darren stopped by, Tia said he brought the divorce papers."

"Was she upset about that?"

"No, she seemed relieved it would be final."

Ryder shifted. Darren could have slipped into the nursery and unlocked the window without Tia's knowledge.

"Tell me about the night the baby went missing."

"What do you mean?"

"Tia said she'd fallen asleep and when she woke up and

checked on the baby, he was gone. She called 911, then you came over when you saw the police."

"That's right."

"How was she?" Ryder asked.

"How do you think she was?" Judy said with a bite to her tone. "Someone kidnapped her child. She was hysterical."

"What exactly did she say?"

"She was crying so hard she could barely talk." Judy sighed wearily. "But she said someone had kidnapped Jordan from his bed. I tried to calm Tia while the sheriff searched the house and outside."

"Did Tia say anything else?"

Judy rubbed her forehead. "She just kept begging the sheriff to find her son. He asked about her marriage. She told him about the divorce, then she said she was afraid Darren abducted the infant."

"According to Tia, he left her because she refused to give him money from her charity."

"True." Judy made a low sound in her throat. "But if he took the little boy for money, why hasn't he demanded a ransom?"

Good question. And one Ryder wanted the answer to.

UNABLE TO BEAR the scent of her clothes any longer, Tia stripped and stepped into the shower. The hot water felt wonderful, but as she closed her eyes, images of her little boy taunted her.

"I promise I'll find you," she whispered. "I will bring you home and I'll never let you out of my sight again."

She scrubbed her body three times to cleanse the ugliness of the jail cell, then soaped and rinsed her hair. When she climbed out, she brushed her teeth, pulled on a clean T-shirt and pair of jeans, and dried her hair.

The agent still hadn't returned.

The hole in her heart continued to ache, and she stepped back into the nursery and ran her fingers over the baby quilt she'd hand sewn. Each square featured an appliqué, a hodgepodge of different breeds of puppies. She'd imagined naming the dogs on the quilt with Jordie. And when he was older, they'd visit the animal shelter and choose a dog to adopt.

She'd painted the room a bright blue and his dresser a barnyard red. She opened up one of the drawers and touched the sleepers she'd neatly folded, the tiny bootees and socks, then hugged the little knit cap he'd worn home from the hospital to her chest. She blinked back more tears as she inhaled Jordie's newborn scent.

She had to do something to find her son.

Maybe a personal plea on the news.

She'd talk to that agent when he returned.

If he didn't agree, she'd find a way to do it herself.

RYDER CANVASSED THE NEIGHBORHOOD, but no one had seen or heard anything suspicious the night before or the night of Jordie's disappearance. Several of them hadn't even met Tia, as she'd only moved in a few weeks before.

Two older women claimed they'd seen Tia strolling the baby in the mornings. She'd looked tired but doted on her child.

He walked back to Tia's, frustrated that he hadn't discovered anything helpful.

On a positive note, he hadn't heard anything derogatory about Tia, nothing to make him doubt her story.

He banged the horse door knocker, and Tia opened the door. She'd showered, and her hair looked damp as it hung around her shoulders.

His gut tightened. She was damn gorgeous.

Not something he should be noticing or thinking about.

"Did you learn anything?" Tia asked.

He shook his head. "Afraid not. None of your neighbors seemed suspicious, but I'm going to run background checks on each of them just to be on the safe side. I want to talk to the hospital staff next."

Tia frowned. "Why? Jordie was taken from my house."

"I know. But we have to consider every possibility. Perhaps a stranger or another patient was in the hospital looking at the babies, someone who didn't belong."

Tia's eyes widened. "You mean someone could have been watching Jordie, looking for a chance to take him?"

Ryder shrugged. "Either him or another child. We could be dealing with a desperate, possibly unstable parent. Perhaps someone who lost a child or couldn't have a baby was depressed, desperate. He or she could have scouted out the nursery. It's happened before."

Tia shivered.

Ryder couldn't resist. He gently took her arms in his hands and forced her to face him. "If someone took him because they wanted a family, that means Jordie will be well taken care of, that he or she will keep him safe."

Tia released a pent-up breath, then gave a little nod. "I want to appear on television and make a plea for whoever took Jordie to return him to me."

Ryder hesitated. "That could work, but it could backfire, Tia. Sometimes going to the media draws out the crazies and we waste time on false leads."

Her eyes glittered with emotions. "Maybe. But if the person who abducted Jordie wants a family like you suggested, seeing how much I love and miss my baby might make them rethink what they've done and bring him back."

He couldn't argue with that.

"Please, Agent Banks," she whispered. "I have to do everything I can to find him."

Ryder inhaled. "All right, I'll set it up."

"For today," Tia said. "I want to do it right away."

"All right, but call me Ryder." After all, they were going to be spending a lot of time together—as much as it took until they recovered her son.

"All right, Ryder," she said, her soft voice filled with conviction. "I want to speak to the press as soon as possible."

Ryder nodded then stepped aside to make the call.

Tia's heart raced as Ryder returned, his phone in hand. "Did you set it up?"

"Yes. At six. They'll air it on the evening news."

"Good. That will give us time to go to the hospital."

Ryder agreed and they hurried to his SUV. Ten minutes later, she led the way to the hospital maternity floor. The nurses at the nurses' station looked surprised to see Tia, their nervous whispers making her wonder what they thought.

Hilda, the head charge nurse, hurried around the desk edge and swept her into a hug. "Oh, my God, Tia. I'm so sorry about the kidnapping. Did the police find Jordie?"

Tia shook her head no and introduced Ryder. "Agent Banks is looking for him."

"I need to talk to each of the staff members who were on duty the night Tia delivered."

Hilda looked eager to help. "All right, I'll get a list and text them."

"Also, I need to know if anyone suspicious has been lurking around the nursery area and this ward."

"Not that I know of," Hilda said. "But I'll ask around."

"Do you have security cameras on this floor?"

"Absolutely," Hilda said. "We take our patients' and their children's safety very seriously."

"Good. I want to review all the tapes the week prior to Jordie's disappearance as well as the week he was born."

Hilda nodded, then stepped to the desk to set things up.

Tia held her breath. If Ryder was right, maybe the person who'd taken her son was on one of those tapes.

Chapter Nine

Tia hurried toward the nurse who'd coached her during labor. Amy spoke to her, then Tia introduced Ryder.

"This is Special Agent Ryder Banks," Tia said. "He's helping me search for my son."

Ryder flashed his credentials. "I'm talking to all the staff," he said. "You were here the night Tia delivered her son?"

Amy nodded. "I worked night shift that week."

Tia offered her a smile of gratitude. "Amy was my labor coach. I couldn't have done it without her."

Amy shrugged. "You did the hard work, Tia." Her voice cracked. "I'm just sorry for what's happened."

Tia swallowed the fear eating at her. "I'm going on television to make a plea to get Jordie back."

Amy squeezed her hand. "I hope that helps."

Ryder cleared his throat. "Amy, have you noticed anyone lurking around the maternity floor? Maybe someone near the nursery?"

Amy fidgeted with the pocket of her uniform. "Not really."

"How about a patient who lost a child?" Cash's story about the McCullens echoed in his head. "A grieving mother might be desperate enough to take someone else's child to fill the void of her own loss."

Amy squeezed Tia's hand again. "That's true. But I can't discuss other patients' medical charts or history."

"You don't have to. Just tell me if there's someone who fits that description."

Amy worried her bottom lip with her teeth. "There was one woman who suffered from complications and delivered prematurely, only twenty weeks."

Tia's heart ached for her. "That must have been devastating."

Amy nodded. "She and her husband were in the middle of a divorce, so she blamed him. She thought the stress triggered her premature labor."

Hilda returned and motioned for them to join her at the desk. "The security guard is waiting whenever you want to take a look at those tapes."

"Thanks." Ryder turned back to Amy. "Why don't you watch the tapes with us? If you see anyone you think is suspicious, you can point them out."

Amy and Hilda exchanged concerned looks, then Amy followed them to the security office. They passed a nurse named Richard who grunted hello.

Amy exchanged a smile with him and introduced Ryder. "I'm canvassing the staff to see if anyone saw or heard anything strange when Miss Jeffries was here."

"I didn't see anyone suspicious." Richard gave Tia a sympathetic look. "I'm sorry about your baby, Miss Jeffries."

Tia murmured thanks, then Richard had to go to the ER.

Hilda led them into the security room, and she, Ryder and Amy gathered to view the tapes.

When the guard zeroed in on the camera feed showing her at admissions, Tia's heart gave a painful tug. That night she'd been so excited. After nine months of carrying her baby inside her, of feeling his little feet and fists push at her belly, of listening to his heartbeat during the ultra-sounds and imagining what he might look like, her son was going to be born.

She was going to have a family of her own.

He had cried the moment he'd come out, a beautiful sound that had brought tears to her eyes. He had a cap of light blond hair, blue eyes and tiny pink fingers that had grasped her finger when she'd caressed him to her breast.

But now he was gone.

RYDER PARKED HIMSELF in front of the security feed, anxious to find a lead. Amy certainly seemed to care about Tia and wanted to be helpful.

Tia's breath rattled out with nerves as she sank into the chair beside him. One camera shot captured her entering the ER—apparently she'd driven herself. She held her bulging belly with one hand, breathing deeply, as she handled the paperwork.

Although her hair was pulled back in a ponytail and she was obviously in pain, she looked…happy. Glowing with the kind of joy an expectant mother should be feeling.

All his life, he'd thought his birth mother had sold him. But if Cash was telling the truth, she hadn't done any such thing.

She died trying to find us.

Cash had insisted that was the truth.

Had his biological mother felt that anticipation over giving birth to him and Cash, only to be grief stricken when she was told her twins were stillborn?

His lungs squeezed for air. How she must have suffered.

Tia was wheeled into a triage room, then a delivery room, where they lost sight of her.

"Let's look at the hallways near the nursery the week before—"

"Go back to the day he was born," Amy suggested quietly.

That must have been around the time when the other woman lost her baby.

The next half hour they studied each section of the tape, zeroing in on parents and grandparents and friends who'd visited—most of whom looked elated as they oohed and aahed over the infants in the nursery.

Couples came and went, huddling together, smiling, laughing and crying as they watched the newborns.

Emotions churned in Ryder's belly. He'd never imagined having a family of his own—a wife, kids. Not in the picture. Not with the job he did.

A long empty space of tape, then another crew of family members appeared, gushing and waving through the glass window.

Just as they left, a young woman emerged from the shadows, her thin face haggard and lined with fatigue. She was hunched inside an oversize raincoat, her hair pulled back beneath a scarf, her face a picture of agony as she studied the infants. The nurse, Richard Blotter, paused as he passed, his gaze narrowed.

"There's Jordie," Tia said in a raw whisper.

The woman hesitated as she walked along the window, eyeing the pink and blue bundles. She paused in front of Jordie's bassinet.

Tia straightened, her body tensing as she leaned forward to home in on the woman's face.

"She's looking at Jordie," she said in a low voice.

Yes, she was.

Richard passed the nursery, but the woman hurried away.

Ryder swung his gaze toward Amy, but she quickly glanced toward the floor, avoiding eye contact as she bit her lower lip.

"Do you know who this woman is?" Ryder asked.

"I don't remember her name," Amy said, "but she's the woman I mentioned who lost her baby."

"I need a copy of this tape," he told the security guard.

The tech team could work wonders with facial recognition software. He'd also get a warrant for medical records and find out her name.

She might be the person who'd stolen Tia's child.

TIA CONSTANTLY CHECKED the clock as Ryder questioned other staff members. Hilda discreetly ran a check for any patients who'd required mental health services.

As they left the hospital, Ryder drove to the county crime lab and dropped off the partial print and matches he'd found outside the nursery along with the tapes for analysis. He wanted the ID of the woman who'd been watching those babies.

He received a text from the FBI analyst as they walked back to his SUV. "One of our analysts located Bennett Jones."

"Where is he?"

"Jones remarried and moved to Texas. Been there four months. His first wife claims he's made no move to see their baby since he met the other woman."

Tia gritted her teeth. "That's not uncommon. He was angry when she left, had a bruised ego, but he quickly replaced his family with another one."

Ryder grunted a sound of disapproval. "I also have an address for the woman, Wanda Hanson. She entered a rehab program after her husband gained custody of their infant."

"Where is she now?"

"A few miles outside Pistol Whip." He started the engine and pulled onto the highway. Tia contemplated the woman in the security tape as he drove. Sympathy for her situation and her loss filled Tia. If she'd taken Jordie, hopefully he was in good hands.

But Jordie belonged to her. *With* her.

And she would do whatever necessary to bring him home.

The sun dipped behind a sea of dark clouds, painting the sky a dismal gray. The farmland looked desolate, with dry scrub brush dotting the landscape, the ground thirsty for water.

Ryder drove down a narrow two-lane road past a cluster of small, older homes that needed serious upkeep. A few toys and bicycles were scattered around, the yards overgrown and full of weeds.

He checked his phone for the address, then turned in the drive of a redbrick ranch. Anxious to see if Wanda had her son, Tia slipped from the vehicle and started up the drive. Ryder caught her before she made it to the front door.

"Let me handle this," Ryder said in a gruff voice.

"She hates me, Ryder. If she took Jordie, the minute she sees me, she'll know the reason I'm here."

And Tia would know by the look on Wanda's face if she was guilty.

RYDER PUNCHED THE DOORBELL, his gaze scanning the property for any sign Wanda was home, but there was no car in the drive. It was impossible to see in the tiny windowless garage.

Tia stepped slightly to the right and peered through the front window. From his vantage point, the house looked dark.

"Do you see anything? Any movement?" he asked.

"No one in the kitchen or den."

He rang the bell again, then banged on the door. Seconds passed with no response. He jiggled the doorknob, but it was locked.

"I'm going to check around the side and back."

He veered to the left and Tia followed.

"You're sure this is her place?" Tia asked.

"Yes, our analyst, Gwen, is good at her job. Apparently Wanda had no money for rent or to buy a house. This place belonged to her mother, who passed away last year. She's been living here since the custody hearing."

He passed the side window. No lights inside. The curtains hung askew, clothes scattered around the room. Dry leaves crunched as they inched to the back door. He jiggled the door but it was locked.

Dammit, he wanted to search the interior. He removed a tiny tool from his pocket just as Tia did the same.

"I've got it," he said, remembering the way they'd met. "Don't touch anything, Tia. If we find evidence, I don't want it thrown out because you were present."

"Don't you need a warrant?" Her brows furrowed at the unpleasant reminder, and she jammed the tool back in her pocket.

Hell, he was breaking the rules. "Technically, yes. But it's acceptable if I have probable cause. I can always say we heard a noise and thought the baby was inside."

Ryder yanked on latex gloves, opened the door, flipped on the overhead light and called out, "FBI Special Agent Banks. Is anyone here?"

Silence echoed back. Then Ryder stepped into the tiny kitchen. Outdated appliances, linoleum and a rickety table made the room look fifty years old. A dirty coffee cup sat in the sink along with a plate of dried, molded food. The garbage reeked as if it hadn't been taken out in days.

Ryder opened the refrigerator, and Tia spotted a carton of milk, eggs, condiments and a jar of applesauce.

On the second shelf sat two baby bottles, half full of formula.

Her pulse jumped. Why would Wanda have baby formula and bottles when there were no kids in the house?

Her child was a toddler, too, not a baby, so why the bottle?

Ryder crossed the room into the den and flipped on a lamp. The soft light illuminated the room just enough for her to see that Wanda wasn't a housekeeper.

Magazines, dirty laundry and mail were spread across the couch and table. A worn teddy bear had been stuffed in the corner along with an infant's receiving blanket.

Tia followed Ryder into the hall. The first bedroom had been turned into a nursery. Tia scanned the room, her heart racing at the sight of a tiny bassinet.

Wanda's baby had long ago outgrown it, but a receiving blanket lay inside, along with an elephant-shaped blue rattle.

A baby had been here recently. Was it Jordie?

Ryder paused to look at it, then walked over to the changing table and lifted the lid on the diaper pail.

"Was Wanda allowed visitation rights?" Tia asked.

He shrugged, then made a quick phone call and identified himself. "Mr. Hanson, was your wife allowed visitation rights to your child?"

Tia held her breath while she waited for the answer.

"No. Hmm," Ryder mumbled. Another pause. "When did you last see her or speak with her?"

Silence stretched for a full minute. Ryder thanked the man then his gaze darkened.

"He hasn't heard from her. Said she hasn't seen the kid, but he's safe with him. The last time he talked to her, she'd fallen off the wagon and screamed at him that she hadn't deserved to lose her little boy."

Tia trembled. Wanda blamed her, not her drug addiction.

Ryder opened the dresser drawer—several baby outfits, all for newborn three-month-old boys. He hurried to the next bedroom while she stood stunned at the sight of the clothes.

Ryder's gruff voice made her stomach clench. "It looks as if her suitcase is gone and her clothes have been cleaned out, like she left in a hurry."

Tia gripped the edge of the baby bed. Had Wanda abducted Jordie and gone on the run?

Chapter Ten

Fear paralyzed Tia. "Look at these clothes and baby things," she said to Ryder. "If Wanda has Jordie, with the border less than a day's drive away, she might have taken him out of the country."

Ryder snatched his phone from the belt at his waist. "I'm going to issue a BOLO for her. Do you know what kind of car she drives?"

Tia searched her memory banks. "She used to drive a black Honda, but that's been over a year or so."

"I'll have Gwen check her out. Look through that basket on the kitchen counter. See if you find a pay stub or anything else that might indicate where she's going."

He riffled through the desk in the corner as he phoned the Bureau.

She focused on the basket. Piles of overdue bills, a lottery ticket, a speeding ticket that hadn't been paid, a letter from the rehab center asking her to call her counselor.

A manila envelope lay beside the basket. Tia opened it as Ryder stepped back into the room. She sighed at the legal document granting custody of Wanda's child to her husband.

She dug deeper and discovered a pack of matches.

Her heart thumped wildly. The logo on the outside read the Big Mug.

The same logo was on the matches Ryder had found in the bushes outside her baby's nursery. "Look at these."

"We need to stop by that bar," Ryder said. "I sent those other matches to the lab for prints. I'll do the same with these and see if they have the same prints."

Hope flared in Tia's chest. "If the prints match, that means Wanda took Jordie."

"Don't jump the gun," Ryder said. "Let's canvass the neighbors and see if anyone noticed Wanda acting strangely or if they saw her with an infant."

He gestured to the laundry basket. "Look through those clothes and the laundry and see if any of the baby things are familiar. What was Jordie wearing the night he was abducted?"

The memory of that baby sleeper haunted her. "A light blue sleeper with an appliqué of a wagon and horse." She rushed toward the laundry piled on the couch.

An assortment of receiving blankets, caps, outfits, bootees and...a sleeper. She quickly examined it. No appliqué of a wagon and horse—a teddy bear instead. She frantically searched the rest of the laundry, but the sleeper wasn't there.

Relief mingled with worry. She didn't want to think that Wanda had taken Jordie because she was angry. If the woman was drinking or taking pills again, she might have an accident or hurt him.

No. She had to remain optimistic. She closed her eyes and said a silent prayer that Jordie was safe.

Ryder touched her elbow. "Gwen is alerting airports, train stations and bus stations to watch for Wanda. She's sent photos of Jordie and Wanda nationwide. If they try to get out of the country, we'll stop them."

"I hope so," Tia said.

Ryder took another look through the house while she checked the chest in the nursery.

Ten minutes later, they walked to the neighbor's house next door. A tiny gray-haired woman opened the door, leaning on a cane.

Ryder identified himself, flashed his credentials, then explained the reason for their visit.

"I'm Myrtle." The little woman gave Tia a sympathetic smile. "I'm sorry about your baby, miss. People coming in your house and stealing your children—I don't know what the world is coming to. It's just plain awful."

Ryder cleared his throat. "When did you last see your neighbor Wanda?"

"About three days ago," Myrtle said.

"You mean Wednesday?" Ryder asked.

Myrtle nodded. "Early that morning, I saw her carrying some kind of bundle out to the car. Then she sped away."

Tia's lungs squeezed for air. Tuesday night was when Jordie disappeared.

RYDER AND TIA spent the next half hour questioning other neighbors. They met a young woman strolling twin toddlers into the driveway across the street. Tia gushed over the children, a boy and girl, who looked to be about a year and a half old.

Ryder made the introductions.

"I'm Dannika," the young woman said. "I'm not sure how I can help."

"Tell us about your neighbor Wanda," Ryder began.

Dannika claimed Wanda liked to entertain late at night, and that she'd seen several men come and go over the last month but had never been introduced to any of them. One drove a black Range Rover and another a dented white pickup. She made sure her children stayed in the fenced backyard instead of wondering to the front because she was worried about Wanda's driving.

Tia's face blanched at that statement.

Ryder didn't like the picture this neighbor was painting. "She was driving while intoxicated?"

"It appeared that way," the young woman said. "She was reckless, weaving all over the road. One night she smashed her own mailbox."

Tia wiped perspiration from her forehead. "Did she have family around?"

"Not that I know of."

"Did you see her with a baby?" Ryder asked.

The woman took a sip of her bottled water. "No, although sometime Wednesday afternoon, she was carrying a bundle to the car. It could have been a baby wrapped up in a blanket."

Ryder's jaw hardened, but he worked to maintain a neutral expression. So if she'd left early that morning, she might have returned for some reason. "Was anyone with her that day?"

"No. But an SUV was parked in the drive that morning."

"What kind?"

She rubbed her forehead. "Black. I think it was a 4Runner."

"Did you see the driver?"

She shook her head. "I'm afraid not. I didn't think much of it at the time."

Ryder handed her a business card. "If you think of anything else that might help, please give me a call."

She accepted the card with a nod then knelt to console the little girl who'd woken from her nap and started to fuss.

Tia looked longingly at the toddlers as they said goodbye and walked to the next house.

A teenage boy answered the door wearing a rock band T-shirt, his arms covered in tattoos, a cigarette dangling from the corner of his mouth. His eyes looked bloodshot. "Yeah?"

"Are your parents home?" Ryder asked.

The kid's fingers curled around the door edge as if he might slam it in their face—or run. "No."

"Where are they?"

"Daddy lit out when I was three. Mama's working at the dry cleaner's down the street." He shoved his hand in his back pocket and shifted nervously. "Why?"

"I need to talk to them."

Panic streaked the teen's eyes when Ryder flashed his badge. "Look, man, I ain't done nothing."

Ryder chuckled sarcastically. "I don't care if you're smoking weed or have drugs here at the moment, buddy. We're looking for a kidnapped baby."

The teen cursed. "I didn't steal any kid."

"It was my baby," Tia said quickly. "And we don't think you took him. But the woman next door, Wanda, might have."

"Have you seen her around?" Ryder asked.

The boy tugged at the ripped end of his T-shirt. "Not today."

"Did you see her with a baby?" Tia asked.

"Naw." He shot a quick glance down the street.

"What's going on down there?" Ryder asked.

The boy looked down at his shoes. "That's where she gets her stash."

"Her dealer lives on the street?" Ryder asked.

The boy shrugged.

"Is he your supplier?" Ryder asked.

"No, hell, no." Fear darkened his face. "And don't tell him I said anything. I don't want him coming after me."

Ryder grimaced. "Don't worry, I won't mention you. I'll tell him we're talking to all the neighbors, which is true."

Relief softened the wariness in the teen's eyes.

Ryder pushed his card into the boy's hand. "Call me if you see Wanda come back, or if you think of anything that could help."

The boy nodded, his eyes darting down the street again.

Ryder turned to leave, his gaze scanning the area in case someone was watching.

PURE PANIC SEIZED TIA. "Oh, my God," Tia said as the young man closed the door in their faces. "What if Wanda is high and driving around with Jordie? She might have an accident or lose her temper—"

"Shh, don't go there," he said softly. Ryder gripped Tia's arms and forced her to look at him. "We don't know that she took Jordie."

"But what if she did?" Tia cried. "I've heard of desperate addicts actually selling their children or trading them for their fix."

"I know it's difficult not to imagine the worst," Ryder said, "but we need to focus. We still have a lot of possibilities to explore. The woman in the security footage at the hospital, for one."

Tia inhaled a deep breath. "All right. What do we do next?"

"I'm going to talk to the drug dealer," Ryder said. "You need to wait in the car."

"But I want to hear what he has to say."

Ryder's jaw tightened. "It's too dangerous. We have no idea if he's armed or if there are thugs working with him."

He walked her back to his SUV.

"Be careful," Tia said as he started down the sidewalk toward the drug dealer's house.

She accessed the pictures on her phone and studied each

one she'd taken of Jordie while she waited. Although she didn't need to look at them—she'd already memorized each detail.

RYDER SCRUTINIZED THE yard and house as he approached. The windows were covered with black-out curtains, the window in the garage covered as well.

Could be a sign that the man who lived inside had something to hide.

He raised his fist to knock, his instincts on alert. The yard was unkempt, and a black sedan with tinted windows sat in the drive. He banged his fist on the door, one hand sliding inside his jacket, ready to draw his weapon if needed.

Inside, a voice shouted something, then footsteps pounded.

Ryder knocked again, and the voice he'd heard called out, "Coming."

Ryder glanced to the side of house, looking for signs of a meth lab—or a runner.

The door squeaked open, and gray eyes peered back, a twentysomething male with a head of shaggy hair glaring at him. "Yeah?"

Ryder flashed his credentials and was rewarded by a panicked look from the guy. "I'm canvassing the neighbors to see if anyone has seen Wanda Hanson, who lives in that house." He pointed to the run-down ranch they'd come from.

"Listen, man, I don't know many of the neighbors," the guy said. "We don't exactly have cul-de-sac parties around here."

No, but maybe crack parties. "But you may have seen the news about a missing infant, a six-week-old boy named Jordie Jeffries?"

"Do I look like I've got a kid in here?" the guy said, belligerence edging his tone.

Suddenly a movement to the right caught Ryder's eye, then the door slammed shut in his face.

A second guy exited a side door and darted to a truck parked at the curb.

Ryder pulled his gun from his holster and shouted for him to stop. But the man he'd been talking to at the door ran out the side after the truck.

Suddenly Tia bolted from the SUV and dashed toward the truck.

He yelled for her to go back, but a shot rang out, the bullet zinging toward Tia.

Chapter Eleven

Ryder grabbed Tia and wrapped his arms around her, then threw her to the ground, using his body as a shield to protect her as they dodged another bullet.

Tia screamed and clutched his back as he rolled them toward the bushes.

"Stay down," he growled in her ear.

She nodded against his chest, and he lifted his head and peered up at the truck. Another bullet flew toward them.

He motioned for Tia to keep cover in the bushes as he drew his gun and fired at the driver. He missed and the man jumped in the truck.

Ryder pushed to his knees and inched forward, gun at the ready. The engine fired up. Tires squealed as the driver accelerated and pulled from the curb. Ryder jogged forward and shot at the tires, memorizing the tag as the truck sped down the road.

He turned and saw Tia running toward him. Dammit. "I told you to stay down."

"They're getting away," Tia cried.

Ryder stowed his gun in his holster and coaxed Tia back to his SUV. She sank into the passenger seat, and he phoned his superior and explained the situation, then gave him the license plate and the address of the house. "Get an APB out on this truck. I also need a warrant to search his place."

"You got it. I'll contact the local sheriff and have him bring the warrant."

Ryder bit the inside of his cheek. He didn't particularly want Sheriff Gaines in the middle of this, but excluding him would cause more trouble. Pissing off the man in his own jurisdiction could work against him.

Connor transferred him to the tech analyst Gwen.

Ryder gave her the home address. "Tell me what you find on the man who lives here."

Tia tucked a strand of hair behind her ear, her hand trembling. He tilted her chin up with his thumb. "You okay?"

She nodded, expression earnest as they waited.

Seconds later, Gwen came back on the phone. "House is owned by a couple in Texas. They've been renting it for the last year to a twenty-five-year-old student named Neil Blount. But…" She hesitated and Ryder thumped his boot on the ground.

"Arrest record?"

"A couple of misdemeanors for possession. Looks like he dropped out of college."

"Job history?"

"Nothing substantial. He worked at a couple of hamburger joints. Last job was at a bar called the Big Mug."

Ryder hissed. The matches outside Tia's place had come from that bar. "Find out everything you can on that bar, its owner and history. They could be running drugs out of there."

TIA WATCHED AS Ryder and the sheriff entered Neil Blount's house. If Jordie had been with those men at any time, what had they done with him?

Her phone buzzed, the caller display box reading Crossroads.

It was Elle. "Hey, Tia, I just called to see how things are going."

Tia relayed what had happened. "At this point, I don't know if Wanda or this man had anything to do with Jordie's disappearance, but Ryder is looking into them. What's happening at Crossroads? Do you need me to come in?" Tia asked.

"No, everything is going smoothly," Elle assured her. "The new family has settled in. I already set up a job interview for the mother. She seems anxious to accept our help so she can get back on her feet."

"Good. That's half the battle," Tia murmured. Sometimes families resisted accepting help or, in some instances, emotional issues and addictions kept them from following through on good intentions.

"I'm saying a prayer for you," Elle said. "I know you're going to find him, Tia. I just know it."

Tia wished she felt as optimistic.

"Call me if you hear something."

Tia thanked her and disconnected just as Ryder exited the house. She rushed toward him. "Any sign of Jordie?"

He shook his head. "No. We did find drugs, enough to indicate Blount is into dealing big-time. Sheriff Gaines agreed to get his deputy to work with one of the DEA's special agents to see just how big his operation is."

"Where is my baby, Ryder?" Tia said in a hoarse whisper.

Ryder wanted to console her, but he couldn't lie to her. "I found a laptop and am sending it to the lab for analysis. If there's any mention of a kidnapping or possible child-stealing ring, they'll find it."

Tia nodded, although anxiety knotted her shoulders. A child-stealing ring? God…that could mean that whoever had taken Jordie might have sold him to a stranger.

That stranger could be halfway across the world with her son by now.

RYDER HATED CHASING false leads, and Blount and Wanda both might be dead ends. Although at this point, he had no other clues. "We have time before the interview," Ryder said as he and Tia got in his SUV. "I want to go by the Big Mug on the way."

Tia twined her hands in her lap, twisting them in a nervous gesture. "What if they're long gone? Maybe in Mexico or Europe or Brazil?"

Ryder covered her hand with his to calm her. Her fingers felt cold, stiff, her anxiety palpable. "That would mean passports, flight plans. We didn't find anything in Wanda's house to indicate she'd made arrangements to leave the country. And with the Amber Alert and airport, train and bus stations on guard, someone would have seen them."

"Not necessarily," Tia argued. "A woman cuddling a baby wouldn't arouse suspicion."

"No, but authorities will be watching for anyone behaving suspiciously. Also, to travel with an infant, you have to provide a birth certificate."

Ryder started the engine and pulled onto the road, heading toward the Big Mug.

"Can't people fake birth certificates?" Tia asked.

Ryder veered around a curve, staying right when the road forked. It definitely had happened, especially with criminals who stole children as a business. But he didn't want to panic Tia any more than she already was.

"It's difficult, but it can be done," Ryder said. "Knowing there's an Amber Alert for an infant, security personnel and authorities will scrutinize documents carefully." At least he hoped they would.

A slacker could miss crucial signs on faked documents, though. Worse, if the kidnapper was smart, he or she might have altered the baby's name, birth date and even his sex.

People were looking for a baby boy. They might not take a second look at an infant swaddled in pink.

Tia lapsed into a strained silence while they drove, the deserted land stretching before them a reminder that a kidnapper could have vanished somewhere in the Wyoming wilderness and stay hidden until the hype surrounding the baby's disappearance died down.

Then he or she would try to make a hasty escape.

They had to find Jordie before that happened.

The gray clouds overhead darkened, casting a dismal feel as they ventured into the outskirts of town. The Big Mug sat off the country road next to a rustic-looking barbecue place called the Tasty Pig, a place Ryder had heard had the best barbecue this side of Cheyenne. His mouth watered at the thought, but one peek at Tia told him that food wasn't on her mind.

All she wanted was to find her baby. He didn't have time to feed his stomach when she was hurting and Jordie's kidnapper might be getting farther and farther away.

He parked in the graveled lot. Pickup trucks, SUVs and a few sedans filled the lot. Country music blared from the bar, smoke curling outside as they walked up to the door. A few patrons huddled by the fire pit on the rustic planked porch to the side, a gathering spot for smokers and people wanting to escape the loud music inside.

"I know Wanda had addiction problems, but I can't see her hanging out here," Tia said beneath the beat of the music as they walked to the entrance.

"But it would be a good spot for drug exchanges," Ryder pointed out. "She slips in, orders a drink and leaves with a small package in her purse."

Tia nodded. "I feel for her little boy. I kept hoping she'd get her act together, for his sake."

"Addiction changes people," Ryder said in a gruff voice. "They lose perspective."

"That's true," Tia said softly. Sadness clouded her eyes. "After my folks died, I was prescribed antidepressants, but I didn't like taking them and quickly stopped. I always thought that if I had a child and took care of him, my child would grow up healthy and happy. But...I failed him in the worst way."

Ryder's gut clenched. "This was not your fault, Tia."

He pulled her up against him. Her labored breathing puffed against his neck as he rubbed one hand up and down her back to soothe her.

"Let's just focus on finding your baby," Ryder said in a low voice. "Hang in there, okay?"

She didn't move for a second, but he felt her relax slightly against him.

He was not going to disappoint her or her baby. Jordie deserved to know his real mother, that she loved him.

The sentiment resurrected the memory of his twin brother's visit. Cash had insisted their mother loved them.

He pinched the bridge of his nose. He didn't want to think or believe that his mother, Myra, had willingly accepted a stolen child.

If she had, she'd lied to him. And if that was true, he didn't know if he could ever forgive that.

TIA BRACED HERSELF for the bar scene. She had to be tough. Not fall apart in Ryder's arms.

It would feel so good if she could lean on him, though.

But leaning on a man wasn't an option.

Especially this man—he had handcuffed her and hauled her to jail.

"You can go back to the car," Ryder said. "I'll handle this."

Tia wasn't a cop or federal agent, but the bar patrons hanging around outside in the parking lot didn't incite a safe feeling. She was surprised there were so many here, too. Judging from the motorcycles, there must be a biker rally nearby.

"This is a seedy-looking crowd," Tia pointed out. "I'd feel better going in with you."

A tense heartbeat passed. For a moment, he looked around, sizing up the situation. When he settled his dark gaze on her, admiration for her mingled with concern in his eyes. "You're right, but keep a low profile. Don't forget that we were shot at earlier."

Tia shivered. "How could I forget?"

Guilt flashed on his face. He didn't have to remind her about their close call. She knew their search was dangerous.

That whoever had taken Jordie didn't want to be found. That he or she would kill to get away.

But she didn't care.

Being close to Ryder Banks was dangerous in another way.

Tia steeled herself against letting her guard down around him, though. He was a tough federal agent. He seemed intent on doing his job.

And he was sexy and strong—just the kind of man a woman wanted to lean on.

She'd seen enough women fall into that trap and come through Crossroads, broken and desperate and in need of help.

She would never forget the lessons she'd learned.

"Just stay beside me," he growled as they went inside.

Tia put on a brave face.

She'd keep her eyes open and her senses alert. Maybe someone in the bar knew who had her son.

Chapter Twelve

Ryder tucked Tia close by his side and visually scoped out the bar as he entered. Protective instincts kicked in, and he looked for male predators, drunks on the watch for a one-night pickup who might target Tia, possible drug dealers or patrons who were high or looking to cut a deal.

Then Wanda.

He didn't know the woman, but this establishment definitely boasted a rough crowd. Booze, conversation, flirting, boot-scooting music and hookups driven by beer and drugs created a chaotic atmosphere. No women with children inside and no couples with an infant.

He kept one hand on Tia's lower back and guided her toward the bar. Two stools on the end opened up as a couple took to the dance floor, and he led her to it, then sank onto one of the stools.

The bartender, a cowboy with an eye for the ladies, slid two napkins in front of them. "What'll you have?"

They weren't here to drink, but he wanted to fit in. "Whatever you have on draft." He slanted his gaze toward Tia with an eyebrow raise.

"The same." She plucked a matchbook from the basket on the counter and rotated it between her fingers.

A robust guy wearing a bolo tie approached to her right,

his short-cropped hair making his cheeks look puffy. He raked a gaze over Tia, then frowned and walked on past.

"Do you know that guy?" Ryder asked.

Tia studied him as she accepted her beer. "No. Why?"

"Just wondering." Something about the way the man had looked at Tia raised questions in Ryder's mind. Had he been simply assessing her to determine if she was single or if she was with him?

Or did he know who she was?

He took a sip of his beer, removed his phone and accessed a picture of Wanda, then laid the phone on the counter. He motioned for the bartender. "Do you know this woman?"

The bartender pulled at his chin as he glanced at it. "Seen her in a couple of times, but I don't really know her."

"Was she with anyone?" Ryder asked.

The bartender wiped the counter with a rag. "Not really."

Ryder had to push. "Was she here to score some drugs?"

The bartender leaned closer, lowering his voice. "Listen, man, I don't know what you've heard, but this is a legitimate place."

"I'm not concerned about the drugs." Ryder eased his credentials from his pocket and discreetly showed them to the man. Then he flicked a finger toward Tia. "This woman's baby is missing. I'm looking for a lead on the kidnapper."

Unease darkened the guy's face. "I don't know anything about a kidnapping."

Tia touched the man's hand, her eyes imploring. "Please think. Wanda may have taken my son. He's only a few weeks old and he needs me."

The man gestured for them to wait, took two young women's orders, gave them their drinks, then returned with the bill.

He slid the check in front of Ryder as if dismissing them. But he'd scribbled a name at the bottom of the bill—Bubba.

"He holes up in an old shack behind the bar," the bartender murmured.

"He took my baby?" Tia asked.

The guy shook his head. "No, but if anything was going on with Wanda, he'd know."

Ryder tossed some cash on the bill to pay for their drinks, then shoved back. The big guy who'd been watching Tia stood by the door as they left, his scowl so intense that Ryder hesitated.

But the moment he returned the man's lethal stare, he jammed his beefy hands in the pockets of his jacket and lumbered out the door.

Ryder stepped outside with Tia, his senses alert as he scanned the parking lot. The tip of a cigarette glowed against the dark night. The big guy folded himself inside a jacked-up black pickup, then sped off.

"Who was he?" Tia asked.

"No idea," Ryder replied. "He was watching you inside, though."

Tia shivered. "If Wanda wanted her son back, coming to this bar wasn't the way to do it."

"She made her choices," Ryder said. He just wondered if taking Jordie was one of them. Ryder took Tia's arm again. "The bartender said Bubba lives back here. Let's find that shack."

She fell into step beside him as they wove down the dark alley. The scents of garbage, smoke and urine filled the air, and Ryder led her past a homeless man sleeping in a cardboard box, which he'd propped behind a metal staircase.

Tia paused, her look sympathetic as if she wanted to offer the man assistance, but Ryder ushered her on. Ryder spotted the shack the bartender had referenced, a weathered structure with mud-and-dirt-coated windows.

Not knowing what to expect, he coaxed Tia behind him, removed his gun and held it by his side as he knocked.

A second later, a sound jarred him. Another popping sound, then an explosion.

He grabbed Tia and dragged her away from the building as the glass windows shattered and fire burst through the rotting wooden door.

TIA SCREAMED, DUCKING to avoid flying debris and glass as Ryder pushed her beneath the awning of a neighboring building. He covered her head with his arms and held her, his warmth and strength suffusing her as wood splintered and popped and glass pellets pinged around them.

She heaved for a breath, trembling as they waited for the worst to die down. Finally the force of the explosion settled, but fire blazed behind them, heat searing her.

Ryder breathed against her neck. "You okay?"

She nodded and turned in his arms to face him. He was mere inches away, his gruff expression riddled with anger and worry.

He felt so solid and strong against her, the weight of his body like a wall protecting her. His gaze raked over her face, then dropped to her eyes. A flicker of something masculine darkened his expression, causing a flutter in her belly that had nothing to do with the fact that they could have died in that explosion.

And everything to do with the fact that Ryder was the sexiest man she'd ever laid eyes on. "What happened?" she asked, her voice cracking with emotion.

His chest rose and fell against hers as he inhaled a deep

breath. "Someone warned Bubba we were coming." Ryder rubbed her arms and lifted his body away from her. "My guess is that he was destroying evidence."

"It was a meth lab?" Tia guessed.

"That's what I'm thinking." He pulled away, retrieved his phone, called for backup and a crime team.

Seconds later, a siren rent the air.

"What if Jordie was in there?" Tia said, panic flaring in her eyes.

"There's no reason to think that." Ryder squeezed her arm. "We'll search the house, but meth dealers generally stick to the drug business."

Still, fear paralyzed Tia as she looked back at the burning building.

THE NEXT TWO hours passed in a blur of law enforcement officers, rescue workers, firemen and DEA agents. The area was cleared due to fumes from the meth lab, forcing Ryder to get Tia away from the scene.

Thankfully the search indicated that no child or baby had been inside. In fact, no one, adult or otherwise, was inside when the building blew. The theory was that Bubba lit up the place to destroy evidence and any links to himself. Ryder was turning the case over to the DEA.

He had more important work to do.

His phone buzzed as he and Tia drove away from the chaotic scene. "Agent Banks."

"Ryder, we have info on Wanda Hanson," Gwen said. "A cashier at a convenience store called in that she stopped for gas, and confirmed she had a baby with her. No word if it's a boy or girl or the age. But when she left the store, she drove across the street to a motel and checked in for the night."

Ryder's pulse jumped. "Text me the address. I'm on my way."

"What was that about?" Tia asked as he ended the call.

"Wanda Hanson's car was spotted. We're heading there now."

"Did she have Jordie?"

He bit his tongue to keep from offering her false hope. "I don't know. We'll find out."

He pulled to the side of the road, entered the address into the GPS, then swung the SUV around and headed west, toward the highway where the motel was located.

Tia's hands went into motion again, fidgeting and twitching. He laid his hand over hers. Her skin felt cold, clammy. "Try to relax. It's about sixty miles from here."

"What if she's gone by the time we get there?" Fear made her voice warble.

"She checked into a room for the night."

"Hopefully she's feeding Jordie," Tia said.

Ryder wanted to assure her that that was exactly what the woman was doing. But if she was high, drinking or coming down from a high, there was no telling what her mood would be.

Or if she'd even be coherent.

"Did Wanda have a gun?" he asked.

Tia's brows pinched together as if she was thinking. "Not that I recall. Why? Did someone report seeing her with one?"

He shook his head and squeezed her hand again. "No, I was just asking. It's better to be prepared." She could have picked up a gun from a gun shop or borrowed one from a friend.

"When we get there, I need you to remain in the SUV," Ryder said. "I'll go to Wanda's room and see if she's home."

"I'm going, too," Tia whispered. "Jordie needs me."

Ryder shifted back into agent mode. "Let me assess the situation, Tia. We can't go in guns blazing or someone could get hurt." Her. The baby.

"You're right." She released a shaky breath. "If Wanda is doing drugs or drunk, she might panic."

"Right." Half a dozen scenarios of how the situation could go bad flashed through his mind. He wasn't green at this. Drug addicts and criminals weren't predictable. And when they were backed into a corner, they did things they might never do under normal circumstances.

Tia lapsed into silence. Dark clouds rolled in as the truck ate the miles, the occasional howl of a wild animal breaking the quiet. Traffic thinned, deserted farmland and broken-down shanties a reminder that this highway led out of town and into the vast wilderness.

A good place to hide or get lost. Or disappear with a stolen child.

Ryder sped up and passed a slow moving car, then checked the clock. The minutes rolled into half an hour.

Wanda Hanson was not going to get away tonight, though. Not if she had Jordie Jeffries with her.

TIA GRIPPED THE edge of the seat as Ryder pressed the accelerator and took the curve on two wheels. His calm demeanor was meant to soothe her, but his big body was tense, hands clenching the steering wheel in a white-knuckled grip.

In spite of what he said, he was anxious to get to the motel in case Wanda didn't stay the night.

She fought panic as the time passed.

"Ryder, what if Wanda is meeting someone at the motel? She could be giving Jordie to that person."

Ryder's thick brow rose. "Just try to keep up the faith."

She ran her fingers through her hair, fighting thoughts of the worst-case scenario—that Wanda had disposed of Jordie.

As they neared the motel she noticed a truck pulling an oversize load was parked on the side of the road, a tiny house behind it.

Cheap neon lights glowed ahead, illuminating a graveled parking lot. Ryder veered into the lot and parked between an SUV and a pickup. Two minivans and a sedan were parked at the opposite end, and another vehicle stood in front of the corner unit.

"That's Wanda's van," he said as he killed the engine.

"Do you know which room she's in?" Tia asked.

"Gwen talked to the motel manager. Room twelve, at the end."

Tia zeroed in on the corner unit. A low light burned inside, shrouded by the motel's thin curtains.

Ryder eased his weapon from his holster and reached for the door handle. "Stay here."

Tia nodded, but as Ryder left the SUV and walked toward the minivan, adrenaline and fear made her open her door and follow. Her footsteps crunched on gravel as she hurried up behind Ryder.

He cut her a sharp look. "I told you to wait in the SUV."

Tia peered through the front window of the minivan, but the windows were tinted, making it difficult to see.

Ryder pulled a small flashlight from his belt and shined it inside, waving it across the front seat. No one there.

He moved to the side window and shined the light across the backseats. Tia's breath caught.

A car seat.

"Look," she whispered. "She has an infant carrier, and there are baby toys."

Ryder gripped her arm. "We have to be careful, Tia. We don't want to spook her. If she has a weapon, this could go south."

Panic seized Tia. If that happened, Wanda might hurt Jordie.

"Trust me," he said on a deep breath.

Ryder's gaze met hers, his dark eyes steady. Determined.

Odd that she did *want* trust him, especially after he'd arrested her. But she did. "You're in charge."

Tension vibrated between them for a long second. The air stirred around them, bringing the scent of damp earth and garbage. An engine rumbled, doors opened and slammed, and a child's voice echoed in the wind as a family climbed out, gathering toys and suitcases as they walked to their room.

They passed several rooms, then a housekeeping cart. Tia lifted a set of towels from the cart along with a pillow. Ryder nodded in silent agreement and they passed two more rooms, then paused at the last unit.

His right hand covered his weapon, which he held by his side as he knocked with his left.

Tia swallowed hard then called through the door, "Housekeeping. I have extra towels and pillows."

Ryder eased Tia behind him. A voice sounded inside, then footsteps and the door creaked open.

Tia's heart pounded as Wanda appeared. Her eyes were glazed, hair stringy and unwashed, and she reeked of cigarette smoke. As soon as she spotted Tia, she spit out a litany of curse words, then tried to shut the door in their faces.

Rydor shoved the door open, drew his gun and shouted, "Stop and put your hands up!"

Wanda came at him fighting and hissing like a crazy woman, but he yanked both arms down beside her and pushed her against the wall.

Tia spotted a blue bundle lying on the bed between two pillows. Jordie.

She raced toward it.

Chapter Thirteen

Tia ignored Wanda's shrill scream as she approached the bundle on the bed. Ryder wrestled the woman's arms behind her and handcuffed her. She kicked and shouted obscenities as he shoved her into a chair.

Hope speared Tia as she slowly sank onto the bed. She didn't want to startle the baby, so she gently pressed one hand to his back.

Cold fear washed over her. He wasn't moving.

"You can't take my baby!" Wanda shouted.

"Shut up," Ryder growled.

Tia's gaze met his, terror making her heart pound. If Jordie was hurt or sick, she had to help him.

She leaned over and scooped up the bundle, but as she turned him in her arms, shock robbed her breath.

There was no baby.

She was holding a doll in her arms. A life-size doll that felt and looked like a real infant.

But it wasn't Jordie.

"Let me go!" Wanda fought against the restraints so hard that the chair rocked back and forth.

Tia whirled on her. "What did you do with my son?"

Ryder's brows puckered into a frown and he strode over to her to examine the baby. "Good God," he muttered when he realized the truth.

Tia carried the doll over to Wanda, "Where's my baby?"

Wanda shook the chair again as she rocked the chair backward against the wall. "You took my boy away from me. You can't have this one!"

Tia shoved the doll into Ryder's arms, grabbed Wanda's shoulders and shook her. "What did you do with my son, Wanda?"

"I don't know what you're talking about," Wanda muttered. "You're the one who took my son from me."

Ryder rubbed Tia's back. "Let her go, Tia. She's so strung out she doesn't know what she's doing or saying."

But Tia couldn't let go. She'd been so sure Wanda had her son. So sure he was here, that she'd take him home tonight and feed him and rock him to sleep and wake up in the morning with her family at home.

That this nightmare was over.

"Tell me, Wanda," Tia said in a raw whisper. "Where's Jordie? What did you do with him?"

Wanda went still, her lips curling into a sick smile, yet her eyes weren't focused. They were glazed over with the haze of drugs.

Tia choked on a sob and stepped back, her heart shattering at the realization that Wanda might not have taken Jordie at all.

RYDER GRITTED HIS teeth at the agony on Tia's face. Wanda started another litany of foul words, and he barely resisted smacking her in the mouth.

"Shut up," he barked.

Tia ran a finger over the doll's cheek. The damn thing looked so real he expected it to start crying any minute.

Forcing himself into agent mode, he planted himself in front of Wanda, dropped to a squat and tilted her face to look at him. "Wanda, listen to me. Kidnapping is a felony offense. You need to tell me if you abducted Tia Jeffries's baby."

Her lip quivered as she flattened her mouth into a frown. "Go to hell."

"That's where you're going if you hurt that baby," Ryder said, his tone lethal. "But if you cooperate, I'll see that you get a fair shake, that you receive counseling and treatment for your addiction."

A bitter laugh rumbled from Wanda's throat. "You don't scare me," Wanda said. Her head lolled from side to side as if she was suddenly dizzy or about to crash. "I didn't take that bitch's baby, although it would serve her right if I did, since she ruined my family."

Tia folded her arms and faced Wanda, her body vibrating as if she was grasping to maintain control. "You lost your child because you chose drugs over him."

Ryder pressed a hand to Tia's arm to encourage her to let him handle the situation. "But we can change that," he said, giving Tia a warning look. "Tell me, Wanda. You were hurting because you missed your son. You were angry at Tia. You found out she had a child, and you wanted to get back at her so you—"

"I hope you never get your kid back," Wanda yelled.

Ryder put his arm out to keep Tia from pouncing. Tears flowed from her eyes, ripping at his emotions.

Ryder spoke though gritted teeth. "I told you I'd help you, Wanda, but you have to talk first. Now, you slipped into Tia's house and you took her newborn—"

"I didn't take the kid." Wanda slid sideways in the chair, her eyes rolling back in her head.

Ryder caught her just before she passed out.

A strangled sob erupted from Tia, her pain and frustration palpable as he phoned 911.

DESPAIR SUCKED AT Tia as the medics rushed in and took Wanda's vitals.

One of the medics gestured toward the doll as they loaded Wanda onto the stretcher. "Is there a child here?" he asked.

Tia shook her head. "She has emotional issues." Whether Wanda's drug addiction or her instability had come first, Tia didn't know.

"She under arrest?" the medic asked.

Ryder cleared his throat. "For now."

"For what?" Tia asked. Being cruel? Traveling with a doll?

"Attacking an officer," Ryder said. "At least that gives us a reason to hold her until she's coherent."

So he hadn't completely ruled out Wanda as the kidnapper. Although if Wanda had taken Jordie, Tia would have expected her to brag about it, to rub it in her face.

Ryder retrieved Wanda's purse from the desk chair and dumped the contents on the bed as the medics carried Wanda to the ambulance. A baby bottle, wipes, keys, tissues, a pack of gum, a small bag of powder that Tia assumed was cocaine, a tube of dark red lipstick, a pack of matches from the Big Mug, a ratty wallet and a cell phone.

He scrolled through her contacts. "Husband's name is still in here. A few others, but not many. I'll have the lab check them out."

Tia looked over his shoulder. "What about her recent calls?"

A couple of unknowns. The motel number. The name Horace Laker. A woman named Elvira Mead. The bus station.

Did one of these people know where Jordie was?

RYDER WENT DOWN the list, calling each number. The two unknowns did not respond. Horace Laker was the owner of Laker Car Rentals. Wanda had rented the van from him.

"Did Ms. Hanson have any children with her when you saw her?" Ryder asked.

"Didn't see any. Said she was in a hurry, though. Had to meet up with someone."

Someone who'd taken Jordie, or her dealer?

"Was she high when she talked to you?"

The man coughed. "Didn't think so. But she did seem antsy. But everyone's in a hurry all the time these days so I didn't think much of it."

Ryder thanked him, disconnected, then called the last number. Elvira Mead answered. Ryder introduced himself and explained the situation. "How do you know Wanda?"

"I'm her neighbor," Elvira said. "She called and asked me to feed her cat for a few days. Said she was going out of town."

"Did you see her with a child? An infant, maybe?"

"No, she lost her boy a while back. Thought that might straighten her up, but it sent her into a downward spiral."

"Did she mention a woman named Tia Jeffries?"

"She hated that woman," Elvira said. "Blamed her for her husband leaving her, but we both knew it was Wanda's addiction. He had to take that boy away from Wanda."

Ryder's gut pinched. Hopefully the woman hadn't gotten her hands on Tia's son. "Did she mention getting revenge against Tia?"

A hesitant pause. "She mouthed off some, but if you think she kidnapped that baby, you're wrong. I saw the story on the news. The night the baby went missing, Wanda was passed out at home."

"You're sure about that?"

Elvira gave a sarcastic laugh. "Damn right I am. She

barreled in driving like a maniac. Left her car running, crawled out and practically collapsed in the driveway. I went out to check on things, turned off the engine and helped her inside."

"That was nice of you."

A pause. "I've been in AA for twenty years. Kept trying to talk Wanda into joining. I promised her I'd be her sponsor, but she refused to go."

Ryder thanked Elvira for her help and disconnected.

Tia was watching him. "Anything?"

He hated to dash her hopes, but he refused to lie to her. "That was Wanda's neighbor. Wanda was home the night Jordie disappeared—she said she passed out and was there all night."

Ryder checked his watch. It was almost time for the early evening news. "We'll drop her phone off at the crime lab. Gwen can check out her contacts while we go to the TV station."

He hated to put Tia through a public appearance. And it could bring false leads.

But sometimes a parent's grief and fear in a personal plea touched viewers and strangers enough to make them take more interest in helping to find a missing child.

They needed all the help they could get.

TIA FRESHENED UP in the bathroom at the TV station, well aware she looked pale and gaunt. Desperate.

God, she *was* desperate.

The past three days had taken its toll on her body and her mind.

But she had to pull herself together to talk to the press.

On the drive to the station, she'd rehearsed in her mind what she wanted to say. In each scenario, she wound up screaming for the kidnapper to return her baby.

You are not going to fall apart. You're going to be calm reasonable, tell the truth and...beg.

She tucked her brush in her purse, wiped her face with a wet paper towel, then dried her hands.

Several deep breaths, and she summoned her courage and left the restroom. Ryder was waiting, his gaze deep with concern.

"They're working on Wanda at the hospital," he said. "Gwen just phoned. She didn't find anything suspicious in Wanda's bank records. In fact, Wanda is broke. Probably depleted her money feeding her habit."

"Then she might have been desperate enough to take Jordie and try to sell him," Tia said, her voice laced with horror.

He shrugged in concession. "I'm not ruling out that possibility, although her phone records haven't turned up a lead. And she has an alibi the night of the abduction."

Tia clung to the theory because they had no other clues. "Then she had a partner or help."

Ryder kept his expression neutral. "So far, nothing we've found supports that theory, Tia. According to a neighbor Gwen talked to, Wanda didn't have any friends visiting. She'd alienated all her family. Another neighbor saw a shady-looking character confront her at her car once. She owed him for drugs."

An attractive blonde woman in a dark green dress approached. "I'm Jesse Simpleton. I'll be handling the interview with you, Miss Jeffries."

Tia shook her hand. "Thank you. I appreciate you taking the time to do this."

"Of course." The young woman's voice softened with compassion. "I'm so sorry about your baby. We'll do whatever we can to help."

"I've set up a tip line." Ryder pushed a piece of paper into the woman's hands. "Here's the number."

"We'll make sure it appears on-screen and rebroadcast it with each news segment." Jesse showed them where to sit by the anchor's chair, and the director instructed them regarding the cameras.

Jesse squeezed Tia's hand. "Just talk from the heart."

Tia didn't know what else to do. Before they started, she removed the photo of Jordie she'd taken the night she'd brought him home from her purse and rubbed her finger over her baby's sweet cherub face.

The director signaled it was time to start. Jesse introduced her. Tia angled the photograph toward the camera.

"My name is Tia Jeffries. Six weeks ago was the happiest day of my life. I gave birth to my son, Jordan Timothy Jeffries. He weighed seven pounds, eight ounces and was nineteen inches long." The memory of holding him for the first time made tears well in her eyes. "I carried him home the next morning, ecstatic. He was a good eater and was growing and healthy and happy. But three nights ago, someone slipped in my home while I was sleeping and stole him from his crib." She swallowed, battling a sob.

"I know he's out there somewhere. I can hear him cry at night. I can feel him wanting to come back to me, to be with his mama where he belongs." She pressed a kiss to the photograph. "I don't care who you are or why you took my baby. I don't want revenge or even to see you in jail. All I want is my little boy back." She swallowed hard. "If you have him, please drop him at a church or hospital. No questions asked."

Jesse announced the information about the tip line, but Tia had to say one more thing.

"I'm offering a reward of a hundred thousand dollars

to whoever brings him back to me or provides a lead as to where my baby is.

She felt Ryder's look of disapproval, but kept her eyes on the camera as the reward was posted on-screen.

If she had to, she'd use every penny she had to get her son back.

Chapter Fourteen

Tia prayed the TV plea brought in answers, that someone had seen her baby or knew who'd taken him and decided to do the right thing.

Ryder stopped at the diner and insisted she eat dinner, although she could barely taste the food for the fear clogging her throat.

An hour and a half later, he pulled into her driveway, the silence between them thick with tension and the reality that night had come again, another night where she would go into an empty house, with an empty nursery and an empty bed.

"I'll come in and check the house." Ryder slid from the SUV and walked her to the door. Tia swallowed back emotions as she unlocked the door.

Ryder flipped on a light and strode through the house, checking each room. "The house is clear," he announced as he returned to the kitchen.

She nodded. She hadn't expected the kidnapper to have returned.

Ryder hesitated, his dark gaze penetrating hers as he brushed his fingertips along her arm. She sucked in a breath.

"You did good during the interview, but—"

"If you're going to tell me I shouldn't have offered a reward, don't bother. If the kidnapper took Jordie for money, this should prompt a call. And if not, maybe someone who knows where Jordie is or who took him might step up."

"I just want you to be prepared in case we receive prank calls or false leads."

"I know." Despite the fact that she told herself not to lean into him, she did it anyway. "But we—I—have to do something."

Understanding flickered in his eyes. "You are doing everything you can," he said. "Trust me. We won't stop until we find your baby."

Tears pricked at her eyes. She needed to hear that, to know that she wasn't alone and that he wouldn't give up. She'd read about cases where leads went cold, other cases landed on their desks and police essentially stopped looking. Children were lost for decades.

Fear nearly choked her. Ryder must have sensed she was close to breaking. He wrapped his arms around her and held her tight.

"Hang in there, Tia."

She battled tears, blinking hard to stem them as she nodded against his chest. His chest felt hard, thick, solid. His arms felt warm and comforting—safe.

His steady breathing and the gentle way he stroked her back soothed her.

But that was temporary. Nothing had changed.

Except that at least she wasn't alone.

She lifted her head to look into his eyes. "Thank you, Ryder. I'm…glad you're here." She hesitated. "Working the case, I mean."

"I'll let you know if I hear anything." He eased away from her, making her instantly feel bereft and alone again. "Try to get some rest."

She nodded and bit her tongue to keep from begging him to stay.

He walked to the door, shoulders squared, his big body taut with control. "Lock the door behind me," he said as he stepped outside onto the front porch.

She rushed to do as he said, then watched through the window as he climbed in his SUV.

RYDER PINCHED THE bridge of his nose as he drove away from Tia.

He didn't want to leave her, dammit.

But he had no place in her life. Except as an agent working her case.

He checked his phone, but no messages or calls yet. He hoped to hell the TV plea and tip line worked. Or maybe Gwen would locate the woman on that tape at the hospital.

Dark clouds rolled above, thunder rumbling. Most people had tucked their children into bed by now so they'd be safe and sound for the night.

Like Tia had thought her baby was.

Predators were everywhere, though. Watching and stalking innocents. Waiting to strike when the victim let down his or her guard.

By the time he reached his cabin, his thoughts had turned to possibilities other than Tia's ex or Wanda. What if the kidnapping wasn't personal? What if it had nothing to do with revenge against Tia, but simply that she'd crossed paths with a desperate person who wanted a baby, and she'd become the target because she was a single mother?

Images of the agonized look on Tia's face haunted him as he went inside. The rustic place was empty, a chill in the den. He shrugged off his jacket and holster but carried his gun with him, then planted it on the coffee table. The envelope of letters Cash had left was sitting in the center of the table where he'd left them.

He stared at it, struck by the pink rosebuds on the wooden keepsake. His birth mother's doing.

Myra Banks was his mother. She'd rocked him to sleep when he was a baby and nursed his fevers and bandaged his skinned knees and…loved him as much as any mother could.

But this woman… What about her?

Cash insisted he read them, that he understand how much Grace McCullen had wanted the two of them.

He lifted the envelope. Just as Cash said, it was filled with dozens of letters and cards.

He thumbed through them. He didn't know where to start.

Pulse pounding, he walked to the bar in the corner, poured himself a whiskey, then returned. He tossed the first drink back, then poured another and set it on the table.

The picture sitting on the table of him and Myra at Christmas last year mocked him. It had been four years since his father had died. They'd both missed him, although the last few years his father had let his own drinking get out of hand. He'd blamed financial problems, a backstabbing partner who'd cheated him out of half his building supply company.

Even if Ryder and his father hadn't always gotten along and he'd been a bastard to his mother when he was drinking, Myra and Troy had been there for him.

Cash's face, identical to his own, flashed behind his eyes. Cash, his twin, who'd been tossed around in foster care all his life.

Cash, who was now friends—and brothers—with Maddox, Brett and Ray McCullen.

Ryder heaved a sigh. He didn't need a brother. Or to be part of that family.

Still…he had to know the truth.

He dug through the pile, checking the dates, until he found the earliest dated envelope. He opened it and drew out a photograph inside a folded sheet of paper.

He lifted the picture and studied the dark-haired pregnant woman. She was holding a basket of wildflowers. She had her hand on her pregnant belly, and she was smiling up at the sun.

This was the woman who'd given birth to him. She was beautiful.

Emotions flooded him, and he opened the sheet of paper and started to read. Her handwriting was feminine, soft, delicate—her words music to his soul.

Dear son,

This morning, I had an ultrasound and learned I was having twin boys. This is the most exciting day of my life!

I'm not only blessed with one more baby, but two.

As much as the McCullen men need more women around Horseshoe Creek, I honestly believe that God meant for me to have a ranch of boys. The world needs more good men and husbands, and I know you and your brothers will fill that role.

I've already experienced the joy and chaos little boys bring, and also the love and camaraderie they share. I can't wait to add you and your brother to the McCullen clan.

Your father, Joe, is a tough cowboy, but a loving man and father, and you will be blessed by having a role model and leader to guide you through life.

I wish my own mama, your grandmother, could have lived to see this day.

I love you so much my heart is bursting and exploding with emotions. Just a few more weeks, and I'll get to hold you in my arms.

Until then, I'll sing you a lullaby each night while you nestle alongside your twin inside me.

Love always,

Mama

"MAMA LOVES YOU, JORDIE," Tia whispered as she stepped into the nursery. The soothing blues and greens of the room reminded her of the day she'd painted the room in anticipation of her son's arrival.

Ina had knitted baby bootees, and Elle had brought a basket of baby toys. She picked up the blue teddy bear Amy had given her, turned on the musical mobile of toy animals dancing above Jordie's crib and hugged the bear to her as she sank into the chair.

The toy train, football, blocks, arts and crafts corner, puzzles, rocking horse and farm set were all waiting. She rocked the chair back and forth and began to sing "Twinkle, Twinkle Little Star" along with the musical mobile, pushing the chair back and forth with her feet as she cradled the bear to her like she had her son.

For a while, she allowed herself to imagine her little boy playing in the room. She saw him riding the little pony, drawing pictures to hang on the wall, learning to walk, running outside in the backyard and splashing in a rain puddle, then waving to her from the jungle gym at the park.

Of course he'd learn to ride and they'd have picnics and feed the horses and ducks.

A smile tugged at her mouth as she envisioned birthdays

and Christmases and marking his growth on the wall chart that she'd hung by the door.

The Hickory Dickory Dock clock on the wall ticked another hour away. Another hour that her son was missing.

ONCE RYDER STARTED with the mail, he couldn't stop himself until he'd read every letter and card. His mother poured out her heart, telling him how much she missed him every day, how she envisioned him and his twin and what they would have looked like, how she put flowers and toys and gifts on their tiny graves, how she quietly celebrated their birthdays.

Then there were disturbing letters where she chronicled her search for the twins. On pink flowered stationery with ink blurred from her tears, she'd written heart-wrenching descriptions of the nightmares that had plagued her. Sleepless nights when she'd wake up sobbing into the pillow because she could hear her babies' cries.

Ryder rubbed a hand over his eyes. God.

Cash was right.

The words on those pages were not from a woman who'd sold her children to fund her and her husband's ranch.

She told about the distance her grief had created between her and Joe, about his affair with Barbara, about how she'd forgiven him because they'd both sought comfort in different ways.

In each progressive letter, she'd promised not to give up looking for them, that she would find them and bring them back to Horseshoe Creek.

The last letter made his heart pound. She'd sensed someone following her. Had felt like she was being watched.

She'd been afraid...

Grief for the woman who'd given birth to him mushroomed in his chest. He traced his finger over her picture, and sorrow brought tears to his eyes.

Next came the face of the woman who'd raised him. Myra Banks.

Dammit. Had she lied about how she'd gotten him, or had the person who'd kidnapped him and Cash lied to her?

He stood and paced. He had to talk to her.

He checked his watch. Ten o'clock.

Dammit, she'd be in bed now.

He'd pay her a visit first thing in the morning. And he'd get to the truth.

TIA DRAGGED HERSELF to the bedroom, forced herself into pajamas and crawled into bed, hugging the teddy bear to her. She sniffed the plush fur, her son's baby scent lingering.

She closed her eyes, but the dark only accentuated the quiet emptiness in the room and in her house.

Her chest ached so badly she could hardly breathe.

Fatigue clawed at her. Just as she was about to drift asleep, her phone trilled.

Tia's pulse jumped.

She swung her legs to the side of the bed and snatched her cell phone. Her hand was trembling so badly she dropped the phone on the floor. Heart racing, she flipped it over.

The caller ID display box showed *Unknown*.

Panic snapped at her nerve endings, but she jerked up the phone and stabbed Connect.

"Hello."

"I saw you on the news."

Tia's breath stalled in her chest. "What? Who is this?"

"Your baby is safe. But he won't be if you keep looking for him."

Terror crawled through Tia. Before she could ask more, the phone went silent.

Chapter Fifteen

Tia trembled as she stared at her phone. The voice had belonged to a woman.

Who the hell was she? Did she really have Jordie?

And what had she meant—he was safe for now? If she kept looking…what would she do to him?

Terror and rage slammed into her. She punched Call Back but it didn't go through.

Tia lurched from bed, strode to the window and peeked out through the blinds. No cars outside. No one in the backyard.

She rushed to the front and looked through the window—no one there, either.

Heart pounding, she pressed Ryder's number. She paced the living room while she waited on him to respond. Three times across the room and he picked up.

"Ryder, I just got a call from a woman who said she has Jordie, that he's safe."

"What?" Ryder said. "Is she bringing him back?"

"No." Tia wiped her forehead with the back of her hand. "She said if I wanted him to stay safe that I should stop looking for him."

Ryder murmured something below his breath. "Dammit, I'm sorry, Tia. I warned you that your interview might draw the crazies and pranks."

"What if it isn't a prank?" Tia cried. "What if she's telling the truth, and we keep looking and she hurts him?" She choked back hysteria. "I'd never forgive myself if something bad happened to him because of me."

RYDER SILENTLY CURSED and walked outside onto the back porch. No way in hell he'd sleep now.

"Listen, Tia, I'll be right over. Meanwhile, I'll call the tech team and see if they can trace that call. Did a name show up?"

"No, it was an unknown."

Of course it was. "Probably a burner. I'll see if anything has come in over the tip line. Stay put and don't panic."

"I'm trying not to," Tia said, her voice cracking with tension. "But I'm scared, Ryder."

"I know." His own gut was churning. If that woman had abducted Jordie, she might be panicking. And if she didn't have him and was just playing some sick, cruel game, she was heartless and deserved to be locked up.

"Hang in there, Tia, I'll be there soon."

Ryder threw a change of clothes and toothbrush in a duffel bag. Then he strapped on his holster and gun, slipped on a jacket, snatched his keys, and headed outside. Out of the corner of his eye, he noticed the mail from his birth mother. He hurried over, stacked everything back inside the envelope and closed it.

The night air hit him, filled with the smell of impending rain.

He jumped in his SUV and sped toward Tia's, calling Gwen as he drove onto the main road.

He explained about the call Tia had received. "I need you to find out where that call came from."

"I'm on it, but if it was as quick a call as it sounds, I doubt we can trace it."

Frustration knotted his shoulders. "I know it, but do your best." They couldn't ignore any call or lead. "Anything from the tip line?"

"Not yet. There have been a few calls, and I have people checking them out."

"What about the woman in the video feed from the hospital nursery? Any ID on her?"

"Afraid not. We're running her through facial recognition and waiting to get the medical records from legal, but so far nothing. I'll keep you posted."

"Thanks." Ryder ended the call, his experience as an agent warring with his worry for Tia and her baby.

You are not supposed to get involved.

But after reading his birth mother's heartfelt words and realizing the pain she'd suffered had only grown deeper with every passing day and hour he and Cash were missing, he realized that Tia was experiencing the same emotions now.

Grace had sensed someone was watching her because she was asking questions about him and Cash.

Tia had just received a threatening call.

Still, he couldn't talk Tia out of giving up her search. Her love—a mother's love—was too strong, just as his birth mother's was.

Only his birth mother's search had gotten her killed.

TIA PACED THE living room, too terrified to sit or lie down. By the time Ryder arrived, she'd worked herself into a sweat.

She yanked open the door and met him on the porch. "Could you trace the call?"

Ryder's boots pounded the wooden porch floor as he strode toward her. "Gwen's trying. But most likely it came from a burner phone, Tia. If she calls again and you keep her on the phone long enough, maybe we can get something."

Tia's chest tightened. "But what if she doesn't call again?"

Ryder gripped her arms to stop her constant motion. "We'll find her another way."

"But how?" Tia whispered.

Ryder pulled her into his arms and held her. "This is what I do," he murmured.

She pressed her hand against his chest. His heart beat steadily beneath her palm, soothing her slightly. Ryder was strong and caring and he knew what he was doing.

She had to trust him.

Hard to do when the last man she'd trusted had been Darren, and he'd tried to con her out of her inheritance, then abandoned her when she was pregnant.

He pulled away slightly, then took her hands in his. "When she called, did you hear anything in the background that might indicate where she was?"

Tia strained to remember. "I don't know, I was so terrified…"

"Think. Was there any street noise? Cars? A train? Water?"

"I think I heard a siren."

"Like the police?" Ryder asked.

She shook her head. "No, maybe an ambulance?"

"So she might have been near a hospital," Ryder said.

Tia pressed her fingers to her temple. "Maybe. I don't know, Ryder. It could have been a fire engine."

He squeezed her hands. "Okay, just think about it. Something might come to you later."

Although later might not be soon enough.

RYDER STRUGGLED NOT to show his own anxiety. Tia needed comfort, encouragement and hope.

Lying to her wouldn't be fair.

He insisted that she lie down, but from the couch where he'd stretched out he could hear her tossing and turning.

Just as dawn streaked the sky, she finally settled and fell asleep. She needed rest, so he changed clothes and made coffee, then decided to pay his mother that visit.

By eight o'clock, he'd swung by his place, picked up a couple of Grace's letters and was knocking on Myra's door. She always enjoyed her coffee in the sunroom in the mornings and greeted him with a cup in hand.

"Ryder, what a nice surprise." She wrapped him in a hug. Ryder stiffened slightly. She might not be so happy when he told her the reason for his visit.

Myra pulled back, a small frown creasing her eyes. "Is something wrong, honey?"

Ryder gave himself a second to grasp his emotions before he cleared his throat. "We need to talk. Can I join you in the sunroom for some coffee?"

"Of course." She swept her hand through her wavy chin-length hair and gestured toward the coffeepot. "Do you want some breakfast, too?"

Ryder shook his head. He couldn't eat until this conversation was over.

He chose a mug from her collection, filled it with coffee and they walked to the sunroom together.

She sank into her wicker chair while he took the glider. His father had owned a fifty-acre farm outside town, but when he died, his mother sold it and bought this little bungalow a mile from town. It was a small neighborhood, but catered to retirees who didn't want to deal with yard upkeep.

"What's going on, Ryder?" she asked, tone worried.

"I've been working a case," he said, stalling. "A baby kidnapping."

"Oh, the Jeffries woman. I saw her on the news last night."

He sipped his coffee and gave a nod. "We're hoping the tip line turns up a lead."

"I'm so sorry for her," his mother said. "It must be horrible to have your baby stolen from your home like that."

He studied her but saw no sign of an underlying meaning that she could relate because of him. "She's devastated. She wanted a family more than anything in the world."

Myra traced a finger around the rim of her mug. "Well, I hope you find the baby."

"I will." An awkwardness stretched between them in the silence that ensued. Ryder took another long sip of his coffee. He didn't know where to begin, so he removed a couple of Grace's letters from inside his jacket and laid them on the wrought-iron coffee table.

His mother looked down at them with a frown, then lifted her gaze to meet his. "Talk to me, son. What's going on?"

"It's about my adoption," Ryder said. "I need to know who handled it. How you and Dad got me."

Myra's hand trembled as she lowered her coffee mug to the table. "We've already been through this, Ryder. We wanted a baby and couldn't have one. Your father met this lawyer who said he'd found a little boy for us."

"What was the lawyer's name?"

A seed of panic flared in her eyes before she masked it. "Frost. William Frost."

Ryder made a mental note of the name. "You said he told you that my birth parents needed money, so they sold me in exchange for relinquishing custody."

Frown lines creased her forehead. "Yes."

Ryder had to tread carefully here. This woman loved

him and had raised him. He couldn't treat her like a suspect in an interrogation.

But…he had to know the truth. If she'd lied to him or if someone had lied to her…

He gestured toward the envelopes on the table. "That's not true, Mom," he said gruffly. "I know who my birth parents are now. The McCullens."

His mother gasped. "You talked to them?"

He shook his head. "No, unfortunately they're both dead."

She rubbed her forehead with two fingers. "I don't understand, Ryder."

"They didn't sell me," he said bluntly. "I was kidnapped, stolen from them at birth, along with my twin brother."

Shock and some other emotion resembling guilt streaked her face.

"You knew I had a twin," Ryder said, his throat thickening. "Didn't you?"

Pain and guilt darkened her eyes, then she turned away and wrapped her arms around herself as if she needed to physically hold herself together.

His anger mounted at her silence. "You did, didn't you? You knew about Cash?"

She stiffened her spine. "We were told there were twins, but that one of them was sickly. And…your father didn't think we could handle a sick child."

"So it wasn't about the money?" Ryder asked. "Not to the McCullens. And you and Dad lied about paying for me, so you could have taken Cash in, too."

She shook her head, eyes wild with a myriad of emotions. "No, we did pay," she said sharply. "That lawyer wanted a fee, and we used every ounce of our savings to adopt you. We couldn't afford hospital bills for a sick baby and…we thought he'd find a place for your brother."

Rage at the situation fueled Ryder's temper. "But he didn't, Mother." Ryder stood, the glider screeching as it shifted back and forth. He walked to the door and looked out at the woods, needing air.

When he turned back to her, he slammed a curtain down over his face to mask his emotions. "Cash was tossed around from foster home to foster home. He never had a break."

"You met him?" she asked, her voice cracking.

"Yes, he came to see me." The turmoil in Cash's eyes taunted Ryder. "He never had a family, Mother, because you and Dad separated him from me." He pounded his chest with his fist. "And before that, someone kidnapped me and Cash from our birth parents."

Tears blurred her eyes. "I…don't know what to say, son, except that I only knew what the lawyer told us. I raised you. I love you."

Ryder jerked the envelopes from the table and pulled out the photograph of pregnant Grace McCullen, looking up at the sun.

"She was my mother, Cash's mother, and she wanted us. She didn't choose to give us up for adoption."

"That can't be true."

"It is true, Mother. She kept cards and letters she wrote to us. She poured out her heart because she missed us and loved us."

She shook her head in denial. "I'm sorry, Ryder, I had no idea…"

"Maybe not," Ryder said. "But she—her name was Grace—Grace and Joe McCullen not only looked for us, Mother—they died trying to find us."

Chapter Sixteen

Ryder sat in silence as his mother read the first letter. She wiped at tears as she picked up two of the cards and skimmed them.

"My God," she said in a haunted whisper. "I...can't believe this. I...really didn't know, son."

Ryder stood, gripping his coffee mug with clammy fingers. "Maybe not, but you should have told me I had a twin." He faced her, his heart in his throat. "I had other brothers, too, Mother. And parents who grieved that I was taken from them." Just as Tia was grieving.

She jammed the card she was reading back into the envelope. "I'm sorry, Ryder. I don't know what else to say."

He didn't know what else to say, either.

Except the disappointment, sadness and regret for the McCullens—along with his own, for missing out on knowing his brothers—was eating him up inside.

Memories of arguments his mother and father had had when he was a child echoed in his head. His father had been harsh at times, demanding, had always pushed to get his way.

"I know Dad was a tyrant at times, Mother, and that you gave in to him. Do you think he knew the truth?"

She pressed her lips into a thin line. "How dare you disparage your father when he's not here to defend himself,

Ryder. He and I both loved you and we did the best we could." She snatched the letters and cards and pushed them into his hands. "There's nothing good to gain by harping on what happened years ago. I've told you the truth, and I'm done talking about this."

Ryder crossed his arms. His mother could be stubborn. She'd always defended his father, even when she knew he was wrong. Now that he was dead, though, he hoped she'd think for herself.

"Fine, then you're right. We're done talking." Furious and confused, he strode back through the house.

Even if his father had known about Cash and the kidnapping, Ryder couldn't confront him. His father was dead.

But…the lawyer might have answers.

His phone buzzed as he sped from the driveway. Gwen.

Hopefully she had news for Tia. He'd also see what Gwen could find out about William Frost.

TIA WOKE TO find Ryder gone. Disappointment mingled with hope that he might be chasing a lead.

Groggy from too little sleep, she showered, scrubbing her hair vigorously to calm her nerves.

Her TV appearance had aired the night before.

Then that call…

But how had the caller gotten her personal cell phone number? They hadn't released the number on TV.

Surely other reliable calls would come in. Someone who'd seen her baby. Someone who wanted that reward money badly enough to turn the kidnapper in, even if that person was a friend or someone he or she loved.

She checked her phone for missed calls or messages before drying her hair, but there were none.

Outside, she heard a noise. An engine? Car slowing?

She peeked through her bedroom window and scanned the yard. A slight movement. A shadow.

It disappeared as fast as it had come.

Her pulse quickened. Had someone been outside? Was someone watching her or her house?

Or was she simply paranoid?

She blew her hair dry, gathered the strands into a ponytail and brushed her cheeks with powder to camouflage the bags beneath her eyes. Lip gloss helped with her parched dry lips.

She hurried to get coffee and forced herself to eat a piece of toast. The rumbling sound of a car engine startled her, and she rushed to the front window and checked outside.

Ryder.

She swung the door open before he stepped onto the porch. "Gwen just called. It might be nothing or we might have a lead."

She snatched her purse and phone on the way out the door, then ran back and plucked the baby quilt from the crib just in case they found her son. Pressing it to her chest, she jogged down the steps and crossed to his SUV. "What kind of lead?" she asked as she dived into the passenger seat.

"Someone reported seeing a woman with a baby at the bus station outside Sagebrush acting suspiciously."

Tia's breath caught. "Was it a little boy?"

Ryder covered her hand with his. "I don't know, Tia. It might not be Jordie or the person who kidnapped him. For all we know, the woman is just a nervous traveler, or she could be in trouble for another reason."

"Like an abusive spouse," Tia said, his logic ringing true. Still, she clung to hope as he sped toward Sagebrush.

RYDER TRIED TO banish the image of his mother's pain-filled face from his mind. He had to focus on Tia now.

But…when he had the time, he'd talk to Maddox. As the sheriff of Pistol Whip, Maddox might have information on that lawyer.

Tia twisted her hands together. "Who called about the woman?"

"A ticket salesperson at the bus station."

"Did she get a look at Jordie?"

"She didn't say." He didn't want to squash the light in Tia's tone, but he also didn't want to feed false hope.

Tia chewed on her bottom lip, then lifted the baby blanket and pressed it against her cheek. Early morning sunlight slanted off her face, making her skin look golden and her face young.

He thought of his birth mother, Grace, in the picture where she was her pregnant. She'd looked radiant and happy, just as he imagined Tia had during her pregnancy.

He wished he could have seen Tia like that, before the horror and agony of this kidnapping had taken its toll.

She remained quiet as he maneuvered through town.

Just as they pulled up, a bus was loading, a line of passengers boarding. Tia leaned forward to search the group as he swung into a parking space. Before he killed the engine, she threw the door open and started toward the bus.

But the bus door quickly closed, the engine fired up and the bus pulled away.

Tia cried out in frustration.

Dammit. Ryder motioned to the entrance of the station and darted inside. He strode straight to the ticket counter, flashed his ID and explained he needed to speak to the person who'd phoned the tip line.

A white-haired woman in a green shirt emerged from the back. "I'm Bernice, the lady who called."

Tia rushed up behind him, her breathing choppy. "This

is my son, Jordie." She shoved the photograph toward Bernice. "Did the woman you saw have this baby with her?"

Ryder placed a hand to her back as they waited on a response.

TIA'S HEART WAS pounding so hard she thought it would explode in her chest.

Bernice leaned over the counter and scrutinized the photograph. "Hmm, I can't be sure. She had him wrapped up tight in a baby blanket and kept him to her chest, so I couldn't see the baby's face."

Tia gripped the counter. "Did you see the baby's hair? Was it blond or dark?"

Bernice settled her reading glasses on the end of her nose. "I…I'm sorry, I can't say."

Ryder gave Tia's waist a squeeze, a silent message to hang in there.

"Why did you think she was acting suspiciously?" Ryder asked.

Bernice worried her glasses with her fingers, settling and resettling them again. "Well…she was awkward, you know, like she didn't know how to take care of the baby. It was fussing and crying and she jostled it to try to quiet the poor thing and kept looking around as if she was afraid."

Because she had Jordie?

Or had Ryder been right—was she running from someone else? God knew, Tia had worked with enough women coming through Crossroads that that was a distinct possibility.

"Did she call the baby by name?" Ryder asked.

Bernice glanced at the other ticket attendant, but the heavyset woman simply shrugged. "I was on my break, didn't see or hear nothing."

"A name?" Ryder asked again.

Bernice shook her head no. "She just kept saying, 'Hush, little darlin'.' That's all."

"What was the passenger's name?" Ryder asked.

Bernice checked the computer. "Vicki Smith."

"Did you check her ID?" Ryder asked.

The woman nodded. "All she had with her was a discount store card, one of those big warehouse deals where you have to have a membership."

"No driver's license?" Tia asked.

She shook her head no. "Said her wallet was stolen. Sounded down on her luck."

"What's her destination?" Ryder asked.

Bernice glanced at the computer again. "Cheyenne."

"Can you give me a description of her?"

"She was wearing a scarf, so I don't know how long her hair was, but it was a dirty brown."

"Height and weight?"

Bernice shrugged. "About your height, ma'am. But she was plumper, although hard to tell how plump with the baby pressed to her like that. Could have been baby weight, too."

"Did she have any distinguishing marks on her body? A tattoo or birthmark?"

"Not that I saw," Bernice replied.

"Did she mention meeting anyone?"

"No."

"Did she make any calls? Maybe on a cell phone?"

Bernice hesitated again then shook her head. "I didn't see a phone. Like I said, though, she was acting strange, like she didn't want to talk to people. So I didn't push it."

Ryder thanked her, then pressed a card on the counter. "If you think of anything else she said or did, call me."

Tia clutched the baby blanket to her as she followed Ryder back to the SUV. "What are we going to do?"

Ryder started the engine, a muscle ticking in his jaw, "We're going to follow that bus."

He gunned the engine and sped onto the highway. Tia buckled up for the ride.

RYDER HONKED HIS horn as a sedan nearly cut him off when he pulled out of the bus station. The black car ignored the horn, sideswiped him then raced on.

Ryder swerved, hit the curb and bounced back onto the road. He wanted to go after the son of a bitch, but following that bus and the woman on board took priority.

Tia's breathing filled the strained silence. She gripped the dashboard and said nothing, though.

Instead she kept her gaze trained ahead, eyes darting back and forth in search of the bus.

Ryder spotted it ahead, flew around an ancient pickup and roared up beside it.

"Look!" Tia pointed to a side window near the back, where a young woman wearing a dark scarf turned to watch them.

Dammit, she had a baby on her shoulder, swaddled in a blanket, and her eyes were wide with fear.

"That has to be her," Tia said in a raw whisper.

Chapter Seventeen

Ryder considered pulling the bus over, but decided to wait until the next bus station. It was only twenty minutes away.

Meanwhile, he phoned Gwen and asked her to dig up what she could find on Vicki Smith.

"I'm following the bus she's on now," Ryder said. "She used a discount store's ID, no driver's license, so it may be a fake name."

"Smith is an extremely common name," Gwen said. "Let me see how many Vickis there are."

A traffic light turned yellow, but the bus coasted on through just as it turned red. Tia looked panicked. Ryder quickly checked the intersection for cars, then sped through.

No way were they going to lose this bus.

"Ryder, I found dozens of women named Vicki Smith, but none match the description you gave, either. But if this woman is the unsub, she could have changed her appearance."

"I know. Cross-check with those medical records we got warrants for and see if any of those women recently delivered a baby or lost a child."

"On it."

The bus slowed at another light. The woman turned around again, fear flashing on her face when she realized they were still behind her.

"Okay, a woman named Vicki Smith gave birth to a baby girl a month ago in Sagebrush."

"Find out where she is now and the status of the baby."

"Okay, I'll keep you posted."

She disconnected just as the bus moved forward. It swung a wide left at the intersection and Ryder followed it into the parking lot of the bus station.

TIA DARTED AROUND the front of the bus just as the door opened and passengers began to unload.

Ryder rushed up behind her. "Stay calm and let me handle the situation," he said in a low voice next to her ear.

Tia felt anything but calm. She rose on tiptoes to see over the passengers, desperate to find the woman and baby. The bus was full, though, and the woman had been sitting near the back, so she couldn't do anything but wait.

"What did you learn about her?" Tia asked as an Asian woman and small child walked past her, followed by two teenagers, earbuds in, immersed in their music.

"Nothing, really. A woman named Vicki Smith gave birth to a baby girl a month ago. Gwen's looking into her."

Several more passengers left the bus, then the bus driver peered to the back of the bus, seemed to decide that was everyone getting off at this stop and closed the door.

"No!" Tia hit the door with her palm.

Ryder stepped in front of her and rapped his fist on the door, then flashed his badge at the window. "FBI, open up."

The bus driver flicked a hand up, indicating he was going to comply, then opened the door. Tia started to board, but Ryder gently urged her to stay still.

"Let me handle it, Tia." He flashed his badge as he climbed the steps. Tia followed on his heels.

Whispers and murmurs passed through the remaining passengers still seated.

"FDI Special Agent Ryder Banks," Ryder announced.

Tia scanned the people on board and spotted the woman in the back huddling down in the seat, her head buried against the baby. A scarf covered her hair, shadowing her face.

Ryder held up his hand. "Please stay seated, folks. I need to talk to the young woman in the back, the one with the baby."

The woman remained crouched in the seat, face averted as she soothed the crying child.

Tia's heart ached. Was that Jordie crying for her?

Ryder motioned for the woman to come with him. She stood slowly, hugging the baby to her as she followed Ryder.

"This should just take a moment," he said to the woman and the bus driver.

Tia shaded her eyes from the sun as she exited the bus into the parking lot. Ryder guided the woman to the sidewalk.

The woman pivoted, covering the baby with her hand to hide its face.

"Miss," Ryder said, "what is your name?"

She cast a terrified look at Tia then patted the bundle in her arms. "Vicki Smith."

"And your baby's name?"

"Mark," the woman said. "Why? What do you want with us?"

Tia cleared her throat. "Do you know who I am?"

Vicki adjusted her scarf, drawing it tighter. "No. Should I?"

Tia barely restrained herself from yanking the child from the woman's arms. "I was on the news last night. My baby was kidnapped I've been looking for him ever since."

The woman backed away. "I don't have your baby. This is my child. I'm going to visit my mother in Cheyenne."

Ryder gently touched the baby's cap. "Then we can clear this up really quickly. Just let us see the baby."

She shook her head vigorously, clutching the child as if to protect it from them. "You can't take my baby. I won't let you."

Tia inhaled sharply. The fear in the woman's voice was real. Whether it was because she was a kidnapper or for another reason, she couldn't tell.

Ryder gently touched the baby again. "I'm not going to take the child. But I need to verify that this is not Miss Jeffries's son."

"It's not," the woman cried. "Now let me go. If I miss that bus, I can't get to my mother's."

"Just show me that it's not my son," Tia said, softening her tone. "Then we'll let you be on your way."

The woman trembled, her eyes wary as she studied them. But she slowly tilted the infant back into her arms and eased the blanket from its face.

Ryder gently pushed the cap back to reveal a thick head of wavy black hair.

It wasn't Jordie.

TIA'S LEGS BUCKLED. Ryder steadied her, sensing her disappointment.

"I'm sorry, you're right," Tia said. "I just thought..."

"Someone phoned the tip line and said you were acting suspiciously," Ryder said, still unwilling to release her before he heard the real story.

She *was* acting suspiciously and hiding something.

Alarm speared the woman's eyes. "I...don't know what you mean." She hurriedly rewrapped the infant and started back toward the bus.

Ryder caught her arm. "Wait, I need to ask you some questions."

Vicki's eyes darted around the parking lot. "Please, you can see I don't have that woman's child. Now let me and my baby go."

"Something's wrong," Ryder said. "Is that child really yours?"

"Of course it is," she gasped.

"Then why the fake ID? Because I know Vicki Smith is a fake name."

"No, I'm Vicki. I'm from Pistol Whip—"

"There is a Vicki Smith from Pistol Whip, but she gave birth to a baby girl a month ago."

The woman sagged against his hold. "Please don't do this. If he finds us, he'll kill me and take Mark. He's already hurt him once. I won't let him do it again."

Tia had eased up beside him. "I'm sorry for scaring you, Vicki."

"Are you talking about your husband or boyfriend?" Ryder asked.

Embarrassment heated the woman's cheeks. "Yes."

"He's Mark's father?"

"Yes—"

"How did he hurt him?" Ryder asked.

The woman rocked the baby. "He can't stand it when he cries. He shakes him so bad. And the other night he threw him against the wall."

Pure rage shot through Ryder. If she was telling the truth, the bastard should be locked away.

"The real Vicki and I are friends," she continued. "She loaned me her discount card so I could use it as an ID to get on that bus."

"Is your mother really waiting?" Tia asked.

The woman shifted, then shook her head, fear and defeat streaking her face. "No... I have no place to go, but I had to get away from him." She dropped a kiss on the baby's head. "I put up with him hurting me, but I refuse to let him beat up our son."

"Good for you," Tia said with a mountain of compassion in her voice.

"I'm sorry about your situation," Ryder said injecting sympathy into his voice. "But if what you're saying is true, you should go through the proper channels."

"I filed a police report once, and they came and talked to him." Her voice grew hot with anger. "Then do you know what he did?"

"He was enraged and took it out on you," Tia said.

"Yes," the woman whispered brokenly. "He beat me so bad I couldn't walk for days. Where were the police then?"

Ryder silently cursed. He'd heard this story before, too.

"I can help you," Tia said. "I run a program called Crossroads. It's for families in crisis. There are other women like you, women who will help you."

"But he'll find me," Vicki cried. "He always finds me."

"No," Tia said emphatically. "I promise you he won't."

"She's right," Ryder said. "If everything you're telling me is true, I'll make certain you and your child have protection."

The woman began to sob, and Tia drew her and Mark into a hug, comforting them while Ryder motioned to the driver that he could leave.

Tia's heart ached for the woman. Unfortunately her story was a common one. The cycle of abuse would repeat itself if she didn't break it. That took strength and courage and help from strangers.

She could offer that. And if Ryder was willing to help…

The woman's body trembled next to Tia as she helped her into the SUV. She wished they had a car seat for the infant. They would take care of that ASAP.

Ryder phoned a friend with a private security company, and he agreed to guard the center for the evening. She phoned Elle to give her a heads-up about the situation. Vicki admitted her real name was Kelly Ripples.

Tia hugged Kelly again as they arrived at the center. "Everything will be okay now, I promise."

Elle and Ina met them at the door. "We fixed a room for you and the baby," Ina said. "I hope you don't mind sharing a room. Susan and her little girl are really nice. They just got here a couple of days ago. I think you'll like them. The little girl loves babies."

Kelly looked skeptical, but thanked Ina and followed her to one of the bedrooms, where a portable crib was set up in the corner. "I need to feed him," Kelly said.

"Of course," Tia said. "We'll let you have some privacy."

Ina gestured toward the rocking chair. "When he's settled, please join us in the dining room. I cooked a pot of homemade vegetable soup and some corn bread."

"That sounds wonderful," Kelly said in a low voice.

Tia joined Ryder in the hallway. "Thank you for arranging for the security guard."

He nodded. "I called Gwen. She's checking Kelly's story."

"I believe her," Tia said.

Ryder crossed his arms. "Time will tell. Until then, she'll be safe here. And if her story is confirmed, I'll see that her husband never gets hold of that child again."

Tia had never trusted a man the way she did Ryder. His fierce protectiveness and drive for justice was admirable.

She wanted to tell him that, but her growing feelings for him terrified her.

THE COMPASSION TIA showed for the woman astounded Ryder. She had gone from suspecting Kelly of kidnapping to an offer to help her in minutes.

Ryder's cell phone buzzed. He motioned to Tia that he needed to take it, so he stepped into the other room. "Gwen, that was fast."

"It's not about Kelly," she said quickly. "We have a hit on the woman in the security footage at the hospital nursery, and I cross-checked it with the hospital records. Her name is Bonnie Cone. She lives outside Sagebrush. She lost a baby recently and suffered serious depression. Her husband claimed she was obsessed with having another baby right away, but the doctor advised against it. The husband said they separated last month. He hasn't been able to reach her for a couple of weeks and he's worried."

A desperate, grieving woman. "Where is she?"

"I'm texting you her address now."

Ryder considered pursuing the lead on his own, but if they found Bonnie Cone, Tia could tell them really quickly if she had Jordie.

Chapter Eighteen

Tia assured Kelly that she and Mark would be safe at Cross-roads. The private security agent seemed to take his job seriously.

His eyes also lit up with a spark when he met Elle.

Tia would love to see her friend with a nice man. She'd had her own troubles before joining Crossroads and deserved happiness. But she definitely had built walls to protect herself.

Just as Tia had done.

Maybe that was the reason they were such good friends.

Ryder explained the phone call, and they rushed toward Sagebrush. She fidgeted, determined not to get her hopes up.

"The woman we're going to see was the one on the security camera at the hospital. Her name is Bonnie Cone. She lost a baby over a month ago. According to Bonnie's husband, she was despondent and obsessed with having another child."

Tia's heart went out to her.

But…her sympathy would only stretch so far.

The afternoon sunlight beamed in the car and slanted off farmland as they passed. Beautiful green grass, cows grazing, horses galloping on a hill in the horizon—a reminder of Wyoming's natural beauty. Normally those things soothed her, but today nothing could erase the grave feeling in her chest.

Bonnie's house was an older ranch, set off the road in a neighborhood about five miles from town. Although the house had probably been built fifty years ago, it looked reasonably well kept, except for the yard.

A gray minivan was parked in the drive. As they passed it, she peeked in and spotted a car seat.

They walked to the front door in silence. A welcome home wreath on the door and a wooden bench on the front stoop indicated that Bonnie had tried to make the house more homey and inviting.

Ryder punched the doorbell, his gaze scanning the property. He was always on alert. A product of his job, she supposed.

How did he live this kind of life, facing danger and criminals every day, and not become jaded? Did he ever relax?

He punched the bell a second time and Tia peeked through the front window. Living room with a brown sectional sofa, magazines dotting the coffee table, along with a baby bottle and an assortment of infant toys. A colorful blanket was spread on the floor, a toy rabbit and squeaky toy on top.

Seconds later, footsteps sounded and she quickly moved away from the window. If the woman saw her, she might bolt.

RYDER FLASHED HIS ID as Bonnie opened the door. "Miss Cone, my name is Special Agent Ryder Banks, and this is Tia Jeffries."

Bonnie's gaze darted to Tia, her eyes widening in recognition. "You're the woman on TV last night."

"Yes, that was me," Tia said softly. "Can we come in?"

Bonnie glanced back and forth between Tia and Ryder. "I don't understand."

Bonnie looked pale and thin, her eyes were dark with circles, her medium brown hair curly and tousled as if she hadn't slept in days. She was also still wearing a bathrobe.

Ryder shouldered his way through the door. "We need to talk. It'll just take a moment."

Bonnie tugged the belt of her robe tighter around her waist and gestured toward the sofa. Baby clothes and crib sheets overflowed a laundry basket, spilling onto the sofa.

Tia exhaled and slid the basket to the floor so she could seat herself beside Bonnie. Ryder claimed the club chair opposite her.

Bonnie plucked a receiving blanket from the basket and wadded it in her hands. "What is this about?"

"We're investigating the disappearance of Miss Jeffries's baby," Ryder said.

"I'm sorry about your son." The woman gave Tia a sympathetic smile. "But what does that have to do with me?"

"You delivered your baby at the same hospital where I gave birth," Tia said.

Pain darkened Bonnie's eyes. "Yes."

"I know you lost a child," Tia said gently. "That must have been awful."

Bonnie's lower lip quivered. "It was."

"I'm so sorry," Tia said. "I understand the heartache."

"No one understands," Bonnie said with a trace of bitterness. "I carried him for nine long months inside me. I had dreams for him."

Tia placed her hand over Bonnie's. "I do know. I carried my baby just like you did, I dreamed about holding him and watching him grow up. I started a college fund for him before he was even born."

Ryder swallowed hard at the emotions her words stirred.

"We were watching the video feed from the hospital," Ryder cut in. "You were on it."

Bonnie narrowed her eyes. "What?"

"After your baby was gone, you came back to the hospital and you were looking at the newborns."

Bonnie made a strangled sound in her throat and placed her hand over her stomach. "Yes, I wanted a baby so badly. I missed my son."

"That's understandable," Ryder said. "You missed him so much that you were out of your mind with grief."

Bonnie nodded, tears welling in her eyes. She swiped at them, unknotted the blanket and began to fold it methodically, as if the task was calming.

Tia picked up a burp cloth from the basket and ran her fingers over it. "We know you were grief stricken and in a bad place, Bonnie. I understand that, I do."

"Maybe you were so distraught you did something you never would have done otherwise," Ryder said. "You wanted to replace your baby, so you found another one."

Bonnie's startled gaze shot to Ryder's. "Yes, I did. My husband didn't understand, but I had to have a baby." Her voice was raw, agonized. "What's wrong with that?"

"Nothing," Tia said. "Not unless you took my son to replace yours."

Bonnie stood abruptly, knocking the basket of laundry over. Clothes spilled out, but she didn't seem to notice. "My God, that's the reason you're here. You think I kidnapped your baby?"

Ryder stood, sensing the woman might turn volatile. "We have to ask."

Bonnie fisted her hand by her side. "That's completely insane," Bonnie stuttered. "I would never do such a thing."

A mixture of emotions welled in Tia's eyes. Ryder wanted to comfort her, but she needed answers instead.

"But you got another baby," Ryder asked.

Fear deepened the panic in Bonnie's expression. "Yes, but that baby is mine now." She whirled toward Tia. "He's not yours, do you hear me? He's mine and you can't take him away."

Tia pressed a hand to her mouth.

"Then where did the baby come from?" Ryder asked.

"I didn't steal anyone's baby," Bonnie shouted. "I adopted a little boy."

Tia's sharp breath rent the air. "Then you won't mind showing him to me."

Anger slashed Bonnie's expression. "If it'll get you to go away and leave me alone, then yes. I'll get him."

She stalked toward the bedroom, and Tia and Ryder followed. For all he knew, she was going to grab the baby, go out a back door and run.

TIA RUSHED TO stay close to Bonnie in case she snatched the baby and tried to get away.

Bonnie stumbled, then grabbed the bedpost to steady herself as she crossed to the bassinet.

"He's sleeping," she said in a voice both tender and filled with fear. "I hate to disturb him."

Tia and Ryder remained in place, though, so she gently lifted the infant, swaddled in a blue blanket with turtles on it, his tiny fingers poking out.

Tia's pulse pounded as Bonnie gently pulled the blanket back to reveal the baby's face.

He had a fuzzy blanket of brown hair, his chin was slightly pointed, his face square. He was beautiful.

But he wasn't Jordie.

Disappointment nearly brought her to her knees.

Tia grabbed the bedpost this time, choking back a cry.

"Tia?" Ryder's low, gruff voice echoed behind her.

She shook her head, then turned to face him, her heart in her eyes.

Ryder crossed the room and took her arm, then glanced at the baby.

"How old is he?" Ryder asked.

"Four weeks today." Bonnie dropped a kiss on the baby's head, making Tia's heart yearn for Jordie even more. "Isn't he beautiful?" Bonnie said in a voice reserved for doting mothers.

"Yes," Ryder said. "You said you adopted him?"

"I did. After I lost…my child, I was devastated. Then my doctor advised against another pregnancy and I thought I couldn't go on." She paused and swiped at tears. "One of the counselors suggested adoption. I thought it would take a while, but someone else in the hospital gave me the name of a lawyer who handled private adoptions, and I contacted him." She rocked the infant back and forth in her arms. "It was a miracle. He said he knew of a teenager who had decided to go the adoption route. I couldn't believe it." She hugged the infant tighter. "As soon as she gave birth, he called me. I rushed to the hospital and there he was in the nursery, all wrapped up, just needing some love."

Her eyes brightened. "Love I could give him. I knew he was meant to be mine. I needed him and he needed me."

"He's lucky to have you," Tia said.

Bonnie nodded. "I named him after my father, David. He was a good man."

"It's a lovely name," Tia said. "I'm sure your father would be happy."

"What was the lawyer's name?" Ryder asked.

"He's a reputable attorney," Bonnie said defensively.

Ryder arched a brow. "His name?"

"Why do you want to know?" She clutched the baby tighter. "Did you talk to my husband? If you did, he probably told you I was crazy, that I was obsessed with having another child. And I was, but that doesn't mean I won't be a good mother to this little guy."

"I'm not questioning that," Ryder said. "But I'd like to talk to the lawyer just in case whoever abducted Tia's baby might have done so to sell him."

"Sell him?" Bonnie gasped. "My God. It's not like I bought him off a black market. What kind of person do you think I am?"

"It's no reflection on you, Bonnie," Ryder said. "But in a missing child case, I have to consider every possible theory."

Tia wanted to reassure her everything would be all right. But if, by chance, she had adopted a child obtained illegally, that adoption would be illegal and the courts would intervene.

That scary realization must have occurred to Bonnie.

"You can't take him," Bonnie said. "I can't lose him, too."

Tia stepped closer to calm her. "We're not going to do that, Bonnie. We just need the name of that lawyer."

Her expression wilted, and she closed her eyes for a second as if in a silent debate. When she opened them, she clenched her jaw. "His name is Frank Frost. His office is in Cheyenne."

"Frost," Tia said. "Thank you, Bonnie. We'll let you go and rest." She stroked the back of the baby's head. "You sleep tight, sweetie. Bonnie loves you and will take good care of you."

Ryder glanced at Tia. "Let's go."

Anxiety tightened her shoulders as she followed him outside. "Ryder, what's wrong?"

"I don't know," Ryder said as he climbed in the front seat. A muscle ticked in his jaw as they pulled away.

"Are you keeping something from me?" Tia asked.

Emotions glittered in Ryder's eyes, but he quickly masked them. "No."

"Yes, you are," Tia said earnestly. "You promised not to lie to me, Ryder. If you heard something about Jordie—"

"I didn't," he said, his wide jaw hard with anger. "But I recognize that name Frost."

Tia pulled the baby quilt into her lap and twisted her hands in the soft fabric. "What about him?"

Ryder heaved a weary breath. "I was adopted myself. I've always known it, but recently I learned who my birth family was—is. I have a twin brother, Tia. We were kidnapped as babies and our parents were told we were dead."

A cold chill swept over Tia. "You were kidnapped?"

He nodded. "My twin brother has reconnected with our birth family. He came to see me the other day."

"Oh, my God." Tia laid a hand on his shoulder, aching to comfort him for a change. "That must have been a shock."

"It was." He hesitated, then cleared his throat. "The lawyer who handled my adoption was named Frost."

Tia froze. "You think it was the same man?"

"No, his name was William. But they could be related."

"Are you suggesting the lawyer knew that you and your brother were stolen?"

Ryder shrugged, but his look indicated he did.

Chapter Nineteen

Another thought occurred to Ryder as he drove toward Cheyenne.

If Frost had intentionally been an accomplice in the kidnapping and selling of babies—him and Cash—was that the first instance?

How many more had there been since?

He'd have to talk to the McCullens—see if they'd looked into the lawyer. But the thought of meeting his brothers made his gut clench.

He wasn't ready for that. Not with the memory of those letters fresh in his mind.

Worse, now he'd divulged his secrets to Tia. She'd grown silent, obviously contemplating the implications of his statement.

He spotted a barbecue restaurant and pulled into it. "Let's get a quick lunch. I need to call Gwen."

Tia nodded, worry radiating from her features as they made their way inside. They grabbed a booth and ordered, then he stepped outside to phone Gwen.

"I checked into Kelly Ripples's story," Gwen said. "She's telling the truth. She's been in the hospital three times over the past year with injuries consistent with spousal abuse. A neighbor reported a domestic at her place six weeks ago. Found a pregnant Kelly on the floor bloody and bruised."

"Son of a bitch."

"Yeah, he's a bad one. Good for her for getting away from him."

"We just have to keep him away," Ryder said. It was a damn shame women needed help to escape the men who supposedly loved them. But better for the child to not have a father than have one who hit him.

"I have someone else I want you to run a background check on. A lawyer named Frank Frost. He has a practice in Cheyenne. Also look for info on William Frost."

"What are you looking for?"

Ryder explained his personal situation, including the history behind his own adoption, brushing over Gwen's murmur of sympathy. "The woman in the video, Bonnie Cone, used Frank Frost for legal services in a recent adoption. I need to know if that was legitimate, if adoptions are his specialty, if there have been any complaints against him—"

"I got it. I'll get back to you ASAP."

He thanked her, then hung up and started inside. A breeze blew in, stirring dust. A ranch in the distance reminded him of the McCullens and Horseshoe Creek.

He had to put aside his feelings and talk to the McCullens. See if they had insight on either of the Frost men. If Maddox had investigated him, it could save Ryder time.

Stomach knotted, he punched Cash's number.

"Ryder?"

"Yeah," Ryder said. "I read the letters."

A tense moment stretched between them. "They wanted us."

"I know that now."

"You want to come by Horseshoe Creek and talk?"

Did he? "Sometime. But I'm mired in this kidnapping case right now. Actually, that's the reason I called."

"What do you need?"

An odd feeling tightened his chest. He'd always worked alone. Been a loner all his life.

Now he had brothers.

Cash had offered to help, no questions asked.

"I need to know if you or any of the McCullens know anything about a lawyer named William Frost."

A heartbeat passed. "Frost?"

"Yeah. He's the lawyer who handled my adoption. I wondered if he was in on our kidnapping."

Cash's breathing echoed over the line. "I'll talk to Maddox and Ray and call you back."

Ryder thanked him and disconnected. He had to get back to Tia. She was anxious for news.

He wished to hell he had some.

TIA TRIED TO eat her pulled pork sandwich, but she could barely swallow the food. Her stomach was churning.

Ryder had been kidnapped as a baby. Her son had also.

And now that Ryder knew the truth, it was too late for him and his birth parents to reconcile.

What if that happened to her and Jordie? Was she doomed to a life where she searched the crowd everywhere she went, hoping to see a child that was her son? As the years went on and he changed, would she even recognize him?

She sipped her tea to wash down the sandwich. "I've been thinking." She set her tea glass on the table. "If this lawyer is involved in something illegal, he's not going to just come out and tell us."

Ryder's jaw tightened. "No. I'll need a warrant for his records."

"That's not easy," Tia said. "Not with adoption or medical records."

"Gwen's seeing what she can dig up, and I called Cash

to see if the McCullens know anything about Frost. They're both going to get back to me."

He dug into his sandwich, and Tia toyed with an idea in her head. "You're planning to talk to Frank Frost?"

Ryder nodded as he chewed. "I'm hoping to find out something to use as leverage to persuade him to talk."

"I have an idea." Tia tapped her nails on the table. "Why don't we pose as a couple wanting to adopt a baby?"

Ryder scrubbed a hand through his hair. "That's not a bad idea, Tia, but you were on TV. He'll recognize you."

Tia's pulse jumped. She hadn't thought of that. "Wait a minute," she said, her mind spinning. "I'll wear a disguise."

He took another bite of his sandwich and wiped his mouth with the gingham napkin. "I don't know. He might see through it."

Tia's mouth twitched. "Trust me, Ryder. I've done this before." At his perplexed look, she continued, "I mean, for other women."

Ryder studied her as he finished his meal. "I don't need to know details," he said.

Because he sensed what she'd done might have crossed the lines with the law. It had a few times. But sometimes the law failed.

"All right. But I think it could work."

Ryder ordered a cup of coffee and pie. "It's worth a shot, although if he recognizes you and realizes what we're doing, it could be dangerous."

"I don't care," Tia said. "I don't want Jordie to be lost to me forever like you were to your parents."

Her comment hit home and brought pain to his eyes.

"I'm sorry. I—"

"You're just speaking the truth," Ryder said. "I admire that, Tia. I've been lied to enough in my life."

Tia laid her hand over his and stroked it. "What do you mean?"

He glanced at their hands, and she expected him to pull away. But he didn't. He turned his hand over beneath hers and curled his big fingers around hers.

"My father is dead, but I talked to my mom. She claims she didn't know I was kidnapped, but she and Dad knew I was a twin. They didn't take my brother because he was sickly." His tone turned gravelly with anguish. "Cash was never adopted. He bounced from one foster home to another and had a rough life."

Tia had heard similar stories.

"That's sad," Tia said. "Is he all right now?"

Ryder nodded, his frown softening. "He's connected with the McCullens and is married. He even adopted two kids."

Tia rubbed his palm. "That's a great ending to the story. He used what happened to make him stronger and to give back to needy children."

"But he could have grown up with me, had a decent upbringing—"

"You feel guilty that you got the better deal," Tia said, sensing guilt beneath the surface of his words.

His troubled gaze lifted to hers, and he gave a quick nod.

"It's not your fault," Tia rushed to assure him. "You were an innocent kid, a baby when you were taken. You didn't know about him."

"Not until this week." Resentment deepened his tone.

Tia's heart ached for him. "You're angry at your mother because she didn't tell you about him."

He nodded again. "How could she keep that from me?"

A tense silence stretched between them.

"I don't know, Ryder," Tia said honestly. "It was obviously a complicated situation. Maybe she was trying to protect you."

"Protect me from what?" Ryder barked. "From knowing I had a sibling?" He shook his head. "No. She was protecting herself and Dad," Ryder said. "She said they didn't have enough money to raise both of us."

"Was that true?"

He shrugged. "Maybe. But they claimed they paid to get me. That the McCullens sold me. That's what I thought until Cash showed up and told me the truth."

"I don't completely understand, Ryder," Tia said softly. "But they must have loved you, so give it some time."

He didn't look convinced, but the waitress appeared and he left cash to pay the bill. His phone buzzed just as she walked away.

Ryder glanced at the number then back at Tia. "It's Cash. I need to take this."

Tia decided to stop in the ladies' room while he answered the call. Her emotions were all jumbled. Hearing Ryder's story reminded her that Jordie was in someone else's arms now.

And that she had to get him back. She couldn't spend a lifetime wondering where he was and if he was safe.

RYDER INHALED THE fresh air as he stepped outside. He shouldn't have confided his story to Tia. But when she'd taken his hand and looked at him with those tender, compassionate eyes, he hadn't been able to stop himself.

His phone buzzed again. He pressed Connect. He had to get his head back in the case. "Cash?"

"Yeah. I spoke with Maddox. When he and Ray were trying to find us, they learned we were left at a church. The name Frost did come up. He was a lawyer in Sagebrush, but he died ten years ago."

"Did he have a son?"

"Yeah, his son is about our age. He took over his father's practice." Cash paused. "Maddox questioned him about us, but he said he had no clue. Adoption records were private and sealed."

"I'll work on obtaining warrants," Ryder said. "Tia and I are going to question Frank Frost this afternoon."

"Keep us posted," Cash said.

"I will." When this case was settled, he'd meet his other brothers, too.

He ended the call, then phoned Gwen. "I need you to work on obtaining warrants for a lawyer named Frank Frost and for his files. Also, see if you can get one for his deceased father's case files."

"That'll take time."

"I think Frank Frost may be involved in the Jeffries baby kidnapping."

"Any evidence to support it?"

"That's why I need the warrants." A double-edged sword. Judges were hesitant to force situations without probable cause.

"Bonnie Cone said Frost handled her baby's adoption. Since the name Frost surfaced regarding my adoption, I think there's a connection."

"I'll get on it ASAP."

He explained about his plan with Tia, and Gwen agreed to rush to set up a profile for the couple, complete with a background, bank information and accounts, and job history along with a cell phone he could use in dealing with the lawyer, one that couldn't be traced back to him if Frost looked. "I had Elle contact Frost's office for an appointment," Tia told him. "They emailed paperwork for us to fill out, so I'll do that before we go. I'm going to say that we've tried in vitro fertilization and it's failed several times."

"Good idea," Ryder said.

"Let's stop by Crossroads," Tia said. "I have clothes there to create a disguise."

He agreed and they drove to the center. When they arrived, Tia and Elle filled out the paperwork from Frost's office and faxed it to them, then she disappeared into a back room while Ryder checked in with the security officer he'd asked to watch the place, an ex-military guy named Blake Bowman.

"Any problems?" Ryder asked.

Bowman shook his head. "No." He lowered his voice. "The people here are something else. They're doing good work."

All thanks to Tia and her generosity.

Elle joined them, her body language exuding anxiety. "Any word about Jordie?"

"We may be on to something," he said. "How is Kelly?"

"She's settled in and seems willing to accept our help."

"Good."

Elle tucked a strand of hair behind her ear. "You are going to find Jordie, aren't you, Agent Banks?" She glanced toward the door. "Tia doesn't deserve this."

"I'm doing everything possible."

The door opened, and a woman with curly blond hair, bright green eyes and wearing a Western skirt appeared. She was almost as tall as Ryder, with big bosoms, and wore a wrist brace on one arm.

"What do you think?"

Ryder's eyes widened at the sound of Tia's voice.

He hadn't recognized her at all.

Hopefully Frost wouldn't, either.

"I didn't know it was you," he said gruffly.

She smiled. "I told you I could pull it off." She offered

him a long Duster coat, hat and glasses to disguise himself, then they hurried to his SUV.

"Let me take the lead when we see Frost," he said.

She slipped something from her pocket and opened her palm to him.

Two simple gold wedding bands lay in her palm. "If we're going to inquire about adoption, we have to pose as a married couple."

Ryder considered balking, but she was right.

Still, for a single man who liked being alone, it felt odd as hell when he slid that wedding band on his third finger.

Chapter Twenty

Tia and Ryder practiced their story on the way to the law-yer's office.

Thankfully Gwen was on top of things, and Frost's personal assistant had already emailed that they had been approved and everything was in order.

Tia adjusted her wig as they parked in front of Frost's office.

"Are you sure you're up to this?" Ryder asked as they made their way up to the man's office.

Tia nodded. "I'll do whatever it takes."

Ryder gave her an encouraging smile. "You're a brave woman, Tia."

She shook her head. "Not brave. I'm a mother. It's just what mothers do—protect their children at any cost."

"Unfortunately not all mothers are that way," Ryder said darkly. "Believe me, I've seen some shocking examples over my career."

Tia sighed. "I'm sure you have. And all your life you thought your own mother had sold you." She pressed a hand to his cheek. "Now, you know that's not true. She loved you and Cash."

She was right. Emotions clouded his expression, and he reached for the door to the lawyer's office. "Let's do this."

Tia offered him a brave smile and entered first. Playing the loving husband, Ryder kept his hand at the small of her back.

"Jared and Emma Manning," Ryder said. "I called earlier to see Mr. Frost."

The perky redhead announced their arrival to her boss. "Follow me."

Tia held on to Ryder's arm as they entered. The receptionist made introductions and offered them coffee, but she and Ryder declined.

Frank Frost was midthirties, with neatly groomed hair, a designer suit and caps that had probably cost a fortune. Framed documents on the wall chronicled his education and legal degree, along with photographs of him and an older man who resembled him, most likely his father. Another picture captured him with a leggy blonde in an evening gown posing in front of a black Mercedes. A Rolex glittered from his left arm.

Tia gritted her teeth. Had he made his money by selling babies?

Frost ran a manicured hand over his tie. "Have a seat, Mr. and Mrs. Manning, and tell me how I can help you."

Ryder started to speak, but Tia caught his arm. "Let me tell him, honey."

Ryder's gaze met hers. "Of course, sweetheart."

His look was so strained that Tia bit back a chuckle. But she focused on Frost and her act. "We've wanted a baby forever," she said earnestly. "But it hasn't been in the cards, what with my endometriosis and all. We've been through all the tests and spent a small fortune on in vitro, but it didn't work."

"I'm sorry to hear that," Frost said, injecting sympathy in his voice. "It always saddens me when folks such as yourself, who would obviously make good parents, aren't blessed in that way when others who aren't parent material spit kids out left and right."

"Thank you for understanding," Tia continued. "I was just about ready to give up, but I met this woman at the hospital when I was leaving the other day. She had the saddest story ever and told me that she'd lost her own child, but that she was adopting a baby." Tia dabbed at her eyes. "So it hit me then, that that's what we had to do."

"There are a lot of unwanted children in the world," Frost said.

"I really want an infant," Tia said. "I…just love babies and want to get a little one so he or she will bond with us from the beginning."

Frost shifted, pulling at his tie. "Infants are harder to come by and in higher demand."

"I tried to tell my wife that," Ryder said. "But she wants a baby so badly." He removed a checkbook and set it on his lap. "I'm willing to pay the adoption fees and any extra costs if we can expedite finding us a child." He tapped the checkbook. "Money is not a problem. I…have done well for myself."

Tia pressed a kiss to Ryder's cheek. "Isn't he wonderful? He's going to be an amazing father."

Frost looked back and forth between them as if searching for a lie. But Tia swiped at tears and leaned into Ryder, playing the desperate woman and adoring wife.

"Please help us," Tia whispered. "I don't think I can go on if I don't have a baby in my arms." That much was true.

Ryder curved an arm around her, pulled her to him and dropped a kiss on her head. "I promised Emma that we'd have a family," he said, his voice cracking with emotions. "You understand how difficult it is for a man to not be able to give the woman he loves everything she wants."

Frost nodded slowly. "I'm sure it's difficult."

"Not just difficult," Ryder said. "It's painful and frustrating." He opened his checkbook and reached for a pen. "Just tell me what you need to make it happen so my sweet wife here will finally get to have the child she deserves and wants."

A thick silence fell for a moment, then Frost gave a conciliatory nod. "I will see what I can do. Although it might take a few days."

Tia gripped Ryder's hand and kissed it, then shot Frost a smile of gratitude. "You have no idea how much this means to me, to us."

"I'm happy to be able to assist you." Frost shook Ryder's hand. "I'll let you know when I have a baby that suits your needs and then we'll make the arrangements."

Tia's heart pounded. She didn't want to leave without something concrete to go on. But Ryder gently pulled her to stand, keeping her close to him and playing the loving husband.

"Come on, sweetheart, it's going to be all right now." He arched a brow at Frost. "You won't let us down, will you, Mr. Frost?"

A sly grin tilted the man's face. "Just have your finances in order when I call."

"No problem." Ryder coaxed Tia to the door.

She chewed the inside of her cheek to keep from screaming at Frost and demanding that he tell her if he had her son.

Ryder pulled her out the door then back to his SUV. As soon as they climbed inside, she collapsed into the seat and closed her eyes.

RYDER'S PHONE BUZZED as they drove away. Gwen again. Hoping she had good news, he quickly connected it.

"Ryder, we just received a call through that tip line. A

woman. She wouldn't talk to me, but said she needed to speak to the woman on the news."

"Maybe she'll talk to me."

"I suggested that, but she said no. It has to be Tia."

Dammit.

"Where did the call come in from?"

"I don't know, she was only on the phone for a minute. Said she wanted Tia's number."

"Did you give it to her?"

"No, I told her I'd have to speak to Tia first. But she insisted that she had information that could be helpful."

Ryder cursed. Then why the hell hadn't she just given Gwen the details? "All right. When she calls back, give her Tia's number. But keep a trace on her phone so we can track down this woman. If this is some kind of prank or if she's the one who threatened Tia earlier, I'll find her." Although the earlier caller had Tia's cell number.

Ryder ended the call then relayed the information to Tia. They were halfway back to Tia's when her phone trilled. She startled, then glanced at it and showed Ryder the display.

Unknown.

He bit back a curse, then motioned for her to answer it and place the call on speaker.

She laid the phone on the console and connected. "Hello."

Heavy breathing echoed over the line. Ryder clenched the steering wheel tighter, braced for a threat.

"Is this Tia Jeffries?"

Tia inhaled sharply. "Yes, who is this?"

"I don't want to give my name," the woman said in a low voice.

Tia twisted her mouth to the side in agitation. "Then what do you want?"

Another tense moment passed. "I don't know if this will help, but I delivered my baby at the same hospital where you did. It was six months ago, so I don't know if it's connected."

"If what's connected?" Tia asked.

"I'm a single mother," the woman continued. "I was down on my luck, moneywise, and lost my job a few weeks before the baby was due."

Ryder and Tia exchanged a questioning glance. Where was she going with her story?

"Anyway, when I was in the hospital in labor, this nurse came in to be my coach. At first he was nice and supportive, but he said he heard me telling the nurse at check-in that I had no insurance and that I was going to raise the baby alone."

Tia took a deep breath. "Go on."

"That's when things got odd."

"What do you mean odd?"

"He asked me if I'd considered giving my baby up for adoption."

Tia paled. "Had you?"

"No…well, maybe it occurred to me, but that was only because I was so broke and was afraid I couldn't take care of my child on my own. But I didn't think I could do it." The woman hesitated, her breathing agitated again.

"What happened?" Tia asked.

"I told him I'd think about it." She cleared her throat. "But once I held little Catherine in my arms, I knew I couldn't let her go. Then the nurse came in to visit me in the hospital room and pressured me. Said he knew someone who wanted a baby really badly, that we could go through a private adoption and I'd be compensated well enough to take care of my hospital bills and set me up for the future."

Ryder's blood ran cold.

"Then what?" Tia asked, her voice shaky with emotions.

"I told him no, again. And again. Then the day I brought my little girl home, he showed up at my house. It freaked me out, and I threatened to call the police if he contacted me again."

"What did he do then?" Tia asked.

"He got angry. But I held firm. When I picked up the phone to call 911, he left."

"Have you heard from him since?"

"No. But when I saw your story, it reminded me of how much that experience disturbed me. I mean, he knew where I lived. That I was alone. He even made me feel bad, that I was being selfish for raising a child on my own."

Tia rubbed her forehead. "You said *he*. It was a male nurse."

"Yes, his name was Richard." Her voice wavered. "Maybe I was just paranoid, but I…just thought it might be important."

"Thank you," Tia said. "Actually, Richard was one of my nurses when I went into the hospital, too."

Ryder swung the SUV off the side of the road and parked. Tia thanked the woman and asked her to call if she thought of anything else.

As soon as they disconnected, he phoned Gwen. "I need an address and everything you can find on a nurse named Richard Blotter."

TIA RACKED HER brain to remember if Richard had mentioned adoption to her.

She'd been half-delirious with excitement and pain that night when she had arrived at the ER.

He had helped her into the wheelchair and gotten her settled into a labor room. When she'd told him she had no labor coach, he assured her he'd help her through the process, but then Amy had stepped in.

"Tia?" Ryder's gruff voice broke into her thoughts. "What do you know about Richard Blotter?"

She massaged her temple, where a headache was starting to pulse. "Not much. He was nice to me, and seemed caring. But that night was chaotic."

"He knew you were a single mother?"

Tia nodded. "Yes, he was actually ending his shift, but he must have stayed, because he came by to see me after Jordie was born."

"So he knew you lived alone?"

"Yes." Bits and pieces of their conversation trickled through her mind. "He said he wasn't married, but he wanted to have a family someday. That he chose nursing because he liked to help people. He especially liked labor and delivery because he enjoyed being part of such a happy day for people."

"Did he seem suspicious to you? Like anything was off?"

Tia struggled to recall specifics. "Not really. He said he was raised by a single mother, and that it had been hard on her and him. That he always wanted a father." She hesitated. "I told him I wanted my baby to have a father, too, but the father wasn't interested."

Horror struck her.

She had been scared and in pain and nervous over the delivery and had spilled her guts about those fears.

Had Richard befriended her so he could gain access to her baby?

Chapter Twenty-One

Ryder gritted his teeth as the pieces clicked together in his mind.

Richard Blotter grew up in a single-parent home, missed having a father and resented it—perhaps he had projected his own bitterness on Tia and other women who chose to raise babies on their own.

The profile fit.

He also had access to patient files, worked in the labor and delivery unit and had personal contact with Tia. Bonnie had delivered at the same hospital, lost her baby and wanted another child.

But if Blotter was trying to place kids in two-parent homes, why would he have helped Bonnie adopt a baby when her husband had left her?

Unless he didn't know about the separation...

"Did Blotter ever call you at home or drop by to see you?"

Tia shook her head no. "But he could have found out where I lived."

"I know." Ryder punched the number for the hospital. "This is Agent Ryder Banks with the FBI. Is Richard Blotter on duty today?"

"Just a moment, please. I'll check," the receptionist said.

Tia bounced her leg up and down in a nervous gesture. Ryder rubbed her arm to soothe her.

"Agent Banks, actually, he was scheduled to work today, but he didn't show."

"Did he call in?"

"No, and that's odd. He's usually very dependable. Maybe there was a mix-up and he didn't realize he was on the schedule."

Or maybe he suspected his days were numbered, that the police were on to him.

"All right, if he shows up, please give me a call."

"May I ask what this is about? Do you think something happened to Richard?"

"I can't say at this point," Ryder said. "Just please let me know if he shows up at the hospital."

He checked his text messages. Gwen had sent him Blotter's home address. "He's not at the hospital today," he told Tia as he turned the SUV around and began to follow his GPS. "We're going to his house."

"I can't believe that Richard would do this," Tia said. "He seemed so nice and caring. I...trusted him."

"He was a nurse at the hospital," Ryder said. "You had no reason not to trust him."

"But I should have picked up on something."

Ryder blew a breath through his teeth. "People can fool us, Tia. Believe me, I've dealt with sociopaths who can lie without blinking an eye. Besides, you met him when you were vulnerable."

"I should have been smarter," Tia said, anger lacing her tone. "I let him get close and he kidnapped my child."

"We don't know that yet," Ryder said, although his gut instinct told him they were on the right track.

Tia shifted and turned to look out the window as they

drove. "I don't know whether to wish that he was involved or to hope that he wasn't."

"You're strong, Tia. If he is, at least we're getting closer to finding your baby."

He pressed the accelerator and sped toward Blotter's.

GUILT NAGGED AT Tia as Ryder drove. If her conversation with Richard was the reason he'd abducted Jordie, she'd never forgive herself.

She mentally replayed the night she'd given birth over and over in her head. Jordie had been a normal delivery—alert, his Apgar score high. She'd nursed him right away and kept him in the room with her all night.

She hadn't wanted him out of her sight.

Amy had assured her that her reaction was normal, that a lot of first-time mothers were paranoid about their newborn being away from them for even a moment.

She'd been right to be paranoid.

She'd just thought she and Jordie were safe in her own house.

They should have been, dammit.

Ryder veered into an apartment complex a mile from the hospital.

He checked the address, then wove through the parking lot in search of Blotter's building. "There it is." Ryder gestured to an end unit. The parking spots in front of it were empty, a sign Blotter wasn't home.

"I'm going to check it out. You can wait here if you want." He opened the car door and Tia jumped out, close on his heels.

Anger surged through Tia, pumping her adrenaline, and she removed her wig and dropped it on the seat. She wanted to confront Richard herself.

"Let me do the talking," Ryder said when they reached the door.

Tia nodded, although if Richard admitted he'd abducted her baby, she couldn't promise that she wouldn't tear his eyes out.

Ryder rang the doorbell, his gaze scanning the parking lot while they waited. Afternoon was turning to evening, and the lot was nearly empty.

Ryder punched the bell again, then pushed at the door. To her surprise, the door squeaked open.

Ryder motioned for her to stay behind him, then he removed his weapon from his holster. "Mr. Blotter, FBI Special Agent Ryder Banks."

Tia peeked past him. The foyer was empty. Ryder inched inside. "Mr. Blotter?"

Silence echoed back.

Holding his gun at the ready, Ryder moved forward. Tia stayed behind him, her gaze scanning the living room, which held a faded couch and chair. A small wooden table occupied the breakfast nook, paper cups and fast-food wrappers littering it.

No sign of a baby anywhere.

Ryder checked the bathroom and bedroom. "Clear. He's not here."

Tia stepped into the small bedroom. A faded spread, dingy curtains—no sign of Blotter. Ryder opened the closet door, and disappointment filled Tia.

No clothes inside.

She checked the dresser drawers. Empty.

Richard Blotter was gone.

"DAMMIT," RYDER SAID. "It looks like he left quickly."

"You think he knew we were coming?" Tia asked.

Ryder shrugged. "I don't know how he could. Not unless the nurse at the hospital gave him a heads-up we were asking about him." He phoned Gwen. "Get a BOLO out on Richard Blotter. He's cleaned out his apartment."

"On it," Gwen said. "I'm looking at his bank account now, Ryder. He cleaned it out, too."

"Were there any suspicious transactions before today?"

Tapping on computer keys echoed in the background. "He made a couple of big deposits over the last four years but quickly moved the money into an offshore account."

Could those have been payoffs for kidnapping babies or convincing single mothers to choose the adoption route?

"What about another house or property that he owns?"

"I don't see anything." She hummed beneath her breath. "Wait a minute, he has a sister."

That could be helpful. "What's her name?"

"Judy Kinley," Gwen said.

"Judy?" He glanced at Tia and saw her skin turn ashen. "Yes, she lives—"

"Across the street from Tia Jeffries." Ryder's pulse jumped. "Find out everything you can on her and Blotter. If there's a second address or other family members, let me know. And examine both their phone records."

If Blotter and his sister were working with Frost or with another party, they might find a clue in their contacts.

Tia was staring at him with a sick expression when he ended the call.

"Judy is Richard's sister?"

Ryder nodded.

"She never mentioned that her brother worked at the hospital," Tia said. "She came into my house and pretended to be my friend. She brought me food and a gift when Jordie was born." She gasped. "Oh, my gosh, she even brought me a dessert that day. I had some that night. Do you think she put something in it to make me sleep?"

Ryder silently cursed, "It might explain why you didn't wake up when Blotter came in. And why there were no signs of a break-in on the window," Ryder said.

Tia dropped her face into her hands. "Because she was in the nursery. She must have unlocked the window that day she visited me and Jordie." Tia pressed a hand to her chest on a pained sigh. "It's all my fault. I welcomed her in. I let her hold my baby."

Ryder rushed to console her. "This was not your fault," he said firmly. "These people are predators."

Anger replaced the hurt on her face. "We need to go to Judy's."

Ryder's gaze swept the room. He doubted she was home. If Blotter had skipped, she'd probably left with him.

"Help me look around here before we go. Maybe he left a clue to tell us where he went."

"I'll check the kitchen," she said.

Tia raced to the other room while he dug through the drawers and closet. But Blotter had cleaned them out as well, leaving no sign as to his plan.

TIA HOPED TO find something in the kitchen, an address or contact they could trace to her son, but the drawers and cabinets were empty.

Pain and hurt cut through her.

They had to find Richard and Judy. They were the key to her son.

Ryder appeared a second later. "Nothing in there. Gwen's searching their contacts, bank records, history."

Tia rushed to the door. "Let's go. Maybe Richard hasn't gotten to Judy yet."

They hurried outside, and Ryder raced toward Tia's neighborhood. She mentally beat herself up all the way.

How could she have been so stupid? She'd trusted Darren, and he'd deceived her. She'd trusted the hospital, the staff and nurses, but one of them had conspired to take her son. Then she'd trusted her neighbor who seemed friendly and helpful.

That was one of the worst deceptions. How could a woman do that to another woman?

Judy had taken betrayal to a new level—she'd consoled Tia the very night Jordie had disappeared.

No wonder Judy had been so quick to rush over. She'd known what was coming. She'd been watching the house, had probably alerted her brother when the house was quiet. When Tia had turned out the light.

Maybe she'd even stalled when she'd come to Tia's rescue to give her brother more time to make his escape with her son.

Ryder took the turn into the neighborhood on two wheels. He screeched into Judy's driveway, and they both hit the ground running.

Ryder gestured for her to wait behind him, then he drew his gun and held it at his side as he pounded on the door. "Judy? It's Agent Banks. We need to talk."

Tia checked the garage, but Judy's car was not inside.

Her heart sank. "Her car's gone, Ryder."

His jaw tightened. He knocked again then jiggled the door. Just like Blotter's, the door swung open. Ryder stormed in, Tia behind him, calling Judy's name.

The empty bookshelves looked stark now, a reminder that Judy hadn't added any personal touches to the place. No family photos or mementos.

Now Tia understood the reason.

Ryder raced through the house searching while Tia checked the kitchen drawers and desk. She fumbled through a few unpaid bills, then found a small note pad with several pages ripped out.

An envelope caught her eye, and she pulled it out and gasped. Several pictures of her when she was pregnant were tucked inside.

She checked the drawer again, hoping for an address or phone number of someone Judy or Richard might be working with.

Her fingers brushed something wedged inside the top desk drawer, the end caught. She stooped down and gently pulled at it until it came loose.

Rage shot through her. It was a photo of Jordie the day she'd brought him home from the hospital.

Ryder's boots pounded on the staircase as he rushed down. "Nothing upstairs."

Tia's hand trembled as she tossed the picture on top of the desk. "I was so stupid. She was watching me all along."

Ryder cursed and reached for the photo, but suddenly the sound of something crashing through the window jarred them both. A popping sound followed.

Then smoke began to fill the room.

Chapter Twenty-Two

Ryder dragged Tia outside into the fresh air as smoke billowed into the room. He pulled her beneath a cottonwood, and they leaned against it, panting for breath.

Tires screeched. Instantly alert, he scanned the yard and street and spotted a dark car racing down the road.

Did it belong to the person who'd thrown that smoke bomb in the house?

"What was that?" Tia said on a cough.

"Someone who doesn't want us finding the truth," Ryder said, jaw clenched.

Tia pushed her hair from her face. "Judy Kinley and Richard Blotter are definitely involved."

"I agree."

Ryder removed his phone to call 911, but a siren wailed and a fire truck careened around the corner. Someone on the street must have seen the explosion and called.

The fire engine wheeled into the driveway and firefighters jumped into action. "Are you okay?" Ryder asked Tia.

"Yes, go talk to them."

One of the firemen met him on the lawn. "What happened?"

Ryder explained.

"Anyone hurt or inside?"

"No. I'm going to call a crime unit to process the inside

of the house, though. I believe the woman who was living here was involved in a baby kidnapping."

The fireman lifted his helmet slightly, expression dark, then gave a nod and went to join the others. Ryder phoned for the crime unit, then made his way back to Tia as they waited.

She paced the yard, looking shell-shocked. "I can't believe Judy would do this to me. Why?"

Ryder shrugged. "Maybe she was protecting her brother or needed money."

"But who did they give my baby to?"

He wished to hell he knew. "We'll find him, Tia. We're getting closer."

"If Richard was involved, do you think someone else at the hospital knew?"

Good question. "Let's go back to the hospital and see." Maybe by then Gwen would have something on Richard and his sister, like an address where they might be hiding out. She was supposed to be checking their prints against the matchbook he'd found outside the baby's nursery.

The crime team arrived ten minutes later, and Ryder explained the situation to the chief investigator while Tia walked across the street to her house to change from her disguise.

"I want the place fingerprinted," he said. "Then let's compare the prints to the matchbook we found outside the nursery." He had a feeling Blotter and Judy were accomplices.

Frost still ranked high on his list as the leader.

One of them might be able to point them to the person who actually had Jordie.

TIA BATTLED NERVES as she and Ryder entered the hospital. Each time she walked through the door, the memory of giving birth to her son returned. She had been so proud when she'd carried him home that day, so elated and full of plans for the future.

That future looked dismal without Jordie in it.

Ryder went straight to the nurses' station. Hilda, the charge nurse, waved to her. "Tia, I saw the news story," Hilda said. "Is there any word?"

"Not yet." Tia motioned for Hilda to step aside and they slipped into the break room while Ryder canvassed the other staff for information on Richard.

"Hilda, I have reason to think that Richard Blotter might have been involved. Did you ever see or hear him do anything suspicious?"

Hilda's eyes widened. "No, he was always so helpful, especially with the single mothers." Alarm flashed across her face as if she realized the implications. "Are you suggesting he was friendly because he was up to something?"

Tia nodded. "I don't think he was working alone, though. His sister lived across from me. I think she was watching me and unlocked the window in the nursery so he could come in and take Jordie."

"But why would they do such a thing?" Hilda asked.

That was the big question. "I don't know yet," Tia said. "But some people are willing to pay a lot to adopt a baby."

Hilda gasped.

Tia's stomach knotted. "Was Richard close to anyone here at the hospital? Did he have a girlfriend?"

Hilda scowled and peered down the hall. "Not that I know of."

Tia bit her tongue in frustration. "Is Amy here today?"

"She just left, sweetie." Hilda's phone buzzed, and she checked the number. "I have to get this. I'm praying for you, Tia."

Tia thanked her and followed her back to the nurses'

station. She punched Amy's number then left a message asking Amy to call her.

Amy had worked more closely with Richard than Hilda. Maybe she knew something about him that could help.

RYDER'S NEWLY ISSUED phone vibrated as he ended his conversation with an orderly who stated that he'd always thought Blotter showed a peculiar interest in the single mothers. He'd thought Blotter was interested in striking up a romance, but it was an odd place to look for female companionship.

Ryder agreed with that.

The phone vibrated again. Frost's number showed up on the screen. Surprised to hear something so quickly, he hesitated. Frost might be on to them.

"Jared Manning speaking."

"Yes, Mr. Manning, I reviewed your information and everything seems to be in order."

"Great. When do you think you'll have a baby for us?"

"Actually, that's the reason I'm calling. Typically it takes months to find an infant, but it just so happens that we were placing a baby today, but the couple we were working with backed out. So, it may seem sudden, but if you and your wife are interested, we could arrange for you to take this child."

Sweat beaded on Ryder's neck. He wasn't buying the man's story. Maybe Frost had checked out the phony bank account and decided the Mannings had more money than the other couple so his profit would be larger.

Whatever, he couldn't turn down this opportunity. "Of course we're interested. Is it a boy or a girl?"

A pregnant pause. "I believe it's a little girl. I didn't think you were particular about the sex."

"We're not," Ryder said, careful to keep his tone neutral. "I just wanted to tell my wife. She's going to be so excited. I'm sure she'll want to pick up some clothes and girly things."

"Good. I'm glad. Now we have some details to work out."

"Just tell me what you need," Ryder said.

"My secretary will send you an account number for a wire transfer and the amount. Once that's taken care of, we'll schedule a time and place for you to pick up the baby."

"How soon will this happen?"

"Since we already had this adoption arranged, the placement can happen tonight. That is, unless that's too soon."

"No, tonight is great. I can't wait to tell my wife."

"Good. You'll receive the details shortly. I hope you and your wife and the little girl will be very happy."

Ryder assured him they would be, then stared at the phone in silence when the man hung up.

He hurried toward Tia. "Frost just called. He has a baby for us."

Hope lit Tia's eyes. "A little boy?"

He shook his head. He'd probably already placed Jordie. "A baby girl. But if we catch him in the act, we can force him to talk."

Renewed determination mingled with disgust on Tia's face. "When do we get her?"

Ryder's phone dinged with a text. He quickly skimmed for details.

"Tonight. Eight o'clock. I'll have Gwen wire money into his account now."

His mind churned. If they were about to crack a baby stealing/selling ring, he wanted to take Frost and whoever else was involved down. His first thought was to call Maddox, the sheriff of Pistol Whip.

But he'd never even met the man.

This was not how he wanted to meet, either.

So he phoned his boss. Statham would send backup with no questions asked.

AN HOUR LATER, Tia dressed again in her disguise. Tonight she was no longer Tia Jeffries—she was Emma Manning.

Looking to adopt a child.

Granted, she'd hoped the baby that the lawyer would bring was her own son, but at least they were one step closer to finding him.

If Frost was selling babies to the highest bidder, they would catch him and put him away.

She certainly didn't want any other mother to suffer the pain she'd felt the past few days.

Ryder donned his disguise as well. They didn't want anyone to immediately recognize him and run. Anxiety filled Tia as they drove to Frost's office to finalize the paperwork.

He wasn't in the office, but his receptionist handed him the documents and they signed them, anxious to complete the exchange.

When the lawyer's personal assistant left the room, Ryder photographed the documents and sent a copy to the lab for analysis.

Then they went to the outdoor café next door to pick up the baby. She and Ryder had both agreed that was an odd place for an adoption exchange, that it indicated something fishy, but they had to follow through, pretend to be the desperate couple who asked no questions but paid to get what they wanted.

Ryder visually scanned the parking lot as he parked. "Are you ready?"

Tia nodded. He'd insisted they bring a rental van in case they were being watched. Richard and Judy might recognize Tia's. She had insisted Ryder install the car seat.

Whoever this baby belonged to, she intended to protect the child at all costs.

Ryder squeezed her hand. "Remember, play it cool. We'll wait until the child is handed over and then move in to ask questions or make an arrest."

"Do you think Frost or Richard Blotter will show?"

"I have no idea what to expect, but we have to be prepared for anything."

Tia braced herself and adjusted her wig. She'd never felt so alone.

Except for Ryder. He was here.

She'd hang on to him as long as possible. And when she got Jordie back, she'd once again learn to manage on her own.

"How are we supposed to know who we're meeting?" she asked.

Ryder gestured toward the entrance and then asked for a table. "Frost's assistant sent our photograph to whoever is bringing the baby."

Tia fidgeted with her purse, trying to act normal, but her pulse was racing. Ryder threw his arm around her, nuzzling her neck, perpetuating the image of a young couple in love as they made their way to the hostess's station.

Ryder pointed out a corner table toward the back of the outdoor seating area. "We want that table."

Tia realized he'd chosen it to give them a good view of the entrance so he could look for the person they were supposed to meet.

She draped herself around him as they walked to the table, half faking the kisses yet needing his strength to help her through the nerve-racking ordeal. When they sat, the waitress immediately deposited water on the table and took coffee orders.

Ryder positioned his chair to watch the entrance and

pulled her close to him again, twining his fingers with hers. She stared at their laced fingers—her hand so small in his, his so large and calloused yet so tender, and a wealth of emotions swelled in her throat.

Suddenly he stiffened, and she jerked her gaze to the door. Her heart stalled in her chest.

Amy, the young labor nurse who'd befriended her, appeared, holding an infant.

"My God, not Amy," Tia whispered.

Amy scanned the seating area, shifting back and forth, her movements jittery. A second later, she looked at Ryder and must have recognized him.

Panic streaked her expression, then she turned and ran.

Chapter Twenty-Three

"Amy?" Tia rose to go after the young woman, but Amy had disappeared.

Ryder shot up. "I'm going after her!"

He jumped the gate to the patio and Tia jogged to the gate entrance, pushed it open and followed. Amy was running across the street toward a white SUV, clutching the baby to her.

Ryder caught up to her and cornered her by the vehicle. Tia's breath rasped out as she wove between cars.

Shock mingled with hurt and disbelief. Tia removed her wig and Amy gasped.

"You took my son?" Tia cried.

Amy shook her head in denial. The baby started to cry and she jiggled the infant in her arms, trying to shush it. "No, I didn't do it, Tia. I swear."

Ryder folded his arms, his big body blocking her from escaping and pressing her against the side of the SUV.

"Who does this child belong to?" Ryder asked, his tone hard.

Tears blurred Amy's eyes. "A teenager. She gave her up for adoption."

"Just like I supposedly did," Tia snapped.

Amy's face contorted in pain.

"Where's my son?" Tia shouted.

"You have to believe me, Tia," Amy said. "I...didn't take Jordie. I swear."

"Then what's going on?" Ryder demanded.

Amy trembled, the baby crying louder. She patted its back, but Tia reached out and took the infant. Her arms had felt empty for so long. This little girl wasn't Jordie, but she could comfort her until they brought her home to her mother.

"Explain," Ryder said sharply.

Amy wiped at her eyes. "I...I swear I didn't know about Jordie or anything about babies being kidnapped."

"Yet here you are," Ryder said with no sympathy.

"I got a call, was told to drop this baby off with its adopted parents."

"Who called you?" Ryder asked.

"Richard Blotter," Amy said. "He...threatened me, threatened my little girl." More tears trickled down her cheeks. "You know my daughter is handicapped. She needs surgery. I didn't have the money..."

"He paid you to steal babies from the nursery," Ryder cut in.

"No." She sucked in a sharp breath. "A while back, I caught Richard Blotter hacking into patient files. He said he worked with a lawyer who handled adoptions. I threatened to tell the hospital that he was violating patient confidentiality, but he assured me he was only helping mothers and families by connecting them with the lawyer. I thought it was legitimate."

Amy looked miserable. "I had to do something to help Linnie. She needs braces to straighten her legs so one day she can walk. I...just wanted to give her a normal life, as normal as she could have."

The baby had quieted in Tia's arms as she swayed back and forth.

"But you eventually figured out what was happening?" Ryder asked.

Amy gulped. "I heard Richard on the phone a couple of days ago. He sounded upset, nervous. He said they had to lie low, that the police were asking questions." She twisted her purse strap between her fingers. "That's when I realized what had happened."

"Then why didn't you come forward and tell me?" Tia cried.

"I confronted Richard, but he said if I told I'd be arrested for my part, that I'd go to jail for aiding in a kidnapping." She gave Tia an imploring look. "I couldn't go to jail, not when my little girl needs me."

Compassion for the woman's situation filled Tia, but hurt over Amy's betrayal overpowered it. "So you just kept quiet and let them take my baby. Where is he, Amy? Where is Jordie?"

Amy's face wilted again and she shook her head. "I don't know, Tia. I…honestly don't know."

"I'm sorry, Miss Yost," Ryder said. "But you're going to have to come with me until we sort this out."

Amy shot Tia a panicked look. "But I'm supposed to go home to Linnie."

"Who's with her now?" Tia asked.

"My mother." Amy's voice cracked. "She'll be devastated if I go to jail. And if I lose my job, I can't support us."

"Let's take it one step at a time." Ryder guided Amy to the rental van. Tia carried the baby, soothing the infant with her soft voice.

She strapped the baby into the car seat in the back beside Amy, who was staring into space, ashen-faced and terrified.

Ryder needed a safe place to leave her, but he didn't want to take her to Sheriff Gaines. He considered the McCullens, but this wasn't the way he wanted to meet his brothers. He still had to bring Frost in for questioning and find Blotter and Judy.

He drove to the FBI office instead then escorted Amy to an interrogation room. "Do you have information on the mother of that baby?" Ryder asked.

She shook her head no. "I was just told that she'd signed away her rights and that another couple wanted her."

He pushed her again for more on Frost, but she didn't seem to know anything else helpful.

A kind woman named Constance from the Department of Family Services arrived to take the baby until they sorted out the custody issue.

"I'm sorry, Tia, really," Amy said for the dozenth time.

"Just cooperate and tell the police whatever you know," Tia said. "I don't want what happened to me to happen to anyone else."

Ryder's chest clenched. Even though Tia was suffering, she still had compassion for Amy. She was an unusual woman.

"My little girl needs me," Amy said in a pained whisper.

"Tia's baby needs her, too," Ryder said. "Cooperate and we'll see what we can work out."

They left Amy in federal custody and the baby with Constance then drove back toward Frost's office.

"I'm sorry your friend was involved," Ryder said.

Tia muttered a sarcastic sound. "It seems like everyone I meet lies to me." She touched Ryder's arm. "Promise me you won't do that. If you find out something about Jordie, promise you'll tell me no matter what."

Ryder didn't want to be the bearer of bad news. He wasn't giving up now, either. "I promise."

She relaxed slightly, and he sped into the lawyer's office

parking lot. Although he was gone earlier, Frost's Mercedes was in the parking lot now.

Ryder led the way, anxious to get this bastard and make him talk. Early evening shadows played across the parking lot, accentuating the fact that most everyone had gone home for the day.

He snatched the warrants he got at the FBI office from his pocket as he reached the office door, then gave a quick rap on the door and pushed it open. He paused in the entryway to listen for sounds that Frost was inside or had a client but heard no voices. Only the faint sound of a familiar machine.

A paper shredder.

Adrenaline pumping, he rushed through the reception area, following the noise. Frost was in the file room behind the shredder, feeding files into it.

"Stop, Mr. Frost. I'm Special Agent Ryder Banks." Ryder waved the envelope. "I have warrants for your files."

Frost shifted, then reached down. Ryder thought he was going for the files, but Frost lifted a pistol and fired at them.

Tia screamed and ducked behind the door. Ryder pulled his weapon and fired back, hitting Frost in the chest. Frost grunted in shock, dropped his gun and collapsed to the floor.

Ryder kept his gun aimed on the man as he rushed toward him. Frost was reaching for his pistol again when Ryder made it to him, but Ryder kicked it out of the way.

"It's over, Frost," Ryder barked.

Tia ran up behind him. "Where's my son, you bastard?"

Frost coughed, his eyes closing then opening again.

Ryder stooped down and grabbed the man around the neck. "Where's the baby?"

Frost gasped and tried to speak, choking for a breath. Blood gushed from his chest wound, soaking his white designer shirt. Then his eyes rolled back in his head and he faded into unconsciousness.

Ryder released the man abruptly. "Don't you dare die, you bastard."

Tia dropped to her knees and shook the man. "Wake up and tell me where my baby is!"

But Frost's only response was to gurgle up blood.

Ryder cursed, afraid it was too late, and called for an ambulance.

TIA FOUGHT DESPAIR as the paramedics loaded the lawyer's unconscious body onto the stretcher and into the ambulance. Ryder instantly went to work searching the files while the crime unit began processing the office space and sorting through the shredded documents.

Tia looked over Ryder's shoulder into the file cabinet. "Anything on Jordie?"

"Not yet." He offered her a smile of encouragement. "But don't give up. We still have mountains of papers to sort through, plus we need to search his computer."

Tia tried to hang on to hope. They couldn't have come this far and not find her baby.

Although if Frost had destroyed the documents pertaining to Jordie and he died, and they didn't find Richard Blotter, her son might be lost to her forever.

Chapter Twenty-Four

Ryder hoped the search of Frost's files would turn up an address for the person who had Tia's son, but no such luck. There was a list of other adoptions, which appeared to be legitimate, but he turned them over to the Bureau's unit that worked with the National Center for Missing and Exploited Children—NCMEC—to verify the adoptions and their legitimacy.

He and Tia sat in silence in the waiting room of the hospital, their nerves raw. A few minutes later, a doctor appeared with a grave expression on his face. "I'm sorry, but Mr. Frost didn't make it."

Tia sagged against him, devastated. Their only lead was gone.

"We're still looking at his computer, and if we find Blotter, he may have the information we need."

She nodded against him, although her despair bled into his own. He didn't want this case to end without answers.

He wrapped his arms around her. "I'm driving you home to get some rest."

"I want to do another press conference," Tia said. "To-night."

Ryder debated on the wisdom of the idea, but what did they have to lose?

He phoned the station and spoke with Jesse, the anchorwoman who'd interviewed Tia before. She was anxious for more of the story and agreed to the late-night segment.

If Ryder had exposed a major baby-selling ring, the public had a right to know. They also needed eyes searching for Blotter and his sister, Judy.

They stopped for Tia to change out of her disguise. She looked exhausted and sad, but she held her head up and faced the camera with a brave face.

Ryder spoke first. "Tonight we have information regarding the missing Jeffries baby, although we do not have the baby back in custody." He explained about the lawyer's alleged adoption setup and his theory about Blotter and his sister serving as accomplices.

"If anyone has seen or had contact with Mr. Blotter or Ms. Kinley, please phone our tip line." The station displayed pictures of the man and his sister. "Or if you have information regarding Mr. Frost and his adoption practices, please come forward."

Tia clenched the microphone with a white-knuckled grip. "I'm Tia Jeffries and I'm pleading with you again. I believe these people abducted my son. It's possible that whoever adopted my baby isn't aware that he was stolen from his own bed, from his mother. If that is the case, there will be no repercussions. I just want my son back safely."

She wiped at a tear but managed to maintain control as the anchorwoman summarized the story and repeated the number for the tip line.

"Good luck, Miss Jeffries." Jesse gave her a hug.

Tia thanked her and Ryder drove her home. When they reached her house, Tia rushed inside.

She darted into the bathroom and shut the door, then he heard the shower water kick on and her sobs followed.

Tia felt limp when she climbed from the shower. She dried off and combed through her wet hair on autopilot, numb from the day's events. She yanked on a tank top and pajama pants and left the bathroom in a daze.

Ryder was standing in the living room, a bottle of whiskey in front of him along with two glasses. He raised a brow and she nodded. Why not?

Maybe it would dull the pain for a while. Maybe when she woke up tomorrow, Jordie would be home in his crib and her life would be normal again.

Then Ryder would be gone.

She wanted her son back. But she realized she didn't necessarily want Ryder to leave.

Not a good sign.

He handed her the whiskey, and she swirled it around in the glass, lost in the deep amber color and the intoxicating smell.

Ryder tossed his drink down, then pressed his lips into a thin line. "We're not giving up, Tia. Don't think that."

His words soothed her battered soul. But she wanted more. His touch. His kiss. His mouth on hers, his lips driving away the pain with pleasure.

She sipped her drink. "I trust you, Ryder. I know you'll find him."

He slowly walked toward her. "You are the strongest woman I've ever known."

"I'm not strong," Tia said in a hoarse whisper.

"You are." He reached out and tucked a strand of damp hair behind her ear. His movement was so gentle and tender that her throat closed.

Yet her heart opened to him, and her body screamed with need. Unable to resist, she placed her hand against his cheek. His skin was tanned, rough with dark beard stubble, his eyes liquid pools of male hunger, desire and strength.

She needed that strength tonight.

She finished her drink, then pushed the glass into his hand. "Another?"

She shook her head no. "I don't want a drink."

He swallowed hard, his jaw tightening as she traced a thumb over his lips.

"Tia?"

"Shh, don't talk." Her body hummed to life with the desire to be closer to him.

She gave in to it, stood on tiptoe and pressed her lips to his. The first touch was raw, his breath filled with hunger. Her skin tingled as he deepened the kiss.

She whispered his name on a breath as he plunged his tongue into her mouth, and she tilted her head back, offering him free rein on her neck and throat as passion drove her to pull him closer.

She fumbled with the buttons of his shirt, and he brushed her cheek with the back of his hand, then lower to trace over her shoulder and down to her hip.

He pressed her into the vee of his thighs, his thick sex building against her belly, a sign that he wanted her just as she wanted him.

That was all she needed.

She was tired of hurting all the time.

For this one minute in time, she wanted to feel pleasure. Pushing the guilt aside, she clutched his arms and pressed her breasts against his chest.

Her nipples throbbed, stiffening to peaks, the warm tingle of electricity in her womb a reminder that she hadn't felt this way about a man in a long time.

She didn't bother to question what was happening. Life made no sense. All she'd known was pain for days.

Tomorrow the pain would be back.

But tonight, Ryder could alleviate it.

Every ounce of Ryder's ethical training ordered him to stop. To walk away.

But his body didn't seem to be listening to his brain.

Instead, the hunger inside him surged raw and primal, driving him to hold Tia closer, to stroke her back and shoulders, to brush her breast with one hand until he felt her chest rise and fall with her sharp intake of breath.

He deepened the kiss, savoring the heat between them as she met his tongue thrust for thrust. Her hands raked over his shoulders and back, her touch stirring his body's need.

He shifted, his erection throbbing against her belly and aching to be inside her warm heat.

She coaxed him to the bedroom until they stood by her bed. Soft moonlight spilled through the room, painting her in an ethereal glow. Yet that glow accentuated the paleness of her skin and the sadness in her eyes.

He took a deep breath and forced his hands to be still, to look into her face. "I won't take advantage of you," he said gruffly.

Her gaze met his, turmoil and pain and some other emotion he couldn't define flaring strong. "Then I'll take advantage of you."

With one quick shove she pushed him onto the bed.

His chest clenched. "Tia?"

"Shh." She pushed him to his back then crawled on top of him, straddling him and moving against him in a sensual move that sent white-hot heat through him.

He cupped her face with his hands and drew her to him for another kiss. Lips met and melded. Tongues mated and danced. His hands raced over her body as she tore at the buttons on his shirt.

She shoved the garment aside and the two of them frantically removed it, then she tossed it to the floor. Her hands made a quick foray over his chest, making his lungs explode with the need for air.

"You're beautiful, Tia," he murmured. God, she deserved better than this.

She kissed him again, then lowered her head and trailed kisses and tongue lashes along his neck. She teased and bit at his nipples, stroking his sex with one hand while she worked his belt and zipper with the other.

He wanted her naked before he exploded, dammit.

He slowed her hands, then settled her hips over his sex, moving her gently so he could cup her breasts in his hands. They were full, round and fit into his palms.

He kneaded them then lifted his head, pushed her tank top up and closed his lips over one ripe nipple. She moaned, threw her head back and clung to him.

He flipped her to her back then straddled her this time, loving both breasts with his hands and mouth, her moans of pleasure eliciting his own.

He trailed his tongue down her abdomen, then shoved her pajama bottoms off and spread her legs. She clawed at his back, but he wanted her, sweet and succulent in his mouth, hard and fast below him.

Pushing her legs farther apart, he drove his tongue to her sweet heat and suckled her. She groaned, writhing beneath him as he plunged his tongue deep inside her and tasted her release.

The sound of her crying his name as she came apart sent erotic sensations through him, and he rolled sideways long enough to discard his jeans and pull on a condom.

Then he rose above her, kneed her legs apart again and looked into her eyes.

The raw passion and pleasure on her face stole his breath.

He wanted to see her look like that again and again.

She closed her hand around his thick length and guided him inside her. He moaned her name and found his way home.

TIA CURLED INTO Ryder's arms, closed her eyes and savored the sensual aftermath of their lovemaking.

Although guilt niggled at her. How could she enjoy herself when her baby was still missing?

Still, her body quivered with erotic sensations, and she clung to him as if hiding in his arms could erase reality.

Finally she drifted into sleep. But sometime later, a ringing phone jarred her awake.

Ryder rolled from the bed, snatched his cell phone and answered. "Yeah? Okay. I'll be right there."

He reached for his shirt as he ended the call.

"Who was that?" Tia asked.

"Gwen. Someone spotted a man they think is Blotter at a motel near the airport. I'm going after him."

Tia pushed at the covers. "I'll go, too."

Ryder eased down on the bed beside her. "No, Tia, stay here and rest. He didn't have the baby with him. He might be dangerous."

Ryder's touch reminded her of their night of lovemaking, the frenzied, harried hunger, the gentle touches, the pleasure his touch evoked. She didn't want him to go.

But he had to do his job. And if he found Jordie…

She lifted one hand and placed it over his, grateful for his tenderness. "Please be careful, Ryder."

He nodded, eyes dark with the memories of their night together as well. "I will." He dropped a kiss on her lips, then gathered his jeans and yanked them on along with his socks and boots.

She watched him dress, silently willing him to come back to bed and make love to her again. But she bit back the words.

Finding her son was more important. She wanted him back in her arms so they could start their life together.

Her heart squeezed. Only Ryder wouldn't be part of that life.

RYDER PHONED LAW enforcement in Cheyenne, explained the situation and requested backup. A detective named Clay Shumaker met him near the airport.

Ryder checked with the motel clerk, who claimed a woman had signed herself in as Mrs. Jerome Powell.

Ryder showed him a picture of Judy Kinley and he identified her as the woman. Finally they were catching a break.

He and Shumaker approached the room with caution. Shumaker circled to the back to cover the bathroom window in case the couple tried to escape.

Ryder knocked on the door. "FBI. Open up, Blotter. Ms. Kinley. It's over."

The curtain slid aside and two eyes peered out. Judy Kinley.

"Give it up and no one will get hurt," Ryder shouted.

But the door opened and a gunshot rang out. Ryder cursed and jumped behind the rail to dodge the bullet. Blotter raced out, gun aimed and firing.

Ryder raised his weapon and fired back, catching Blotter in the shoulder. Blotter twisted and fired at Ryder.

Ryder's body bounced back as the bullet skimmed his arm.

Chapter Twenty-Five

His arm stung, but the bullet had only grazed him.

Another one skimmed by Ryder's head, missing him by a fraction of an inch. Ryder cursed and released another round, this time sending Blotter to his knees with a gunshot to the belly.

"He's down!" Ryder shouted to the detective.

Shumaker appeared, pushing Judy in front of him, her hands cuffed. She was crying. "Richard!"

Ryder kicked Blotter's gun aside and knelt to check his wounds. Blood oozed from his abdomen, and he'd lapsed into unconsciousness. Dammit.

He wanted Blotter alive and talking.

Ryder called for an ambulance then confronted Judy at the police car. Fear and panic flared in the woman's eyes. "Where is Tia's son?"

"I don't know," Judy said.

"Don't lie to me, Judy. You pretended to be Tia's friend, then you unlocked that window for your brother to come in and kidnap the baby. Why?"

Judy closed her eyes and released a pained sigh. "Money. Richard…he needed it. The people he owed threatened to kill him if he didn't pay up. I…told him I'd help this once, but that was it."

"So you and Richard conspired to kidnap Tia's baby,

then sold the child for cash," Ryder said, not bothering to hide the derision in his voice.

"It wasn't like that. That lawyer convinced me that the baby would be better off with two loving parents."

"That wasn't his or your decision," Ryder said. "Tia loves her son and would be—will be—a wonderful mother."

Judy hung her head in shame.

"Who did he give the baby to?" Ryder pressed.

"I told you, I don't know," Judy said.

"Nothing? Didn't your brother tell you a name or where the couple was from?"

Judy shook her head. "He said it would be better if I didn't know."

Then she wouldn't be culpable. But that was a lie. She was an accomplice to a felony.

The siren wailed, lights flashing as the ambulance arrived. Ryder gestured to the detective. "Book her."

"Please don't let my brother die," Judy said as the detective guided her into the back of his car.

Ryder didn't respond. He told the medics he'd follow them to the hospital.

As soon as Blotter regained conscious, he was going to talk.

He followed the ambulance to the hospital then stayed with the man in the ER.

"He needs surgery," the doctor told him.

"Make sure he survives," Ryder said. "That man kidnapped a child. I want to talk to him."

The doctor scowled. "I understand."

Ryder went to the vending machine for coffee then phoned Gwen for an update. "Please tell me you found something on Frost's computer or in his files."

"We've collected information on at least half a dozen

adoptions that might be in question and are assigning a task force to investigate them individually."

"What about a couple who got Jordie Jeffries? An address where he might be?"

"I'm afraid not. We won't give up, though, Ryder."

He closed his eyes in frustration, then returned to the waiting room to pace while he waited on Blotter to get through surgery.

A SOFT KNOCK at the door woke Tia. She stirred and stretched, then realized that it might be Ryder returning.

Maybe with news.

She pulled on her robe and knotted it at the waist, then hurried into the living room. Morning sunlight spilled through the front sheers and warmed the floor against her bare feet.

She hesitated at the door. "Ryder?"

"Yeah, open up, Tia."

Tia jerked the door open, her heart in her throat. Ryder faced her but stepped aside. "There's someone here who wants to see you."

A slender twentysomething woman was stooped down beside a baby carrier. A baby carrier holding a small blue bundle.

Tia gasped and dropped to her knees in front of the baby. "Jordie?"

Ryder cleared his throat. "Yes, it's him, Tia. He's fine."

Tia's gaze met the young woman's and she scooped her son up into her arms, tears spilling over. "Oh, my Jordie, I thought I would never see you again." She kissed and hugged him, then held him away from her to soak in his features before she planted more frantic kisses all over his face and head. "Oh, baby, I've missed you so much."

His little chubby face looked up at her, a tiny smile pulling at his mouth. "I love you so much, Jordie." She glanced at Ryder. "How did you find him?"

"Blotter was shot but he regained consciousness long enough to tell me the name of the adopted party."

He gestured toward the woman. "This is Hilary Pickens."

Hilary sniffed and dabbed at her eyes. She was shaking and looked terrified and sad at the same time. "I'm sorry... I didn't know." The woman's voice cracked on a sob and she touched the baby's head lovingly. "I didn't know he was stolen. The lawyer told us that he was ours, that his mother didn't want him."

A myriad of emotions flooded Tia. Rage at the people who'd done this.

Compassion for this woman, whom she believed had been a victim just as she had.

"I took good care of him, I swear," the woman said. "I wanted a baby so badly, and when he came to us, I couldn't believe it finally happened."

"You went through Frank Frost?"

The woman nodded, tears streaming down her face. "But then I saw you on the news and...at first I ran. I thought I couldn't give him back." She gulped a sob. "But then I kept thinking about you and hearing your voice begging to have him home, and I looked into his eyes and knew I couldn't keep him. That it would be a lie, that he wasn't really mine." She glanced at Ryder. "I was packing his things to bring him here when Agent Banks showed up at my door."

Ryder nodded in confirmation.

Tia cuddled Jordie closer, then reached out and took the woman's hand and led her inside.

Then she and Hilary hugged and rocked Jordie together while both of them cried.

Ryder stood aside as Tia and the young woman cooed over the baby. He had never met anyone like Tia.

She had suffered while her son was missing, yet she'd accepted the woman who had her child into her home and forgiven her within seconds.

The other woman was suffering, too, he realized. She had wanted a child, but she'd done the right thing when she discovered Jordie had been stolen from his mother without the mother's consent.

His own mother's face taunted him. The pain in Myra's eyes when he'd shown her his birth mother's letters.

He had been hard on her. Had walked away.

He had to see her.

Knowing Tia would be fine now she had her son, he slipped out the back door. She no longer needed him. She had her family.

It was time he reconciled with his own.

Anxiety knotted his gut as he drove to his mother's house. He knocked on the door, childhood memories bombarding him.

The times he was sick and his mother nursed him back to health with her homemade chicken soup and tenderness. The bedtime stories and holidays baking cookies together. His father teaching him to ride a bike and a horse.

The door opened, and his mother appeared, her face pale, eyes serious and worried. "Ryder?"

He offered her a smile. "Mom, I…I'm home."

A world of relief echoed in her breathy sigh, and she pulled him into her arms and hugged him.

Ryder hugged her in return. Nothing could change the way he'd come to be in this woman's life, or the fact that his birth mother had loved him and suffered when he was taken.

But Myra Banks was family, and he loved her.

Three days later

IT WAS TIME he met the rest of his family—the McCullens.

Nerves crawled up Ryder's back as he drove to Horseshoe Creek.

He had tied up the case. With Gwen's help and the task force in place, they had found three more cases in Frost's files of unlawful removal of a child from its birth parent, all three teenagers he had coerced into handing their babies over to him for placement. However, the young women had not been blessed with the hefty payment Frost received— he had kept that for himself.

The mother of the baby Bonnie Cone had adopted agreed to leave her with Bonnie, although Bonnie encouraged the teen to be part of the child's life. Tia's Crossroads program stepped in to facilitate the arrangement.

Tia did not press charges against Hilary, but Hilary joined Crossroads. Helping other families was filling the void left by her own loss, and she'd decided to become a foster parent.

Tia's kindness and Crossroads program were a blessing to so many.

He had been blessed to have met her.

Rich farmland, pastures and stables drew his eye as he wound down the drive to the main farmhouse on Horseshoe Creek. Cash had asked all the McCullens to join him at the house for the meeting.

God. Ryder was so accustomed to being alone, he wasn't sure how to handle this.

Although being alone had its downside. He missed Tia, dammit.

The beauty of the land reminded him that this property had belonged to his birth parents, that they had worked the land and animals and built a legacy for their sons.

And that he was one of them.

It was still difficult to wrap his head around that fact.

The sight of trucks and SUVs at the rambling farmhouse made his pulse clamor. They were all here waiting to meet him.

What if he didn't fit?

Dammit, Ryder, you're an FBI agent. You've faced notorious criminals. This is family.

Except he felt like a stranger—an outsider—as he parked and walked up to the door.

Before he could knock, Cash met him outside. "Hey, man, glad you came."

Ryder shook his twin's hand, an immediate connection forming. He was no longer alone.

Cash had been out there all along.

Cash looked slightly shaken as well. "The others are waiting."

Ryder nodded, his voice too thick to speak. He'd done his research, knew all the names and faces.

But he wasn't prepared for the warm welcome.

"I'm Maddox, the oldest," the man in the sheriff's uniform said. "Welcome to Horseshoe Creek." He gestured for him to follow. "Everyone is out back on the lawn. Mama Mary fixed a big dinner. We thought we'd do it picnic style."

Cash gave him a brotherly pat on the back, and Ryder shot him a thank-you look, then he walked through the house to the back porch and onto a lush lawn with picnic tables and food galore.

A chubby woman with a big smile and wearing an apron greeted him first. "I'm Mama Mary," she said with a booming laugh. "Nice to finally have all the family here together."

Cash had told him about the bighearted woman who

had served as mother to the McCullen boys after Grace was murdered.

She swept him into a hug and he patted her back, emotions thrumming through him when she released him and his brothers lined up to meet him.

TIA HUMMED A lullaby to Jordie as she rocked him, the warmth of his little body next to hers so wonderful that she didn't want to put him in his bed. Each time she did, she feared she'd wake up and find him gone again.

Since his return, she'd had a security system installed, along with new locks. He had been sleeping in the cradle in her bedroom, but one day he would outgrow it and she'd need to move him to the crib.

Still, for now, she clung to him. Listening to his breathing at night gave her peace. His little movements and smiles filled her with such joy that she thought she would burst from happiness.

Except…she missed Ryder.

Her bed seemed big and lonely without him. His scent lingered on the pillow. Images of his naked body tormented her. And when she closed her eyes, she imagined Ryder beside her, holding her, loving her, his big body there to protect her.

But…she hadn't heard a word from him. He'd brought her baby back to her as he'd promised, then disappeared.

Probably onto another case.

He didn't need her or a ready-made family.

She tucked Jordie into the cradle and stroked her thumb over his baby soft cheek. "I love you, little man. Mommy will always take care of you."

She had to be both a mother and father for her son. Somehow she'd find the strength to raise him alone.

And to forget Ryder.

Chapter Twenty-Six

One week later

Ryder parked his SUV on a lush stretch of Horseshoe Creek and studied the pastures, the horses galloping along the hill and the open spaces and imagined a log home built on the property. A swing set out back. A screened porch overlooking the pond.

Family dinners and picnics.

He had tried to stay away from Tia. She needed time to settle with her son. Time to recover from the trauma.

He had helped her on the case, but he wanted more. But he didn't want to play on the fact that she might feel indebted to him.

His feelings for her had nothing to do with debt.

He'd fallen in love with her, with her kindness and compassion, with her strength, with the way she loved her son and helped others.

But what did he have to offer?

He was a loner who worked a dangerous job. What kind of father would he be?

He wanted to be like Joe McCullen.

The past week he'd spent hours visiting and getting to know the family. They'd taken him in as if he'd always been part of them. He'd also gotten to know Deputy Roan

Whitefeather, who turned out to be his half brother. The McCullens had even welcomed Myra into the fold.

He studied the piece of ranch land they'd given him to build on with emotion in his throat. He had a home here if he wanted it.

He did want it. But he didn't want it alone.

What are you going to do about it?

Damn. He swung the SUV around and headed toward Tia's, even though doubts filled him as he left the ranch. Tia had been burned by so many people. She'd admitted she didn't trust anyone. Darren had betrayed and hurt her.

What if she didn't want him?

TIA FINISHED HER morning coffee as she read Jordie a story. Granted, he was too young to really understand, but he seemed to like the sound of her voice.

The doorbell buzzed just as she laid him in the crib. She hurried to the door, brushing her hair into place as she went, then peeked through the window.

Ryder's SUV.

The fear she'd lived with when Jordie was missing returned, yet she reminded herself he was safe now. Richard Blotter and Judy were in jail. Frost had died.

Her son was home and no one would take him from her again.

She took a deep breath and opened the door. Ryder stood in front of her, looking big and tough and so handsome that her lungs literally squeezed for air again.

"Tia?"

His face looked so strained that fear returned. "Is something wrong?"

He shook his head. "No. Can I come in?"

She swept her arm in a wide arc. "Of course."

"How are you and Jordie doing?" he asked.

She glanced toward the nursery door. "Good. I...still get nervous sometimes when I put him in his room, but I have a security system now and baby monitors everywhere."

He nodded, his body rigid. Finally he released a breath. "Would you and Jordie like to take a ride with me?"

She rubbed at her temple. "A ride?"

"Yes, I have something to show you." His dark gaze softened. "Trust me."

She did, with every fiber of her being. "All right, I'll get him. But you'll have to put my car seat in your SUV, or we can take my minivan."

"I've got it covered."

He had a car seat?

She didn't ask questions, though. She went and scooped Jordie up, then wrapped him in his blanket. Ryder brushed his finger over Jordie's head, his expression tender.

"He's growing."

"I know," Tia said, proud that the ordeal hadn't stunted him.

They walked outside together and he opened the back door for her to settle her baby in the infant seat.

"Does he mind car rides?"

"He sleeps through everything," she said with a smile. She was the nervous one.

Ryder seemed stiff and uneasy, but he slowly relaxed as he drove. She studied the farmland as they left town, then was surprised when they reached a sign that read Horse-shoe Creek.

"You met the McCullens?" she asked.

"Yes," Ryder said, his voice gruff. "I've spent a lot of time with the family this past week. They took me in like I was part of them."

"You are part of them," Tia said, sensing the pain that

he'd felt and how difficult it was for him to accept the change in his life.

"They even welcomed Myra, my mother," Ryder continued.

"I'm happy for you, Ryder." She leaned her head on her hand. "Family is everything." She still missed her mother and father and brother and wished they were alive to see her son.

Emotions glittered in his dark eyes as he met her gaze. Then he turned down a drive and wound past several stables. Finally he parked at a stretch of land by a pond.

He cut the engine and angled himself to face her. "This is beautiful, Ryder."

A broad smile curved his serious face. "It's mine."

Tia gasped. "Yours?"

"Apparently Joe McCullen left the ranch to all his sons."

"I'm so happy for you. Do you plan to build a house and live here?"

He lifted her hand in his. "Yes. I thought a big farmhouse with a porch with rockers on it." He pointed toward the left side. "A play yard with a swing set could go right there."

Tia's heart began to race. "A swing set?"

He nodded. "And there's a lot of room to ride bikes and horses, and we could teach Jordie to fish one day."

Her breath caught. "Ryder?"

He squeezed her hand, then pressed a kiss to her palm. "I don't just want a house, Tia. I want to build a home here, and I want you and Jordie to be part of it."

"You do?"

"Yes. I love you, Tia." He dug in his pocket and lifted the gold bands they'd worn during their disguise. "I like the feel of this on my hand. I thought we might make it real." He shrugged. "Of course we can get new ones. A diamond for you if you want."

She'd seen the discomfort on his face when she'd handed him the rings that day. But now…now he seemed relaxed. Happy.

Sincere.

"You aren't doing this just so Jordie will have a father?"

He shook his head. "I want to be his father, if you'll let me." He kissed her fingers one by one. "But I miss you and love you, Tia. I want us to build a life together. To be a family."

Tears welled in Tia's eyes. Happy tears this time.

She gently brushed her hand against his cheek and Ryder swept her in his arms and covered her mouth with his. The kiss was deep, passionate, sensual, filled with promises and yearning.

"Is that a yes?" he murmured.

She nodded and kissed him again. "Yes, Ryder, I love you, too."

She didn't need diamonds. She had her son back. And with Ryder and the McCullens, she would have the big family she'd always wanted.

Epilogue

Six months later

Tia's heart overflowed with love as the reverend announced she and Ryder were husband and wife.

Ryder kissed her thoroughly, the passion between them building. But that would have to wait.

Their family was watching now.

"Later," Ryder whispered against her neck.

She gently touched his cheek. She would never grow tired of touching him. Or hearing his voice. Or looking into his impossibly sexy eyes.

She certainly wouldn't get tired of loving him. "That's a promise."

He gathered her hand in his and they turned to face the guests. Mama Mary smiled from the front row. Just last month she'd married the foreman of the ranch. But she still held the family together with her big warm hugs and comforting food and motherly love.

Maddox, Brett, Ray, Roan and Cash had bonded with Ryder and helped build the house she and Ryder were moving into, while their wives had helped Tia organize the wedding on the lawn.

Cheers and clapping erupted, shouts of joy and happiness and congratulations as she and Ryder stepped from the gazebo to accept glasses of champagne.

She looked across the beautiful ranch and the wonderful McCullens, grateful for their boisterous chaos.

Rose jiggled her baby boy, Maddox's son, Joe, in the stroller while Ryder's mother, Myra, nestled Jordie to her. Willow and Brett's son, Sam, was chasing fireflies with Cash and BJ's adopted boys, Tyler and Drew.

Maddox lifted a champagne flute. "Let's toast to the last McCullen."

Ryder laughed and so did everyone else.

"Hell, he's not the last." Brett touched Willow's bulging belly. "We're just getting started."

"So are we," Ray said as he pulled a pregnant Scarlet against him.

Megan, Roan's wife, smiled sheepishly. "So are we," Roan admitted with an affectionate hug to his wife.

Ryder and Tia exchanged a secretive look. They planned to have more children as well and so did Cash and BJ, but Ryder vowed not to push Tia. Jordie was only a few months old.

Still, as she sipped her champagne and nuzzled his neck, love and passion exploded inside him. Tia wanted at least four, maybe six kids.

Tonight might not be too soon to start.

* * * * *

Look for more books of gripping suspense from
USA TODAY *bestselling author Rita Herron,*
coming soon!